# The Legend of the Viking

## CLAN MACLAOCH CURSE SERIES
### BOOK TWO

## BECKY BANKS

Ha'iku
Press

Published by:

Maui, Hawaiʻi | Portland, Oregon
haiku-press.com

Cover design by James T. Egan of Bookfly Design.

beckybanksbooks.com

ISBN: 978-0-9882614-5-7 (e-book)

ISBN: 978-0-9882614-4-0 (paperback)

*To the MacNáradhaighs, who gave birth to the Manarys,*
*who gave me one helluvah story.*

# Prologue

*Outer Hebrides, Scotland*
*The Year of Our Lord 1210*

Quiet fell in the stone hall as the old woman made her way back down the long table, an engraved bone cup in her hand. This time she would not be turned away. The rushes scattered on the floor muted her steps and absorbed the echoes and murmurs of those gathered there.

"Grandson," she called, her craggy voice carrying over the heads of the raiders. As she continued under the gaze of cruel men, she closed her eyes and moved toward her grandson and, with an ability she should not possess, around those in her way. She tightened her fist about the engraved cup she'd been given by a guard loyal to her. "Hear me, Grandson. Do not dismiss my warnings. For now, I have seen it thrice." She held the cup for him as though to indicate the tea leaves within it.

"Silence," he commanded her.

"You must know." Her voice carried to him clear as crystal in the humid and smoke-tinged air. "You must hear me, Grandson."

The room shifted as they looked to her then back to their self-proclaimed king.

"Once the boughs of love are gently rocked—"

"I said—"

"Rocked by her embrace," she shouted over him. There was gasping and a small cry of outrage. "You will want of nothing else; it is foretold, in the feral times of man, that another will come to stand between you and that which you love most. If it should come to pass, if his vengeance against you should succeed, your spirit will forever walk this land. This will be the truth until your retribution breaks the bounds of nature and settles the balance. Blood will be spilt, hearts will be shattered, and vengeance once started will not be stopped—"

The Viking's fist slammed down with a bang. "Enough!"

Earthenware cups and the boar's carcass jumped as wine spilled, and another cry of alarm was heard. The old woman stopped and opened her eyes then.

He smiled distastefully at the seer the village folk called Völva. "His vengeance? Yes, you have said it again and again. So, tell me, Grandmother, what is the name of my enemy? I will slay him now." His laugh shook the foundation.

The old woman hissed out in disgust, "Grandson, 'tis not a man you will know until you have crossed him. Only when his blade touches your skin will you comprehend my meaning. Only now is it not too late; you can stop him. Stop your lust for things you cannot have."

His gaze cooled dangerously, and he gave her a warning he seldom gave to others. "What you speak of is treason. Will you condemn one of your people to a traitor's fate?"

"I did not say that the sword would be held by your kin—"

"That is right—you said nothing other than 'a man'!" After his icy outburst, he smiled at his people. "An ordinary man, whom I have yet to meet, will someday strike at me in anger." He laughed again. His wolflike smile in place, he said, "Grandmother, you speak of every man who wishes to sit upon this seat." He gestured to his intricately carved throne.

The old woman nodded and worked the rest of the distance down the long wooden table to him. She trailed one hand on the backs of the chairs for balance as the crowd murmured and laughed with their chief. She made her way to his seat and smiled, placing the cup down; she held her hand out to him.

"Then, peace, Grandson."

"What is this? You wish to read more into my future? Perhaps get a name that I can use?"

She continued with her placating smile, her hand outstretched. "Let us be at peace."

"Peace!" He laughed but placed his palm in hers. She grasped it then spat into it. The Viking tried to pull his hand back, but her grip was unusually strong. She traced the lines of his palm with her thumbs as her murmured words washed over him.

Trying still to pull his hand back, he hissed, "You are a pitiful old woman. Nothing but a bogeyman to scare children into obedience. I will make sure you pay for this." To his guards, he barked, "Remove her!" and shoved her back with his other hand.

She stumbled but, catching herself, stood upright as if possessed. Her filthy wrap slipped from her shoulders. The room's light dimmed.

Her eyes, having gone cold as snow clouds, looked sharply at her grandson, the most feared man of the Outer Hebrides. "Remember this warning"—the stone walls shook—"for it will be your last: Seek the unobtainable, and you will be blinded by love. She will outlive you and, in your absence, will suffer a fate worse than death. And your spirit, unable to succumb to the call to Valhalla, will roam these lands for eternity."

Light snapped back as she folded down into the old woman she was. She picked up her heavily worn blanket and wrapped it tightly about her shoulders. A firm hand with a gold-clasped wrist gripped her shoulder.

Ormr Minorisson, Viking chief and self-proclaimed king of the Outer Hebrides stood then, towering over her. "Those words will be your last to me." He gestured to his man who was holding her arm. "Take her to the church of the Misty Cliffs." Then, to her: "You will stay there from now until your last breath."

*One*

Castle Laoch, Glentree, Skye, Scotland
*Present Day*

Rowan sat in the circle of light cast by his lamp. He glared at the bright screen of his laptop as he keyed in numbers.

As a child, Rowan had watched his uncle work the ledger, a large leather-bound book with lines that reminded him of rows of barley sprouting new and crisp in the spring's rich soil. As soon as he took the helm of the MacLaoch estate, he transitioned the whole lot to computers, saving the knuckle of his right middle finger from the permanent ink stain his uncle had always worn. That ink stain was a tattooed reminder of how tied the clan was to the coffers. How tied the castle was to the coffers. How *he* was now tied to the coffers.

The cell where the Gathering monies was bloomed a big round zero, a black hole in the spreadsheet. The annual net revenue line had a seven-figure number. Seven figures below zero.

Rowan pinched the bridge of his nose. The clan was fucked with a capital *F*. Not "attempt to sell the Rembrandt in the upper hallway and hope the posh want to pay millions" fucked, but enduringly fucked, because next year, he'd have to do the same, and the year after, ad nauseum, until there was nothing left in the castle save for the stone itself. Add ten years in arrears on bank payments to the devil, and now the Reaper was calling to collect his dues.

Clan members had run for their lives last summer as thunder and lightning and bullets rang out and took their Gathering registration fees with them. No one bid on the million-pound silent auction items, and the hunt up at the lodge—a ten-thousand-pound-per-night experience —never happened. Instead, his cousin tried to kill him, and his uncle attempted to murder his newfound love.

Rowan's mind skipped at the bittersweet thought of Cole.

Cole was asleep in the cottage. That cliffside cottage that was easier to live in and heat than an entire castle. Cole was his ray of hope in all this bleakness, like the rare Glentree summer sun when it kissed his cheeks. He took a pleasant sojourn away from the defeat in front of him and reminded himself of Cole's sunset-colored curls reflecting the copper heat of that same sun and the fire she stoked in him. He wished she were there now. He desperately needed to do what he loved, to clutch a fistful of that fire and breathe her in as her arms wound around his waist, squeezing him tight. She was the only creature on earth who made him feel soothed, comforted, and completely at peace simply by being near him.

He knew that to pay respect to all she was to him he needed to offi-cially make her his wife. It felt wrong to not have done it already, but as he looked back to the numbers, he couldn't shake the feeling that to legally tie her to him was akin to tying her to an anchor and throwing both of them into the loch.

Then there was the bother of the ceremonies, vetting, and rites to follow, though the clan was currently occupied with raking him over the coals for the way the Gathering ended and squabbling about whether to chop his uncle Gregoire's branch from the clan. It seemed selfish to ask them to rejoice in his love when everything else was going so wrong.

He leaned back in his great-grandfather's Chesterfield desk chair—a three-thousand-pound appraised value—with a creak and blew out a breath. The phone call that had precipitated him sitting there for eight hours straight came back to him. If everything proceeded as the bank man had threatened, there might be no castle for he and Cole to live in much less a clan chief for her to marry after his people hanged him from the old oak in Glentree's town square.

Rowan felt the pinch of his ulcer and reached for the pills he hid in the upper desk drawer. He dropped two powder-yellow tabs into his palm and tossed them back then picked up his tumbler and washed them down with whisky.

*Two*

It was late afternoon when, phone to my ear, I stood behind Rowan's old oak desk up in his office in the castle's fairy tower. It was a lovely place to be and made me feel closer to Rowan now that he spent most nights away from home.

"Uh-huh," I said distractedly into the handset. I was at cord length on my tiptoes trying to see out leaded-glass windows, over treetops, down to the loch below. The late-afternoon sun was obscured behind the thick clouds, making the sky a hundred thousand shades of gray. I got a view of the black, rocky beach of Loch Laoch, but too little. I needed to be able to view at least fifty yards worth of that beach to ensure I didn't miss that afternoon's phenomenon.

An anticipatory energy filled my body, as when hearing an ice cream truck. I was going to have to end my call. Just thinking I might miss out made my heart skip a beat and stole my breath.

I touched the rubber band at my wrist and snapped it for some focus. It was on my wrist to help me reign in my temper after, a year ago, I punched a woman at the Gathering gala. She'd deserved it, but now, I simply wore it as a physical reminder to remain present. I hadn't been angry in months.

I shifted my weight. The potential student intern I was on the phone with was excited to get a call back and was regaling me of a story about her and her granddaddy de-braining a particularly aggressive Highland bull. Her granddaddy was Glentree's local large animal veterinarian, and she an undergrad in zoology.

"Adara—"

"But tha's when we gave him a quick snip and—"

"Adara, thank you, yes, thank you—"

"Oh no, I've talked too much? Grandda' warned me of talking too much if I were to get a call, and now, here I've done it. I've talked too much, haven't I?"

I stretched again, another attempt to see more of the beach—the exact same place where Rowan had tossed me into the ice-cold water, gala dress and all, last year.

"Adara," I said, "I was calling to say that you've got the position. I'm sorry, I'm in a bit of a rush, so I'll email you the details tonight—"

Her ear-splitting scream had me yanking the handset away from my ear.

"Oh, my grandda' will be so happy! We're MacLaochs, ye know, and to study a site that hasnae been touched in..." Her Scots got thicker as her voice broke into a sob.

"Adara, honey, I'm so happy for you. That's wonderful to hear that he'll be proud of you"—another peak out the window and a look at my watch—"but I really have to go. I'll email you." And with an apology to her—and silently, my mother for my poor manners—I hung up. Quickly, I made a Post-it reminder, then began gathering my things. I picked up my to-call folder of folks and the miscellaneous résumés I had on the desk. Swiftly, I shoved them into the open folder and reached for my pack behind me on the desk chair. In my haste, the folder yawned, and the papers slipped out. They scattered like a blizzard over the Persian rug.

"Shit!" I shouted and went to my knees in the mess. Another look at my watch. Another curse. I only had a minute left.

Noticing that sheets had scattered across the room and under furniture, I cursed again and left them there. I scrambled to my feet, slipping on the papers, and was down the tightly winding staircase and out into the upper hallway in short order. The sun made an afternoon debut hitting the western flank of the castle, sending long, blazing beams of light over the parquet floors and down the main staircase. I was midway down the staircase myself, the sun warming my back, when Marion called to me.

She stood at the front administrative counter, her silver hair tucked behind an ear, and her cardigan was pale pink in celebration of spring.

Her blue eyes went wide with hope when she saw me. "Excellent timing, my lady! It's teatime. Join us in the sunroom—"

"Nope! Nope, nope, nope," I said with each step.

I ran past her and around the lower staircase then through the main hall to the rear of the castle.

She called from behind me, "Where are ye always headed at this hour?!"

"Nowhere!" I called back. It was my special secret, and I was telling absolutely *no one.*

Off the back steps I jumped, my rubber boots slapping my calves as I did so, and crossed over the closely cropped, aptly named bowling green. The scents of crushed grass and foliage tickled my nose as I stole a glance down to the loch. It was still obscured, this time by the stone balcony, and down those steps I jumped too, with another boot slap, then started up the rear gravel trail toward the whitewashed stone cottage.

My heart raced as I sprinted.

*Was I about to miss it?*

The trail split, forking toward the research field and the cottage that Rowan and I shared. I was going to neither. I hung a sharp left toward the cliff's edge in the distance. My boots slipped as I exited the gravel path, making my arms whirligig to catch my balance. I slowed my pace as I got close—minding my step and the rocky edge between me and the tidal pools fifty feet below, I chanced a look up as the loch, all of it, came into view.

I was giddy with excitement and clasped my hands together. I hadn't missed it after all. The entire swath of the black-rock beach, melting into the curve of Loch Laoch, was visible from here, making it *the* spot for my wildlife viewing. The spot where Rowan and I had our first real lip lock was small in the distance but clearly visible.

I turned my wrist, looking at the time, and smiled—soon. It would happen soon.

My insides pleasantly churned as I waited for my ice cream truck of a moment to arrive. The onshore breeze brought with it the tang of seawater and twang of birdsong as they flit and flew, darting over the exposed tidal pools. A few more minutes passed before heat spiked in my veins, and he strode into view.

The MacLaoch clan chief wore a form-hugging dark-blue button-down. I'd buttoned him into it just that morning, stealing a kiss off his distracted lips with every round mother-of-pearl shell I thrust into its matching hole. His black slacks fit his athletic, lean hips and legs like the pants had been stitched around him, showing off the high and tight ass that I smacked with erotic glee each time I was within arm's reach. His sport coat, I frowned now, was gone. It would not flap like a flightless bird as he wrenched it off today. I conducted myself as I did during any of my wildlife biology observations and deduced: The laird was furious again today and would partake in his afternoon ritual. It wasn't unlike sitting riverside, concealed downwind, from a grizzly as he fetched spawning salmon from the stream. It wasn't wise to approach the bear but instead just enjoy from afar the display of prowess.

Things with the Gathering the year prior had not ended well. In fact, it was still going. The clan wanted answers and were holding Rowan to giving them. They were split into two camps: some said Kelly and his father, Gregoire, should be stripped of their clan rites, and others said to turn a blind eye. Each day Rowan "consulted" in his laird and chief roles, and he needed an outlet to vent.

It just so happened to be a beautiful outlet for me to watch, a capable man solving his problems.

A stone's throw from the water's edge now, Rowan stopped and toed off his shoes while working the buttons of his crisp, collared shirt, giving me mini flashes of warm skin. I sighed, ready for this angry cater-pillar to shed its cocoon and thrust himself into the cold loch water and emerge after a mile of open-water swimming the beautiful, powerful butterfly he was. Finally, he sloughed off his shirt, and even from my distance away, I could see his shoulders were taught. The muscles of his upper back and arms firmed as he gestured angrily, stabbing pointedly into the air as if in argument with the people and their noise he had had to consume that day.

My fingertips itched to touch his bunched muscles, to dig into them and massage them loose. I kept my thoughts quiet lest they call to him and break this gorgeous routine.

With a flick of his fingers at his belt buckle, his pants loosened. His mouth opened, and after a second's delay, his roar reached me. His warrior physique was primed for a fight. It appeared today had been extra hard. I noticed now that his black hair looked tossed and roughed up from his impatient hands running through it. Button and zipper undone, his pants and underwear were shoved down to rocks and kicked aside along with his socks.

I sucked in a deep breath and steepled my fingers, pressing them against my lips, holding in my erotic joy.

*There he was.*

Standing naked as the day he was born, Chief Rowan MacLaoch was the image of the Celtic warrior stripping bare to unleash his ferocity without a single item to hamper his movements. His heated skin was a sharp color contrast with the obsidian-colored rocks and the dark hair that ran from his navel to his cock. It stood impressive despite the cold.

His thighs and buttocks flexed their musculature as he navigated the rocky ground. The water, even though he'd been prepared for it, stole his breath, making him suck through clenched teeth. I could hear that intake of breath like a memory in my ear, a wordless tell that entering me in a surprise lovemaking session in his tower office was pleasantly intense for him as well.

He took four quick breaths before diving into an incoming wave, plunging himself into the depths of the loch. In awe, I watched as he expertly carved a path through the punishingly cold water. His bent arms kept time with the pace of a Highland jig, or a pub brawl. His fingertips were pointed and punishing, slicing the water out of his way, and then turned languid and caressing on his way back.

While he would go a short, and if by boat, easy, distance, it was the evening wind that kicked up a small chop on the water, making it Iron Man worthy. Each time he breathed, he had to do it through his teeth so as not to inhale wind-whipped water droplets off the chop. It would take all his focus to swim the round-trip mile.

If him sliding into the water was gold, him stepping out was diamonds. As he entered the shallow waters, his naked form became visible; it was a greenish hue under these waters, like a moving jade sculpture. I inhaled and bit my lip, waiting for it. Sensual excitement warmed my skin. It was one thing to ogle a man with whom you had no experience; it was another to watch a man with whom you did, knowing how that pelvis moved against yours and the petal softness of those lips on the skin of your breasts.

There in the shallows, he stopped moving, and like a monolith emerging from the water, he stood, the loch sparkling off him, running down his sharp edges. He wiped water out of his eyes, making his biceps go firm and round. My gaze wandered his body like a caress down to the *V* of his pelvic muscles where they were drawn deep, accentuating the lines of his abdominals. Each of his exhales was punctuated with water droplets that had run down his nose and off his upper lip. He pushed his way through the water with heavy steps, each one revealing more and more of his sculpted magnificence. I knew the weight of that body when it was on top of mine. I followed the tight midline of his stomach to his navel and then the dark path of hair down to his relaxed manhood. Despite the chill of the air, he was warm, hot even, and he hung longer and thicker than the average male would having just stepped out of forty-degree water. I bit my knuckles to suppress a shout and a wave to get those sapphire eyes to find me.

When Rowan reached his discarded clothes, his expression changed. Despite the distance, I knew his was a happy look—it was the one he gave over shoulders when his eye caught mine across a crowded room. Suddenly, I shivered. My skin now felt as cold as Rowan's as our connection ignited, letting me feel the ocean water on his skin. His slow-blooming smile dimpled just one cheek. A hum moved across my skin before his face turned up toward me. I didn't need to shout or wave; today, those sapphire eyes found me in silence.

*Three*

R owan crested the trail a few minutes later, a moment that I
would come to hold like a photograph in my mind when he left
for his next clan fundraising trip. He wore not his pants and
shirt but eight heavy yards of tartan around his waist, one end tossed
over his shoulder. How had I missed seeing him carry that to the water
with him?

I gave him an appreciative whistle and laughed as I walked to meet
him. He could have been walking that same path for centuries and not
have been out of place. He was a portrait waiting to be painted.

He grinned back and stopped a few feet from me. The cliff breeze
pushed at a curl of raven hair loosening from the dense wetness of the
rest of his thick head of hair.

"Miss me?"

"Who, me? Nah. How can I miss you when I've been stalking you
this whole time? I'm surprised you didn't hear my thoughts."

"Must have been clean until just now."

"Pure as the driven snow." My smile turned gentle. "How was your
day?"

"Fine," he lied. "How was yours?"

"Fine," I echoed. "Now that we have the formalities out of the way..."

I stepped up to him. His left hand went to my face and cradled my cheek as his other reached around and cupped my rear end, pulling me in against him. My own hands skated up his arms, enjoying the feel of his skin, both cool and hot.

"I'm not ever going to get used to having ye call to me like that."

His eyes devoured me, and I bathed in their light. The flicking sapphire and Mediterranean blue against the gray day. "Good," I said and went up on my toes, offering a kiss. It had been a fun year, exploring together how the love of our ancestors had created in us a bond that sometimes quite literally thrummed within us. But right now, I appreciated a connection more tangible.

He brought me in higher against him but did not provide the answer to my begging lips. He looked into my eyes, studying them like I assumed Einstein would if the theory of relativity were in his arms.

"Your eyes change color. Did ye know?"

"Hard to forget when you keep telling me. Now, stop delaying your gratification. Be more like me: if there's cake on the table, eat it...ASAP."

"I like cake..." His voice went soft.

"Then feast, my love."

"I like to watch you a wee while before I consume you whole."

Rowan was the master of delayed gratification. If he could reflect on the color of the sky mid-coitus to prolong the experience, he would.

We'd spent much of our last year apart, and reminding ourselves of each other's features had become part of our routine each precious day we were together. The biggest thing I noticed about him was that his aggression in the water was taking calories out of his body faster than he could replace them, and as such, a new feature on his face was visible, long crevasses next to his full mouth. On one hand, I wanted to sit with my chin on my fist and stare at this new angle. On the other hand, I wanted back the exact face I fell in love with. I felt the urge to make a ten-course meal in his honor, then sit astride his lap and feed him every morsel from my fingertips. Now, my finger trailed that long crease.

"Your eyes change," he continued, "different when you look at your field notes and when you're standing here with me."

"Is that so?" I wasn't really listening. "I wonder why that is?" I didn't really care.

His thumb swiped across my cheek. *Yes*, I begged in my mind. "Oh aye, I can guess."

"It might be that my botanical studies don't grab my butt. Nor do they tower over me and make me think of sex in castles, and discarded kilts," I said, giving the fabric a tug. I wrapped my arms around his neck and pulled myself up against his firm body. "You know this kilt in particular ties me in knots," I murmured against his lips. It was the first one I'd seen him wear, and even if I lived to be a hundred, I'd never forget it. With my nose nestled next to his, I continued, "I didn't know you were wearing it today. I would have started stalking you a whole lot earlier than an hour ago."

He dodged my lips, enjoying the game. "Found it in the locker room down there, seemed faster than pants."

I knew that locker room—loved that locker room. It was the first place he'd put me on my back and kissed the hell out of me.

"Did you know you have nothing on underneath?" I whispered.

"Is tha' right?" he said with mock shock.

"It makes me think you might want to kiss me, MacLaoch. So, do it, and tell me you love me as much as I love you, you beautiful human being."

He took a deep, shuddering breath. He was losing his battle with himself. There was an obvious long and firm protrusion at his hip height pushing against me, telling me the exact direction of erotic due north.

"Come, Cole"—his pupils going wide; he was enjoying the words I was feeding him and the moves my body was putting onto him—"let's go inside."

I relaxed down against his front. Then pressed my hips against his and rubbed my body back up. "Sure, just one kiss first?"

His eyes went half-mast as the massaged north star under his kilt took control over his brain. Rowan groaned out a plea before lowering his face and losing his lips to mine.

The smell of brine and his exertion swallowed me whole. I dove into our connection like he had the loch. He'd been gone a few days the week prior and the week before that too, and on, and on, for months. He was going to be gone again.

I shoved at the fabric on this shoulder and as it fell discovered that his kilt had been hastily gathered about his hips and restrained only with the thin belt of his trousers. A belt that was built to withstand the fabric of a lightweight cotton blend and keep everything together in situations no harsher than sitting. It was not meant to hold up against a figurative ton of plaid and a lustful partner hell-bent on seeing her Scotsman naked. The belt snapped.

Rowan cursed; he was now in his birthday suit.

I smiled against his lips. "Oh no," I murmured, "I'm so sorry."

He grinned back. "Turnabout is fair play." And those hands that had sliced through the water, powering him forward through the chop, grabbed the hem of my sweater. It was up, off, and tossed aside, soon followed by my pants and boots.

He picked me up, and I wrapped my legs about him, trapping the length of him between our bodies. It was warm and velvety, and as the cold sea air swept across my naked back, I suddenly thought we should be quick about it.

"Holy sh—" I shivered. I'd been in Glentree for a year, and my blood had yet to acclimate to the consistently cool coastal temperatures that Rowan's had been born into.

Rowan's mouth was on my neck as he made movements behind me and then lay me down on my back on the massive blanket his eight yards of traditional tartan fabric made. Into the warmth of the wool and sponge of the grass we nestled. Rowan settled himself over me before tossing the end of his heavy tartan over his back. We were plunged into a woolen cave there on the grass at the base of his castle and in the shadow of our distant cottage. Rowan looked down at me, the laughter in his eyes matching mine. We were outside and naked, wild like the animals in the forest nearby.

I laughed as he set us back on task, his nose going to my neck then his mouth to my breast. His mouth softly tugged and suckled as his pelvis shifted over mine, moving his firm thickness to the entrance of my Narnia. "Ready?" He grinned.

It was a rhetorical question. Our bodies were one and the same. Still, I answered him. Beneath the plaid, I let my knees fall open farther, giving him more room. "Are you?"

"Aye, born ready, lass," and he slipped inside of me.

We let out a collective sigh.

"Oh..." I groaned. "I miss you already."

"I'm right here," he whispered against my neck. "I havenae gone yet."

My hands smoothed his neck up to cradle his jaw and bring his gaze to mine. "Yes...that's true. You're right here, aren't you?" I reminded myself and sealed it with a kiss.

He groaned and pushed farther in, then relaxed out before lazily pressing back in again.

"I love you," I whispered.

"*Tha gaol agamsa ort fhèin,*" he responded. *I love you too.*

There in our temporary tartan home at the cliff's edge with the earth at my back and the moody gray skies above us, we came together like we were always meant to: cradling each other, our bodies and hearts held within each other's embrace until we collectively clenched and released. Our voices mixed with the sea breeze until they too were carried off in the wind.

# Four

~

The next morning, my wellies caught dew droplets on their toes as I trekked the well-worn path from the cottage front door up to the rear of the castle. By now the boots could make the short trip by themselves. The grass was still flattened from our romp, which made me smile. Rowan had been gone before daybreak, this time south to Glasgow. Just as I had predicted, my heart hurt to see him go again. My days were busy, though, helping to cut the time he was gone.

That morning I was meeting with Clive, clan historian and Minory history buff, for our weekly tête-à-tête we'd kept to since I decided to stay in Glentree. He'd been the staunchest supporter of my Minory heritage since before I was reluctant to admit it myself—and the architect of my written family tree. My first few visits with him had been almost daily, meeting relatives and shaking hands with folks I tried hard to memorize the names and connections I had with.

I was up the rear stairs and across the bowling green when an onshore squall threatened and gusted up the cliff's edge, tossing my hair before kicking leaves off the stone patio. They swirled around the plaque that caught my attention the first time I set foot at Castle Laoch.

It was coated with leaf litter. I went to it and wiped my hand across the brass, pushing dew drops and pine needles off it, giving it an impromptu cleaning. I read it again, this false version of my and Rowan's shared history where the MacLaoch family was in the right. Their version had them "saving" their Lady MacLaoch from a marauding Viking a thousand years ago. That false narrative was engraved into metal, then set into the very foundation of Castle Laoch. But the Secret Keepers, the family's oral historians who guarded every truth passed along from the lips of those who had lived it, said Lady MacLaoch had been in love with the Viking and didn't need or want to be rescued. She definitely didn't want him to be killed, and she'd cursed the clan chief's descendants—her descendants too—in punishment. Then I came along, the long-lost Minory heir, the Viking's descendant.

I'd come to Scotland and all the way up to this tiny Skye town in search of this family name, Minory, and discovered a truth so wild it wouldn't be believed by anyone outside of Glentree. While Castle Laoch had become my home, its people my people, there was another side to the curse. It was my side. It had been Rowan's bloodline that had initiated the curse, but it was the blood of the man she loved, from my lineage, that had spilled, staining Lady MacLaoch's island over a millennia ago.

Before I went into the castle to meet Clive, I looked out to the slate-colored water stretching along the horizon. "Who were you?"

Who was that arrogant Viking who sailed these seas and fell in love with the one person he couldn't have? Who was that vulnerable man, felled by a love that couldn't be hidden, who got beheaded for it? I had no idea.

Making my way into the castle, I was so ensconced in my romanticism of that past that I only realized there was shouting when I was a few feet from Clive's door.

"No!" I heard a familiar voice shout, "I will take these this instant back to the library. You will not have these for your personal use. They were given to the Glentree library, and it's there that they will stay! You MacLaochs expect that any item pertaining to ye means you can hoard —oh aye, I said hoard!—information, denying scholars and school children alike. No! I will not calm down, ye blasted man!"

I peered through the open door into Clive's book-filled office to find Clive cornered behind his desk chair and Deloris, the Glentree librarian, in a rare moment away from her archives counter, looming large like a library dragon coming to collect her bejeweled book eggs. Clive's face was blotchy red, and his glasses were steamed up in the corners.

"Ye have no right here! Ye may not take this nor those back to your institution—"

"You may, as everyone else can, check these out at your leisure. There, they will be safe—"

"I will not be made to stoop so low as to pay membership into your club to get access to materials that belong to Clan MacLaoch!"

"It's not membership, you fool! It's called a library card, and yes, ye must obtain one to help us keep track of materials!"

"Ah-hem." I cleared my throat and plunged in as both pairs of specs turned to face me. "Hi, what's going on?"

"This man has been hoarding a document—a historical artifact— among other books of national import here in this sty he calls an office!"

Clive, now seated at his desk, looked around the room as he went puce. It was a stormy academic sea: overflowing shelves, books tucked in every available crevice, books stacked waist high on the rugs that dotted the stone floor.

"Sty!?"

"A historical document?" I cut in.

Deloris had papers in her hands, and Clive had both hands flattened over something in a plastic sheet. I assumed it was the item Deloris was hell-bent on retrieving.

Clive blustered on, "The paper I've been painstakingly deciphering for the MacLaoch solicitors." It sounded like something he'd told me already.

Deloris scoffed, "Oh aye? Peabody had that archival page for the better part of last year, and he surmised that unless ye were an Old Norse orthographer, ye wouldn't know what a Blood Rock or Raining Grass might mean in modern language. If ye can decipher it at all."

Dr. Edwin Peabody had been in Glentree at the behest of Rowan for research into the origin of the MacLaoch curse. While here, he began electrostatic measurements of Rowan and eventually me in an attempt to understand how the curse energy moved from generation to generation as well as our connection.

Rowan had also spent much of the prior year helping Peabody navigate the complex relationship that Glentree's dueling archivists had. In hindsight, I now knew I'd witnessed him doing this. I'd arrived in the library a year ago and unknowingly passed Rowan as he took books and papers from Deloris to Clive. It was a moment I wish I could have rewound and watched with my current knowledge—it had been an early moment in my brush with my destiny. Rowan enjoyed this task, but now without him as a go-between—he was dealing with bigger, more troubling business—they were back to getting on like a spark and dry brush.

Rowan had explained to me that Deloris and Clive had been extremely close when the library first opened its archival section and hired Deloris some thirty-odd years ago. It had been a beautiful relationship between two scholarly minds...until Deloris urged Clive to move the MacLaoch chief's journals from the 1800s and before to the climate-controlled archives in the Glentree library.

"What's this paper you need, Clive?" I said now.

"The paper, Miss Minory—"

Deloris scoffed hard enough to have her spectacles bounce on their chain, "Minory! Aye, her name is Nicole Baker, ye—"

Clive interrupted, hands still pressed to the protected page amid a sea of yellowed papers. "As I have discussed with Miss Minory in our weekly gatherings, I honor her original bloodlines, not the fickle nature of her great-grandmother's heart and choice of marriage partner." To me: "Do you see why I must defend my work and the work of my forbearers to prove you and you alone are the only savior and descendant of the Minory of the curse and as such belong within the familial arms of Clan MacLaoch?"

Savior was a bit much, but I let Clive have his moment. Despite the curse against Rowan's chief seat being lifted, things had yet to vastly improve for Rowan and the clan.

He Clived on, saying, "Arguably, this time will be the last time I will need to defend the Minory name, before you dispose of Minory for MacLaoch. Therefore, my work must be absolute; we will not have another chance with Casswell."

While Deloris muttered about Clive living in another century, his words gave me pause. The thought of my marriage to Rowan was like a little bird that fluttered into my palm, and I cradled it and looked at it with fondness. We were handfasted, what I'd come to consider as engaged, but we hadn't talked much of making it legal in the modern sense.

Clive pulled down his glasses, a question in his gaze, and Deloris mirrored him.

"Miss Minory, you look as if this is the first you've thought of marriage to the chief. Please tell me that the laird has at least promised marriage to you, yes?"

"I, well," I said, thinking that he had, or would, if given the time. His actions were more what I based our relationship's security on, and my answer was "Yes, of course." But I couldn't help but think Rowan's plate was so full that planning a wedding with half the family in another country was something that would have to wait until the right time.

Clive squinted at me and then toward my empty ring finger.

Deloris chimed in, attempting an explanation, "Yes, dear, when you marry the chief, there's a bit of pomp and circumstance that happens. I vaguely remember his uncle...when he attempted several of his marriages... There is some sort of process that happens."

Clive confirmed with a nod. "Precisely."

"He never officially wed any of the women he promised marriage to, so it's hard to say whether it was his philandering—I don't mean to speak ill of the dead, but the man was a well-known lover of women—or this MacLaoch clan process that did it."

Clive gave Deloris a covert smile, one that said the whole town knew the thirty-third clan chief proposed marriage to women out of formality and not any sense of wonder and love.

Then to me, he said, "As you may know, the Minory heir occurrence is a once and a lifetime project for me, one I relish and wish my own father were here to enjoy the surprises and—"

"Clive," I interrupted with a get-on-with-it hand roll.

"Yes, well, whilst I can't confirm any of those rumors about our previous chief, I will say that I've never been so involved with the process as I am this time. Whether it was that or his wandering eye, I can assure you, this time, it'll not be the process."

My stomach pinched in concern with the unknown. "Well, it won't be a wandering eye for Rowan and me. So, what do you mean, Deloris, that it was the clan process that did it? Like his fiancées were run out of town by the clan solicitor?" Then I mumbled, "We're handfasted—that's engaged enough. Right?"

The look of disbelief was back on Deloris's face but then fell away, "Oh aye, not to worry, Cole, love—everyone knows your bond is deep with the chief." She came to me, and patted my shoulder with her free hand. Then pressed the subject further with a bold question asked in a delicate tone: "But he has asked ye to marry him, aye? Ye've casually talked of it?"

Both spectacles were back on me. I opened my mouth then closed it, unsure what to say. I diverted hard onto another subject, the one I was actually there for. "Sure, yeah, absolutely. Now, Clive, I just popped by for our normal session... Need me to call my mother and get any more names of Daddy's kin? If not, I'll just be headed back to work now." I threw my thumb over my shoulder and took a step back. Then another. It felt a little like fleeing. It was one thing to mediate a skirmish between them—it was another when they both turned their eyes upon me.

"Yes, well, now, I have a note here," he said, lifting his hands off the paper for the first time and looked around for it. Deloris's eyes went to the paper artifact and took a small step toward his desk. "I've spoken directly to your mother," he said.

"Come again?" I was nearly in the corridor when he said that, and I gave myself whiplash turning back. "You did what?"

"I've spoken with your mother. Half of our sessions have been you conversing with her to get the details I need of your father's lineage. I took it upon myself to discuss with her directly, and I must say," he said, giving me a smug look, "she is quite agreeable. Not at all the force of nature that you insinuated she'd be if I were to talk with her alone."

I took a moment to digest what he'd said. I was wholly surprised that Mother would be agreeable with Clive about the Minory lineage. A lineage search that she so adamantly wanted me to put to bed last year. Though the part that made me shiver was the way he said *agreeable*, as if he'd had a delightful bite of figgy pudding.

"Clive, you know I love coming here for our regular harassment-

and-history sessions, but I'll have to quit you if you make a habit of hitting on my mother."

Deloris giggled.

He made a guttural sound of disgust. "Och! Don't be so American, will you please, Miss Minory?"

"Aye, Mr. Clive. As ye wish." I bowed.

He sighed, adding dryly, "I will miss our meetings ever so much, Miss Minory."

"Yes, we are getting to the end of it, aren't we?" I had to admit that I'd grown fond of our scheduled visits. He reminded me of a grumpy uncle who hid his love for jaunty social discourse.

"Done, then?" Deloris asked and looked at the plastic-covered sheet. She was surprisingly close to the desk now.

Clive clomped his hands back down over it.

Deloris pressed. "Ye've introduced her to Eli Campbell, then? And Mary?"

It was Clive's turn to scoff. "Mary? Come now, Miss Minory is closer in relation to me!"

Deloris waited.

"And Eli, no."

Their conversation felt like an old argument being rehashed.

"Eli who?" I asked.

The spectacles were back on me, matching expressions of surprise.

"What?" I asked.

"Eli Campbell? Ye've not heard of him?" Deloris asked gently as if I were a grenade who'd lost her pin.

Clive helped her. "I do not think she knows."

"Knows what?"

"If ye've no clue who Eli Campbell is—"

Clive interrupted, "Then it's settled."

Deloris looked at him. "Far from it."

"She knows not who he is—can we ask for a better control group?"

"Who's Eli?"

They beamed at me. Deloris added, "Ye'll see. It's settled, then. I've a mind to bring her 'round Mary's house. I'll set it up."

I was glad they were suddenly on even ground, chuffed with each other even, but I was still in the dark on this Eli person and the surprise it brought them that I didn't know him.

"Just one hint? Who's Eli?"

"Tower control down at the coast guard station."

I looked at Clive then Deloris. They might as well have said, "Brian in Portland"—I still had no clue.

"All right." I let it go. "But back to this paper," I said, nodding toward Clive's hands. "If I leave to go back to work, there won't be bloodshed, will there?"

They both laughed good-naturedly, as if earlier they hadn't been a moment away from a physical brawl.

"Absolutely not." Clive beamed at Deloris.

"Agreed," said Deloris, "as long as the paper comes with me."

I closed my eyes and groaned.

"It will not!"

I cut in before Deloris could fire back. "I understand that Rowan isn't here to see this transfer of materials back and forth between you two, but if you would be willing to work together to return the materials to the library, Clive, I'd be grateful. And, Deloris, about the library card—let's just make him one and keep it at the library for us to use when he borrows stuff."

"Well, I never." Clive harrumphed.

I smiled, "Thank you, Clive," I said, pretending to take his retort as an acquiescing to my request.

Deloris clicked her tongue. "It's fine. But who will pay his overdue fines?"

"I will not pay—"

I held up a hand. "I'll pay."

Deloris raised her brows at me. "It's three thousand pounds, Nicole."

My brows matched hers as Clive shouted, "Highway robbery!"

She turned back to him. "Well, ye've had these for a decade—even after I've put in formal request after formal request to have these back—and I'm feeling puckish!" she shouted, holding up the three delicate-looking manuscripts.

"We'll figure out a way to raise the money."

Deloris looked me up and down then nodded. "Aye, fine."

"So," I said, looking back to Clive, who was looking on edge, "Deloris will house our books until you need them next, and when you do, all you need is to arrive in person and request them." It felt odd to have to describe the purpose of a library to Clive, but I just chalked it up to one of those things you do because the situation was better for it.

"And return them on time," Deloris said, making Clive go puce once more.

"I will not be limited to fourteen days!"

"It's four weeks, ye dolt, and if ye need for scholarly articles, you can extend for twelve weeks or a custom time as long as there's no wait list."

Before Clive could reply, I said, "Great! It's settled. Deloris, I'll see you back to the car park?"

"Psht," Deloris scoffed and turned to leave.

I sidled up to Clive's desk, my satchel bumping a tower of books as I did. "When you're done with the archival document, you'll take it to Deloris?"

He gave me a petulant look.

I put my hand out. "Do we have a deal?"

"Aye, fine."

We shook, and as his hand left the paper, I looked down, and it was as familiar to me as the first page of my master's thesis.

"What the..."

Clive gave my limp hand a shake. "What is it, Miss Minory?"

"That paper."

Deloris came back. "What of it? Is it stained?"

Clive was about to object when I said, "I've seen this before."

They both looked to me and my open-mouthed expression and back to the page.

"Ye, have? With Dr. Peabody?"

I shook my head. "No, it's— I've—" I attempted.

Clive turned the page around so that it was upright to me. "You have seen this before? Where?"

"'Fishing was poor that day, rain kept the mud deep and the animals stuck...'" I read. The skin on the back of my neck tightened as if a familiar hand was placed there. I straightened up and looked around, then back down to the page. The feeling was gone, and the page was now illegible. Sepia animal skin paper deeply lined with runes and scribbles.

"You can read it," Clive said and with the loud scrape of his chair on the stone stood. "Miss Minory can read her ancient grandfather's handwriting."

"Nonsense..." Deloris said, looking to me as if she wanted me to agree. It was nonsense, right?

"That paper was written by a Minory?"

"Not a Minory. *The* Minory."

I was flabbergasted. "Clive, how—"

He shut his eyes and waved his hands in the air. "Fine, I knew not that it was absolutely from him. I'd a strong inkling, and now you've confirmed it!" His eyes popped open, "It had just been rumor and speculation. I needed more time with it"—he gave a pointed glance at Deloris—"to be quite sure. Though, I believe you've confirmed the rumors. You can read it."

"I can't."

"Ye just did."

I was at a loss for words but despite not liking the idea, I was open to it. "Maybe."

"My God," Deloris whispered.

## Five

Clive gestured to the paper there on top of his chaotic paper-and-book-filled desk and dove into the heart of it: "These papers were in the possession of Dr. Edwin Peabody—"

"Aye, we know," Deloris cut in.

Clive continued, "He was a special guest of our laird, Rowan James Mac—"

"Aye, she knows who he is, more than the rest of us."

I smiled. Yes, I sure did, I thought. "Continue, Clive."

"Yes, well, if Miss Minory cannot read them now, we must find someone who can. Unless you can again?" he added, looking at me with eyes wide in anticipation.

I looked back down at the sheet that looked as if a razor had been take to its gutter edge while the other three sides were fuzzy like loose-leaf was wont to do over time.

"Nope."

"Fine. Then let me say that it is this guest of our laird—Dr. Edwin Peabody—who has advised me that a local, not in Glentree proper but north of here, who can possibly decipher these. The Misty Cliffs."

"Sure, let me see if Rowan's not too busy—maybe he can give us a name or a number to ring."

Deloris and Clive watched me like a TV set with the local football game on, happy to witness what Rowan and I did, our "magic trick." I gently reached out to Rowan with my mind and got a gentle but distracted mild sizzle back. "He's a little distracted." I pulled out my cell to text Rowan what I was contacting him about but then groaned. The dark screen told me that I'd once again forgotten to charge its tired, minuscule battery. I'd been too busy losing my mind to that dark-haired man last night. I shoved it back into my pocket.

Clive puffed his chest out like a rooster and declared to us, "We need answers. Let us head north, then. We can take some provisions from the kitchens; it will be a full day's walk."

Clive turned, grabbing his walking stick, which was the result of two saplings twined together and polished to a high shine, and knowing Clive, it was likely the walking stick his father had had, and his father before him, et cetera, ad nauseum.

Deloris scoffed. "I'll not be walking to the northern tip of Skye, Clive MacLaoch, and in case you hadn't noticed, Ms. Baker has a plethora of things she must look after while the laird is gone and cannot walk all the way up there."

I was about to head off the ensuing kerfuffle when Clive said, "Fine, I shall head out on this journey solo."

"Och, you're so daft! I have a coupe we can all fit in, except that walking stick; that surely will not fit."

It was only six feet in length, but I think I understood. Regular Clive, she could barely get on with. Quest Clive, she wasn't having any part of. Clive looked to his stick and the offer Deloris made to take us up to Misty Cliffs via car and not foot and placed his walking stick back against the stone wall. "Fine. Let us depart."

Deloris tucked the books under her arm and headed for the door. "Come now, can't you go anywhere without it sounding like you're heading out on a quest?"

Clive stomped indignantly. "We are searching for an elder with runes expertise in the ancient north of Skye in order to help us decipher a Minory document. What else, pray tell, Miss Deloris, would we be setting out on?"

I shrugged. "I have to agree, feels quest-y."

Deloris made a guttural sound of disbelief. "Why did I bother going to university when I could just make up my own realities..." she mumbled as we exited for the car park.

OUT AT THE MISTY CLIFF'S CHURCH, CLIVE, DELORIS, AND I all stood in the gravel car park adjacent to the low stone wall that kept the casual passerby from entering the graveyard and wide expanse of pasture that was like a green sea around the boxy whitewashed church. There on that grassy plateau we were treated to a forceful breeze. My hair shot backward, and my jacket flapped like a kite in the wind. It was the kind of good, bracing wind that reminds the soul that there's a power greater than it in the world.

The clouds were high and clustered around the mountains in the distance behind us, while back down the way we'd come was the shoreline. The black, rocky bluffs of Skye's northernmost point stabbed the blue-gray of the Atlantic Ocean. Back up and beyond the ancient white church, sitting like the plump green backs of enormous hippos, were the outer isles. The Hebrides.

Clive pointed out to the cliff and down the coast and said over the wind, "There is the path that leads back to Laoch. If ye follow it, it leads you to the castle in just a handful of miles. 'Tis not for the faint of heart, but it's a path well-known to the chief in his days before you arrived, Miss Minory, when he opted for spending more time closer to Laoch than roaming his vast estate."

"And ye wanted us to traverse it." Deloris glared at him.

Clive's statement about Rowan was somewhat news to me. I'd known Rowan had had difficulty adjusting when he returned home to civilian life from the hospital in Germany, leaving the war and his military career as a Royal Air Force pilot behind. He found that living in his forests was a kind of soothing balm for his rattled mind. He could tap into his youth when he spent more time among the trees than people, allowing him to thrive in nature like a wild animal, judgment free, then return to the castle with clearer mind because the rest of him was physically and emotionally worked out.

I nodded and followed Deloris, with Clive in the rear, to the garden gate set into the hand-built stone wall. Deloris paused to tell something to Clive, letting me go first, and as I touched the gate I, too, paused. The kind of pause you feel just before the phone rings and its news about a parent's death or a baby being born. It was just a gate, but opening it felt consequential even though the church was small in stature and little known to Glentree residents there on the outer edge of MacLaoch land. The paint was peeling off the gate; little white flakes dotted the gravel. I lifted the latch with a metal click and opened it; the gate swung open with a squeak, and I passed through it. Standing on the other side, I took in the church and its outer walls where untamed climbing roses rioted. The thorny beauties reached up past the church's glazed windows on their wandering race to the top of the steeple. Their thick, fragrant heads bobbed in the moist sea air, reminding me that they had likely done the very same thing for centuries. Our lives were infantile there in that yard of the deceased.

I held the gate open for Deloris and Clive. They both were taking in their surroundings like tourists on a walk. On either side of us were tombstones in erratic rows. Those closer to the path all seemed to be made of chalk. They'd aged badly in the salt air, and lichen was doing its best to revert the stone back to its elemental state. They sat like broken teeth jutting out of the grass, their inscriptions eroded and mostly indecipherable, save the shape of Celtic knots. Within the low stonewall of the graveyard the grass was mowed to within an inch of its life and tediously trimmed around each headstone as if His Royal Highness resided there, or at least the clan chiefs of MacLaoch. But that I knew for certain was not true; MacLaochs had been residing in the MacLaoch churchyard and crypt since—if you believed Rowan's version—before time itself.

The setting was heartbreakingly beautiful, the kind of beauty that hits your bones, because with it comes a touch of darkness. The place was the resting place of the dead and situated on a cliff under moody skies. It made you want to cry and write poetry or the kind of novels where no one in the end survives. That place had seen things—bore witness to—unspeakable acts, and that energy permeated the air and the soil, and halfway down the trail, I thought better of knocking on the arched wooden church door.

Deloris, it seemed, felt it too. "Oh, I'm not liking the feel of this place," she said, looking behind us as if a ghost were walking there.

"Yes, well," Clive said, getting as close to an agreement as he was able in the hushed moment; then he added, "We've come this far. Just a quick knock to see if anyone is 'round; then, we'll leave."

"Clive, do you know what Rowan said about his encounter with this person? Any details like go to the back door and bang three times... then run for your life?"

Clive was also spooked and looking about said, "Not quite, but it now makes sense in this context. He came across them in the woods just south of here on the border of MacLaoch lands. He said they spoke in a tongue unfamiliar to him, then in an incomplete translation, something about 'it begins' or 'so it begins.'"

I was surprised again. I'd not heard Rowan talk of this person or what sounded like a prediction. "When was that?"

"Oh, a while back, my dear. Before you arrived."

I nodded; it was what I was starting to call "before my time," or BMT. We had Eastern Standard Time (EST) and Pacific Standard Time (PST), even Hawai'i Standard Time (HST); now I had BMT.

"As a matter of fact, I believe it was the...oh, day before an American tourist passed out in his arms."

It was odd hearing myself be dryly called an American tourist by Clive, but I smiled when I finally recognized his joke. "Oh yeah, when was that?"

"I believe the day you walked into the chief's life and set everything on its end."

Deloris smiled back at me.

"That was a good time," I said and meant it. I brought us back to the person Rowan encountered. "Well, they weren't wrong. A lot began then. So, that person was a seer?"

"I've not a clue," he said and knocked loudly on the arched wood door. His knock reverberated into the vaulted space on the other side of the door. While we waited, we looked around to the empty graveyard and lawns and tried to not think that someone was watching us. Despite the lack of other visible human beings, I shivered anyway as Clive knocked again. When again no one answered, he called out, "Hello? Anyone here?"

It wasn't much longer before the creeps won out, and with a cautious eye on the place and the tombstones, we made our way back to the car park and the bracing wind.

"Is it just me," Deloris asked, "or did it feel like we needed a ritual sacrifice to get that door to open?"

Clive harrumphed and opened his car door. "Aye, and not be of MacLaoch blood standing on that sacred land."

They both looked at me, expectations high in their gaze, that I go back solo to that door.

"You can't pay me enough to sacrifice myself." I'd witnessed the power of the supernatural. Lady MacLaoch showed me that a spirit like hers could tear a hole in our branch of time. I didn't know who this rune person was, but if they could see Rowan's future, I wasn't going to approach them alone. I'd need someone firmly holding my hand.

We silently rode back to Glentree along the winding coastal road. Clive kept checking the rearview mirror, and it wasn't until we were back on MacLaoch land that we all breathed a sigh of relief.

*Six*

It was late morning by the time I got to the research site and early afternoon by the time I finally lost all the heebie-jeebies I acquired at Misty Cliffs. Glad to be on MacLaoch soil, I got to work. Squatting in my assigned quadrant, I worked as bush tits flitted from perch to perch in the thicket just beyond me. Lifting a plant's fledgling leaves with the eraser of my pencil, I notated leaf lobes and coloring. *Sorbus aucuparia*, I thought and sighed with a kind of proud joy; it was another glorious native species. Rowan's namesake was *Sorbus aucuparia*, and from our data collection, it was thriving in our little plot of land. With a fat smile on my face, I could almost hear Rowan making a mischievous joke about the number of seeds necessary to grow all these rowan trees. Which of course made me think of his seed, and just like that a thought began to grow: he and I and a wee one. Just this morning I'd been introduced to the delightful daydream of marriage, and now babies were making me warm and fuzzy. I definitely liked the idea, but it was a daydream for the future.

My name was called from down the trail behind me, interrupting my thoughts. Smothering my fuzzy daydream, I notated where I was on my chart and turned to meet Marion, who was making her way from the castle to me, waving.

"Hello, Marion," I said as I stretched out my legs and back from crouching for so long. A gentle breeze from behind her brought with it the scents of the Circle Garden's green foliage and blooming azaleas.

She was wearing a wool skirt of the MacLaoch plaid and a cream cardigan with matching pearls, her salt-and-pepper hair pulled back with a broach she'd had made into a hair clip, as she'd told me when I first admired it. She had a fresh-looking coat of pink lipstick on.

She smiled. "Hello, my lady."

"How goes it?" I asked, tucking my pencil behind my ear and aluminum clipboard under my arm. Calling me that was Marion's and Flora's way of reminding me who I was to the castle and the clan. As in, Lady Rowan James Douglas MacLaoch. But they knew I saw myself as just Cole, studier of plants, so I suspect it had become not just their way but their private joke, to call me "my lady" to see how long it took my brain to break.

"I've got a message from Ruth—apparently there's a chap in admin to see you?"

"Me?"

"Yes," she said, looking at the piece of paper stuck to her finger, "he's from the University of Glasgow and said the Fund sent him?"

"Oh, that's quick," I said. "They told me just yesterday they didn't have enough qualified people to come out just yet." The National Cultural Preservation Fund, or the Fund, for short, had classified us a conservation project, and we were receiving monies from their general support fund. In exchange, a distracted Fund director had told me over the phone when we finally connected, they'd want to send an archaeologist out to poke around. I could hear the clink of glasses and laughter on his end while we talked. He hadn't seemed too concerned about sending someone immediately. Most of their archaeologists were busy with the massive unearthing of an ancient drinking hall on Orkney, he told me, so the bits and bobs my team had accidentally uncovered were relegated to literal old news. I had agreed and gotten off the phone, unsure if he'd just given me a code for "actually, we're too drunk to care." I had assumed we'd end up packing up the few odds and ends at the end of the summer and driving them over to Aberdeen to have an archaeologist look at them there.

"Shall we?" Marion asked, indicating I walk with her.

I looked down at my watch then around to the field. I had more work planned, but it wouldn't do to keep the archaeologist from our sole funder waiting. Plus, maybe I could find out what in the disorganized heck was happening. "Maybe he could come up here—"

"Yes!" Marion injected. "This is a very good idea!" She beamed hustling back down the trail.

I couldn't decide whether her hustle was to get the man up here as quick as possible or because something she had going on in the kitchens was at risk of scorching. With one more curious look after her, her pale-pink cardigan a soft light amid the phosphorescent azaleas, I went back to work.

It was less than a half hour later when Marion was calling to me again. I stood up in the knee-high shrubs and meadow grass, notated where I was, and looked down by our workstation; a tall man was with her. His brown hair was a full two heads above her white twist, and in that tweed, he looked like a model showcasing the latest in Cambridge fashion. Even from this distance, I could tell the Fund's doctor of archaeology was no older than I.

Halfway to them, I heard Marion's chiming waterfall giggle. I smiled to myself as the puzzle of her earlier hustle came together. Glentree was a small town, Laoch Castle estate was even more isolated, and if a handsome stranger with business at the estate showed up at the administrative offices? He was front page news.

Closer now, I could see that Marion's cheeks were pink, and her eyes glittered clear and bright. Nearby, only one of the six of my crew thought that Marion was more curious than the tasks they were bent to. I smiled back at Holly, who raised her eyebrows in response. I was glad I wasn't the only one beholding this joy.

Holly Alexander was a local whose father and his father before him managed the whisky production at the corporate distillery the next town over. They were Clan MacLaoch, and Holly, much like the rest of the clan, felt like family to me already.

Finally face-to-face with the archaeologist, I had a solid oh-my moment, as my mother called them. He was a tall and lean young buck with the face of an angel. Sharp cheekbones flanked eyes that made me wonder if it was their color or their perfect setting that made him so strikingly handsome. Or was it the soft, full lips that stretched wide into a welcoming smile that drew in a person, disarming them, preparing them to say yes to anything he was about to ask?

I stuck my hand out. "I'm Nicole Baker, the representative on this project here at Castle Laoch." I watched the light play against his skin, casting angular shadows in all the right places to highlight his facial features. His brown hair was threaded with gold, the ringlets, long enough to brush the bottom of his strong jaw, tucked behind his ears.

"It's a pleasure to meet you," he said, squeezing my hand gently, the lilt in his words drawing the ear to him like it would be to a song. "The name is Dr. Mickey Gillian, University of Glasgow. Call me Mickey."

"A pleasure," I said genuinely. I was instantly charmed by his Irish brogue. In just a few words of introduction, he somehow elicited a feeling of joy and eroticism.

As he released my hand, I saw the smallest slip of his gaze to my bare ring finger. I smiled to myself—he was no fool about what he looked like and the feelings he drew out of others. I'd wager his bed was only empty when he wanted it to be. My brother had charms like this man's. He had made chasing women into an Olympic sport in the small town in South Carolina where we were born and raised. TJ spent most of our youth extolling his wisdom to me, his subordinate, as if I too were a young man wanting to get women into bed.

I made a mental note to call Rowan and tell him I loved him.

I said, "It's an honor to have someone of your professional caliber visit us up here at our research site."

A rarity in these parts, his American-straight teeth glinted at me. "My caliber," he repeated and put his palm over his heart. "Ms. Baker, please, it is you who are doing me a great honor in seeing me on such short notice. I am here at the behest of the Fund to assist your team, if you'll have me."

"Of course, anyone from the Fund is welcome here at the site. Of course," I said again. I cleared my throat and took a beat. I was the vision of eager. "How do we proceed?"

There was something in my question that seemed to catch him off guard or made him think harder than seemed necessary.

"Very simply, consider me your summer shadow," he said with a smile that informed me he was nothing but a gift.

This gave me pause. Without a clear directive from the Fund, he was just some dude hanging about, and an aimless archaeologist was dangerous for my plants—folks like that had a pension for digging for things underground. My stomach pinched. I carefully dug for some guardrails to put on him. "Is that so?"

"I've got my marching orders from the Fund. Now, you needn't worry about their strict standards, as I'll be in touch with them on how things are going here."

Marion's cheeks blushed pink.

I smiled again at him while my mind unpacked the load of information stuffed into his short sentence. I hadn't just been sent an archaeologist; I'd been sent a minder. Normally, I'd love not having to deal with the paperwork associated with the artifacts and reporting, but I didn't like handing that control over to someone possibly working at odds to my goals. Then Marion giggled again, shifting my focus; she was now literally clutching her pearls against her own dirty thoughts. I gave her a kind smile. "Thank you, Marion, for escorting him out here." If I acted now, I would hold steady the man's body count; if she stayed any longer, he was going to give Marion a heart attack.

Dr. Gillian held his hand out to her. "Thank you very much. I know it was a trouble out o' your day, and I appreciate it."

"Oh, you're welcome," she said, sliding her hand into his. He kissed her knuckles before giving her hand back, "It was no problem at all"— she beamed—"and when you come back tomorrow, I can escort you out here again. Or," she said to me with a hopeful smile, "he can stay in one of the castle rooms so he doesn't have to travel so far from town?"

While the castle did have rooms for guests, they were all tucked up tight, furniture covered in sheets and windows shuttered. It also wasn't my call. "So thoughtful, Marion, thank you. We shall defer to the laird?"

She beamed at Dr. Gillian before looking at me. "What? Oh aye, of course."

He watched our back-and-forth with obvious pleasure.

"Thank you," I said again and looked pointedly at Marion then to the path. When she made no move to return to the castle, I said, "Marion, I'll take it from here. Ruth is calling." I looked over her shoulder, going up on my tiptoes, feigning I was watching Ruth waving to us through the trees from the castle.

She swiveled around. "She is?" and looked through the trees while she headed a few steps back along the path then stopped, coming back to Dr. Gillian. She held her hand out again, and he kissed it again. "It was a treat to meet you." She exhaled with a dream in her eyes. "See you tomorrow."

I was going to have to speak to Rowan when he returned home. He needed to toughen up our admin ladies—he needed to flirt with them relentlessly every morning, get them immune to hot young men, or we'd lose the castle to the next pretty face.

Halfway into the Circle Garden, Marion turned back and waved.

Dr. Gillian raised his hand and turned to me a private smile on his lips. "Apologies for my intrusion. I understand that the first weeks of a new site require intensive work from its managers. But do you have a moment to talk?"

I nodded and gestured for us to walk down the lower path to a spot where we could view the entirety of the site, the purple mountains in the distance while the waves crashed behind us against the cliffs. It was where I'd taken clan members curious about what we were up to in that side field.

"I'm glad that you've come, but I must tell you that I'm surprised. The Fund's director himself made it sound like we wouldn't be getting anyone right away. He said this just yesterday."

Dr. Gillian walked easily next to me, hands clasped behind his back. "Ah yes. Sounds like our communications were like ships passing through the night. I had gotten word a few days ago that my fieldwork in Sudan fell through, so I reached out to them and to my dean's office letting them know my summer was now open. The Fund snapped me up, and here I am," he said and smiled then nodded to the castle towering next to us. "This place is incredible—a blend of architectural styles as it was built out over the centuries, and still functioning."

I stepped over a few loose rocks. "Yes, Marion will give you a tour tomorrow, I'm sure, or this afternoon, if you like?" I asked as I came to the spot I'd been seeking and pivoted, looking back up the field.

Dr. Gillian followed suit, and we were quiet for a while. I was hoping he could see the beauty in what grew above ground and not be eyeing it only for buried treasure.

"It's a wonderful place," he said, and we fell into more silence.

"In the course of our work, we haven't stumbled upon much that would be of interest to you," I eventually said. "But we've found a couple things." I felt like I was walking a tightrope between making us sound too boring for him and giving him another sparkle so that he didn't suggest setting up an official dig himself. I could maybe make use of what he'd told me—he hadn't been expected, probably not even wanted to be here himself; he just found himself with time on his hands, and a gap in paychecks. Based what I'd experienced with the Fund, Dr. Gillian probably didn't know much himself about the process they wanted from him. I quickly surmised, the next few days I'd show him what he needed to report back to his higher-ups: nothing here! Then he could take his lovely but distracting face to Orkney with the others and check in again later as the director originally planned.

I gave him the tour and eventually stopped back at the tented "central command" where I picked up the box of artifacts we'd already collected. "What do you make of this?" I asked, retrieving an item made of wood.

As he took it from me, our hands brushed each other. His touch was warm and dry. He was thoughtful as he turned it over, analyzing it.

"It's part of a quaich, the original word *cuach*, from Gaelic, meaning "cup" or "bowl." I'd say from the late 1600s. This is wood, the easiest material to make them out of. Later, after the introduction of herd animals, they would have made them of horn. And later still, pewter or silver either inlaid or wrapped around the rim. People have theorized that the earliest quaich would have been shaped to mimic scallop shells, which coastal people surely used as their earliest drinking vessels, but I have always thought, as soon as we learned to carve, wouldn't we have made something with handles? Much easier to hold drunk," he said and grinned at me. His smile faded as he gracefully ran his finger around the invisible whole rim of what would have been a complete quaich. "Maybe this one broke in a drunken brawl. Likely we'll find innumerable fractured and degraded pieces—this area is close to the castle yet downwind, a perfect location for a trash pile. Not fact, just a possibility."

I was surprised and looked back over my field. Could that be a contributing factor to the field's biological makeup? Dr. Gillian was perhaps more valuable than I had assumed. He handed the shard back to me. I gingerly took it and turned it over in my hands, catching the archaeological fever now, wondering whose lips this cup had sated.

He misread my contemplation, though his misunderstanding also provided useful information. "As exciting as a midden is, I'm not sure this site has the potential for a big dig. Sorry." I felt a light wash of relief before he amended. "No doubt you've heard about Orkney," he said. "If we do find something, know that we could have diggers here in a second, rest assured."

"Yes, a...drinking hall in Orkney?" I asked, changing the subject.

"Viking drinking hall."

"Huh..."

He was looking in the rest of our "trash bin," so to speak. He plucked a smooth bone and angled it this way and that between his fingers. He paused for a moment and searched the long expanse of worktable, cluttered with tools, water bottles, and write-in-the-rain paper. He stabbed his fingers into the open toolbox belonging to Holly and extracted her ten-times magnifier. Folding out the lens, he took a closer look and said, "Not from kingdom animalia but rather plantae." I blanched. How had I, a botanist, taken this bit of plant for an animal? "Specifically, skeletal seaweed. Is there a white sand beach nearby?"

Feeling like I was being taken for a ride, I pointed out the obvious. "Seaweed has no skeleton. But, please, do go on."

"I take it you're not familiar with maërl, Ms. Baker," he said, his tone changing to that of lecturer. "The cell structure of this seaweed results in heavy lime deposits, giving it a skeletal-like structure. As I'm sure you know, lime is—"

"Calcium carbonate, yes," I said, looking down at the piece in a sense of wonder.

"Exactly, making it much like bone, and excellent fertilizer, among other things. This piece," he said, "shows the wear and tear of seawater and of being ground against sand. A casual glance, and that buffing could make it look like a bird bone."

I took the piece from his proffered palm. "Fascinating."

"This place really is," he said. "In fact, would you and that fine American accent tell me more o' the fascinating area that we'll be studying?"

"How 'bout tomorrow?" Giving him my best South Carolinian drawl, then boldly winked at him because two could play the indulgent game, and from the look on his face he was loving it.

"Well, then, I suppose I'll have to...delay my gratification until later."

I had to take a moment and gather my wits, then put my hand out to shake. "First thing tomorrow I'll walk you around the field and explain everything. Thank you so much for coming by, and when you get a chance, send me your contact information."

His smile caught me up short. He was angelic with his rainwater curls tucked behind his ears, but when he wanted to, he could turn up the amperage. His voice went low, "I look forward to giving it to you." The innuendo so heavily laced his simple reply that I knew he was using the opportunity to offer his body. Naked.

"Jesus Christ," I said under my breath.

He shook my hand and then brought it to his lips. "What was that?" he asked.

My eyes stared at his lips a hair's width from touching my skin, his breath warming the backs of my knuckles, "Nothing," I said, giving myself a mental smack to the back the head.

"I thought you said something that involved Jesus?"

A cool breeze began playing with the ends of my hair and clearing the heady pheromones that had nestled in me. I said quietly, a hint of a knowing smile on my lips, "It is just that I usually call on Jesus to help me when a devil is in my midst. Now, are you going to be a gentleman and kiss my knuckles and give me my hand back, or am I going to have to take it from you, young man?" I didn't know about Jesus in this case, but I could always count on Mother for an assist.

His chuckle came from deep in his throat; he was enjoying my admonition. "Yes, ma'am," he said and, keeping his eyes on me, brushed a kiss across my knuckles. He gave a mock tilt of a cap before leaving through the Circle Garden. I unabashedly watched him leave.

Holly came up behind me, the light crunch under her boots sounding before I heard the flick of a water bottle spout and her long drag from it. She sighed out in relief, "Oh aye, my god, who was that chap?"

"A devil in disguise."

"Mother Mary, keep me safe...and in his arms. Please tell me he's looking for a job here. I could use a good wrestle with a devilish man."

I looked over my shoulder at the younger woman. She had her hair pulled back in a tight French braid, her baby hairs swirled expertly down her high forehead, and a choker around her neck. "Then you should know I think he pocketed your magnified glass."

She squinted, studying his backside before he disappeared between the hedges of the far side of the Circle Garden. "Aye, and so it begins."

# Seven

Later that evening, I sat on the bench under the wall phone of the cottage, receiver to my ear and Rowan on the other end of it, wrenching my boots off. I felt like a teenager again, tucked in a nook for a call with my boyfriend. He'd just gotten to his accommodations, and I could hear him typing while we talked.

"Who's this Mickey Gillian chap?"

I could see the low light of dusk beyond the cottage's windows; it would be a cloudy but dry evening.

"You spoke with Marion?" I guessed and felt downright envious she got to talk with him midday and wondered how she usurped me in preferential treatment with him.

He stopped typing, and there was a low laugh. "Yes, *mo ghràdh*, your phone was going straight to voice mail."

I put my hand to my forehead. "Ah yes," I said, remembering my dead cell.

"So, who's this chap? Marion says you got on like two best friends."

He was like a dog with a bone. I put my toe to the heel of my boot and wrenched my foot out of its wellie, I told him all that had happened, even about Marion giggling.

He sighed. One of those sighs that's far from content but rather is an expulsion of extra air because your blood pressure has increased and now there's less room in your body for anything else.

"What is it?"

"I need to be there."

"I'm here. Maybe I can help?"

"With a handsome stranger who's shown up and halved the wits of the people working there? Marion? Giggling and escorting him out into tha' wee pasture you're looking at? She and Flora don't abide getting shoes in the muck, and yet she risks it for this chap."

I smiled at his use of *wee pasture*. It was a term of endearment, used just with me. I said, "That probably explains why, when looking into his handsome features, I had trouble remembering my own name.

"As long as you don't forget mine. Handsome features, you say?"

I switched ears. "Like an angel fallen to earth—"

Rowan made a long loud sound that was half groan, half frustrated growl.

I gave an indelicate snort of laughter. "Fear not, my love," I said. "I sent him off. I amazingly had wits enough to do it."

"Och, good. Seriously, though, I hope he doesn't find a place tae dig."

He knew my soft spots. "Exactly."

We were quiet for some time, me working my socks off and him typing.

Something in Rowan's silence made me ask, "Are you really worried about something regarding this Mickey Gillian and the Fund?"

"Och, no' worried so much as I don't trust him tae do what you need there. And only what ye need."

"Only what I *need*? You're going to have to unpack that for me—"

"How old is he?"

I was about to answer, but it was a rhetorical question.

"He looks no older than ye. Ye say he's a PhD?"

"Yes, are you looking at a picture of him?"

"University website."

"And?"

He grunted cryptically.

"Does it say under his name, 'Loves to dig up biologically significant research sites'?"

"No," he said, dragging out the word.

"What is it?" I asked.

"What did the Fund say to ye about the artifacts?"

I knew where he was headed with this, and it was something I didn't want him to add to his plate of worries. "Look, I think it's just a miscommunication. The Fund is amped over this new dig out on Orkney, and—"

"The whole summer, though? What's the angle?"

I hated when Rowan got like this. The stressed-out version of himself that made him question even the most basic of motives. Though, to be fair, he had good reason. His cousin put a bullet in his shoulder last year, and that can really dampen the instinct to trust first. If your family was willing to shoot you, a stranger held zero trust credits.

"Did ye ring the Fund?"

"I left a voice mail," I said, "and he's not up to anything nefarious, Rowan. He'll be here for a few days, see we have nothing for him, and bounce to the hot new dig on Orkney. He even said he was dubious why the Fund sent him. I think he'll prove his point to the Fund and head out of town and check in again at the end of summer."

I heard him gust out a sigh. "Aye, fine."

"You don't sound fine."

"I trust ye," he said with sincerity.

"Then let me keep this on my plate of worries, love; you have a big enough helping on your own."

"I love ye. Not sure why I was worried."

I smiled. "I love you too, and you, worried? Never."

He gave a short laugh. "Oh aye, I'm down here, and a handsome stranger has shown up with a strong interest in ye and your research site—"

"Not to worry—it's a field for research, not hay primed for a good roll." I wasn't good at reassurances; I had my own PhD in antics.

"Oh aye, now you're having a laugh. I pray for the chap who tries to roll through your wee pasture before you've a chance to log each and every one of your species bairns."

"True," I said then amended, as his fingers started clicking on his keys again, "unless it was you. I'd fuck the hell out of you up and down that hillside."

"Uh-huh," he said absently.

I'd lost him to his work again. I felt a pang of longing wishing him back home; at least when he went back to his work here, I could sneak kisses.

"I miss you," I mumbled.

Rowan absently answered, "What was tha'?" Then, snapping clear, he said, "Oh aye, I feel it too. I want to be home now, but something has come up, and I'll need to be in Glasgow a while longer. I should be back home Saturday morning and all weekend."

"No worries," I said and tapped the back of my head softly against the wall behind me to knock those pining thoughts out my ear. "What you're doing there is important, I know. It's just..."

"Tha' house is cold without the other..." he finished.

"Yes. It is," I said, and we were quiet on the phone together, the silence having us both reaching for the other one until our skin lit up and my blood rushed along with his. I closed my eyes and ran my hand up my sparking arm and heard him sigh. "I haven't seen you in what feels like forever."

"It has only been two days..." I could hear the smile in his voice.

"What are you wearing?"

"Now?" I could hear him look down. "I think what I was wearing when I left."

"Oh babe, you should change."

"Oh aye? Are ye asking me to take my clothes off, lass?"

I felt a smile stretch across my lips. "I guess I am... Do it...slowly."

I felt his rough laugh like a dry brush over my skin sending a thrill down my spine.

"How many buttons?"

"All of them."

"And ye? What have you got on tha' needs to be on the floor?"

"Everything."

"Then let's get to it. Slip those buttons out, one by one."

"Are you?"

"As I do mine, I'm doing yours. My fingers are your fingers," he said in a baritone that reminded me of warm nights and skin-to-skin contact.

My arms lit up with more energy than I'd had before; it was as if he were pointedly pushing his hands through space and time to caress me. Fingers of moonlight rippled down my arms.

"Mmm..." came from deep in my throat. "It feels like you're here with me."

"You can feel that?"

"Yes," I whispered, both impressed and turned on.

"Good."

Feeling warm, I undid my top and slipped it off; cool cottage air kissed my skin, and I returned the heat Rowan was sending me. He exhaled softly, telling me, with satisfaction, that he'd felt it too.

I could feel the edges of his pearl buttons and the force he used to push them through the holes. We hadn't been so connected before. I inhaled long and deep, pressing my thighs together, wanting more of him.

Ghostly fingertips brushed the tops of my breasts, and I murmured, "More."

"Undo tha' top button," he said of my pants, and I responded in kind.

"You too."

I pushed my pants down to my knees so my thighs could open for him and my hand. Only things had gone cold as the line clicked.

"Hello?" I said, "Are you still there, babe?"

He grunted in dissatisfaction. "Cole... Cole, I am getting another call. I have to take it."

"Oh..." I let disappointment color that single syllable, telling him with tone that taking that other call wouldn't be wise.

"It's the bank man," he said, but it sounded more like *hangman*.

"Oh, all right," I said, giving him some latitude. "Everything going, OK?" Then I realized he'd already switched calls, hanging up on me.

I was surprised; he rarely interrupted our calls by taking another one. Much less one so damn intimate.

Between his time with solicitors, bank managers, and prospective investors and my time getting the research field prepped, our time to catch up with one another was rare, making these minutes precious for us both.

I reached back and slammed the handset onto its cradle, cursed unladylike, pulled my pants up, and rammed my feet back into my wellies. I had work to get back to.

It was dark out the windows behind me, and the cold of the evening pressed against the glass as I sat in Rowan's old desk chair up in the fairy tower office. Laptop open, I quieted my need for more of him, for the simple joy of telling Rowan that the first analysis of the field was looking like it was full of native species and that I'd successfully navigated a Deloris and Clive squabble. Instead, I reviewed the most recent data we'd gathered at the site and then began filling out purchase orders for our next round of field supplies.

I finished and, sitting back, shoved my fingers into my hair and gripped, pulling my scalp into an impromptu massage. My mind wandered off work and to the room I was sitting in. In that very room, that very chair, just a year ago, Rowan asked me to the gala. The laird of MacLaoch estate hiding behind his whisky and a wall of feigned indifference, letting the invite I'd held in my hand do all the talking. He told me later that he'd expected my answer to be a "go fuck yourself" and rightly so. I smiled then at the memory of him kissing my knuckles and telling me that when I said yes, it was the first real moment of untarnished joy he'd felt in years.

I sighed as the castle groaned and knocked around me as her stones released the day's warmth. I had grown accustomed to the sounds Castle Laoch made, but there were more nooks and crannies in the place than a prairie dog den. I tried to not be spooked being in the tallest tower alone.

I sat forward to check my email one more time before going back to my internet-less cottage for the night. There was a new note, copied to someone at the University of Glasgow's College of Archaeology, from Mitchell Gillian, PhD. I felt my eyebrow rise. His given name was Mitchell, not Michael, as I'd assumed from his nickname. As a cover letter to his attached professional CV was the one-line email:

*In case you need to quiz me again, proof that I can handle it.*

I popped the résumé open and was instantly impressed with the laundry list of accomplishments, including papers written, digs he's participated in, and courses he taught. As I was reading the email, another email came in, this time from the university administrator who had been cc'ed:

*Missed one, Dr. Gillian.* 🤍

*Historical artifacts conservator 3 years, Volga Trade Route Exhibit, London Museum of History.*

*Ms. Baker, please feel free to contact me with any questions. I've worked with Dr. G a long time and am happy to help.*

*All the best,*

*Harry*

I smiled at the administrator's email and couldn't help but think that this Harry was another casualty of the Dr. Gillian charm. A man with his education and connections was impressive enough—couple it with wit and good looks, and he became a danger everywhere he went.

I shot off a simple thank-you email to them both, letting them know I'd received it. And before I could close my laptop, Mickey responded:

*Good night, Ms. Baker. I look forward to seeing you in the morning. Sweet dreams.*

*This,* I thought, *is the trouble with trouble. It starts out as fun.*

I hoped, for his sake, he would complete his site analysis and be out of Glentree before Rowan returned.

Then with a light step, so as not to disturb the clan ghosts that haunted the castle at night, I made my way back to the cottage and my wide, cold bed.

# Eight

The next morning saw me up at first light and moving though the dawn mist, coffee in hand, hoping to be at the research tent before anyone could interrupt me. The air hung heavy with the smell of loamy soil and crisp foliage. Early red-breasted robins sung to each other in the trees as bush tits peeped and cajoled from their perches among the flowers of the Circle Garden. My breath became fog as I got to unboxing our equipment for the day.

I'd gotten things halfway set up when an unfamiliar footfall on the gravel in the distance caught my attention. I looked toward the Circle Garden...and Dr. Gillian, making his way toward me, his head bent, deep in thought or mindfulness of the uneven ground.

He was in a pair of rough-hewn heavy-canvas pants, and his forest-green wool sweater hugged tight his shoulders and chest, making him *Archaeological Digest*'s sexiest man of the year. One hand carried a to-go mug and his other a kit of some sort. It was a Pelican case like mine but bright yellow. Even from a distance, I could see that his case looked like it had been dropped off a moving truck, rolled through gravel, and been subjected to gunfire. He'd been unearthing things for a long time.

I realized belatedly that I'd just raked my eyes from his boot toe up to his just-washed hair and back down again—the understanding came when my gaze landed on his face, now upturned toward mine, his mouth quirked in a way that said he knew I'd just appraised the dickens out of him.

"Sorry for my staring..." I decided to own up to it. "You're, ah, here so early."

He gave me a disarming smile that said he didn't mind my staring, not one little bit. He took a sip of tea. "I am," he finally said. He was gathering small bits of joy watching me attempt to form sensical thoughts.

I took a long pull of my coffee. It was like he had arrived in my dressing room before I was ready, and now I was hastily tossing on clothes while he watched.

"Did you have a pleasant evening, Nicole?"

*Say something, Cole.* I could be honest. I could tell him my boyfriend stoked my fires last night and then left me cold. And now here he was, looking like a fresh specimen that I'd like to insert under my microscope and take a long hard—*OK, not that!*

The birds filled in the quiet between us as my mind bathed in butterflies. This time he bailed me out. "Since it's just the two of us right now, could you be enticed into giving me a private and in-depth tour of the site?"

I coughed into my coffee. "Excuse me?"

"First, though," he said, gently prodding the bits and bobs in the now open cases, "may I remove the archaeological items to a safer location?"

I cleared my throat, finding my voice. "Yes, when Marion and Flora get in, I can speak with them about finding a good spot in the castle."

I purposefully avoided saying, "Finding a dry spot." Staying outside, where they'd been perfectly fine for centuries, may be the best place for them, really. Rowan was constantly poking at the castle foundation and stringing together Gaelic words punctuated with what my mother called French.

Dr. Gillian gave me a winning smile and said, "Wonderful," then came around the table, standing close enough for me to feel his body heat. He offered me his arm. "Shall we take that stroll, and you can show me what I've been missing?"

I smiled up at him. How easy it would be for me to just ignore the world, relationships, responsibilities, and put my arm in his. Just, *Sure, handsome!* and skip off along the hillside. Instead, I patted his arm like he was a good horsey and said, "Sure, let's start this way."

"Lead the way, m'lady."

I could grow to like that term, with him saying it.

Under his seemingly genuine interest, I warmed and indulged my love of plants, drawing the tour out as the site came alive with other people and my stories. Holly sneaked me two thumbs up and a grin that said, *We'll talk about this later over a pint.*

We got to the top of the hill overlooking the field. The work tent was in the near distance and the castle stood beyond, brooding like the fortress it was. Even darker were the steel waters of the loch, dotted with green humps of the outer isles before giving way to the expanse of the Atlantic at the horizon. There at the top of the hill Dr. Gillian squatted and looked down over the tall tips of soon-to-be-blooming thistle.

"O'aye, what are the bumps in the field?"

"Good eye. It's hard to see them when you're down there. We kept smacking into these longish structures as we were cordoning off the field."

He stood and tilted his head. "An' what have you noticed? It seems they're in a pattern." Then back to me with a wide smile. "But you already know this, of course."

I nodded and took a moment to put my hair into a ponytail. The morning wasn't warm, but overdosing on his smiles and complements was making my blood warmer. "It's likely we have a dense geologic rock outcropping that's being eroded away at a slower rate than the surrounding ground."

He nodded and made a sound that could easily be mistaken for a mid-coitus groan. Well, easily to me, in that moment. "Have ye had a look, then? A close look, pulled back the shrubs and brush and such?"

He wasn't looking at me now but the mounds again, so he didn't see his spell on me break.

"As a woman who has devoted her life to botanicals, no, I have not ripped plants out by their root hairs just to have a closer look at what lies beneath them. I do, however, know that the MacLaochs have been here since the dawn of time," I said quoting Rowan, "and they know of no stories about this area to indicate that anything like a Viking drinking hall is buried here. For as long at the MacLaochs have been here, this area has been a coastal Highland meadow, telling me the humps are geologic in origin."

He looked at me. "Oh, I believe you. Now, care for an adventure, Ms. Baker?"

"Depends on what you have in mind."

"Would you be so kind as to walk me through your booby traps to that first mound?" He gestured at the string grid we'd laid on that section of the field.

Refraining from making a joke about boobs, I led the way. Easily ten feet in length and five in width, it domed at only knee height.

"May I?" he asked, kneeling and grabbing a fistful of herbaceous ground cover.

As gorgeous as he was, so were those plants. My voice went lecturer serious. "What do you have there?" I noted that the tender shoots all were common enough in our plot and the rest of Glentree that I nodded.

He pulled and delicately placed the uprooted plants aside and then scraped and dug at the accumulated soil. Dug some more. He grasped the knife from the leather pouch on his belt like a farmer bent in the field and dug at the soil that encrusted rocks. Eventually the ping of steel on rock sounded, and he switched to abrasive hand swiping to reveal in that little section what looked to be rocks piled on top of rocks.

It was not what I had assumed. What any of us had assumed. It was not rock jettisoned up by tectonic plate movement. My mind went blank as the loud sound of my internal voice shouted, *Oh, shit.*

"Cairns," he whispered and looked over the rest of the field.

I shivered, feeling like someone had just walked over my grave.

"Interesting," he said.

Finally, I said, hating myself a little for the pain in my voice as I should be happy for any good discovery, "Burial markers?"

He stood and dusted the front of his pants legs. "Cairns don't always mean that. Often they mark a trail or trade route, for example. However, there are so many here... These could be part of a ritual.

Graves. Or I know of those that have been stacked before battle, with the returning men removing one stone each to mark their homecoming and remind them of those no longer alive to claim their stones. That is mere speculation, and I'd want to pursue further investigation. However, as I watch your face go from glowing to green with sickness, I am reminded that this area is already being delicately studied, and I shall endeavor to follow your lead and not just have my way with things."

He gave me a roguish grin, and I thought less about bouncing his ass out of Glentree—better yet, burying him under that very cairn.

"As long as you don't intend to rip up the biologically significant ecosystem here, Dr. Gillian, we'll get on just fine."

"We will, won't we?" Dr. Gillian smiled. "Get on. Just fine."

I gave him a singular brow lift, now immune to his meaningful pauses. I was in full plant-protection mode.

He saw it. "I will inquire about getting ground-penetrating radar. A noninvasive way to give us more insight and data for a risk assessment."

"All right, so today you can identify the items we've already collected; then I'll call you back here when the radar comes?"

Brain full with the possible fallout of what he'd discover, I absently heard him say, "Nicole, it sounds like you want to be rid of me." His voice had delved into deep, warm tones like sunny beach sand.

"Uh-huh," I said. If he was here for much longer, there was a likelihood he'd attempt to convince the Fund to excavate. Now it was a race to see if I could prove the validity of my hypothesis, that the site was ecologically important, before—

He took a tiny step toward me; it was intimate and familiar, like Rowan stepping toward me. My immediate bodily reaction, one based solely in the subconscious, like closing a car door after exiting, was to step into him and tilt my head up. Prepped for a kiss.

Too late, my brain hit the brakes. Dr. Gillian had been waiting and took that wrong cue. Just as his hand came up to touch my cheek, a whistle had me snapping my head around. It was Bernie and Angus, looking up toward us from the research tent.

I turned back to Dr. Gillian. "Two old friends come to say hello. I must go."

He gave me a self-satisfied look that said he knew how close to a lip lock he had gotten. "Probably best. You are a force to reckon with, Ms. Baker; to be alone with you will be a dangerous game for me."

Not sure what to say, I just left, or fled. I wasn't sure.

As I hustled toward the tent with Dr. Gillian close behind, he said, "You know, there are rumors of MacLaoch gold buried in these hills."

*There's gold in them thar hills.*

I glanced over my shoulder and caught a glimpse of golden-brown stubble. He was so close. "Something tells me the MacLaochs would have melted it down by now if that were the case."

"O'no, rumor has it that it wasn't theirs to begin with, and it'd come with a curse, so it was buried with the dead men who delivered it."

The words were dark, but his murmur was seductive, drawing me in and under his spell. Curses, yes. But gold? No one ever mentioned gold or dead men. Other than one prominent dead man. My Minory ancestor.

"Just think, it could be pirate's treasure buried out there." Born on warm breath, his words printed themselves along my neck just as we came up to Bernie and Angus.

I tried not to shiver or groan. I was nearing empty, needing Rowan's skin against mine. Involuntarily I turned toward where I thought he was, but Dr. Gillian was already walking away.

"Cole!"

I was shunted into my next role, and with genuine happiness I threw my arms around Bernie's then Angus's neck and hugged each of them hard. I hadn't realized how much I'd missed them until I was standing next to them again. They smelled of dried brine and fish. While the gray skies didn't tempt me out into the ocean every morning, the gray-haired MacDonagh brothers were fishermen to the bone and spent every morning of their lives out there fishing, giving tours, or pretending to do both. The two men guffawed and pulled back, patting me on the back and shoulder.

Bernie's tan skin and Angus's crooked teeth, matching his crooked nose—they were just as I remembered on the shores of Lady MacLaoch Isle right before Rowan's cousin Kelly bashed them in the heads with an oar and set off a string of events that culminated in an explosion only they themselves were able to end.

I had to take a deep breath before shoving that memory back down. "It feels just like yesterday I watched you two bring about the end of a centuries-old curse." I exhaled as I took in their too-small argyle sweaters and loose-fitting jeans. I wanted Rowan there with us. He'd been shot that day, and memories of it all still had a way of slithering into my insides, stealing my breath and stilling my heart.

"Oh aye, it's been nearly a year."

I'd seen the brothers over the months but just to wave.

"We'd be deeply hurt, but we've heard ye have been a little busy with the laird here," Angus said with a bawdy wink.

I wasn't going to tell him that reality had kicked in long before, and sex in dungeons and oddly shaped hidden alcoves had plummeted in frequency.

"How have you been? How are your noggins?" I asked touching the top of my own head.

"Och! Fine. Kelly's in worse shape now, being that he's just a wee one in his mind now, aye?"

Getting struck by lightning would do that to a fellow. This was after his father attempted to lift the MacLaoch curse and usurp the chief title by forcing marriage upon me, the Minory heir. Then having lost his very last marble, Kelly pointed the gun at me but ended up shooting Rowan through the shoulder. When the metaphorical dust settled, Kelly received a spanking from Lady MacLaoch for his role in it all in the form of a bolt of lightning. Hence his current "wee one" status.

"Then you two are still two of the most powerful wizards I know," I managed.

They were pleased at my use of *wizard* but tamped it down. "Aye, but more like recipe keepers for our Lady MacLaoch; she gave us the recipe to undo the curse when it was time, and we just followed the plan. We still can't light fireplaces with a snap of the finger—"

"Or load our boat with fish—"

"Or gold, for that matter!"

They looked at each other and honked with laughter.

The sound settled me, and it felt good to have familiar faces with me. Like joyful extended family come to visit.

Their comment made me think of what Dr. Gillian had said, and as

I showed them around what I'd been up to this past year, I asked them about it. "Do you know if gold was ever thought to be buried here?"

Angus answered, "Gold? Maybe, from the time of the Clearances? I know quite a bit of gold and power exchanged hands then from our clan."

The Clearances were something I knew a little of. It was the name for the last great exodus of people from Scotland. While the Clearances made way for the wool industry that Scotland was now well-known for, it was a hideous way to get there. Families were driven from their ancestral lands by the thousands, and after all was said and done, nearly a quarter million Scots were displaced.

"No, farther back than the mid-1800s—more like the time of Lady MacLaoch, twelfth and thirteenth centuries."

Bernie thought on it as he stepped around roots in the flattened grass path. "Not that we've been told, but it would have made sense if the Minory had come to claim the chief's daughter, but it would have been buried with him. I've never been one to want to dig up old bones, and I certainly wouldn't start with the digging here."

I agreed. "It would be where he was beheaded."

"Aye."

"Maybe ask Chief MacLaoch if he knows what the cairns are about? There's lore we all know; then there's the lore only the chief knows, aye?"

"Here now, I was thinking you two knew all there was about the old love birds," I said about Lady MacLaoch and her Viking lover.

"Och, well, when it comes to Lady MacLaoch and the curse she placed on the clan and the importance of the Minory and the power of their love, yes."

Angus cut in, "Gold sounds like the bartering price of a maiden if you're a Viking. If he did any bartering, tha' gold would be on MacLaoch accounts and sit with the laird."

*Ew*, I hadn't thought deeply enough of what a fine marriage proposal in the thirteenth century looked like. Women were considered property in much of the world then—and in many ways still now. And what'd you do when you wanted to buy property? You showed up with a bag of cash. A laird's daughter? That bag of cash turned into a trunk of gold. I made a mental note to text Rowan when I charged my phone again.

We'd gotten to the tent, and Bernie and Angus took a long look at Dr. Gillian, whom I'd told them about on our walk, one of those looks that was assessing not only his level of skill but that of his mother, father, and any relation that could call him kin. When I'd told them he was from Glasgow, they both shot me a look as if I'd said Antarctica.

Before I could introduce them, Holly called to him from the field and held up a small piece of something. He was barely out of earshot when the brothers said, "He's a blessed lad, isn't he?"

"Blessed?"

"Face of an angel," Bernie added.

Angus finished, "Guts of the devil."

"As he is the designated and well-renowned archaeologist with the Fund, we're happy to have him spend his summer with us," I said pointedly to them both. And to myself.

Angus sniffed. "Has the chief seen him?"

"Met him? No, but he's reviewed his credentials."

"And?"

"Did I mention he's well-credentialed?"

They both now gave me matching expressions that said they knew full well Rowan liked him as much as they did.

"Speaking of the chief, " Bernie said, "has he made your stay here...permanent?"

That sounded ominous, like death and taxes. "Permanent?"

Angus tried. "Yes, got down on one knee and all that?"

It was twice now I'd been asked that in the past twenty-four hours. "I'm sure he has plans to. The fallout from the Gathering has proven to be more difficult than Rowan expected. When things settle down, we'll make it official, I'm sure." At their skeptical glances, I said, "Don't worry—it's on our minds."

"Aye, fine." Angus let it go, but Bernie didn't.

"Not even the mention of it?"

Angus cut back to his brother. "Bernie, let it go. What if it's a surprise, aye?"

"A surprise? The girl's own wedding, a surprise? Now yer having a laugh."

"Marion's none the wiser—she said as much—and now our lass? It's trouble is what it is."

"Guys," I cut in, "Rowan has every intention of making my stay here permanent. Now, until then, I've got my work visa, and I don't think that the government will send me back before it expires. It's all right."

They were quiet and then reluctantly nodded as if that wasn't the point.

I walked Bernie and Angus back to the car park with a renewed agreement that we'd see each other that weekend when Rowan was home. I had the distinct feeling they were going to press for a wedding before the month's end. I said goodbye to the Secret Keepers. Angus tucked into the old sedan that looked to be as old as them, but Bernie paused, putting a hand on the car roof.

"Nicole," he said, concern creasing his already craggy features, "there's four days before the one-year anniversary of Lady MacLaoch's curse being broken." He looked to get in the car but stopped again and added, "Be careful."

"Be careful?"

"Aye, just...careful, ye ken?"

I nodded despite not knowing what he meant.

I watched the car go down the drive and around the forested corner and out of sight. I felt the word, *careful*, hum around my mind. I shook my head to clear it. I had bits of artifacts to find an indoor home for, a date later with Deloris to meet another relation, and over a hectare of land to catalog before a ground-penetrating radar showed up.

# Nine

〜

Heading around the backside of the castle after my visit with Angus and Bernie, I made a mental list of which rooms I could beg Marion and Flora to help me clear to make space for our growing pile of artifacts. The clouds had congregated as the day wore on. I thought of the last time I'd looked down at the shale and instantly missed Rowan. Today, I couldn't see the spot—a swift-moving fog was creeping up the shore in a black-out density.

I couldn't fathom how it could be so thick so quickly; both earth and air felt to be the same temperature. Not to mention, if it kept going, the research field would suddenly be socked in.

Turning to get back to organize folks to pack up for the day, I almost ran into someone. "Oh!" I said as I dodged a short woman in a shawl coming down the steps.

"Bah!" she shouted and sidestepped me.

"Sorry," I said, thinking her a tourist, though she wasn't dressed like it. She wore a long wool shawl woven into Celtic patterns with the variegated greens of the deep forest. She carried a gnarled staff and held me in a shrewd glare.

"There's a fog—" I started to warn her to not use the lower sea steps when I spied a corner of the plastic-coated runes paper peeking out under the edge of her shawl. "Hey," I said and approached her.

Her hand flared out at me, and her gaze widened. "Stop!"

I did.

"You..." she said and faced me fully, "it really is *you*."

Castle tourists sometimes recognized me from the newspaper clippings from our welcome bulletin board behind the front desk. "Hi, I'm Nicole Baker, and you are? Or more to the point, why are you absconding with papers that I last saw on the clan historian's desk? We sell keepsakes, you know. They're in the gift shop off the main foyer."

She took a step toward me. "I'll keep these for you, Minorisdóttir."

A shiver shook its way down my spine. Minory's daughter? "I'm sorry, you are?"

"Minory's grandmother."

"Minory," I echoed her rolling *R* and breathy *O*. I came back to the pertinent thing. "I'm sorry, but I can't let you leave here with those papers. They're old and need to be in the care of historians who can keep them safe," I said with a little less vehemence than before, but I still stepped forward with my hand out to her. Even though she knew my Minory name, I was going to need a damn fine reason not to wrestle them away from her.

"You called me to them. Are you unaware that he still looks for you?"

I thought immediately of Rowan. He was the only man I knew who had ever actively looked for me. Nothing she was saying was making sense. I took another step.

As if reading my mind, she tucked the papers in deeper as the fog now crept up the base of the steps, thick as night.

"He looks for you in earnest now. A year and a day, some may say, will bring back the day he went away. Is that what you want? Do you actively seek him to return by using this?" she asked, gesturing to the page.

When the confusion on my face didn't clear, she continued, "What was lost is now found. Minory blood ignites on MacLaoch ground, and this will do no good here in the heart of MacLaoch power. Your touch, his touch, has called me to take it home."

I looked at her fingers on the corner of the journal page and felt it slipping away from me. "Look, lady, those papers *are* mine, so give them back." I added, because I had a strange feeling the fog was being commanded by her, "If you tell me who you are, I can get Clive, our clan historian, to set some time aside—"

"If you cannot see me for who I am, then you and I are not ready to meet. These, however," she said of the papers, "will return home. Tick tock goes the midnight clock. Goodnight, child," and she attacked. Gently.

She flicked me between the eyes. I stumbled back with the surprise of it and felt the ground coming slowly, first to my knees, then to my face. I rested my head on my arms. The grass felt so soft, so inviting, and I felt so tired. I was nice to lie down and close my eyes. I'd chase after her. I would get those papers. I just needed a short rest.

I WOKE WITH A START AND ROLLED ONTO MY BACK. SUNDAY mornings were the best. There were doughnuts, coffee, and later, football. I'd nowhere to be but there, home in my pajamas. Was that bacon I smelled? I stretched my arms wide in my bed, enjoying the feel of flannel...grass. I patted the ground; it was indeed grass. I opened my eyes. The cool loch breeze kissed my face, chasing away my childhood Sunday dreams. I stared up at the castle next to me and the bright-white cloud cover of the sky beyond its turrets. It all came crashing in: that woman in the shawl had put me on the ground.

Minory's grandmother, she'd said before taking off north up the coastal trail Clive had wanted Deloris and me to quest with him on. I remembered watching her go as I fought to keep my eyes open. I groaned. That path led right up the tip of Skye, to the Misty Cliffs church.

I knew who I'd just met.

If I thought of the MacDonagh brothers as wizards, that would make her...

"That witch." I cursed and scrambled up to my knees and then to standing, but my head swam. "Fudge buckets..." I breathed and collapsed back to all fours. The fog was gone save for a long tail of it beyond the sea gate and up into the cliffside forest. There it was slurping up the hillside and into the small stand of pines and deciduous trees.

I heard light footsteps on the gravel and saw Holly's hiking boots then yellow jeans through the hedges as she came around the corner.

"There ye are!" she said just before she swift-footed it up the short steps to me on the bowling green.

She knelt in front of me. "Ye all right, mate?" she asked and put her hand on my back.

"I..." I went back onto my haunches. "What time is it?"

She looked me over. "You look rough and have grass imprints on your cheek. Have a lie down, did ye?"

I shook my head. "If I'm not still dreaming, an old woman just stole something from the castle and knocked me out."

Her eyebrows shot up. I wasn't sure she believed me, but then she said, "She clobbered ye? You've been gone for hours. Have ye been lying here the whole time?"

I blinked and looked at her, her brown eyes wide and worried. "I think so."

"Shit."

"Yeah."

"Want me to get that intern, the skinny chap, and we can go hunt her down? I don't like her putting my mate out like that."

I didn't want to tell Holly that the most unhealthy human being I'd encountered—our epidemiological student who only consumed Doritos and Mountain Dew, a habit he acquired while at an exchange program in the States—was not going to cut it. "I'm not sure that he's the kind of backup we need with her."

"Och, you're right. Maybe that hot new chap from Glasgow, calls himself archaeologist. I was thinking we could use one of 'em could charm her—ye know how biddies love the young men, and he's decent at flattery. If it goes sideways, we can always use the skinny one like a stick and beat her with him until she gives up what she stole?"

I couldn't help but laugh at all of that. "No, it's OK. I meant, I don't think any of us can stop her. I think she's a witch of sorts." And if she was the Minory's grandmother, lineage dictated she was also my great—to the millionth power—grandmother.

Holly's eyes went wide. "I told my mum the other day that this place has a kind of power to it. I believe it, a witch, ye say? Maybe I should call my mum, and she can send us some herbs before we go get what she stole."

I smiled in relief at Holly; she was pure Scots, with her plan: "Witch, ye say?" she had started and then without hesitation, "I've got a bag of tricks for tha'."

IT WAS ANOTHER HOUR TO CONVINCE HOLLY THAT I WAS fine, that one "lay down" for the day was enough, I didn't need another, and no, she didn't need to call her mom for herbs. I'd sort it out later. What I did need was another visit to the Misty Cliffs; this time I had a feeling its caretaker would be there.

Only, things were a hive of activity at the research site, and before anything else could be done, my boots needed to stay at the field for as long as I could manage it. The quadrants were almost complete, with GIS tags, and in those sections, our students were squatting, recording the wildlife they were discovering. It had that buzz of amazement already. While we hadn't come across any one item that was classified as extinct or rare, what we were seeing was an abundance of native wildlife and flora, and it was that abundance in one central location that was rare.

Holly was next to me shielding her eyes from a bright ray that broke through the clouds. We stood in the field analyzing the cumulative data coming in from the network program we'd set up on the research field's tablet.

"It's really something," I said, tapping the screen. "I was looking through it last night, and the native species we're cataloging are so thick that we've yet to come across any invasives. I could understand some struggling invasive species, but none? It's really unprecedented."

"Like an original carbon copy of the early times, aye?"

I nodded, looking at the data set; we were taking in an impressive list, and counting, of native sedges, bush tits, coastal butterflies, spring bloomers, and saplings of rowan and pine. It was a veritable laundry list of who's who of Glentree's flora and fauna. The excitement of what that meant for updating texts and images throughout academia was palatable. This would be a refresher on so many levels.

Holly looked to the forest several hectares away and said, "Maybe we'll come across something really rare. I can feel it."

I smiled, feeling it too. "Yes."

"*Felis silvestris silvestris,*" Holly said out to the horizon in dreamy tones.

"Fully mature *Sorbus aucuparia,*" I added.

Holly laughed, her spell broken. "*Sorbus aucuparia,* a rowan tree, aye? Besides being ubiquitous, you've already seen it, mate—you're dating the tallest one I've seen, and the hottest."

I grinned. "But what's this Felis you're hoping to see?"

Holly moved off the innuendo-ridden subject of Rowan's cock and explained her pussy...cat. "Scottish wildcat, *Felis silvestris silvestris.* I know I'm a bees-and-ticks gal—they have their important place among our wee ecosystem, but to see a Scottish wildcat, now that would be something."

"Fauna holy grail."

"Yoo-hoo!" Marion's call carried over the field like a mother calling to her babes. Holly and I turned to see her waving and putting down a platter stacked tall with scones, along with her signature whipped cream and homemade strawberry jam. Before Dr. Gillian arrived, Marion had brought small things, hot chocolate when it was absolutely miserable out, tea when things were slow with tourists at the castle. Scones was a sharp escalation.

Holly nearly threw the tablet at me and made a beeline for the tent, carefully stepping over lines and around plants as she did but never breaking her stride. I watched other students appear from the field, pulled by a siren song from the sea of scholarly pursuits to her shores of homemade baked comfort. Dr. Gillian, who I suspected this show was really for, was in the castle basement, shelving artifacts.

I laughed and made my way through the field to the tent too.

As faces, including my own, were being stuffed with cream, jam, and buttery baked goods, Marion and I caught up on the day's events.

"It's been a fine morning," she said, "just a handful of visitors, cousins of the McClures, ye know them, aye?"

"Relations to Mary McClure?"

"Of the forge? Glory no, they're the Ulster branch of the McClures," she said as if I should have known.

Holly cut in, "Friends of the auld twin fishermen, aye?"

"Aye, that's them, up from Inverness to tour the castle and see if they can feel the MacLaoch ghost. I told them all the details of that day and yours and the chief's part in it," she said with a proud smile.

I just nodded as the scone crumbled and mixed with the silky cream and sharp strawberry jam. Bernie and Angus must have been up with their cousins when I saw them earlier.

Marion continued talking with me. "We have several of the cottages rented out for the remainder of the month, a writer, banker, and film-maker, to name a few. I said if they wanted interviews with you and the laird, I could take appointments down."

I nodded, not sure what Rowan would normally do in these situations, but I'd do my best to relay all of it to him or Clive, who had started taking on more of the administrative tasks now that Rowan was on the road more. I wondered about the banker and if that had anything to do with the estate's finances.

"Oh." She added, "And there's a bit of a squabble happening at the library at present. Flora had a call from her nephew studying there that Clive was demanding something back while Deloris shouted insults in return. Maybe ye can intercede while the laird is away?"

I felt my eyes go wide, the rune paper. I cursed with my mouth full, and I took off at a run toward the library.

"Mate!" I heard Holly as she came running over the bridge. "Oye, mate!"

I turned, jogging backward. "Sorry, Holly, no time!"

"I know—take my car, ye ijit!" she said and tossed me her keys. I caught them. "If you run, you'll puke up your scone, and by the time you finally get there, Clive will be dead!"

I laughed and coughed on a scone crumb. She made a face like *See what I mean?*

# Ten

At the library, I rammed Holly's little two door into park and ran through the parking lot, through the glass front doors of the library, and down the concrete steps to the warm basement and thought I would follow the sounds to Clive and Deloris shouting. Only the loudest person there was me panting, standing in the middle of the open study space. The young people there were bent over books and computers, and the older crowd held newspapers aloft. I waited in case I got there at the exact moment Deloris and Clive and taken a collective huge breath and were soon to start wrestling each other and would soon make a sound. There were only murmurs and hushed conversations.

I waited a bit longer and then groaned. I was too late—they'd killed each other.

A boy at a workstation against the wall, surrounded by books and lidded paper coffee cups, looked up and pointed to the stacks behind the counter.

I nodded, thanking him. He must be Flora's nephew, who'd called in the homicide.

Starting down the first aisle of bookshelves, I found no one but heard murmuring in the far corner. As I wound my way through shelves upon shelves of books, files and boxes, the air got thick with must and dust. Coming out the end of one aisle, I looked right and found them shoulder to shoulder, looking down at something on the table in front of them. They were talking excitedly to each other and didn't hear me as I approached. Just as I was about to clear my throat, Clive gave a small laugh and put his hand to Deloris's back.

I paused, unsure what to do. They were getting along. I backed out softly and was halfway to the first aisle I could escape into when my wet boot squeaked.

Clive and Deloris spun around looking startled as if I'd caught them red-handed. Which part of me felt like I had—they might as well have been necking in the corner they were so chummy.

"Oh, Miss Minory."

"Cole"—Deloris put her hand to her chest—"it's just you, love, thank heavens."

I smiled and waved and pretended I had not just seen them getting along. "Hi, guys, I'm glad I found you—"

"The rune papers have been stolen," they said at once.

"I—"

"We've got a bit of evidence here that we're analyzing," Deloris said and showed me a note. Only it wasn't your average, everyday Post-it saying, "Hey, borrowed your stuff, I'll give it right back." No, it was in a runic symbol language that they were shoulder to shoulder trying to decipher.

Clive added, "We believe the woman calls herself a witch, or Völva, from the Old Norse language. The language of the Vikings," he said, leaning hard on the last word, Vikings. "I believe, Miss Minory, that we have a witch in our midst, and she's taken that paper, which is the only proof we have of the location of your ancestor's origins."

Deloris's eyes were bright with the thrill of their investigation. "A witch! Or at least she calls herself that—"

I cut in, "She's a witch all right."

Their faces twisted. They both were prepared to argue their case and didn't think I'd flat-out agree.

"Come again?" Clive asked.

"I intercepted her on the back bowling green with the papers. She flicked me between the eyes, and I woke from a nice nap not long ago."

Deloris crossed herself. "Ye didn't." It was a statement not a question.

"Miss Minory, that's extraordinarily brave and reckless of you. Witches are not souls to be trifled with."

I shrugged. "To my untrained eye, she was just a short, older woman absconding with papers I needed for research."

"Did she say anything, lass?"

"She called me Minorisdóttir? And said that she was Minory's grandmother."

Deloris clutched her pearls, and Clive's hand dropped.

I looked back at their stunned faces. "Right? That's exactly how I felt."

"She's... You're..." Clive stumbled over words. We all were too experienced living with myths to deny the reality of something just because we'd never seen or experienced it before.

Deloris urged me on, and I told them everything, including about the fog.

Clive asked, "Are you well? Should we call the laird home?"

I hadn't even thought of that. "No, I'm fine."

Clive looked at me, then to Deloris, and then back. "Do you suppose with your connection that he might have also been affected?"

"Oh," I said and had to think about it, and thinking about him brought a faint response back from him. "He's fine, and come to think of it, it doesn't really work that way. Just like when I sleep at night, he doesn't conk out. Our connection just goes silent. And he's so far away down in Glasgow, I'm sure he didn't notice."

They looked at me, and then Deloris asked, "What should we do?"

Feeling weird at being asked my opinion, I tried to summon a confident tone. "I think we need to pay another visit to this woman who calls herself Völva of the Misty Cliffs and ask for the papers back. Only this time I'll need to brush up on any superstitions before I knock on that church door. Something tells me those superstitions are law at Misty Cliffs."

.  .  .

THE CHURCH STOOD WHITE AND GLEAMING AGAINST THE
moody cloud cover, matching the limestone of the tombstones in the
neighboring graveyard.

I closed the car door; it slammed with the help of the onshore wind.
I clutched my windbreaker at my throat and ran to the lee of the church.
Leaning against the church door, I remembered the advice Clive had
given me: run around the church in the direction of the sun three times.
My mother still threw salt over her shoulder whenever she spilled some,
to keep the devil away. Running clockwise around the church? Sure.

Deloris and Clive watched me out the car window.

I took off at a jog. Despite the wind's bluster, running with it was a
joy—I felt like I could fly all the way to Aberdeen, toes barely touching
the earth.

My third time around, she stood in the doorway. "Why do ye keep
running past my window? I know who ye are, and it's obvious now you
know who I am. Come in then; we'll have a cuppa and see what I can do
for you."

I was sure that sharing a digestive and polite conversation with my
assailant was not on my recommended activities list, but with a woeful
glance back at Clive and Deloris, I followed her into the dimly lit
church. The stone floors echoed our steps and created a coolness. On
the whitewashed walls were crests that I didn't recognize. Daggers and
belts, shields and thistles, dragons and swords all crisscrossed on bright
primary colors. The tall, frosted windows let in light filling the ancient
wood pews with a glow.

"You have questions," she stated. "Let me start with who I am. I'm
the keeper here. Some call me Völva, or the witch. Maybe even Witch of
the Misty Cliffs, seeress, or auld crank." She cackled and led me into a
small room off the back of the church. In a rear corner was a wood
stove. The room was hot, and I shucked my coat along with my sweater
onto a chair tucked under the equally fragile-looking wood table. Both
looked to be centuries old, their edges worn down over time with the
countless hands that had touched them. The room was lined with ash-
colored wood cabinetry bisected by a wide porcelain sink on the wall
opposite the table. Counters were covered in glass jars and ceramic pots
holding utensils of all shapes and sizes.

She gestured for me to sit as she took down two cups for tea. "But to you, I'm more than that." She nodded at the document sitting on the table. It had been removed from its plastic sheet and sat inert next to a book that looked equal to its age. "That is what ye are seeking."

I pulled out the chair, its foot catching the edge of a stone in the floor. Sitting, I looked back up to find her smiling at me. She was a lot less mysterious when she did that. "You look much like him."

"Who?"

Her brown eyes twinkled; there was something familiar in their expression as if I knew the mystery she was about to divulge. "My name outside these walls is Ethel Campbell, and you may call me, simply, Ethel," she said by way of explanation as she put a copper kettle on top of the stove, it making a hushed hiss as she did.

Settling into the chair, I watched her move her hands over each teacup, whispering something under her breath before dropping a small spoonful of loose-leaf tea into each. She then poured hot water into each cup before looking back to me and the page she'd taken off Clive's desk.

The leather of the book was dried and nearly opaque, neither soft nor brown like the leather I was accustomed to.

"What is..." I started but felt my breath catch in my throat. I knew what it was. It was the original book the page had been cut from.

She gave me a steaming cup and sat across from me. "To learn about your grandfather, you must start by knowing his past."

I liked the way she spoke about the Minory being my grandfather, and Lady MacLaoch was Rowan's grandmother. There was a simplicity to it that didn't get bogged down by exact measurements of greats to the tenth power or twentieth.

"This book is his diary. It begins very simply with a few..." she said and looking down her nose at the book upside down, she ran an ungloved finger across its surface. "Here, just a few entries of the items he acquired on his trips."

I pulled my sleeves down over my hands to keep the oils from my fingers from getting onto the book and opened it. The musk of old paper wafted up. The front cover creaked like a saddle.

Ethel made him sound like a well-traveled gentleman, a businessman visiting ports of importance, and not a Viking.

The script was faded and only partly legible; the parts that were symbols I couldn't decipher. His original hand. I touched it, and through my sleeve it felt like a connection to a lost world and way of life and in the same breath familiar and kin.

She went on. "In here is everything that you seek, should you want to find it. But I warn you, you may find more than you wish to know."

"I see." One word in the looping, shaky script I could make out: Minorisson. Minory's son. Somewhere down the line it went to plain Minory. A Norse Viking. He wasn't a posh businessman on his worldly travels—he was a fierce man aboard a dragon ship terrorizing places until they gave up their riches and resources. The tome in front of me was a ledger of his exploits.

I didn't like this part of my history. "I see..." I said again and sat looking at the yellowed pages spotted with brown in this dank kitchen off a hovel of an ancient church. "And the first entry dates to?" I squinted at the page, trying to find a numeric value.

"The time before Scotland gave birth to kings."

"That is...?"

"Several hundred years ago. No," she said and thought on it, "eight. Or no, seven hundred. Yes, seven. After so long, the centuries blur together."

I nodded, keeping the shock off my face, but my voice squeaked. "This book is seven hundred years old?"

I looked up to the cupboard where it was being held and thought of all the historians who had just rolled over in their graves and fell over in a dead faint with that knowledge.

As if reading my thoughts, she said, "Magic," then did something that would give any archival person an instant cardiac arrest. From a drawer, she pulled out tape and began taping the page from Clive's office back into the book.

"Oh my god," I gasped, "you don't... I don't think tape is...wow. All right, you're just taping that right back in there," I said as she flipped from the back of the book to the front and turned the book back around.

Her eyebrows drew together. "Well, I cannot share this information with you if it is not in the right order."

"OK," I whimpered and was resigned to her way of things. "But can't you just weave it back together, you know, like with a spell or something?"

She looked at me sharply and clicked her tongue. "And why, pray tell, would I do that? You young ones know nothing of the ways," she admonished. "There is a push and a pull in this universe; the sun rises so that night may fall on the other side of our world. If I should wake these fibers and force them to heal themselves, what is the pull to that push, child? What should come unstitched in my church to solve this minor problem?"

"Oh," I said, feeling slightly admonished, then asked another, as it turned out, stupid question, "then since you knocked me out earlier, does that mean you have to lie awake for extra hours tonight?"

She looked at me through resigned, heavy-lidded eyes that made me think of bored Sunday patrons and replied blandly, "As I've said, to stitch this shut, I must wake fibers and have them regrow. Please tell me how that is akin to suggesting to you to sleep when it is obvious how tired you are?"

I looked back down at the tome to break the eye contact and whispered as I searched its pages for something, anything, "Yes, right, makes sense."

We sat in silence as I read the bits of Latin text and stared at the other symbols and basically thought of all the information stored in that seven-hundred-year-old text. One day it could become the accident site of some spilled cup of tea, and before you could say poof, a millennia's worth of lineage could be gone. "May I come back tomorrow with my laptop? I'd like to get this information digitized."

"Yes, that'll be nice," she said and took the last swig of her tea. As she placed the cup down, she peered into it as if reading something and then looked up at me. "Are you done?" she asked and stood pointing to my teacup, where there was one last gulp.

I picked it up and drained it and handed it to her, "Yes, thank you so much."

Her brows scrunched as she looked into the bottom. "You drank the leaves."

I paused, putting my sweater back on. *Yes,* I thought, *that's what happens when you float them loose in there like that.* "Yes... Is that, OK? Should I not have?"

She harrumphed and put the cups into the large, chipped porcelain sink. "No, that's all right," she said, sounding as if it were a grave disappointment.

# Eleven

Deloris and I dumped Clive rather unceremoniously back at the castle after she realized we were late for the meetup she'd set with Eli Campbell. I wondered if he'd be as curious as the last relation Deloris had introduced me to, Mary of the forge, Mary McClure. Mary had been delightful, if a little forward, producing a key to her house for me, despite both Deloris and me assuring her I was just a very distant relation. Now we were heading south off MacLaoch lands on the coastal road to see someone who promised to be just as interesting.

Pasture rolled over the hills above us; lichen-covered rock walls bisected with wooden gates delineated the fields before we passed through downtown Glentree on Harbor Road. Glentree harbor was lit in the low afternoon sun that had poked out under the clouds. Long shadows were cast across the water below. I watched fishermen restocking their ships for their early-morning trips. Tour guides were launching evening cruises on the fishing vessels that did double duty each day. Catches in the morning, cruises in the afternoon. It seemed that money was tight for everyone these days, not just the laird of Clan MacLaoch.

Deloris navigated us out of town and back down on the coastal road while she prepped me for the visit.

"Now, just like Mary's visit, this one will be well structured too. Eli Campbell is the tower control down at the coast guard facility." Deloris gave me a quick look as if to see what my reaction was.

I shook my head. "Nope, still don't know him. Any reason I should?"

She looked back to the winding road and pretended to squint at the road signs, each written in both Gaelic and English.

After a while she answered, "Ye'll see. We'll have just a few moments with him. Don't mention the chief."

"Rowan?"

"Aye."

"Why?"

"It's just that—oops!"

An earlier sign told us of an upcoming driveway, and just before us, the road dove inland, and a driveway forked sharply in the opposite direction. Deloris yanked the wheel hard into the driveway.

"Whoa!" I grabbed the door as I slid in my seat.

The trees flanking the one-lane drive whizzed by.

"Och!" Deloris exclaimed. "I cannae believe I nearly missed the entrance."

I was pressing my foot to my imaginary brake as we took the small road up to a guard station at a good clip.

Beyond the yellow gate arm was a small air strip with helicopter pads, a double-propped helicopter visible, and hangars whose tops could be seen beyond the stout control tower. Out at the end of the docks in the far distance stood a massive white coast guard cutter with wide orange bands. All were inscribed with HM COAST GUARD. Deloris hit the brake, making us slide before stopping with a chirp. Rolling down her window, she leaned out of the now-wheezing vehicle—it had not liked the low gear of the hilly journey nor the rally-car entrance— and chatted up the man in the guard booth.

Midway through their conversation, I heard my name and saw the guard peering in Deloris's window. He took off his cap in greeting and said to Deloris, "Aye, I see it. Eli will be pleased." Then slipped her a twenty-pound note.

I could feel my left brow rise in question; it sounded like I was to be offered up to Eli as collateral and there was money on the line.

"All right," I said as we ambled down the road toward the air station office and control tower, "what's going on?"

"Och! Never you mind. Clive and I disagree on something, and I told him I wouldn't bias you about it before ye meet him yourself. Ye'll see soon enough."

"You're twenty-pounds sure."

"Aye, as you can see, we've a wee wager going. If I'm right—and I am—I'll have enough tae buy one new computer this summer for the library."

Deloris pulled us into a parking spot where the motor of her car rattled, shook, and spit until it finally gave up with a bang.

I had to hand it to Deloris—she knew how to fundraise.

I gave the dash a pat and ran after Deloris, who was already down the sidewalk, dusting off my Southern manners for what had the potential to be a lucrative meeting.

The interior of the rectangular control tower offices was 1950s steel and particle board. The walls were painted classic institutional dinge-white with steel office desks lining up side by side behind the welcome counter. In back were stairs I assumed led to the control tower above us. The chipped particle board welcome counter running the length of the office had a bell on it next to a sign-in sheet.

Deloris called, "'Allo there?"

"Deloris, is this place always so empty?" I whispered.

"Och, it's fully staffed; it's just tha' they don't get many visitors," she said and then, louder, "'Allo!"

We waited a bit more. Deloris looked at her watch, then around the room, craning her neck to see farther down the hall. "They should be expecting me. Now we'll be running late, and he doesn't have much time—he's verra important here."

The room might have been empty of people, but its desks were piled with paperwork. The computers were relics, and the room smelled of printer toner and stale black tea.

With a frustrated expulsion of breath, Deloris smacked the counter bell repeatedly.

I winced as the shrill *ding! ding! ding!* echoed through the building, and my teeth.

When nothing but the *bang-clang* of the radiator replied, Deloris adjusted her cardigan and struck the bell again. I winced again.

A few more moments passed before a stocky woman in a uniform of sweater and matching dark slacks came down the hall and into the room, stuffing the last of a sandwich into her face, "Oh, eh. What do ya want?" she asked around the bite. The short braids she sported on each side of her head seemed in complete opposition to her attitude. Playful and childlike she was not. A swarthy, ocean-going woman who was in the presence of crude sailors daily? Absolutely.

Deloris promptly asked if Eli was in.

"And who's doing the askin'?"

I noticed then that she didn't sound like any of the Scottish dialects I'd heard. Hers reminded me of proper British English, if it had met a seagoing bunch that found little use for the ends of words.

And she was making Deloris bristle.

"His grandmother," she said, rolling the *R*, emphasizing her Scots and her *O*s stretching out as if she were purposefully putting pressure on the vowel.

The woman looked her up and down, then to me: "And who are you?"

Before I could answer, Deloris did. "The Queen of Sheeba." Then added: "My granddaughter, ye daft lass. Now go get my grandson before I ring this bell until yer ears bleed."

I looked at Deloris in disbelief; the book dragon I'd seen earlier in the week was back. It was as if when she left the library, she left behind the rules requiring her to be quiet and deferential. The woman was unimpressed; she just shoved the sign-in sheet at us. "You'll 'ave to sign in. An' I'll need to see your identification," she said and turned, leaving us with the clipboard with attached pen.

It was a drastically different reception than that of the one we received by the guard at the entrance. I looked after the woman as she disappeared up the set of stairs and then back to Deloris, who was writing *Barney Rubble* on the sheet.

"Deloris..." I whispered, and trying to distract her from her flared temper, I put a reassuring hand on her arm. "Are we really meeting your grandson?"

She looked down at my hand and patted it motherly, "No, love, it's all right, but he could be, and who is she to deny me to see him? I've cleared this meet with Eli, and I've had no troubles in the past."

The sign-in sheet was forgotten as a deep voice bellowed down the stairs, "Deloris? Aye! Where is she?"

The sound of heavy footfalls moving swiftly down the steps was soon matched with view of the largest man I'd ever seen. "Deloris!" he bellowed again as he ducked under the doorway and moved through the desks toward us. He was a towering man hovering close to seven feet, with a solid barrel of a chest and a smile just as big. The stacks of papers fluttered in his wake.

"'Allo there!" As he embraced Deloris, she disappeared within his tree trunk arms. "How are ye?"

She was beaming up at him as he released her. "Bonnie well, verra well, it was good to catch up with you and Elsie on the phone the other day. Now, as I promised, a surprise," she said and reached back for me.

It was an odd sensation to see my own eyes looking back at me. My brother and I shared few physical similarities, as he'd gotten the dark hair and tan complexion of my mother's French ancestors while mine ran toward creamy, freckled skin and golden-flecked green eyes. Just like the ones on the face looking back at me. We stood staring at each other. This must be what a baby feels like seeing their own reflection for the first time.

"I'm Elias Campbell, the tower control 'ere. Ye can call me Eli, and am I tae call you cousin or," he said, blinking fast as if taken aback by his own thought, "sister?" he croaked.

"This, Cole," Deloris said to me, "is yer cousin. Elias, this is Nicole Baker; she's tae only be related to the Campbell's by marriage, but yes, isn't it striking?"

The long, strong line of my nose, good jaw, and neat golden brows stared back at me, and he answered still in shock, "Quite."

I asked Deloris softly, "Cousins. Are you sure we're not blood related?"

"Exactly." Deloris clasped her hands together, a wager won.

"I take it Clive thinks he and I are not related."

"Oh aye, he thinks that, leaning so hard on his great-grandfather's work, refusing to admit that they might have overlooked something when doing genealogy search for the Minory, but I have two eyes, and ye both see it too."

We turned our heads this way and that.

"Aye."

"Yes."

We said at once, like mirror images.

"Cousin," I finally said and smiled, holding my hand out to him.

He ignored it and caught me up in a bear hug that squished my ribs. Air whooshed out, and just as I thought I'd need to tap out to breathe, he released me.

He held me back out at arm's length, smiling, emotion starting to well up in his eyes. "Oh, it's bonnie good tae meet ye."

I smiled back up at him. "It's very good to meet you as well. I—"

"We have so much catching up tae do! Ye need to meet my wife, my kids, our relations—" He spun, looking for Deloris behind him and nearly put her on her rear. "Oh, ye OK?"

She caught her balance. "Yes, yes," she said, waving him off.

"Who else has she met?"

"Mary McClure."

When he smiled now, it was as if Christmas and his birthday arrived in the same day, gift-filled and treasure-laden. He turned back to me. "Ye are related tae Mary, then! Oh aye, what a surprise! And where are you staying? If ye've no place, we can put you up at my place with the wife and kids; we'd be more'n happy to have you."

I laughed—his joy was infectious. "Thank you, but I'm staying with my boyfriend down—" I stopped, looking at Deloris, who was making stop signs with her hands.

Eli's face was still cheerful. "And ye have a beau with you! How long are you and your man friend in town for?"

"Indefinitely. I've moved up here just last year." It seemed as if he didn't know Rowan and the MacLaoch curse at all. It was a change of pace to tell him who I was rather than he already knowing half my backstory as everyone up in Glentree did.

"Och, that's bonnie well indeed! Which house are ye letting? We have one we can let to you; my wife manages properties for the isle, you see."

Deloris again was shaking her head.

I cautiously replied that we were happy where we were on the grounds at Castle Laoch.

Deloris sighed and sat down in defeat in one of the many plastic chairs that lined the front wall.

Eli thought for a moment. "I didnae think that the estate let out houses. I'll have tae tell Elsie about it. Well, it's right good tha' ye and yer American friend are staying on such a historic property!"

"Elsie is your wife?" I asked, changing the subject of where we lived.

"Aye! And we'll have ye and him down for dinner this week; she and the kids will be tickled tae have American kin here on Skye!"

The immediate connection was like a click of a seat belt—it just fit. "That would be great. And actually, my boyfriend is Scottish. He'll be back later this week."

Eli's face went blank, then guarded. "MacLaoch estate... Is he, Rowan MacLaoch, the clan chief?" He did know Rowan. Taking Deloris's advice, I steered us away.

"Now," I said, brightly looking around the place as if I'd just discovered I was in a building and not on a walk somewhere, "what is it that you do here?"

Eli gave a quick smile. "Tower controller. Rowan is really with ye?"

I sighed in despair and gave Deloris an apologetic look. "Yes. Do you know him?"

"Oh aye, he was my best friend before he headed off tae fight for Queen and country," he said and seemed to think about what he was going to say. He put his big paw of a hand on my shoulder. "It's all for naught, and let us not worry about old skirmishes. I take this as a sign to put the past behind, to start fresh. Bring Rowan when he's home, but you and I, we'll have dinner this week, if you're up for a walk. Our home is just five miles off the coastal trail that leads to Castle Laoch."

I was still digesting that my bear of a cousin had been Rowan's best friend before he went off to war. "Oh yes, I, sure, let's do it," I said, using only half my brain. "May I come by tonight...? It's too last-minute, I understand—"

"Oh aye, I know Elsie will want to!" His Christmas-and-birthday-combo smile was back.

We arranged the details before Eli was called back to work.

As Deloris and I walked out to the car, she watched me closely.

I looked back at her. "His best friend? I've never heard of him!"

"I was hoping he'd have told ye."

"Told me what?" I asked. "I'm so, so surprised." And I was. I was also taken aback by how much Eli and I looked a like. Not even my own blood-related cousins in South Carolina looked as close to me as he did. Between the Eli surprise and his history with Rowan, it kind of felt like I'd walked into a spider's web of secrets.

"The laird and he used to be as close as brothers, but that darkness that followed him back from war kept them apart."

"I wonder why he never told me," I mumbled as I got into the car.

Back out on the road, I watched the scenery go by—the water for stretches then pasture as the road tilted inland before weaving back out along the water.

I pulled my cell, dead again, out of my pocket. I had so much to talk with Rowan about and no Rowan to talk with. I stared out at the water as my hand played with the rubber band at my wrist. Rowan and I needed a come-to-Jesus meeting this weekend; the space between us was getting too big.

# Twelve

B ack at the field after meeting Eli, my day continued to turn up pleasant surprises. As I flew high on a cloud of intellectual bliss, for once the damp chill that had settled into my Southern bones evaporated, making me think my wool sweater was maybe, just maybe, too heavy.

As I packed up for the day, all the other researchers already gone to the pub, I noticed it. A gentle humming in my veins, so similar to when Rowan and I had first met that I kept looking at my phone expecting him to say he was returning home. It just looked back at me, black and inert. I was so inside myself that I jumped when I heard Marion's voice.

"Nicole," she said breathlessly, and I saw her clutching her hands.

"Is everything OK?" I asked, knowing that it wasn't. She never called me Nicole.

"I thought you should know... Flora said I shouldn't bother, but then I put two and two together, and I thought... Well, I thought..."

I put the rest of my things away, and when she didn't continue: "What is it, Marion?"

I followed Marion to the castle; she kept one step ahead of me and avoided my questions. Through the heavy oak front doors, she waved me on, but she stayed behind at the castle's front desk with Flora, who was glaring at Marion.

"Up in the office. It's the MacLaoch solicitor... I'm sure it's nothing."

I nodded and hit the stairs, the red plaid carpet softening my foot falls. My blood was still itching. I looked back at Marion and Flora, their faces full of concern, a bit like they were when they'd found a dead rat floating in the upstairs lavatory. This time I hoped it was just a rat.

The upper hall was quiet and softly lit. We'd been cutting costs, right down to the electricity bill. This created excellent shadows for things or people to hide in ambush. At the top of the stairs, the door to the library office was closed. I heard a man's voice like Rowan's grunt and a woman's voice also grunt then gasp and squeal as something hit the floor. My stomach churned. I touched the doorknob and slowly turned it.

The door opened silently, revealing a slice of the room just as a woman's voice exclaimed, breathlessly, "Rowan!"

He was there against the desk. He was there and not in Glasgow as he'd said, but rather on the other side of the door I held ajar.

My mind suddenly stopped working. It came to a full stop like a camera taking one last photo before its mechanisms froze up. That photo held two people. A woman was on the desk, her knee bent against Rowan's side. Rowan was between her legs, and his hand... It was his hand; that wide and capable hand was gripping the top fleshy part of her thigh just under her pushed-up skirt.

Sweat, cold and frightening, slithered down my chest and over my belly as the door latched silently shut. I walked back downstairs, confused. I was out the front door before the impression of Marion and Flora looking at me really registered—Marion was clutching her string of pearls.

Rowan was in Glasgow.

As I hit the stairs outside, the sun had sunk, throwing long shadows over the front gardens and car park. The stones under my feet crunched, and I watched my Wellingtons crunch them. Then the pebbles turned to grass, and I watched my feet crush the blades. My feet walked the well-worn path into the research field and stopped at the far edge where the shrubs began. They surrounded me, cool and unimpressed with what I'd just seen.

Beckoned into their ambivalence, I sat hard on the ground and asked myself, "What the fuck did I just see?"

The sky was turning blood red in the twilight. I welcomed the chill in the air as it iced down my skin.

Why? Why was Rowan home without telling me he would be? Why was there a woman with him? Why was Rowan's hand gripping her thigh? My mind's eye cracked wider, and the vision of him sharply pulling her toward him emerged. Her legs opened easily, and she welcomed him against her, and it wasn't the first time her legs had done that. She was familiar with him being there. Between her legs. And that was the biggest why of all.

Time began to play in fast-forward and fast-rewind as I relived the moment over and over. Each time the feeling of betrayal got stronger and stronger. As did the feelings of stupidity and regret. I'd been told time and time again that Rowan was a well-known man about town before I'd arrived, and how wrong had I been in thinking that the buck stopped with me?

In my mind's eye, there he was thrusting again.

I was in a fairy tale, thinking I could build a truth on a curse that this whole stupid town, that I, was clinging to, but no one had to adhere to it. Least of all the chief of the most powerful family in Skye.

I grit my teeth. This fantasy world would stop. It would stop with me. I might have been naive up until then, but now my eyes were wide open. Rowan couldn't fuck a woman on his desk in this town and not expect me to find out. And now he was going to find out what it meant when I did. I took a deep, stabilizing breath and stood.

# Thirteen

I was somewhere between the castle and south of town before my conscious mind caught up with my body. Darkness was starting to test the capabilities of my night vision when I remembered I had made a dinner date with my cousin, Rowan's old friend. My aimless walk grew a purpose, and I detoured toward town to pick up something to bring. As I rapped on Eli's door sometime later, my visit to the store a blur, I was relieved to see I held a bottle of wine, not a knife or something else made for homicide.

Maybe I should have knocked earlier, back at the castle? Maybe that simple courtesy would have prevented the sickening twist that was starting to take up residence in my stomach.

No, I thought bitterly. A single knock wouldn't have helped. Not when he'd been gone fundraising so much that my being alone for a family dinner had become normal. Opening doors in the castle had become my right, maybe even my duty.

My mind analyzed afresh. When your house is a mess, it can feel tempting to abandon the sink full of dirty dishes, but now I attended to them. Each one. Had fundraising been what he really was doing? Or reconnecting with old lovers?

I grit my teeth at the surge of rage I felt. His hand grabbing the woman's thigh and pulling her in against his crotch. My imagination played it out longer, showing me him thickly thrusting into her. I shook my head at the unhealthy twist of the memory, but when I knocked again, I pounded harder on the door than I had intended.

Before I could snap the rubber band at my wrist, the front door yanked open, and Eli stood there, a wide grin on his face, and boomed, "Hellooo, cousin! Welcome tae my home!" A white kitchen towel was tossed over his shoulder, and as he stepped aside for me to step in, three boys tore out the open door, screeching into the front yard in a game of tag.

"Oye, kids!" he hollered at them. Two fell out of a tree—how had they gotten up it so fast?—and as soon as they hit the grass, the third, and what I suspected as the youngest, jumped atop them and began to wail on them with his fists. "Git yer scrappy arses in tha' house this minute!"

"Eli!" I heard from within the house. "Watch your language," said the woman's voice as she came out and smiled at me and shook my hand. "Has the manners of a bear, this one," she said, elbowing Eli. "I'm Elsie, his wife, and these are our children," she said as Eli put his wide hands on Elsie's shoulders. "Children, come here." When they didn't, the tone of her voice changed. "One...two..." And in a flash of jeans and T-shirts and grass stains, they stood before me from tallest to shortest.

"This," Eli said, putting his paw on top of the tallest boy's head, "is my oldest, Emmit. My daughter, Ester, and my youngest, Evan."

"'Allo," they said in unison before tearing back into the house.

Relieved for the distraction, I smiled and shook hands with Elsie. "Nice to meet you."

She tucked me into her arm and escorted me into the kitchen. She took my offering of wine and immediately set to opening it.

"Now, tell me," she said around Eli, who began setting the table with platters and bowls of food as the children washed up, "how did you find Glentree when you first arrived?"

"I love Glentree!" I dove in with a kind of manic delight. Like I'd stumbled into their dinner party immediately after surviving a horrible accident. The town wasn't my problem, after all.

Elsie said with a sharp bite, "Evan!"

The youngest was brandishing the butter knife like a sword—and was knowledgeable on how to use it like one. His gaze darted to her, and as they held each other's stare over the tabletop, which was at his chin height, he gently placed the knife down next to a dinner plate as if that had been his intent all along.

Elsie nodded. "Aye, right, good boy." Then back to me: "I'm so glad ye like town. We've taken pains to expand the historic feel all the while giving our locals ways to express themselves in a contemporary manner —like with the arts fairs and climate change lecture series. We look auld, but we're modern at heart."

I felt the tension in my shoulders ease as her warmth tucked me into the shelter of her family. Our family. I took the glass she offered and clinked it to hers.

"*Sláinte*," we said in unison.

"In town," she continued, "we have all kinds of shops; have ye been to the batik shop? The artisan who runs it he does all his own dyes and designs, and you must—"

"Dinner," Eli boomed, "is ready!"

All three kids blasted into their seats and grabbed a bit of everything for their plates.

With wine in hand, I sat at the heavily laden table. Ceramic crocks of hand-whipped butter, fluffy soda bread, and long-cooked roast with wine, sautéed leeks, and creamy potatoes sat like offerings to the gods down the middle of the table. The first few bites, though, were like dirt in my mouth. I had consciously set aside Rowan for the moment, but my subconscious was laser-focused on him, and it was beginning to overflow and rob me of real joy, turning my dinner into dust.

Setting my fork down, I focused on my new family. Dinner was a high-volume acrobatic theater production that truly warmed my heart. My own close family enjoyed dinners that could compete with rock concerts. The adult conversation here was bisected into bite-size chunks as one child's bottom would leave their chair and Elsie would make a guttural noise, making that child's bottom go back in their chair. Then while she was distracted, another would turn a gross face, making the other laugh comically loud, showing well macerated food to the entire table. I smiled; it was a deeply normal moment.

Eli began. "So, how's work finding you—Evan," he admonished the boy who was inching toward the fat, warm slices of bread in the middle of the table again. Evan paused, slouching back. "Finish your tatties before you take another slice. Now, Cole, tell me about yer work?"

I hid my smile in my wineglass as Elsie gave the other two a sly wink, a reward for momentary good behavior before looking back at me.

"We're—" I started.

"Evan—" Eli gave his youngest's hand a gentle pat as it was coming back with a fat slice of bread. Evan gave his father a triumphant smile knowing that since he'd touched the bread, he now got to eat it.

The soft clap of skin made me forget the question and look off to the sideboard under the far window. I didn't see the old books or pitcher of dried lavender there but the ghostly aberration of Rowan grabbing thigh. Had I really heard Rowan's hand as it came up against the woman's leg? I heard it again in my mind's ear, and it rang louder and louder until it was a gunshot snapping me back to reality.

Eli asked, "Ye all right?"

"Fine." I smiled my lie.

After dinner, it was a bath and then bedtime with stories, which were a hot ticket by their aunt with the funny accent. Elsie excused herself to go to bed, as she had an early appointment the next day, leaving Eli and me relaxing in the snug living room. Eli refilled his whisky as I sank into the long, plush sofa and pulled a wool tartan blanket over my knees. Eli folded himself into his leather chair and nodded at the albums on the coffee table between us.

"Family history, if ye'd like to meet some more relatives? Most are deceased, skeletons of past lives, but worth a peek, aye?"

"Absolutely," I said and grabbed the one off the top.

"Aye, but that one is more recent, still has some flesh on it."

I recognized young Eli, a version of young me, and a raven-haired little boy: fishing in some; in one they were balancing atop a rock wall, the cattle on the other side staring at them, ears perked and eyes wide. It wasn't until the middle of the album when the boys had gotten a few years older that I recognized the raven-haired boy. The photo was of Eli's birthday party; the other boy was right next to Eli in the crowd of kids. Head propped on his hands watching Eli as he opened his presents.

Only in his blue eyes wasn't a look of excitement or even envy at Eli's mound of gifts, just sadness.

I put my fingers to the little boy in the picture.

"Recognize someone?" Eli asked. The windows were all dark now, and over the hush of the wind, the faint crash of the ocean against the cliffs could be heard.

On my fourth glass of wine and past speech, I just nodded.

"Aye, he was my best friend for the whole of my childhood." He toasted the air with his whisky and took a healthy swallow as if he were toasting a dead man.

"What happened?" I whispered, touching Rowan's sad face.

"Oh aye, I ask myself that very question every day. Never had a brother, save for him."

I looked up at Eli; he seemed to know and understand my pain.

He looked down at the amber liquid in his glass glinting in the soft lamplight. "Rowan was the kind of prankster who might get ye a few days in lockup, but ye'd have a story to tell that no one would believe. I would not have been able to tell my children what it's like to ride a Highland bull on a full moon night if it weren't for him. Nor that the current of the loch will take ye to the Orkney's a day's ride in a dinghy."

I smiled despite myself.

"Then," Eli continued, "he came home from war." Eli was looking out the glass patio door as if toward that distant place, seeing only his reflection, as if conversing with himself on what he witnessed. "I met him at the airport, but he was haunted. Literally didn't see me. He just walked by me and got into the car the estate had sent. I can still see in his eyes, dark circles beneath them, the shattered man he was. I've friends and acquaintances that came back also changed, but not like him.

"He took up the chief position with a dogged determination, and weeks passed before I finally reached out, since he hadn't. No replies to my messages. Then Elsie saw him in town, and he was brash with her, didn't care to see the kids—only those damned Jakeys, Eryka and Kelly, whom he kept as close advisers. I'd not recognize the man as a friend anymore."

I wasn't sure what a Jakey was, but his tone meant *scum*. I didn't disagree with him. Both Eryka and Kelly had tried to kill me, after all, let alone, in Eryka's case, upstage me in the fashion department at the clan's gala—something that might have been worse than death, in Mother's eyes. "He keeps pain and suffering close, like a guilty balm to his burnt heart."

"Aye, that's it.

"The mischief masks it, has always masked it," I whispered down at the picture in the album in my lap. "The pain has always been there, only some days he hides it better than others..." *Like today,* I thought. "Which birthday of yours is this?"

"Aye, my eighth...no, tenth?" he said and looked questioningly at the room. "Aye, tenth."

Rowan hadn't showed me any photos from back then. I'd seen a few professionally photographed ones from clan events, which he started attending at twelve. I took in the deep creases of his brow, already, even at only age ten, and the subtle but present downward tug of his lips and eyes. I felt a pang for him. "He's so sad."

"Aye, he is."

I wasn't sure if we were talking about now or then, or both.

"Tha's right," Eli said. "He lost his mother just before my tenth birthday."

"Oh."

"Ye know," he said, "she dinnae die in an asylum, like most think."

"Rowan told me."

Eli looked incredulous. "He's told ye?"

"Yes."

"Told ye that she was in a car wreck?"

"Yes."

"Did he tell ye how she got there?"

"Apparently she drank a fifth at one of the Gatherings and ended up driving off the cliff."

It was Eli's turn to nod. "Aye, tha's the gist of it. I doubt he's told more than just you and I."

I nodded. His mother's recklessness made me think of Rowan's. "He's just as reckless," I said before I could stop myself, feeling the four glasses of wine, feeling a knife in my gut twist.

"What do you mean?"

I stared at the little boy in the photo. A dark presence in the middle of jubilation, a sad boy who had lost his mother just a few days before surrounding himself or being forced to surround himself with someone else's joy. I realized that there was a good possibility the man I'd met the year before had been emotionally crushed too many times in his three and a half decades on earth and was now just a broken boy looking for a serotonin boost between the legs of any woman.

Eli sat forward. "What has Rowan done?"

# Fourteen

I hiccupped.

"Oh," I said, realizing I'd spoken aloud. "Yeah…" I drew the word out and then decided, what the hell. "I walked in on him playing hide the sausage with some filly right before I came over here."

Eli put his whisky down with such force that it sloshed. "He fucked some other woman?"

I found the Scottish French so pleasant: *He fooked some other woman.*

"I cannae believe this," Eli growled loudly as he stood, dragging a whisky-slick hand through his hair. "He has ye living with him," he continued. "Then—"

Elsie came around the corner, tying her robe shut, "Eli!" she hissed, "Keep yer voice down."

"I cannae believe this!" he said.

"Lower," his wife said and came to sit next to me on the couch. "What are ye going on about?" she asked up at him.

"Rowan! Boffing another woman, and my cousin walked in on it!"

"What?" Elsie voice was soft and calm.

"I don't know…" The image remained unmistakable, but I wanted it to change for kind Elsie. "I was told she's a solicitor of some sort?" Could I turn what I saw into a business meeting, if only I said it was?

They both were silent, looking at me.

Eli spoke first. "Crow's nose?"

Elsie scowled at him. "No' a beak, per se, but prominent?"

My gut twisted. "Yes."

"Curly black hair pulled back against its will?"

I groaned. "Who is she?'

"The girl he was boffing a little over a year ago, Charmaine Chevalier," Eli said.

My brain stuttered. "Pardon?"

Elsie suddenly looked pained and in one move swept up my half-finished wineglass, put it to her lips, and drained it. She coughed, winced, then said, "Oh. I see." She wiped her mouth with the back of her hand as she put the glass down. "I'm sure it was nothing," and patted my knee.

I just looked wide-eyed at her.

"Nothing?" Eli boomed.

"Voice!" Elsie hissed.

In a harsh whisper, he said, "Nothing? Ye think tha' a woman as rich as tha' and connected as she is tae Rowan and the clan all these years is nothing?"

My stomach churned. The memory was beginning to take on a life of its own, becoming a raging porno of sweat, thrusts, and body fluids. It was crushing my heart and lungs.

Elsie put a steadying hand on my knee and rubbed my back with her other. She looked at her husband. "Ye are freaking her out, love." Then back to me: "It'll be all right—"

"No," Eli said.

"Eli..."

"No."

"This is not the same as—"

"She is my cousin, and he's my—was—my best friend. I am honor bound to—"

"Judge not, Eli. Ye haven't talked with him in over a year, ye don't know—he could have changed."

"Changed?"

Eli gestured toward me. "She should know."

"Never mind that this is Rowan's business."

"But she is my cousin," he said. "We've been here before, haven't we?"

They looked pointedly at each other.

"That was different. Your sister—"

"Exactly! She was my sister!"

"Eli," Elsie hissed, "voice."

He plowed on, "And she's my cousin—"

I was a whole ocean away from home, and the only people I had known as my shoulder and steadying hand were there. But here was a different kind of blood. Eli and Elsie might have become my family only today, but they took that role as seriously as those who knew me as a babe.

"And if she's anything like the rest of our family, Eli, Rowan will be dead by morn. Please, she can handle this. Use your time more wisely, like picking out a casket for yer best friend and drafting his eulogy."

Eli snorted. "They're living together. Did ye know tha'?"

Elsie looked confused. "Ye and Rowan are living together? You're married already, then?"

"No," I said, defeated. I flopped back, closing my eyes, wishing the couch cushions would suffocate me.

"Oh," I heard Elsie say. "Rowan has gone a bit daft, hasn't he?"

"You know, in the States, a woman can live with a man without the need to be married; it's so common that some states consider them to be legally married after so many years."

"Oh," Elsie said again. "She doesn't know."

"No. He hasn't told her. Or has other ideas."

"Other ideas?" I asked.

"Cole, the curse, it's just... Has he proposed to ye?"

"Not officially," I said, counting this as the third time I'd been asked. "We were hand-tied, almost a year ago."

Eli leaned forward. "Traditionally, here in Glentree, cousin, there has tae be an official proposal and a special ring, and from tha' moment forth, he is tae court ye until the day ye are married. Lots of feasts and a clan gathering. Then after ye are married, ye can homestead together. It's an old tradition, and no' one he's seen because of the curse, but he knows about it and as chief, must uphold tha' tradition. No' just willy-nilly plan a wedding and marry ye as ye live together. This is not America," he said, then added in a very American way, "No offense."

"None taken." I looked down at my right ring finger and noted how utterly naked it felt. It was as if the promises Rowan made to me in the dark were now, in the observant and critical light, vanishing. With him, I questioned nothing; I was at peace and trusted him implicitly. Away from him, and now with the vision of him between the legs of another woman embossed on my brain, I found the strands that bound us unraveling more and more with each passing second.

"I'm sure he'll propose," Elsie said.

"But should she accept?" Eli boomed, mirroring my own thoughts.

Together, we had broken the curse, but we had been complete strangers plunged together. To sever our bond would be dangerous. It may also be the sanest thing.

Eli cut into my thoughts. "Elsie, if Charmaine was at the castle, that means—"

"Eli," she pleaded again.

"Money, Elsie...it always comes down to money."

"Not necessarily, it could be a clan request."

"The MacLaoch estate is a money pig, sucks it right from the coffers. I lived there most days as a child—if it wasn't the flooding basement, it was something else. It's old, needs constant maintenance," he said. "And we've heard of a London woman with loads of money working with the chief to help the clan out."

"Oh aye," Elsie said sarcastically, "you've 'heard of' a London woman. Would tha' be from your cousin who was fired from MacLaoch estate for pilfering the landscaping tools?"

Eli flushed. "He does have sticky fingers..."

"And a wild imagination."

"Money," I said, "I don't have loads of money."

"Och. Dinnae worry about it. He'll come to his senses. You'll see to it, I'm sure. If not, ye'll give me a ring, and together as a family we'll work through it with him," Eli said, smiling at me. I had a sudden vision of Rowan in a headlock while Eli hollered at him to apologize.

We were quiet for a while, Elsie and Eli sitting in companionship with my despair. Elsie sighed and upended the wine bottle into my glass and took another deep swallow.

"This...Charmaine Chevalier," I said with a bitter taste in my mouth —her name even sounded like a supervillain's—"who is she?"

Eli winced. "Och, now, dinnae worry about her."

I was drunk enough that when I leaned forward, I had to brace myself on the coffee table. I did it, though, and looked him dead in the eye. "Who the fuck is she?"

Eli scrubbed his face. "She works for the Casswell company."

There was a definite *and* at the end of that sentence, and he was hoping I was too drunk to hear it.

"And?"

He sighed.

"Eli..." Elsie's warning was sharp.

I put my hand out to her. "No, no, I need to hear this."

Eli looked at his wife in apology. "I heard Rowan had gotten a proposal from Casswell. I wasn't sure who it was they were talking about then, just some rich woman who might be able to help the clan with its financial troubles."

Elsie said sadly, "Cole, Casswell is the estate planning and public relations firm tha' has been protecting MacLaoch lands for hundreds of years. Some say they are the clan."

"How so?"

"They've been writing contracts and making others heel to those contracts for centuries. Each agent for the clan has to memorize all MacLaoch laws and rites before they're allowed to be sole agent to the clan. This latest agent, the Chevalier woman, apprenticed at twenty-eight and by thirty was running the management of it. The chief says jump, Casswell agents say how high, and draft the paperwork for it. In turn, they manage the estate and advise the chief on historic precedence and give legal advice."

I buried my face in my hands. "How do you know all this?" I meant,

*How did I not know all this?* Right, I hadn't asked, and Rowan hadn't told.

"They contract out their real estate holdings to my firm. It's just common knowledge for us, ye see?" she said kindly and rubbed my back as if I were ill. "So, she made a deal with him last year sometime tha' they could merge their...assets."

I felt my mouth go salty. "Assets? As in, get married," I said and looked again down at my empty ring finger. What was this reality that was permeating my storybook life? It was sobering.

Eli said quietly, "Aye, tha's the gist of it."

"I think I'm going to be sick."

# Fifteen

I spent the night at Eli and Elsie's and sneaked out with Elsie, who gave me a big hug when she dropped me at the research field on her way to her appointment. The jagged edges of the mountains in the distance were purple, and the research students wouldn't arrive for another two or three hours. I counted my blessings that I could get things going and disappear into my work without talking with a single person until I was ready.

The quiet of the field gave space for the morning birdsong. Setting up the equipment for the day was relaxing. In this peacefulness, I tried to rationalize what I'd seen the night before and believe that Rowan wouldn't do anything to hurt me. I romanticized that he was having an argument with the Charmaine woman and was so close to her telling her off. But his hand on her thigh kept replacing my nice thoughts with murderous ones.

The distinct sound of heels through gravel interrupted my thoughts and quieted the morning songs. I looked up to the gravel path that wound through the Circle Garden and waited. Expecting Marion or Flora, maybe even with a note from Rowan, I instead received a shock when the Chevalier woman in a knee-length black wool dress, not what she had been wearing last night, strode out from between the towering hedges.

"Ah, there you are, Ms. MacLaoch." Her voice was like a cat's purr, deep and thrumming.

I looked back at her, unable to speak. And right then, in my mind's eye, she was on the desk again. Only now I saw a smile on her face. A tug at the corner of her mouth stretching it into a cat-like meow for Rowan to give it to her. In that moment, I knew she had seen me in the doorway. This was no trick of my memory. That recognition had happened. The adrenaline surge that I'd been nursing since the moment I'd witnessed the two made me want to step around the table and give her a smart *good morning* with my fist to her smirking mouth. I'd done it before, just last year, with Eryka—I could do it again. Instead, I snapped the rubber band at my wrist and, standing a bit taller, corrected her. "It's Baker."

She smiled down her nose at me as she stepped under the tent, her heels giving her an absurd height advantage. She placed her notebook down atop my pack. "Oh, do explain," she said crossing her arms.

Taken aback by her curt manner and lack of howdy-do, I forgot I had manners and that my mama would expect me to not be baited. I jumped in headfirst. "I'm sorry... Are you asking me to explain my name? You see, in the United States, where I'm from, the children typically inherit their surnames from their father. My father's name was Baker, and as I just said, so is mine."

At this, the Chevalier woman's smile evaporated. "Ms. Baker, I was alluding to the fact that the MacLaoch chief, Rowan MacLaoch, has stated that you two are married. As a point of reference, *here*," she said, mocking me, "in the United Kingdom—where your customs come from—the woman typically takes her husband's surname."

"If he says we're married... That is just an odd conversation for you two to have had while desiccating an ancient oak—"

She interrupted me with a husky laugh that made me think she really didn't find me funny. "It would be, wouldn't it?" she said; then she added, "So, would I be correct, Ms. Baker, that you if two are not legally married, who cares about any indiscretions he may or may not have had?" She smiled that cat-in-the-cream smile again.

My insides twisted hot and furious, and I tried not to say, *Who the fuck are you?* But it was evident in my tone when I hissed, "And who are you to want this information?" I snapped my rubber band again. I was going to need a whole armful.

She looked to the rubber band at my wrist then to my eyes. "Oh, I apologize," she said, looking anything but apologetic. "My name is Charmaine Chevalier, agent, representative, and solicitor for Clan MacLaoch. The firm I represent, Casswell and Associates, has been tending to clan business for over three hundred years." She slid her hand out. "You'll not find a person with more affinity for this clan than I."

"I see." I attempted an ambivalent smile but ended up grimacing as I clasped her hand. "It's a pleasure to meet you, Ms. Chevalier. And what exactly is the business you have with Rowan?"

"It's—" She tried to pull her hand back from our shake, but I hadn't rung out why she was there, and her thin, cold hand in mine felt so weak. I was going to crush her, one finger at a time.

Her eyes narrowed. "Professional and," she said, looking down at the grip I had on her, "*personal.*" She stared at me long and hard, now returning my tight grip with her own squeeze. "Mr. MacLaoch and Casswell have a long-standing relationship that will never be penetrated by an American with ideals so high above her peasant roots that it is to be laughable at best."

I let my feelings flow into my hand. "You have a long-standing personal relationship with the laird? Then you must know he's had the most interesting year. And where were you? Oh yes, that's right. In his rearview."

"This...dalliance with you," she spat, "has had its day in the sun. It's over. And in the good name of the clan, I'm here to end it."

I looked at her, really studied her like a specimen under my microscope. The high cheekbones, the skin drawn taut over them that spoke of restricted calories and a self-punishment to exceed all expectations. Her thousand-dollar belt wrapped around a tiny waist draped in a sumptuous wool that was meant for queens. The gaze as if I were filth on her shoe. I was going to have to fight like hell for my place there in Glentree, or she was going to rip me from the tower the curse had placed me in.

"Here to end it..." I repeated it like the threat it was and met her gaze and whispered, "I'd like to see you try."

She matched my ever-tightening grip.

We were in the midst of a good old-fashioned pissing match, woman to woman. One lioness to another. What she'd yet to realize, however, was that while she'd spent her youth abusing pencils and keyboards to become the wicked witch of my nightmares, I'd spent my youth in the fields of my father's peach orchard. The pissing matches I'd found myself in before were with farm boys who didn't pull their punches.

I squeezed her hand like it were a peach and I was seeking its pit.

Her face blanched.

"Ms. Chevalier," I said with a perfect drawl that any woman in my family, past or present, would be proud of, "you'll pay me respect as Rowan's chosen partner by keeping a nickel between your knees and a country mile between your bodies, understood? And if I am to become a speck of dust in his rearview, Rowan, as in, the chief of your employer's employer—not you—will decide that, with me," I said, letting her hand go. The white of my grip still evident on her hand, I pushed her folio off my things and into the dirt before shouldering my pack. "You have a nice day now," I said, and keeping my faux smile on, I walked away.

My insides were roiling. I was nearly to the garden bridge when I heard her demand from behind me. "Stop!"

I didn't. I snapped my rubber band and kept walking.

Her heels scuffled through the gravel with speed. "Ms. Baker, I demand that you stop this instant."

The woman had gall, and letting my ire get the best of me, I turned and walking backward called to her, "I've said all I will say to you." Until I found Rowan and got all our issues ironed out.

She was an indignant shadow working through Circle Garden's flowers. "I am here to vet you, Ms. Baker. If I am unable to complete my task, you will not be able to marry the laird, and if you do so without Casswell and Associates' approval, Rowan will be removed as chief. Is that what you wish?"

This news crashed over me like a tidal wave, stopping me in my tracks. I was fed up, right up to my eyebrows, in surprises. Rowan had said nothing of this. Sensing the crack in my resolve, she dove in.

"Let us work together, Ms. Baker," she said, changing her tune like a snake handler would only when the basket was securely over the coiled serpent. She'd just met me and already had a leg up. Literally.

"And what exactly are you to vet me on? Table manners, Ms. Chevalier?" I again tried not to punch her; instead, I snapped my rubber band. At this rate, I was sure to have a welt soon.

"While I doubt you'll pass even the easiest of the questions, I'm still required by Casswell code to shadow you for the next five days. The points on which I am evaluating you are private."

She couldn't be serious. *She*, a woman who so evidently did not want me with, much less marrying, Rowan was to evaluate *me*? It was going to be like showing up to a chili cook-off with peach pie.

"You are obviously kidding. And if you're not, I'll see to having you removed as clan agent—someone with less bias would be more appropriate," I said, feeling like Clive at the very least would support me in this. Stepping closer to her, I said, "And when I make that call, Ms. Chevalier, I will make note to your supervisors of your *personal* relationship with your client. I doubt they will be pleased."

Charmaine's lip curled back. "Oh yes. Spoken like a true American with no concept of how things are done here despite being in the heart of MacLaoch power for a full year. What you have yet to realize, Ms. Baker, is that while Rowan is fond of the diversion you provide, which gives you a sense of power, you have no clout with the clan or with Casswell." She produced a card. "Feel free to contact my supervisor, the eighty-year-old Casswell patriarch. If there's one thing he despises more than wasted time, it is a woman who complains about his decisions. And let me be clear—this will not be the first time that an ill-fitting marriage prospect has called to share their petty grievances."

I was huffing by the time she finished with me. I could feel the blotchy rage on my cheeks and the damp on my forehead. I took her card slowly, trying not to black out with the suppressed need to wrap my hands around her throat.

"I doubt, Ms. Chevalier"—I heard my own voice shake—"that your supervisor has ever heard from a woman with more consequence than *I* have with the laird and his clan."

"We'll see, shan't we?"

We stood there for some time, waiting for the other to back down, the rat wheel of epithets rolling through our minds until one of us blinked.

Finally, she broke, smiling as if she'd won, and held out her hand. "Until tomorrow."

I tilted my head, trying to figure out how she held all that gall in one petite body before I gripped her hand again and reminded her of the farmer's daughter I was. "Until tomorrow," I said, dropping her hand as her face went white again, and I turned, heading straight to the castle entrance. I would find Rowan and bend his ear. Maybe even bend him in half.

Just inside the front doors of the castle stood Dr. Gillian, talking with an enamored Marion, who still had her purse on her shoulder. He said, chipper, "Good morning, Nicole—"

"*Yeah, right,*" I said to him, and stomping up the stairs on my way to Rowan's tower office, I threw over my shoulder, "Get the rest of the artifacts down to the basement rooms like you promised. Have Holly help you. And for the love of god, keep your pretty-boy eyes to yourself. And Marion, find Dr. Gillian a room in the eastern wing of the castle. You were right—he shouldn't have to commute every day when we have plenty of space." Rowan didn't trust the guy? Perfect, let's have him *live* in the castle.

I cackled. I was going to tear down the walls of his fantasy world and start with the reminder that I was here every day, and he was not, making me a dangerous thing to forget about.

I threw open the door to the library. No Rowan. I lit up the hall to the tower stairs and scaled the in-wall steps like a leopard. No Rowan.

Fuming, I stood on the same rug I had a year ago where I accused him of bribing me and closed my eyes. I tried to catch my breath and quiet my mind. I'd find him. I just needed to be quiet enough to feel him in my blood. In moments of deep peace, I'd been able to know which room of the castle he was in by just listening to the hum in my veins. Only in that moment, I had angry sweat down my back and across my brow, my heart was hammering, and my mind was working with pure fight-or-flight emotions. I took a deep breath and counted to ten. At ten I realized that not all the agitation I was feeling was mine. And the other's distress was getting stronger. He was close.

I stomped back to the office door and whipped it open hard. It bounced off the stone wall, and I was on the first step when it smacked me on its way back closed. Cursing, I crashed down the stairs before coming to a halt halfway down, pain throbbing up my backside.

"Ugh!" I shouted, and my voice echoed back at me. I had a moment of clarity there in that narrow stone stairway: I needed to have more time to think; if I talked with Rowan right then, I'd regret everything I did.

# Sixteen

I paced the stacks, slapping Charmaine's card against my palm. "Who does she think she is?" I asked Deloris as she put research titles back in the shelves.

"Och, clan agitator, I presume," she said absently. I'd already been there for thirty minutes venting in a stream of uninterrupted consciousness. Angry consciousness. Deloris listened, interjecting calm agreement of my findings about the woman.

"Her or Rowan? I'm not sure on who to be more inflamed at."

"Oh, I've no doubt you'll have it sorted by tomorrow," she said, pushing a blue hardback into place.

I stopped pacing. "You're right. Can I use your phone?"

I HUNG UP AND CAME BACK. DELORIS WAS FARTHER DOWN the rows, near the desk I'd found her and Clive at just the other day. I flopped down in the chair. My anger was gone. I had left it all on the telephone line.

"And?" she said, wheeling the cart a few feet before setting the foot brake and finding her place again in the shelves.

"He laughed at me," I said. His incredulous bullfrog laugh still clanged in my mind. "I hadn't gotten out more than who I was and why I was calling before he started bark-laughing into the phone."

Deloris put the book down and looked at me. "Oh?" Her voice was tinged with worry, for the man on the other line or me, I didn't know.

"I may have lost it...a touch." I stared off into the distance in a kind of peace that comes from venting pent-up anger. I latently snapped my rubber band.

"Oh aye?" she said, bidding me to continue.

"I said, 'Listen up, you son of a bitch,' then was overly graphic in my description of Charmaine's relationship with the chief."

My reserve was back. I didn't tell Deloris what I'd told Charmaine's boss, the owner/president/CEO of Casswell and Associates. I'd mixed a bit of truth and fiction. I had them much farther along in their position. Both had been oblivious to the priceless artifacts smashing to the floor —things did crash to the floor, though they were probably more junk mail than artifacts. I figured a man dedicated to preserving MacLaoch status wouldn't take to smashing of clan artifacts. I also told him that she was holding sex and financial bribes as collateral for the chief to do her personal bidding, none of it beneficial to Casswell and Associates. But I had been right, the man was a son of a bitch; his only moment of pause was her financial bribe to Rowan. It was as if he knew of it, hated being reminded of it, and hung up because of it.

I had gotten nowhere with him. But I felt better

Deloris looked at me owl-eyed. "Ye did what?"

I gave her a sad smile. "Hi, my name is Nicole Baker, and I have a temper," I said as I snapped my rubber band.

Deloris returned my smile and said, "Around here, it's called being Scottish."

CHARMAINE WAS WAITING FOR ME BACK AT THE RESEARCH field.

I paused in the middle of the Circle Garden, watching her. The spring blooms surrounding me waved, beckoning me to dive into the bed and watch the sky for the rest of the day, or life. Whichever was longer.

I took a deep breath and saw my grad students up in the hillside working, finalizing the grid while others documented plants and fauna.

Steeling my soul, I ditched the flower bed idea and faced my doom.

"Ms. Chevalier," I said as I approached, sounding as if her presence wasn't an absolute nightmare.

One perfect pencil-thin brow raised as she turned. "You work fast, Ms. Baker. I've already received an inquiry about any personal relationship or personal agreements I have entered into with the laird. Not to worry, I reassured him that my relationship with Clan MacLaoch is 100 percent professional."

I thought I'd taken enough time at the library to keep calm, but as her hawkish eyes pierced me, I realized I was wrong.

Reigning in my temper for the sake of Holly and Dr. Gillian, who were sitting there, I bit out, "Walk with me." I set down my pack and picked up a clipboard before moving out to the field.

When I heard her breath behind me, I turned and spat, "You and I are getting on like tinder and fire, so why are you still here? It's obvious that until Rowan returns—"

"Don't address him so informally with me. You are a mild diversion he's indulging himself in at present; do not pretend with me that you are anything more."

I ground my molars and snapped my rubber band.

"What I'm trying say is that you've already decided what your opinion of me is—everything else is just theater. Git, shoo, get gone, and do the thing you need to do, and when the *chief* returns, you and I will have another conversation." By the end of it, I was sounding as Southern as the cousins my mother called *backwater*. *Hopping mad* was also a phrase that applied.

She had smiled at my use of *chief*, but now she growled, "I'm here to vet you, Ms. Baker, or did you think I was disingenuous when I mentioned it earlier?"

My lip curled back. "I think you can just say 'joking,' Charmaine—"

"It's *Ms. Chevalier* to you."

"Charmaine," I said purposely, "if you trail me, you'll get your thousand-dollar suits dirty and likely turn an ankle in those heels."

Charmaine looked at me like a large feline licking the remnants of fish guts off her chin. "I think not. I'll escort you back to the library where I can commence with our introductory interview. Now."

I took a long look at her, calming my angry pounding heart and hoping I had enough restraint to not bounce my clipboard off her temple. Instead, I put my hands behind me and quietly snapped my rubber band again. "No."

She gave me a fake smile. "Your obstinance is refreshing."

"Put that in your report," I said and turned. I'd bet my research site that she'd not step one heel into the mucky soil of the field. "Now, if you'll excuse me," I said, using exaggerated politeness, "I have work I need to attend to."

"Ah, work, yes." She raised her voice so that it carried up to me and out over the field for all to hear. "You mean the examination of the empty lot next to the castle? The insignificant plot of land the clan has agreed to pay you to *look at*. Was this decided by the chief or the entire clan?"

I stopped. I turned around, glaring at her. "Entire clan," I said equally as loud, "and they don't pay me; this is part of a Fund program, and those third-party grants do."

"Ah," she said, "but they do incur other expenses and are not financially benefiting from your inspection."

I took the few steps back down to her. "That's not true. The MacLaoch estate is reimbursed for incurred expenses, and should we find anything of historical or biological importance, Clan MacLaoch will have rights to it. And any press associated with it will no doubt bring financial profits to the estate and clan," I said, keeping my voice even. I had defended my master's thesis a little over a year ago, a process that was far more intensive and aggressive than her probing questions.

"Yes, but, Ms. Baker, you cannot assume that merely digging through the heather and bog will—"

I put my hand up. "Ms. Chevalier, let's avoid subjects you know nothing about. You'll only embarrass yourself. First, the 'heather and bog' is actually not a bog but rather a coastal Highland meadow with native species that date back to the ice age. It is a miracle that it wasn't marred by the destruction during the Clearances or during everyday grazing. One hundred percent of the flora and fauna we've recorded to date has been native. This means the probability of any artifacts being of historical importance increases exponentially. We have a Fund-appointed archaeologist working with us to help us unearth archaeological treasure. Would you like to meet him? Follow me," I said and charged back down the hill toward the tent.

"Dr. Gillian, on your feet and impress," I said as Charmaine caught up.

"O'aye?" was all he got out before she caught up.

I turned to her. "Ms. Charmaine Chevalier with Casswell and Associates, meet our site's Fund liaison, professor of archaeology, Dr. Mickey Gillian, PhD."

Dr. Gillian's eyes laser-beamed into hers, their odd color catching the filtered rays of afternoon sun through the cloud cover as he stepped out from under the tent. I could have sworn he stepped into the light for that purpose.

He murmured something in Irish Gaelic and looked sheepish before giving her a shy, aw-shucks look. "It's a pleasure to be formally introduced."

Charmaine shook his hand and returned his smile. "I'm surprised you didn't mention your credentials when you introduced yourself earlier."

"You are a stunning woman—I cannot remember a word I said, much less what I didn't say."

Watching him slip easily into exactly the kind of role—the bashful, subservient male role—he suspected would appeal to her reminded me of watching an octopus on the sea floor changing color to mimic its surroundings.

Her hawk eyes studied him, looking for a crack. When they found none, she looked over at me. "We're not done here."

"Of course not."

She gave Dr. Gillian a smile that startled me; she was impossibly beautiful, and her pearly-white teeth illuminated her face, making her look kind too. "Lead the way, Dr. Gillian," she said, waving him down the path.

I breathed a sigh of relief at the reprieve. If Dr. Gillian did nothing else for us, at least he had sacrificed himself well. He was a young buck—I hoped he'd keep her busy all afternoon.

Holly scoffed behind me. "She's a pretty miss, isn't she?"

"Is she? It's hard for me to see past the biting snake she calls her soul."

Holly laughed and came to stand next to me, her stainless-steel clipboard in hand, gloves tucked into her back pocket. "Too bad she can't have him. I'm going to marry him."

I looked over at her and smiled. "Oh, are you now?"

"Oh aye, he's yet to know it, though. I may have to slog him over the head and drag him into the heather-covered hills, but I'll do it."

"I believe you."

## Seventeen

G IS device in hand and a sack of irrigation flags under my arm, I made my way to the far quadrant of the research field to mark off the rest of the area. It was also a great place to disappear into the forest if Charmaine returned. I dreamed that it was quite plausible that I'd live there from now on, away from society like Rowan had when the damned man returned from war.

As if Charmaine's absence drew out the sun, the clouds parted and bright Glentree sunlight struck me, making my wool sweater too warm. The grasses and soil all captured the heat, intensifying their smells. Insects buzzed loudly in my ear. I pushed a flag into the ground, walked boot tip to boot tip, until I had traveled two feet, and planted another. It was then I realized the buzzing was pitched oddly. Rowan was near.

I groaned and rolled my head in a circle to loosen the tension in my shoulders. I looked down to the flags under my arm and debated continuing to work or going to find him now. I would give him a chance to explain why he did what he did. I'd only ask myself to try.

Sounds of raised voices made my decision for me. I looked down over the field toward the rear of the castle, where Charmaine rounded the corner, sure-footed Rowan right behind her. Charmaine's staccato words punctuated the still afternoon air.

My stomach churned.

Rowan passed her on the lower trail, making his way up toward the research tent; Charmaine's heels slowed her pace on the gravel path. Halfway to the tent, Rowan skidded to a stop and pivoted back to her, stopping kissing distance from her face. I took a step when suddenly it was clear it wasn't what I'd assumed. Rowan wasn't going to kiss her; he was telling her off. He stabbed his finger over her shoulder like a peeved parking attendant telling a vehicle to turn the fuck around. Charmaine took a step back, her face going from indignation to an emotion I couldn't place on her. However, I recognized the next shift into anger. She whipped her own pointer finger to the ground and lobbed something equally as potent back to him.

Rowan's shoulders bunched, and I reluctantly acknowledged that I knew that stance of his well; this was far from a lovers' quarrel. Some of the knots in my stomach loosened. He looked much like he did a year ago when faced with a belligerent drunk uncle at the fundraising gala. I selfishly prayed he'd punch Charmaine too.

The researchers began to take interest at their escalating quarrel, and Dr. Gillian at the research tent stood staring at them. Then, abruptly, he put his things down and slipped away into the Circle Garden. I wished right then to have heard what he did, and I realized then that I should probably be the adult I was and step in instead of enjoying my spectator view.

Rowan, having run out of things to say to Charmaine, turned away from her, returning to his original trajectory toward the research tent. Only he didn't get far. Charmaine grabbed his arm above his rolled cuff.

I heard her words clearly then: "...a duty to your clan."

Rowan turned back, and while I couldn't hear what he said, her hand flung off him as if his words had scalded. She stumbled back, and he turned away, looking like he was about to rain hell down onto anyone attempting to bar him from his objective. Charmaine glared after him before turning on her heel.

Up until that point, I was like a fly on a leaf in the tall brush, but as she disappeared down the trail, in the quiet that followed, I felt a sizzling across my skin. Rowan's temper had ignited my mitochondria; he was a kinetic ball of energy looking to spark with mine in an explosion.

He spoke with Adara, our recently hired field botanist intern, and in a few heartbeats, I watched as she smiled and nodded and then lifted her finger in my direction. Rowan smiled and looked up; his gaze swept the field like a trained fighter pilot would searching for his target.

I felt a bull's-eye on my chest.

This fly was now found. Our eyes connected, and the same sizzling heat detonated behind my breastplate.

*Finally,* I thought. We were about to have words.

Lots of words.

As he moved up the path, his smile vanished. A MacLaoch determination came over his face, and his eyes were unflinchingly dead set upon mine.

I noticed his shirt was the same as what he'd worn the day before, now a wrinkled light blue with dark pinstriping that hugged his body like I wanted to. His shirt sleeves were rolled up, revealing tense forearms that connected to capable hands that I'd last seen on the thigh of the hateful Chevalier woman.

In the last bit of distance he covered, my chin tipped up as I crossed my arms over my chest.

"We need to talk," he said and stopped a few courteous feet from me; despite the hill, his height still put him at an advantage, looking me dead in the eye. He gestured into the forest behind me. His actions were polite, yet his body vibrated.

I looked over my shoulder into the forest then back to him and obliged. The forest would be a good place for us to talk. It would be quiet and private, and if I needed to dig a hole to bury a body, it was just the place.

Once the full force of the forest's cool air and deep shade took over, I stopped and turned to Rowan.

Rowan's gaze was hard and dark. "Farther."

While he was looking like something that had been dragged through hell, I had feelings of my own, and it was about time I shared them. "If you're worried about my researchers hearing your screams, trust me, here is far enough. And let's be honest, I love you enough to not let you scream for long."

"I'm not playing around, Cole. Farther."

I gave the soil a kick. "Nice loamy soil. The hole I put you in will be easy to dig. Here's fine."

"I need to tae keep walking, so I don't say—"

"Stop," I said, putting up my hand and thinking of that moment when he had Charmaine up on the desk. "Right here is far enough for me to hear what you have to say about Charmaine Chevalier—"

"I don't want her to hear a bloody word I'm about to say. Farther. In. Now."

I grit my teeth, reluctant to admit he had a point. I continued walking, but it wasn't fast enough nor, apparently, in the right direction for Rowan.

He grabbed my upper arm. "This way—there's a clearing in a bit."

My temper was hot enough to match his, and I yanked my arm out of his grip. "Don't touch me. I've followed you this far, and that's far enough."

"I don't want—"

"I heard what you said, but frankly I'm about zero give-a-cares away from having a real nice sit-down with you, and if you drag me anywhere without my permission, I'll snap you like a twig," I said, snapping my fingers, "and take this whole curse, future, destiny crap you and I have going in a whole new direction."

"Ye are making it difficult for me to—"

The birds held their breath as I cut in. "*Difficult,*" I said homing in on that single word and felt it roll about in my mouth. "I'm making *what* difficult, Rowan? What exactly is *difficult* for you? Is life so hard when you have an ex-girlfriend flush with money make you a part of her asset management program right after she tended to your personal needs?"

Ugly red spots bloomed on his neck and cheeks. "I'm sorry you saw that..."

Anger detonated right over my heart. "You...you're sorry? So, you won't deny it? Bold as brass," I said, shaking my head, my voice sounding hollow in my own ears.

He wiped a hand over his face and cursed. "I dinnae mean to—"

I almost doubled over with fury. "Didn't mean to?! Did you fall onto her? How do you 'not mean to'?" I gestured wildly.

"I can explain."

My fingers jammed against my temples; my voice was rough around the edges as anger and betrayal made me cry-scream, "I see it like a photograph in my brain—I don't need your explanation. What I do need is for you to get all of this," I said, gesturing at him, "out of my face until I've thought about what to do about us, but let's get one thing clear, our relationship is officially toast. Having sex with a woman on your library desk is a hard limit for me. A limit that I didn't think I'd have to—"

"Cole, I—"

"Shut the hell up," I snapped. "A limit that I didn't think I'd have to set—since anyone with more than a half a brain cell who knows me knows that if you dip your wick into another woman, I'll break you. It's programmed into my DNA to do bodily damage to any man who does. So, stay safe, pack your shit out of the cottage, and when I figure out what to do about my work situation here, I'll let you know."

So much for my being calm when I saw him next.

He was quiet, the fight drained out of him. He looked exhausted. "Can I speak?"

"Patronize me, and I'll light you on fire, MacLaoch."

"Noted," he said and wiped a hand over his face. "What ye saw was behavior that was inexcusable," he said, "but I did *not* have sex with Charmaine."

I sneered. "I think you have forgotten that not only am I a grown woman, I also have eyes. Eyes that saw you. I knew you were a proud man, but I never thought you a liar."

His mouth was in a firm line, and his eyes held mine. "I was not having sex with her. But she is an ex, and she and I have been intimate before. In the past. The distant past."

"She says otherwise—"

"It's a lie. What you saw was a struggle—"

"Don't."

"No," he said, crunching over the dead leaves of the forest floor and firmly getting in my space, his exhaustion having morphed into flint, "you'll listen tae me. Tha' is what we are supposed tae do. *Listen.* You listen to me, and I listen tae you. But you have tae let me speak, or I'll do more things I'll regret."

I felt my back go up, "Did you just threaten me?"

"Aye. I'm glad ye noticed," he said and continued, his darkness moving over his features, carving shadows under his cheekbones and eyes. His five o'clock shadow darkened the lower half his face, and now his eyes were like gunstock. "She had something that was meant for me, and she refused to give it. I didnae care how I got it. For that, I am ashamed. But, Cole, I'm nearly out of my head when you didn't come home last night. I've been looking for you everywhere. And my skin feels like it's going to crawl off me with shame and rage. I know the rage is ye. I'd not lie with anyone but you, ever," he said and took a deep breath and punctuated its expulsion with *ever*.

We stood there in the forest, the crush of leaves under our feet perfuming the air with the musk of gentle organic decay. The ocean against the cliffs in the distance was muted, and the once-chirping birds were silent above us. Filtered light made the forest a gorgeous spot for a romantic interlude, but for Rowan and me, right now, it was ominous. One false move, and the momentary truce and obligatory listening would be over, and we'd instead be prime for a forest fire.

"When were you going to tell me that you were coming home early?"

"I dinnae think I would, but then I received word that the bank man wanted to meet here yesterday."

"The call you took leaving me with my pants around my ankles?"

"Yes, I'm so—"

"Again, why didn't you tell me?" I might have had a dead cell phone the majority of the time, but everyone knew that if you told Flora or Marion, I'd be informed in the very next breath.

"I did."

"Right."

"Cole..." He sounded pleading, but his eyes said he'd had enough shit for a week and wasn't having a fantastic time taking more on.

"This shit sandwich you're eating right now is one of your own making, MacLaoch. You don't take time to talk with the people who are important to you? To prioritize them in your life? You'll find yourself standing in a forest having to explain why you had your hands on a woman who's used to having you between her legs."

I decided that if I said more, I might blasphemy his whole lineage back to the stone age. I wasn't made into a hothead that second—I'd been one my whole life—and I knew the signs for when I should stop.

I turned smartly and headed out of the forest. The leaves crunched under my feet, but I unfortunately heard him ask from behind me, "Where were you last night?"

# Eighteen

I heard the words; I also heard the innuendo under them. That while I thought he had cheated on me with Charmaine, I, in some sort of rage-fueled haze, had taken another man to bed. This unspoken accusation stopped me. I pulled the rubber band at my wrist back so far that it snapped right off.

Holding air in my fingertips, I counted to ten. At ten, I turned slowly.

"Come again?" I asked and was utterly impressed by the calm tone.

"Don't fuck with me, Cole. I've had enough of people fucking me over. Where'd ye spend the night last night?"

I felt a maniacal giggle start in my chest. He was asking me where I was? My eyes widened as the laughter burst out of me. My gaze was seared onto him as I took a step toward him.

To his credit, he didn't flinch. We were forged out of similar stock, and neither of us knew how to back down when we thought we were in the right. We both were used to staring down explosions without blinking.

"Where was I?" I said and took another step. "Where were you?" My voice slithered through the forest like a serpent before biting him.

His right eye flinched as the realization of how it sounded dawned somewhere deep, deep in the recesses of his mind. "Looking for you. You'd know that if you were there at the cottage."

I tried to tamp down my fury, but somewhere between his saying *you* and *cottage*, I detonated. Reason floated off into the tree canopy, and words I created to purposefully to brand him flowed out of me. Later, much later, I'd deal with losing my damn mind.

"Tell me, Rowan, did you finish rutting Charmaine before you sauntered out to find me? Did you use a condom, babe? I sure don't want herpes or a case of excessive affluence when we fuck again." The effect was immediate.

His hands clenched. "I didn't fucking rut her. Did that pretty fuck, Gillian, give you the comfort you needed? Cry into his pillow, did ye? And in my castle, no less."

"So, you heard about that, then?" I said, meaning that I had hired Dr. Gillian and he'd moved into the castle, but before I realized what it sounded like, he cleared the distance between us and gripped my upper arm.

Others in my position would have had every right to be scared, to start screaming for help, and should have. However, I'd spent my early life being manhandled by an older brother and cousins. I knew the minutiae of a grip. Sometimes it said, "Come! Let's play!" and other times it was trying to make a point or communicate that a fist was inbound. Rowan was getting a really good grip on reality, which happened to be my upper arm.

I may not have been afraid. I was, however, mad as hell. "Get your goddamn hand off me."

"Answer me!" His eyes sparked.

My skin had gone hot, and I looked down to where he held me and then back into his eyes. "What's the hardest you've ever been punched, MacLaoch?"

His eyes studied mine, squinted. "I've been punched verra hard. Knocked out. You'll have to—"

I swung my fist. He blocked it, but I was covering for my knee.

He went down like a ton of bricks and brought me down with him. He shouted and groaned, rolled over onto his knees, and pressed the top of his head against the forest floor. My arm was pinned under him.

When the world stopped spinning, I yanked my hand back, and this sparked him.

He lunged for me, and I rolled away. He caught my shirt and yanked me back. In seconds, Rowan had me pinned under him.

His skin was flushed, and he was panting. "Ye are mine. Mine. Do ye hear me?" The veins at his temple and throat rose, pulsing.

Somewhere in the back of my mind, I was reminded of the heather-laden hillside the week we met. It was nearly a year to the day.

I breathed just as heavily as he did but relaxed back into the uneven earth behind me. His palms were sweaty on my wrists and hot. More sweat had broken out over his forehead, and he looked down at me, begging for a reason to keep wrestling. I gave him an equal yet heavy-lidded stare back; my fury was intoxicating.

Through his teeth, he said, "Ye hit my fucking nuts."

"Sorry."

He heard my sarcasm and hissed back. "Calm down."

"I am calm."

"Ye are as calm as the center of a hurricane."

A drip of sweat undulated off his forehead, and I made a face as it stared me down, threatening to bomb my eyeball.

"You're sweating on— Ugh!" I said, snapping my head to the side to avoid the drip hitting me. It splattered on my cheek. I glared at him. "You're sweating on me."

Rowan did what he always did when he came home sweating from a run on the days the loch was too choppy to swim—he swiped his sleeve across his forehead, this time unthinkingly releasing my arm.

I punched his other sweaty hand off my wrist and brought my elbow back and into the side of his neck. It nicked his chin as he grunted, leaning back. My boots were freed from under him. I brought my knees to my chest and kicked his shoulder.

Rowan, having had proper combat training, was taking each of my blows like professional cowboy would while wrangling a calf. It was only a matter of seconds before he'd have the upper hand again or acciden-tally break my nose, because we'd both solidly lost our marbles.

He fell back onto his hands, and I was up on my feet. Rowan's leg swung out; the ground was uneven, and his shoe caught my ankle. I stumbled down the small incline to my knees before I felt him grab me. I yanked my arm back, but instead of freeing myself, I pulled Rowan to me. He slammed into me, and we log-rolled to the base of a massive tree, me on top of him. It cut out the sun, creating a dense mat of moss and lichen under it.

The tumble had shaken my brain like tofu in its tub of water, but Rowan was clearheaded as he wrenched me over him, putting me onto my back as he straddled my hips. He reached for my hands, and I had the wherewithal to try and buck him off. Now thinking clearly, I arched up and grabbed his shirt to wrench him to the side like he did to me, but something else happened. Rowan's shirt was a proper cotton button-down not meant for roughhousing in the forest. The top button popped first, but the next refused—just like its owner—to be tugged to the side. Instead, the shirt tore open as he pitched forward. His hands slammed to the ground on either side of my head. The fabric was in my clenched fist, and naked Rowan chest was now open to the breeze. The humming in my head was loud. I absently flicked my tongue against my lips, tasting the salt of my own sweat.

Rowan breathing hard above me sizzled, his fury undulating into something rough and wanting, right along with me. Decency was long gone, and we did a swan dive together into the wilds of our animal natures. I watched his muscles flex as his fingers dug into my hair and gripped. My scalp tingled in sumptuous response.

I groaned as my eyes went half-mast in pleasure.

Rowan pulled my head to the side, and his withering gaze stayed with mine until he dove down below my jaw. His teeth scraped the side of my neck, stopping with a bite. I arched slowly against his exposed skin. My world quieted, and all thought went to where he was putting pressure. The bite was gentle enough to not break my skin but hard enough to make me focus on it.

I expelled my breath in a hot gust.

"Stop fighting me," he said against my skin before kissing where he'd marked me. He nuzzled the skin under my jaw and kissed me again.

Then, just like turning on the light in a dark room, my intent changed.

I looked to the fabric in my hand and had the sudden urge to have all of him naked against my own naked skin. My emotions bottomed out, leaving me raw and needy, and I pulled again, only this time I was purposefully taking off his shirt.

I felt a hot tear leak out from the corner of my eye as I shoved his shirt off. He shook his shirt from his arms and covered me again with his body, his lips chasing down the tear. He kissed it off the side of my face and groaned as I dragged my nails up his bare back.

His muscles pulled, making a ravine down the length of his spine; they bunched over his shoulder blades, and I dug into their crevasses. His mouth sought mine. We collided, and as our lips fused to each other, we collectively groaned.

*This...* I thought.

This was what we were fighting for. Our brains had gotten in the way and ruined everything.

I sighed, feeling his body weigh me down, his pelvis grounding me, pressing me back into the earth.

My shirt was tossed atop his. Now we fought with each other's buttons and zippers. Rowan and I were frantic. I made quick work of the button of his dress pants; he yanked open my button fly. His blunt fingertips roughly dragged down my waist before grabbing the top of my jeans and underpants and pushing them down. I was kicking off my boots as I wriggled. Rowan was wrenching down my jeans as I pushed down his, our mouths never releasing.

His mouth opened to me, and I plundered, reminding myself what he tasted like. Worry, whisky, and the tinge of blood. Exertion smoked his skin and slathered it with briny sweat. He groaned and pressed me harder into the soft and flaky moss, lichen, and tree needles and leaves. He settled down between my legs as his hand went back into my hair and pulled my head back. My knees fell open, and I commanded him inside with a shove of my heel. Half-dressed and full-crazy we reconnected there beneath that ancient tree.

I called out as Rowan cursed lovingly in Gaelic. He was thick with rage and yearning, impatient with need. He didn't wait or go slowly; he pressed himself possessively to the hilt within me, bumping his pelvis against mine. He relaxed back a fraction and shoved in harder, smacking his skin against mine. My insides pinched and stretched as he made room within me, shoving his thick, velvety length in deep. I groaned and pushed him in farther still as pain and pleasure swirled, mixing like vodka and honey.

There, tumbling out of our furious state, I wanted things rough and hard. There, sky high and broken off from reality, I wanted him to meet my fierceness tit for tat. I needed my skin to burn against his and for him to scour me beneath his teeth. I needed him to reassert his claim on me like I was some clan-seeking cavewoman. I needed him to settle me so I could descend back down from the stratosphere of emotion I'd rocketed into.

I wasn't alone with that need.

"Cole...please...I love you."

My hand snaked into his hair, and I gripped, pulling his head back before putting my forehead against his. We both were breathing heavy as I looked into his eyes. There he was under my microscope, emotionally open and naked deep inside of me, yearning and begging me to end his purgatory. The obsidian flecks in his irises bled with the depth of the moment.

I closed my eyes and ran the bridge of my nose down his before sealing it with a kiss on his lips.

"I love you too, Rowan MacLaoch. I always will. No matter how goddamn mad at you I am. I love you."

He pushed into me as our lips came back together, and his wide thickness relaxed back out as he whispered, "You're mine," and pressed in again.

Warmth sizzled out from our connection, and my body opened deeper to him. I shoved him farther in and said, "And you're mine. Only mine."

"Always," he whispered back.

He breathed me in like I were a brisk ocean wind and he a man who'd finally stepped out of an airless cave. His nose ran over the tops of my breasts, and he settled on one before moving to the other; he put the first back into his mouth as his pelvis pressed.

Tossing about with him in the forest allowed me to see the flex of his strength, my buck against him, watch indulgently as he faced down each of my metaphorical lashes. Somewhere deep in my subconscious, I'd lost trust in our connection and needed to reestablish our baseline of trust. The baseline that said, no matter what, no matter when, Rowan MacLaoch would forever be faithful. We were indeed tied together first by love and then by something deeper and earth-shattering in its metaphysical weight.

My hands went to his face. I needed to see it in his eyes, the answer to my question. I stilled him and looked into those eyes that matched the color of the sea beyond the walls of his castle. It was as if he were forged from the loch and delivered whole upon the lower sea gate one June morning.

There in his eyes was the matching pain to mine. And then deep in the recesses of them was the proof positive that he'd never let his eye, body, or mind wander from us. That for him it was just me, only me and forever me. It rolled over my skin like a comforting balm, like the feel of sliding beneath warm, heavy, flannel sheets in the dead of winter.

"*Tha gaol agam ort*," he whispered again, and I nodded, emotion welling up. His grip in my hair loosened, and relaxing my head back, he brushed curls off my forehead. His pace slowed, and he pushed gently within me, watching my face.

I gave him a soft smile before putting my lips to his, able finally to murmur, "I love you too."

He put an arm underneath me as I dragged my fingertips down the side of his body feeling the bump of ribs below his warm skin and muscle, stopping at the scar at his hip.

"Keep going," I said, losing my breath.

He gave me a shy smile and nudged my chin to the side with his nose. "I planned on it."

I felt his teeth tug gently on my earlobe before he breathed me in along my jaw. I let out a shaky sigh.

"I missed ye."

I gave a soft laugh. I kissed his lips that smiled back at me.

I clenched around him inside of me and watched as his eyelids fluttered. He answered with a gentle, slippery push deep inside and then relaxed out before pressing back in. He swiped all my erogenous zones and hit upon a point nestled somewhere near my soul that had me groaning. It was my turn to close my eyes, and I felt his belly and hip move against mine as he picked up his rhythm again, pushing us toward a mutually beneficial orgasmic outcome.

As he propped on one elbow, his other hand reached down to my naked rear and lifted. He knew my body well, knew all the spots to grab, bite, and caress. With my pelvis tilted, he drove home our connection, igniting another fire within us; this time it crackled across our skin and pulled us sensuously together.

Warmth rolled out from between my thighs where we pulsed together, and my desire began to pull my breath out of my body in gasps and breathy pleas.

"More, Rowan...please."

His mouth opened to mine, and our tongues skittered across our lips, tasting again. Faster, his pelvis pushed in and out, and we felt something crash against the cliff of our pleasure. I arched, pressing out, begging him to hit against our connection harder still. As the first fingers of orgasm bloomed, Rowan's breath hissed in, and fireworks exploded within me, and I cried out.

Rowan feasted on my neck as his sweat-slickened body rode me to peak again. I shuddered in release again and dragged my nails up his back once more. Rowan groaned loudly as warmth poured into me, and we descended from where we'd flown, back into our mossy bed together.

# Nineteen

W e lay under the gnarled old tree looking up through its lichen-covered branches to the hint of sky. We were smoldering shells of the individuals who had started this whole feud. Our clothes were the charred husks as we lay there pink and new on top of them, surrounded by deep forest and the resumed chirp of birds.

My fingers were wound between his as I lay half atop of him.

"*Tha mi gad ionndrainn*," he said. His Gaelic sounded from the back of his throat.

I smiled and kissed his sparsely haired chest, looked up at him as he looked down at me over the plains of his cheeks. "I missed you too."

"I'm sorry I am rubbish at talking about things that are on my mind."

"Apology accepted."

Then something went across his features, darkening them; his brows drew together as he came up on an elbow, sliding me flat on the ground as he looked down at me. "Don't leave me," he whispered.

I was surprised until I remembered what I had said earlier. "I...I've no plans to leave."

"That day in the library," he started, "she was being childish and holding something out of reach. I lost my temper, I grabbed her to get to it, *mo ghràdh*. Tha' 'tis all."

I nodded. "I don't like that you grabbed her like that, but..." I said, feeling charitable and reminding myself that, setting aside my wild imagination, they both had been clothed, "I believe you that you didn't have sex with—"

"Rut, I believe ye said."

I groaned and closed my eyes, smiling as I covered them further with a hand over them. "You make me an irrational person, Rowan MacLaoch."

"Aye, fine, but, Cole, I'm a daft prick because I have to have an answer for my next question," he said, lifting my hand to see my eyes. "I know ye'll probably light me on fire, and I know in my heart the answer, but my ears have to hear it..."

He didn't have to ask; our hearts were talking to each other again, and his had already asked me. "No, I didn't sleep with Dr. Gillian. I spent last night at my new cousin's house."

I heard the interest in his voice. "I didn't realize you'd found one. Oh aye, that is what part of...aye. I'm sorry. I haven't been a good friend to you, have I?" He touched his lips to mine softly, another apology.

I kissed him back but then gave a sardonic smile as I said, "Something tells me that after hearing who it is and what he had to say, you might prefer I had slept with Dr. Gillian."

He squinted, looking out to the tree next to us then around to the ground. It was as if I were watching him literally dig around in his brain for the person. "The bank man?" he whispered, fear in his eyes.

I grimaced. "No, babe, to my knowledge, I have no relation to this bank man who, it seems, scares you."

"Not scares so much as makes me so angry I think I might pitch him into the fairy hole and not bother checking on him until he begins to stink."

My eyebrows scraped my hairline. "Wow."

"I really dinnae like him."

"I see. No, my cousin—by marriage, I'm told, but Deloris and I aren't certain—is Eli Campbell."

He looked at me for a long beat. I didn't know what for, maybe a "Just kidding!" or "Gotcha!"

"Who?"

"Eli Campbell—"

"Oh aye, I know who Eli Campbell is. I know him very well, and he knows me verra well too." He was staring at me accusingly.

"Don't look at me like that!" I said and laughed.

"He's not a cousin."

The way he said it deadpan made me consider that I'd possibly been hoodwinked by Deloris, but I'd seen Eli. He was me, but bigger and masculine.

"I have to question Clive's paperwork. Minory blood got into Eli's bloodlines for sure. If you've seen him recently, you know we could be mistaken for siblings, not even distant blood cousins."

Rowan managed, "Why... How did ye meet?"

"First you looked like I was lying to you; now you look skittish, MacLoach. Is there something you're worried that I uncovered from my visit with him?"

The hardness returned to his gaze. "Aye and no. He's a friend. A close one at tha'."

I was still feeling a touch masochistic and asked, smiling, "What are you afraid he's confided in me?"

"He's not tha' kind of man. If you want to know more about me, Cole, all ye have to do is ask. I'll tell ye anything you want."

I nodded but felt like I needed to sit up and start putting on my clothes. I started by coming up onto an elbow. "Here's the problem with that, Rowan—we've been together for a full year, and the things he told me, I'd not once heard from you. Like the name Charmaine Chevalier and the proposal she offered you and the details that went with it."

His nose flared as the color drained from his face. Rowan sat up. "He had no right."

I sat up too. I wasn't sure how we'd returned to Quarrel Central, but there we were. Only I did know—it's what happens when too many big things occur between the times you come together. Somehow, somewhere along the way, we'd stopped talking to each other about substantial things. It was too much to go into when we had just snippets of time together.

"He had no right?" I asked incredulously then laughed. "I dare you to tell that bear of a man that he can't tell his *cousin* anything he likes. I *dare you.*"

Rowan reacted more intensely than I'd anticipated. Much more. "Och, fucking bollocks," he said, ran his hands through his hair, and cursed like a fighter pilot. He lay his forehead against his bent knees.

I had expected him to sneer at me, to tell me that Eli wouldn't hurt a fly, because that was how I saw it. But the protector I'd witnessed the night before seemed like the version closer to reality and Rowan knew that man well. And quite possibly Eli held more weight in Rowan's life that I realized.

"I see that news was more troubling to you than I'd anticipated."

I heard from under his knees, "How do ye know he's your cousin?"

"Simple. Clive had a list I exhausted last year; then Deloris added a few who were related to some on the list."

He looked at me out of the corner of his eye. "Eli is not a cousin."

I felt my jaw clench. "Tell me about my family, babe; I love it."

His eyes squinted in a glare. "Be calm. Eli is only a friend—"

"Oh, really? Last I heard, you've blown him and Elsie off, slept with and left his sister. You haven't spoken to him in over a year. And now he's taken a personal interest in why you haven't moved quickly to ensure you and I were married before the one year and a day deadline. Apparently, this is a thing, a real thing. I've heard it three—three—times this week that the handfast is only good for a year and day; then it's null and void. Like a relationship trial. A trial. Is that what we are? Everything we've been through? A test run?"

"No—"

"I thought we were on the same page, you and I, that we'd live together; then sometime next year, we'd get hitched. But why didn't you tell me that the clan has to approve, that there're rites and ceremonies? That part of those rites is Casswell being required to vet me. And all this is to be accomplished within a year and a day. Dammit, Rowan"—I glared at him—"what the flipping hell is going on?"

He took a stabilizing breath and as he blew it out said, "The ring

I'm giving ye is what I was struggling with Ms. Chevalier over. I didn't want to tell ye because I wanted it to be a surprise." He turned to me, worked up as well. "Fuck everyone else, these things are private. As soon as I had asked ye, I'd be going through the formal channels. A year to the day is an old tradition, and I had planned to ask ye before then. It's the modern world; a few months more and the old guard can wait. Glentree knows who ye are; as far as they're concerned, you're a MacLaoch clanswoman from time in memorial. Ms. Chevalier arrived here because she personally couriered Lady MacLaoch's ring to me. I'll be giving you Lady MacLaoch's wedding ring. The ring the Minory gave to her."

"The...what now?"

"The original."

My stomach felt like it took a stumble down a flight of stairs.

"What now?" I repeated but Rowan wasn't done.

"She came in, Cole, just as the banker left. We're closing the doors to the castle. We cannot limp along anymore, and we have no one who will fund us. Or who I'll let fund us. Traditions be damned, ye are mine, we are handfasted, and...and...I'll not have anyone tell me that we cannae be together." His voice rose several octaves before he grabbed my hand. "I need you to believe me. I need you to love me as I love you. I cannae do any of this, Cole, unless ye are with me. I've been alone in this world since I was a boy, but the moment ye entered it, it feels like I've never been alone. That all I've been through has been worth something. I'd relive it all again for you. Vick, everything. You have to believe me; I'd not do a thing to break tha' trust.

"Am I ashamed for how I treated Ms. Chevalier? Yes. I see now that I should have told ye everything. But I feel, too, that time has not been on my side."

I forgot about the ring at hearing Vick's name. Rowan would live through the darkest days of his life, including watching his copilot be shot to death, all over again. For me. For us.

I wiggled in against him, and sitting facing him, I put my hand on his wide, warm chest and ran it up over the round of his shoulder to his stubbled cheek. "I love you. I'll always love you..." I whispered. "I can do both, be mad as hell at you and love you."

He put his forehead against mine and closed his eyes. "Are ye still mad?"

"No, I think it's down to annoyance now." I smiled and, my hand to his chin, pulled his mouth to mine, kissing him soundly. "But we're going to have to unpack everything you've just told me: the castle, the ring, the... What now?" I said with a soft smile.

"Ye know me to my bone and marrow, Cole," he whispered. "I forget tha' I had another life before you. I'll try to tell you more."

"Like, closing the castle?" I asked softly. "That's a big deal."

"Och, I dinnae want to talk about it now. I feel like I need to be fully clothed with a whisky in hand to be out with it." He looked around to his discarded pants and mumbled, "What I really want tae to do is make this real as soon as possible."

*Twenty*

Rowan found his pants under my bum and with his arm around my waist pulled me back in against him and situated me there between his legs. His warm body gently bumped me as he dug into his pants pocket. He retrieved a black velvet bag. The air charged. It was as if the thing in the bag were having a chemical reaction with our surroundings. Out of the corner of my eye, Rowan's face became serious; the thing he was about to do held weight and considerable significance.

He upturned the bag into his palm and then set the bag aside, and there in his hand like a small golden crown was a ring. We looked at the ring, the both of us, with awe. It was an unadorned gold band, save for the hand-engraved detailing that was so well preserved it looked as if it had been worn for just a few hours and then taken off and stored for another millennium. Which, it had.

Rowan plucked it from his palm.

"Christ," he whispered, "it's warm." He reached for my left hand and placed the ring on my ring finger. My mind was still trying to overcome the gravity of the ancestral ring as he held it there, when the forest closed in around us.

"Nicole Ransome B-B-Minory," he said as if being forced to use my ancestral name.

Birds went silent as a soft breeze picked up, rustling over the ground and around tree trunks, brushing past us.

Rowan's breath caught, and we both held still, looking at my finger.

"Holy shit," I whispered, feeling a movement, a spring-like awakening.

"Aye," he said; then we watched as the ring slid down my finger. He grimaced. "I'm no' doing tha'."

"Oh..." I uttered, not knowing what else to say as goosebumps slid out over my skin. "Where is that coming from?"

"I dunno. I'm no' moving it."

"No, that feeling. Where is it coming from?"

"God, it feels—" he said back at me, his lips brushing against my neck.

"Like it's coming right out of the ground," I finished.

"Aye." The heat of his breath was warm against my skin.

Energy, the kind that rushes through your system with your third espresso or at the sight of your first rare species discovery, was moving out of the ground and into our bodies.

Rowan's Scots went thick. "I've words to tell ye, Cole, and once I start, I dinnae think I can stop. I feel a strong urge tae tell ye things, and none of it's what I've practiced."

I could only nod. We were getting caught up in something, like a firm hand at your back, pushing you forward through the door you've stood unknowingly at the threshold of for a very long while. The breeze was now continuous and picking up its pace.

I smiled faintly, remembering the last time he and I were in the midst of ethereal events, and whispered, "I'm really hoping balls of lightning don't come rolling across the ground."

Rowan pulled me in closer, tucking my back in against the heat of his naked body once more, and wrapped his free arm around my middle, clutching me tight. "It's all right, *mo ghràdh... Tha mo ghion ort...*" He continued in Gaelic, but I understood him. As if I were remembering the lines to a song, the meaning of his words came out of the recesses of my memory:

*My love... I love you with all my heart. I am here. And always will be. I gift you this ring. A testament and symbol of my love for you. Upon my own hand I will wear its exact match, and through this infinite bond, we will be together forever, entwined as one body that no one shall come between. As one body, we will be loyal to each other, will form one mind, and be of one heart, and when we join our bodies in consummation, we will be of one flesh, united, until death claims us for her own. Wear this always, as a proclamation to all those who behold it, of our love, dedication, and unfaltering devotion to each other. I will never be without you, my love, and you will never be without me in this life and into the next.*

As Rowan spoke, the lyrical tumbling of his Gaelic rolled into me, rocking my body slowly until the ground seemed no longer to be beneath me. The forest faded, and in the blur of reality, the new dimension that we slipped into drugged my senses. Floating as Rowan's chanting blew cold air across my skin, I felt his grip tighten on me, and all dipped toward black. The memories that I'd held flipped through my mind like the pages of a picture book, but there was something more, something in my blood. As if the strands of DNA within my cells held the memories of an ancestor. Each of them rustled through my mind, but it was not just anyone that my mind searched for. It was driven by the energy surging from the ground, trying to connect with it. It searched until the memory formed: I was no longer a woman but a strong, towering man. The smell of the sea calmed my bones, and I was at peace when my feet were on the deck of my dragon ship with salty water pummeling her prow. There was a yearning in my heart. I watched as arms three times the size of my own encircled a raven-haired woman; golden clasps encircled my wrists, and her body was soft against mine. Rings slipped onto our fingers, and promises were spoken that day out on the calm, open seas.

But as we spoke our vows, the horizon filled with ships, her father's ships. Dread and defiance filled me. It was a feeling I knew well, and soon the man who called himself Laoch, the woman's father, stepped aboard my ship, under the guise of peace.

With a gust of hot air expelled from my lungs, a different kind of memory took over. This one also wasn't mine.

The library room of the castle was warm that afternoon. I could smell the sour tinge of stress-sweat in the room. I was in Rowan's mind. I knew the bank man had just left, and Rowan stood holding his second dram, and across the room seated on the corner of his desk was a woman I recognized only too well.

Charmaine took a sip out of the crystal tumbler of the whisky he'd poured her earlier. "So, what will it be, Rowan?" she asked, studying him. "It's been a year. I assume that's enough time for a man like you. You've yet to return a phone call or communique that I've sent. It's as if you've disappeared. Yet here you are. With an antiques request from our vault, no less. I am busy, as are you, but all is forgiven. I'm grateful for the request, even. It's given me an excuse to come here. If I hadn't over-heard Smith talking about delivering to you," she said and scoffed, "it might have been another year." She took a long breath and another sip of her whisky and let her eyes linger on his well-pressed slacks and snug-fit dress shirt and sport coat. She met his gaze. "It's *very* good to see you. You seem little less sulky from when we saw each other last, but very well nonetheless."

The stress that had been dogging him all afternoon was back with a vengeance. He didn't want to do this. Not here, not now. "Charmaine—"

"No," she said, putting up a finger and turning to her attaché case, placing her whisky down, "business first." She pulled from her case a small black velvet bag and placed it on the desk and then pulled on white archival gloves.

Rowan placed his whisky next to hers and moved closer. Despite his stress the thing she'd brought called to him.

"Nervous?" she said, looking up and smiling at Rowan, who continued to look at the velvet bag.

"Quite the opposite."

Charmaine upended the bag into the palm of her hand. A single gold ring slipped out and despite its obvious age, gave off a glimmer as if it had been polished daily.

"Magnificent, no?"

Even within the dreamlike recollection of Rowan's memory, I could feel how the ring had a heavy presence in the room. It was finally there. Home. The match to the golden ring that sat in her white gloved hand was lost to history. Some said his ancestor threw it off the seawall; others said her father melted it down and kept it as a coin in his pocket. It was just another part of Lady MacLaoch and the Minory's story that they'd never know.

But what they did know—and what I now knew—was that the ring kept on-site at the castle was a fake. The real one had always been in a vault at Casswell and Associates, and only Rowan and the company had known that. I was still enough of myself to catch my breath. He hadn't been lying about why Charmaine was there.

"Amazing, isn't it, Rowan?" Charmaine said, bowing to the unseen power it commanded. "The history of this single ring... Who would know by just looking at it that it has seen more than a thousand years of this clan?" Her London English crisped the edges of her words.

Rowan took a step closer. "It's," he said, thinking of how the gold of Lady MacLaoch's ring would look against my skin, "beautiful." And it was now here, *home*.

There was no doubt that the ring was the very one that the Minory had had made for his lover.

"Isn't it?" she asked and paused as if she'd just uncovered an intricate conspiracy. "Is this your way, Rowan? Are you answering my proposal with this? To have me here with you, with this?" She quietly studied his profile as if the answers to her questions were written in the sharp slash of his brow. "You always were cagey with your true feelings."

She slipped it over the end of her gloved ring finger. It slid down and seemed as if it were going to fit, then suddenly became much too tight.

Rowan looked at her, and I felt his dismay. Buying time to formulate an appropriate response, he said, "I'm not sure I follow you."

"It *has* been a year, Rowan." Her demeanor changed; the moment of her own vulnerability was shuttered and tucked safely away, and she yanked the ring off. "My offer still stands. You were free to agree to it then. But a year later you've yet to return a call. I understand needing some time to think about it, but a whole year? We agreed it was a win-win. You don't want commitment, and I don't want to be a home-maker; we agreed it was perfect."

Rowan took a step back. "I do remember but—"

"As for the paperwork, I can stay an extra day and have new dates put on the contracts, and we can have them signed while I'm here." She smiled softly and looked down at the ring. "I know you don't like talking about your feelings. And I don't mind not hearing them. But it's just that this is a huge benefit to you, to your beloved clan."

"I'm... Charmaine," he said and attempted to be polite, "things have changed."

Charmaine raised an eyebrow. "So have I, but the essentials still work," she said, giving him a teasing smile. "And how is the estate? Making money?"

"No—"

"Exactly, so you still need me."

Rowan was starting to feel boxed in. "Charmaine, what we had, who I was, has changed. The estate isnae doing better, but I'll figure a way out of it; you don't need to be personally involved."

"How can you say that? I'm head agent here and care about this old pile of rocks just as much as you do. The wealth it holds, the history, and that your grandfather kept it from crumbling to the ground after the Depression without selling a single artifact is astounding." She looked down at the ring in her hand. "You aren't planning on selling this, are you? If you are, you will have to convince the clan first—"

"No. I've not got plans to sell the ring."

"But you've plans to sell something else? The Rembrandt in the hallway?"

Rowan sighed, trying to release some of the pressurized stress in his chest, and looked down into his whisky. "I did not invite Casswell up to the estate to discuss finances."

Charmaine closed her hand over the ring and shook her head. "If you're telling me that you're close to defaulting, I have to advise you that it's not your decision to make. Casswell makes that decision, and you will have to bring this to the clan's—"

"I know," he replied and felt the heat of his temper fighting with his patience.

Charmaine stood and crossed her arms tightly. "Look, Rowan, I know the MacLaochs can be a stubborn bunch, but why won't you agree to my proposal? I'll barely be around, and the times that we will be around each other, we'll be doing nothing but rolling around in the sack. It's hardly a difficult choice. You can save your precious clan with very little fuss."

He looked sharply at her. "Charmaine, I'll not except your proposal. Ever. And that is final."

Her eyes narrowed; she seemed to have finally heard him. "Rowan, I feel like you're hiding something from me."

"And I'd prefer Mr. MacLaoch when ye speak to me. What we have is now a professional relationship only; dinnae confuse the two."

"Now I *know* you're keeping something from me," she said, her demeanor having gone wintery. She picked up the velvet bag once more. "I'm not sure you understand what you're giving up. But if that's what you want... If you want to sell artifacts instead of letting me help you, I'll comply to your wishes."

It wasn't the full truth, but Rowan closed his eyes for a moment in relief. "Thank ye."

"But," she said, looking down at the ring in her gloved palm, "what is your real purpose with this?"

He looked up; she was seated again on the edge of the inlaid wood desk, briefcase still open behind her. "It's personal."

"Are you getting married?"

He blinked slowly, gauging his words, choosing them carefully. "As I said, it's personal."

"Who is she?"

He took a step forward and held his hand out. "I'll take the ring now. I believe we're done."

The mood in the room frosted over. "I'm not asking who she is because I'm jealous. I'm asking because it's my job."

Rowan could feel his patience slipping, his Scots getting stronger in his words. "I know what yer job is and is no'. And it isnae to advise me on whom I choose to marry unless I say so."

Charmaine's face took on a careful blend of gloating and disdain. "We've represented the clan and protected its assets for nearly three hundred years. It's my duty to know all the contractual negotiations that the clan has entered into, grandfathered into, and will enter into."

His temper flinted. "Dinnae lecture me on traditions tha' are in my blood. I know them so well," he said, his voice rising; his jaw began to tick.

"Then you know, as your agent *and friend*, Rowan, I have to advise you that any marriage you enter into will need to benefit and propel the clan forward both monetarily and culturally. There are very few women of society who match that description—"

"Yoursel' being one of them?" He heard his own voice go bitter.

"Yes, but as long as you're not marrying a nobody, Rowan, you should be fine."

"Who I married is none of your concern. Drop the ring on the desk and leave," he said.

Charmaine lifted her chin, *"Married?"*

Rowan felt the fiction of his literal word usage and the truth in the spirit of it. "Leave. I'll not justify my choice in partner tae ye or anyone else."

A small muscle pulled at the corner of Charmaine's eye as if her blood pressure suddenly spiked and she was nearing a stroke. "As your agent and representative, I have to inform you that you must comply with the contractual obligations of the chief's seat, or you will lose your inheritance. As such, your children will never preside over this clan as chief, nor will you be allowed to continue as the MacLaoch clan chief."

Rowan's voice went dangerously low. "Ye cannot take awa' from me tha' which is in my blood. Get out."

"Fine, but I will be forced to pursue this. You will be removed as clan chief if you don't allow the woman you have obviously rushed into marriage with to be vetted by Casswell and, subsequently, your clan."

"Get out."

Charmaine's breath came out in a hiss. She turned and picked up the ring and slid it back inside its bag. "Just so it's clear, I'm taking this with me."

Rowan stepped forward. "That will be staying." His heart began to pound heavily in his chest, as if preparing for a fight.

"No, it doesn't belong to you. It belongs to the clan, and Casswell and Associates has been tasked with keeping it safe. You've openly admitted that you want to give this to some woman unknown to us, who could be a thief, for all we know. I'm bound by my duty as Casswell agent to the clan to keep the ring safe in the vault. You can have it after you go through the proper channels."

Rowan had used the last of his vocabulary and instead moved in on Charmaine.

Backed against the desk, she held the bag back away him and challenged, "You wouldn't."

Rowan's eyes were like dark snow clouds, chilling and ominous. "Ye have no idea what I would or wouldnae do. That's always been the problem with ye and me, Charmaine—you've always chosen to look away when I don't suit ye. No space tae look away now," he said and pinning her to the desk with his body, reached for the bag.

As my mind connection with Rowan began to fade, I found myself back on the ship, where the rings—both rings—were now in the hands of my love's father, and it was I who was reaching for them.

Fading into the library, Charmaine squeaked and slipped backward onto the desk to keep from falling. Her case careened off the desk along with pens, a desk lamp, and paperwork. The visions blended, and swords were drawn as library items crashed to the floor. Rowan grasped for the wrist of her hand with the bag as the battle aboard the ship began.

Charmaine attempted to slip sideways off the desk. Rowan grasped her thigh and yanked her forward. And that was where the library evaporated completely, leaving me with the legend I knew as well as the back of my own hand.

As the Viking, I watched as my love was ripped from me. I was tied down like a sea serpent and made to watch her witness my own blade come down upon my neck.

The feeling of the blade as it cracked through my spine shattered the vision. I gasped for air as I came to, screaming.

Something tightened around me as I gulped forest air. I struggled with my ties.

"*Cole.*"

As soon as Rowan said my name, I felt grounded. The realization that I'd just lived another life so vividly collided with my ability to witness Rowan's memories, and suddenly I couldn't contain the wave of emotion. I doubled over between my knees, grabbing handfuls of my own hair, and sobbed violently to release it.

I heard Rowan curse softly and begin to gently sway us back and forth. His hand was warm and soothed my back with a circular rub.

Rowan eventually slowed his rocking, asking, "Tell me? What happened?"

I took in a shaky breath and looked over my shoulder up at him; the green of the forest leaves, moss, and underbrush hugged me, reminding me that I was present in this moment in time and not the one a thousand years prior. "What the hell was that?"

Rowan looked scared as he wiped tears from my cheeks. "I thought, I thought ye left—" he said, his voice catching. "Ye were dead in my arms, *mo ghràdh*. Och, let's not do that again."

I was shaking with adrenaline fatigue; the feel of the blade on my neck was still so strong that I put my hand back there to make sure that it was just in my mind.

"Are ye hurt?" Rowan said, pulling my hair aside.

"No, it's just— Did I pass out?"

"Ye must have. I tried shaking you to wake, but...I'm not sure how we got this way, it's as if I lost a moment, just as I was slipping the ring on your finger." He looked at the back of my neck and then back at me. "It's all right; ye just have a little red line."

I felt a swell of emotion again. "There *is* something there?" I squeaked, "Like the mark of a sword blade?" I rubbed it hard, as if it could be washed off.

Rowan grabbed my wrist gently. "What do ye mean, sword blade?"

I suddenly felt sick and put my head between my knees again. "Oh god..."

"Cole." Rowan said putting his warm palm against my back again. I felt him lift my hair to check. "It's fading."

"I had a vision while I was out. I think I embodied both my ancestor and you for a moment—in his last moments, and, and, and," I tried, but I couldn't say it. The thought was so strong, I feared that verbalizing it would manifest it into life. I didn't have to say anything, though.

"And ye were him when he was beheaded while my ancestor watched."

I grimaced and shook the thought out of my head, groaning, "Yes."

Rowan rubbed my back for a moment or two more then grabbed my clothes. "I have a strong urge to go home, have a hot shower with ye, and lie quietly upon our bed with a whisky in hand."

"Yes, let's."

We got up and dressed. I helped Rowan button his abused shirt in a way that only sort of looked like it had been shredded in a fight. He then pulled leaves from my hair, and we dusted each other off.

Dressed and a little less shaken, I slipped my boots back on and leaned against the massive tree we'd made love under. Sinking my heel into my boot, I looked down at the wide base and realized something profound. It was the biggest tree I'd seen in a long while. Not unusually tall but girthy. I could imagine little kids linking arms to see how many of them it took to wrap around it. Its limbs branched out like multiple octopi had taken up residence in its trunk and flung their arms out to the four winds.

"I don't think I've ever seen a tree this large on the estate," I mumbled to myself.

I walked to one side; the branches sagged low as if they'd been there for centuries and were tired. Coated in fine moss that made the branches green, I went to the other side, slipping on the damp leaf litter.

Rowan was buttoning his cuffs in an automatic gesture, his shirt was surely not better for it. "Aye, it and two others on our site are legacy trees."

"This is," I said, looking high into the canopy to make sure the moss-covered bark was indeed what I thought it was; now that I wasn't stark naked or raving mad, I could stand around and gawk, "this is the biggest yew I have ever seen."

"I see I'm losing ye to science already," he said with a smile.

I turned and grinned at him as he came to where I stood and pulled me into his arms. "Do ye at least have an answer for me, before ye run off like a Highland hare into the brush?"

I looked down at the engraved golden ring on my finger, noticing for the first time that it fit perfectly. "I'm not sure you asked me a question; it was hard to understand since I'm not fluent in Gaelic," I said, coming up on my toes to give his lips a peck.

"Gaelic?"

I leaned back in his arms, looking up at his face. "Yes, you uttered everything in Gaelic. Come to think of it, that's what felt like was pulling me to sleep or into a trance or whatever just happened."

"Oh."

I looked at him as he processed this information and picked up my left hand.

"Don't repeat it," I whispered, urgently.

He looked at me and put a soft kiss on my lips. "Will ye marry me?"

I waited a beat, listening to the crash of the ocean in the distance. The wind laced with salt moseyed through the upper branches, making them creak; birds happily called to each other in the canopy; his words infused me with pure and simple joy. Like a nice, normal day in Glentree would. Relaxed, I kissed him back. "Yes."

## Twenty-One

We were just as Rowan had longed for, in bed, whisky on the side table, and the forested cliffs of the cove adjacent to our window. There, immersed in the pillowy softness of the bedclothes, he explained what he couldn't earlier about the proverbial knife in his gut.

"We're closing the castle doors."

I ached for him and put a hand on his arm. "I'm sorry, Rowan."

"Och. I haven't wanted to believe it myself, and I've yet to talk with the clan... But we lost half of our operations budget when we had tae cancel the Gathering last year and refund monies. We've had some uptick in tours, but they barely cover the cost of keeping the doors open. And if I'm being honest with myself, the Gathering would have barely helped us through the next four years; we would have needed another source of income. Since I inherited the estate from my uncle, the clan has had tae cut back, be more frugal. My uncle, ye see, liked a party or two regularly. Many of the auld-timers like tae remind me of it and feel like I'm stifling the MacLaoch name and robbing from them their birthright to have that kind of clan prestige. But truth be it, we'll not have a castle in three months' time." He took a deep breath and released some pent-up emotion. "Then where will we marry?"

I felt my eyebrows touch my hairline. "Three months?"

"Aye. I'm sick with it. I'd reasoned that I could not ask ye to marry me because in just a short while, I'm not going to have a home or money tae pay for it."

I was quiet. There were small amounts coming in from my grants and Air Force monies from Rowan's time in the Royal service. None was large enough to sustain a castle-size mortgage payment or see the estate past its utility bills. *My grants... What would happen to the research field?* I didn't have the heart to bring up my own dawning worries just then.

"I want to give you everything you can imagine in marrying a MacLaoch chief, but it's been a year, and the clan is worse off now than we had been. I kept thinking something would come through, someone would make a sustainable investment. Tha' hasn't happened. And now I'm here with ye, having nearly lost the only thing in this world I care of."

I closed my eyes and hugged him. "We'll get through this. This castle has made it through hundreds of years of war, the Clearances... We will make it through being dead broke."

"I wish I could believe tha'."

"We will find something in the fields—I can feel it. The rare botanical findings alone could generate thousands of dollars, not to mention the chance we find early Pict pottery."

"We need one million pounds just to keep from defaulting."

I felt my jaw go slack. "That's...that is an incredible amount of money... How did the clan get so deep into its coffers?"

"Aye. It's difficult to keep an eighth-century foundation solid. My uncle inherited a tidy debt and a good income but let the castle and the grounds go fallow to please *appetites*. He lost his income in his later years to taxes. We've gotten by too long on our good name. The last housing crash scared the banking institutions. We'd been paying just enough on our loans to keep them at bay, but this last year, we couldn't make the annual balloon payment, and now they're calling in the loan."

"Your uncle, was he done in by beluga caviar and imported Kobe beef or women and blow...because I assume this was the eighties? Ultimately, it doesn't matter, just wondering." I waggled my eyebrows at him to try and get some light back into his eyes.

He cracked a smile, then sighed. "A bit of it all—he was an amiable man who wanted others to have a good time, and vicariously, then he would too." He looked up at the black beams of our cottage. "Och, but tae be fair, it's mostly inheritance taxes and the interest rate on the five and half million pounds that's killing us."

"That's...that's..." I blinked at the astronomical number.

"The cost of the lead-and-slate roof and the handicraftsmen needed to replace it per the requirements of the Fund is half of it; the other bit is other repairs, inheritance tax, and keeping staff employed."

"Oh," I said lamely, then: "There has to be a way to renegotiate the rates or get historical site grants to pay some of them off or go through bankruptcy to halt creditors or something?"

"If we enter bankruptcy, we will have to at some point negotiate repayment of at least some of the debt—we are cash poor but asset rich. We are quite wealthy on paper; bankruptcy will not be kind to us. Our clan artifacts will be seized. Everything we own, everything visitors to the castle see, belongs to no one else but Clan MacLaoch. We'll have to gift it to clanspeople for safekeeping else the bank will seize it when they take the castle.

"Our family has sat in those chairs, used those tables, and read those books for a thousand years. They're the clan connection to our heritage. To sell it, any of it, would be auctioning off a family member and a piece of my soul to the highest bidder. I'd rather give it away or burn it all to the ground."

"Oh..." I said, thinking of the shard of quaich, tattered fairy flag, and Renaissance painting of his great-great-great-great grandfather hanging in the upper hallway.

"And even if we did find something valuable, we need tha' million pounds by Friday as a good faith payment against the loan that is defaulting," he said and blew out a breath. "My plan had been to use the Gathering monies for that while we made plans to tackle the rest... barring the North Sea wall didn't finally collapse intae the loch."

"Friday..." I swallowed. "That's...that's not a whole lot of time."

He was going to lose his childhood and ancestral family home, and while he was at the chief's helm. It was like fleeing famine by sailing to the Americas, only to crash and drown in sight of shore. I was now having stress pangs for him. I could see how trying to fulfill an ancient prophecy was back-burner, and as long as we were together, that was all that mattered.

Rowan spread his hand out under mine, looking absently at my freckled one in his. "I've no idea at the present moment how to untangle us from the creditor's noose." He added, "Let's change the subject."

I'd heard him, but this was serious. "I feel like I understand more of where you're coming from. I'd be a knotted ball of stress if I were in your shoes. Though, I'm a sharer, so there's much of what you've done that I don't understand. It would have been nice if you had taken the time to tell me all this before. Though...I know a lot of the problem is we've been apart so much. If we spent more time together, maybe we would have talked about this more, probably all of it."

"Aye..."

"Speaking of talking about things," I said, "tell me more about this Charmaine woman. She's a force of nature, and from the things she's said to me, and frankly, what I *saw* in my vision in the forest, I don't think she's wrong about you two having a long-intertwined history together..."

He looked surprised. "Come now, what was tha'? A vision?"

I told Rowan what I saw and experienced...before it had all been overshadowed by a beheading.

"Oh aye. That's exactly how it happened. You saw into my mind, then?"

"I think our connection heightened when you put the ring on. Though, I'm not sure."

"So ye see now the lengths she'll go to get what she wants. She lied to you to get to me. Charmaine is a woman who's not willing to compromise on anything."

"Agreed."

I waited as he debated about continuing.

"She and I," he said and blew out a breath, rubbing his hands over his face, "didn't love each other. I've never loved any of the women I've... I've *been* with," he said as if he were going to confession and pushing out each of the words like a constipated Scot who'd skipped his morning porridge. "Save for a random stranger who told me tae go fuck myself the first moment I met her."

"I did not—"

He kept going, a smile on his face, enjoying the new angle of his thoughts. "When ye passed out in my arms from just one look at my fine face."

I laughed. "I did," I said, remembering how electric our connection was in those first moments. "I sure did." Then I intertwined my fingers with his. "We had no idea what we were getting into right then, did we?"

He shook his head. "Aye, we didn't. I'm so glad it wasn't a tumor that was making my head buzz but rather a ginger-haired maiden—it was like looking directly at the sun the first thousand times I attempted to look directly at ye."

I narrowed my eyes at him. "I know my skin is as pale as a daisy, but I don't glow as the sun, mister."

It was his turn to laugh; he nestled me against him as he rested on his elbow over me. "Your radiance pulled me in, and I couldn't look directly at you without having the feeling like I was about to drown in sunshine. It wasn't until you taught me that I could not only hold sunshine in my hands but that I was worthy enough to have it in my heart that I began to have long, uninterrupted stares at ye."

My own heart broke for the man he had been, and I put my hand to his cheek. "I love you, and yes, you are worthy of my love, of everyone's love. You, my handsome Scotsman, are worthy."

He turned into my palm and kissed it, then covered it with his before sighing as if he were sloughing weight off his tired body. "Charmaine was using me to fill a hole in her life, and at the time, I was fine with it. The castle, running it and protecting the clan from the potential default of the loan, was my main concern and something I should have been delegating to Casswell and Associates. So, when she did step in to help, I was grateful. It was in that position that she offered up solutions —one, the easiest for me, was to merge assets through marriage. I was in a dark place, with Eryka and Kelly as my confidants, so taking advantage of her philanthropic ventures held no emotion—it was business, and something that the clan needed. Marrying her for her assets is now justifiably seen as...unprofessional, but when ye surround yourself with succubae and have seen the things I have, unprofessional is just another tax to pay. And in the history of the clan, we'd been doing it for centuries. The Casswell family and their friends have intermarried with the clan over the company's years of service—a daughter here, a cousin there—so tae marry her for her philanthropic services seemed fine. And back then, she was the sanest person I was close to. Even with all those things making me seriously consider it, something inside said no, so I told her I'd get back to her," he said, smoothing a wrinkle in the sheets. "Then I met ye," he said, his voice changing, deepening. "It became very clear that I needed ye more than anything else in my life. I ignored her calls and emails because the Gathering fell through, and I was in mad need of an infusion of cash and was pounding on every door but hers. It became obvious then how disgusting her offer had been."

I gave a sad smile at his epiphany and added, "But she found you anyway."

"Aye," he said and kept going. "The ring we have up in the upper hall is just a replica, as you know. The original had sat on that same cushion, until we had a break-in; then it was decided that we'd increase security and put it somewhere safe—"

"At the insurance company," I finished.

"Aye, Casswell."

"I knew it," I said softly with a smirk, thinking back on the first time I'd seen it.

"I remember tha' day you came to the castle; my hands were clammy even before I walked in that room—I had so looked forward to seeing you again. Then, there ye were, entranced in front of the ring case. Looking at your face in the reflection of the fairy flag frame when you spoke about the ring, it sent chills down my spine. It's a year later, and I still am surprised by your connection to this place, to the Lady MacLaoch, to me." He shook his head as his mood darkened. "I thought for sure you'd know what was going through my mind or be called by the ring when Charmaine showed up with it the other day. As ye know, she fought me for it when she realized I was going to give it to you." He shook his head at the memory of that moment. "I needed it badly. I had it in my mind already that the ring was yours, that it represented our love, and she was keeping it from me."

I nodded, understanding. "You freaked out and went Rambo on her."

"More like gave in to being a damn MacLaoch and snatched it from her with force."

"*Bellator ad mortem.*"

"Och, nay..." he said and flopped back into the blankets then amended, "Aye."

"A warrior unto death," I translated his motto at him as if he needed me to.

I sat up in our nest of cloud-colored flannel and soft fleece; it was my turn to prop myself above him. I tucked my hair behind my ear and placed a hand over his heart. I could feel the steady thump of it under my palm. "Unburden yourself, MacLaoch. I've seen the truth; now tell me in your own words what happened in that library."

He placed his hand over mine before looking back at me. "I feel like I'm in the confessional."

"As you wish. Tell me what happened, and I'll tell you how long you'll have to be on your knees." I gave him a single brow lift signaling my lewd intentions.

"Oh aye, I'll only be on my knees if it's you, lass, who puts me there. And only if it's on ye I'm using my mouth to atone for my sins," he said, sitting up, his T-shirt tightening across his shoulders as he flopped me back into our soft nest and then moved over me.

"Uh-uh," I said, putting my hand to his chest. "Sins first. Get confessing, my son," I said and crossed him with my thumb.

# Twenty-Two

"So, you see, when she kept it out of reach, I didn't think through how tae get it from her. Had she been a man, I may have punched her lights out." He shook his head. "Both shameful. But too late I felt ye there, a chill down my spine; I looked back, and I thought I saw the doorknob turn shut."

I blew out the memory, which still twisted my guts if left too long inside me. "Yeah, it was me. I wasn't sure what I saw, just that it seemed wrong. There's been so much going on that my brain kind of just shut down until I could cope."

He touched my cheek. "Aye...I kept telling myself that if ye had seen it, that you would have barged in and knocked sense into both of us. Her for keeping the ring from me and me for grabbing her in an inappropriate way. The rage that sizzled along my skin, however, told me otherwise."

"Yes, that was me... When I was able to think about it, I raged, but I'm trying a new thing called restraint," I said and held up my wrist, then remembered I'd snapped my rubber band right off that afternoon. "Oh, that's right. I'm going to have to get a new band."

He wrapped his fingers around my wrist and rubbed. "I wish ye hadn't started being restrained." His breath expelled. "I even checked the hunting cottage for ye. And Will and Carol's. I was about to do a door-to-door search when I realized ye would never miss a day in the field."

"You know me well," I said quietly and brushed a kiss against his lips. "And your penance must be..." I linked my arms around his neck. "One hundred sixty-two days on your knees in solemn prayer to, and in pursuit of, pleasure."

"Amen," he agreed and grinned at me before kissing me solidly on the lips, a message hidden in them asking me to forgive him, to love him, and to never leave him.

I had missed him, that quiet roguish way he had about him hiding the man within who was sensitive and longing for connection. The man who was a match to my own heart.

"I love you," I whispered.

He groaned, leaning his forehead against mine. "Ye have no idea how much I needed to hear those words. Especially today. I woke this morning not thinking I'd hear those words again from ye."

I nodded. "I didn't think I'd say them again to you. I'm glad it was just bad timing and not all the things I was afraid of."

He scoffed. "Oh aye? There's something you, my fearsome lass, are afraid of?" he asked, gathering me and the soft flannel sheets against him.

I gave him a shy smile. "Of course there is..."

He shook his head. "If you could only have seen yourself today," he said, nestling his nose in my neck as if to infuse me with his body and words, "you'd believe what I have come to, that the sea itself would change its tide if tha' woman in the forest I tangled with today told it to."

I put my temple against his jaw and said under my breath, "That's the moon's job..."

"You are as powerful as she. And a right menace," he said, a glint in his eye before he kissed me hard on the lips. "I'm a lucky sod having known her long enough to know just when to pounce." He breathed hot air over my nipple under my T-shirt before pouncing on it and giving it a tiny, gentle bite. I yelped then laughed. I was thoroughly enjoying this ode to Cole from Rowan; it felt good and long overdue, for us to love on each other, uninterrupted by tasks or looming departures.

"When that fierce firebrand," he whispered and kissed my lips, "looks like she might eat me or fuck me," he said with dark smile and slipped his hand under my shirt. "I know which one I'd prefer. And I know it won't stop. She traveled over an ocean and loch to hunt me down." Eyes still on mine, making me smile. He lifted my shirt and kissed my navel, continuing his confession down to the cotton top of my underpants. His intent was clear: he was going to finish his sermon by taking communion at the altar of my erotic tableau. My heart clenched, spreading honeyed joy throughout my limbs as anticipation warmed and tightened my pelvic bowl. Rowan was beyond godlike on his knees, mouth to me—he was a demon out to feast on my erotic energies.

He continued, "She, a red wolf from the Americas coming to claim her pack in her motherlands? Oh aye, I've never been so alarmed, confused, or bloody fucking loved in all my life." He lifted my knee and kissed the sensitive skin on the inside of my thigh, warming it with his breath before tucking his thumb under the band of my underpants and sliding it down. My insides swirled as my knees turned to water. His fingers, brushing my bottom, set off delightful chimes that the southernmost part of me was about to have a guest. A tall, handsome guest we'd had before many a time but who had been absent of late. Rumor was he was back now, with a vengeance, and was due to make a delicious social call. I heard my breath catch before it deepened into one long drag of an inhale. The air was getting thick with sensual pheromones, making me feel drugged with anticipation.

"I'd never," he continued, "stray from her. I live in awe and fear of her, knowing that red wolf will rip my head from my shoulders if I did. And in my awe is the love I have for her; I'm unable to love or be loved by anyone but her. She traveled thousands of miles to tell and show me that, and I believe this red wolf because for the first time in my life, I've tasted joy, the balm of sweet, peaceful love, and the aching need to live and see life through her eyes."

He kissed the chaste cotton of my undies before using his other thumb to bring the opposite band lower until they were at my knees and then on the floor. Rowan put his lips back, now against my autumn-tinged forest. "I love ye."

I inhaled sharply at the relaxing pleasure of his lips, both what they said and what they did. "I love you too." I ran my fingers up into his raven-black hair. "Now, show me?"

His smile was that private smile he kept only for me, the one that said he knew just how I felt, what I was thinking, and liked it. The stare across the dance floor met by that smile, the one at the loch's edge at the end of a long hard day, the one that was followed by the sensual, "Oh aye, yes, ma'am."

He nuzzled in, making me groan as he created a burgeoning warmth within my body that started at the apex of my thighs then ran like rushing water out to my extremities. Closing my eyes and letting my head fall back into the pillows, I felt his tongue slip out and explore, taste, and create his own longing with a groan.

"When I'm done with ye, lass, I hope ye'll see that my heart only beats because you exist."

I hugged his words in my brain and let them soak like a soothing bath into my battered heart and soul. I let them wind down into me and water the new, stronger growth of our love that was emerging from the charred soil of our fight.

I felt his adept fingers on the outer petals of my labia; he parted them to speak directly to my femininity, like a pilgrim at his shrine. Against my clitoris, he spoke, "I'm sorry to have caused ye pain. I hope to make amends now and each time my knees are on the earth before ye."

The whisper of his lips against the sensitive nub of my pleasure center sent my foot sliding out as energy excitedly loosened my joints and whispered for me to arch against it, to arch against him. To take him, all of him, deeper. Another soul-shuddering sigh escaped my lips, and I wove my fingers into the soft flannel of our bedsheets.

"Oh aye, that's it," he said, watching me as he braced himself on one elbow then touched me again with the tip of his tongue before teasing it and sending me further down the erotic precipice. His other hand pressed his blunt fingertips into my glutes like a deep-tissue massage, then released before caressing feather-light up to the back of my knee.

His hands on me, memories of the little touches and grips that built our sensual connections swirled like warm honey inside me. Rowan brushed his cheek over the deep-gold curls between my thighs, then the other cheek, warming her up before he sunk onto her with his full mouth.

As his mouth covered me, I groaned and tilted my head back. I felt the heat of his breath, the firm pressure of his lips as he suckled and teased with his tongue. My hands were once again in his hair and gripped it in earnest. He was taking me for a pleasure ride so beautiful that I had to hold on lest I fell off. My pelvis lifted, begging for more and harder. To chase that building pressure, harder and faster until it cracked open in orgasm.

I felt him hum in pleasure against me, the vibrations titillating, and as he shifted his weight, he slipped a finger inside of me.

"Yes," I moaned then suddenly wanted more, infinitely more, the heavy weight of Rowan and his thick and firmly erect penis inside. I said, "Noooooo, no, no, no," but moaned as he pushed and pulled his fingers in and out of me. I gripped his shoulders as I arched, pushing his fingers farther in. I needed more, something bigger and harder hitting. With a great feat of personal strength, I pulled his fingers out. "You, inside," I uttered like an early human struggling with complete phrases.

Rowan raised a brow. "You're not enjoying this?"

"No—"

"No?"

"It's not that. I really want him." I pointed to his crotch. "*Him*, him. In me, please? Now?"

"But I want to give you pleasure and not take my own..."

"Your pleasure, though, Rowan, is also *my* pleasure," I said, pulling him up. "And I know he's rock-hard and ready."

He gave me an arched brow and confirmed. "I've just had my mouth on ye. Licking and devouring... Of course he's rock-hard." And like a character out of an X-rated novel, he stepped back and slowly grabbed the hem of his shirt and lifted. His eyes watched me as I stared at him. Devoured him. We'd been together for a full year, but the sight of him undressing still made me pause and my heart skip a beat, made me rush to the loch's edge to watch. I felt like a schoolgirl skipping to the candy store with fistful of cash.

Rowan made a show of forcefully wadding his shirt up, letting his biceps and pectorals bunch like the wave-smashing loch monster he was. I groaned and leaned back on the pillows, watching the cut of his muscles dance just for me. Our eyes met, and he gave me a sly smile before he had me watch his gaze move down over my breasts and stop at the apex of my spread thighs. He wet his lips and undid his jeans with the kind of slow, dedicated purpose reserved for chess matches. Rowan popped his button then slid the zipper down with delicious intent before slipping his thumbs into the tops of his jeans and underpants, pushing them down until the blushing tip of his erection was revealed... then slid his pants back up.

"Aw..." I groaned, "such a tease..."

He gave me a wicked grin that made my heart stammer at the bone-white glory of it, the way it split his face with joy and connected to his eyes. "What? This?" he said, playing peekaboo with me and the tip of his engorged erection.

I groaned back at him and sat up. "Come here with that."

"Isn't this how the male strippers in the States do it?"

Knowing he'd never seen anything but a trailer for a movie about male strippers, I replied, "Something like that, only there's a lot more baby oil."

"Aye," he said, moving his hips back and forth, teasing more of his large cock out.

"Yes," I said and lunged for him, laughing.

He shouted and leaped to the side. "Och! Come now, ye have to wait for it."

Off the bed now and just in my shirt, I thought I was going to lose my mind; I was going to have to tackle him to get him inside me.

He laughed and sauntered backward toward the window, making a show of teasing me with his cock. "Chase me, she-wolf," he said as he pushed longer and longer lengths of his erection out.

"Come here," I demanded, following him around the end of the bed, waiting for the right moment to lunge.

"Och, now, so demanding— Shite!"

I had lunged for him. Rowan made to leap to the side but slipped on my panties on the flagstone and laughed as I tackled him backward into the wide, low dresser under the window.

Arms around him, I fell against him on the dresser, which screeched back and slammed against the wall, sending small objects crashing to the floor.

Rowan caught me up and, laughing hard at being tackled, kissed me just as hard; he grabbed my ass and lifted me off the floor, slid me down his front and gently onto his erection. I cry-groaned into his mouth as I grabbed the back of his head and kissed him with pent-up fervor. With his butt on the edge of the dresser, he lifted me up then down again. I shivered with sensory delight; it was soul filling and exactly what we'd needed.

Rowan groaned; his abdominals contracted, pushing himself farther in; his whole body firmed up, arms holding me, legs supporting us, and hands gripping me. He started to glisten with the exertion of doing pelvic crunches while standing, holding the woman he loved while chasing the white rabbit of an orgasm all the way down its dark tunnel.

"Yes, oh-my-Jesus-Lord, yes," I gasped before his mouth was back on mine and his tongue deep against mine, tasting me and dancing with me as our bodies tried to meld into one human being.

My knees scrambled for purchase on the polished wood top, further shoving decorative boxes and candles to the floor. Rowan hoisted me up, and in two steps, we were back onto the bed without breaking our connection. There he fully got rid of his pants and my shirt; the latter he whipped across the room as if he were insulted by how much it kept me from him. His mouth found my nipple and sucked hard as his pelvis tucked in, pushing his thick erection in and against the erogenous zones nestled at the entrance and deep in my vagina. He, being the only man able to reach them all at once. Rowan slid out then in again, and again, pounding us toward a moaning and groaning pleasure peak.

I arched against the hot weight of him, my thighs wrapping around his hips, consuming more and more of our skin-to-skin contact.

Rowan broke our kiss to pant, his skin taking on a sheen as he uttered against my neck, "Fuck, my love, I love ye so damn much."

I moaned my response; the throb of his repetitive pulsing made my body feel as if it were filling with silken honey rolling up and out of my own honey pot and making me clench down at the erotic shiver that was coming.

"Oh, Rowan, I'm coming..." I gasped as he pressed us back to business, harder and faster. My insides clenched, sending ripples of orgasm bursting out like sunshine piercing my soul and exploding out into the universe.

Rowan smacked his pelvis against mine in quick succession until something of a smothered scream of release escaped his throat.

Warmth filled my insides as I shoved my heels into his buttocks, pushing him farther in, helping him empty his entire body into mine.

Sweat slickened, and up on an elbow, Rowan exhaled a long and loud breath and then rested his forehead on my collarbone and laughed. Our bodies were now hyperaware of every movement, skin against skin, and sent shivery tickles though our bodies.

I laughed with him, satiated and breathing hard, feeling the sweat and heat of him. "I love you."

He raised his head and looked down at me, giving me an equal smile back. "I love ye too. *Tha gaol agamsa ort fhèin.*"

## Twenty-Three

R ain pounded on the window of the cottage, while out in the
dark forest, the earth shuddered under an old yew tree. Wind
whipped through the leaves as the creatures of the night
skittered to their holes, dens, and nests—there would be no nocturnal
foraging this eve. The rain-saturated soil moved, cracked, then gaped
as if giving birth. Overhead, the starlight was blotted out as thick,
black clouds moved in and consumed every last spark. Wind grew
first in whispers then in gusts until the saplings bent to the forest
floor. The sky, in blinding threads of light, illuminated and punctuated with the clapping, pounding thunder, until the earth moved.
Water sunk deep into the mossy soil around the ancient yew's roots,
soaking them through and through until the blistering winds and
earth's shattering thunder broke it loose from its foundation. Shaken
and shoved, the old yew tree gave a mighty groan and gave up its
ghost.

"GOOD MORNING." ROWAN SAID, COMING INTO THE KITCHEN
as he buttoned his collared shirt. "You're up early."

I smiled over my shoulder at him. "I usually am after stimulating vigorous activity, and since I got the workout of my life last night, I'm particularly—"

Rowan put his lips against mine. "Mmmm..."

My mind went pleasantly blank as I put the mug of coffee I was holding down on the counter and embraced the man. Warm feelings of satisfaction and being enveloped into safe harbors swam through my system. I pulled him tighter against me as if I could inhale him like a serotonin boost straight into my lungs.

A few moments later, Rowan pulled back. "Ye were saying?"

I blinked lazily up at him. "Completely lost track."

"Aye," he whispered, "I like doing that to ye."

"I wish it worked both ways," I said, kissing his lower lip.

"*Ghràdh*, ye just need to walk into the room, and I lose track of everything on my mind. Even my own name," he said, kissing me again.

"What do you have on your agenda for today?"

He gave a long, loud sigh. "Killing the bank man," he grumbled then squinted out the window as if the man were out there right now waving at us. Letting the conversation slide away from carnal lusts, I picked up the coffee carafe as he added, "I might really fucking do it."

That gave me a jolt of surprise, and the coffee sloshed. "What?"

"He's threatened to return this week to plague me with eviction notices or prison threats. Aye, he'll find himself at the bottom of the fairy hole if he does."

I looked at him in this new light, the way darkness seemed to steal a bit of the brightness from his eyes; this was indeed a crucible moment for him. These moments he had while he was away—he had tried to protect me from them, but now it was nice to share them with him, not nice as in pleasant, but as in the way soldiers head into battle. Together.

"Kill him, and the constable will have to contact Scotland Yard, love. And getting body fluids out of the rocky bottom of the fairy hole will be a nasty job—not worth tossing him down."

"Ye don't clean the hole. You leave them in there until the stink is gone. It's a nice, aerated hole with enough bugs to decimate his body in weeks. Old diaries say that there's nothing but bones in a few short months. Not to mention, the constable is a MacLaoch, and he is first a clansman and a lawman second."

I took a sip of my coffee and regarded him over the rim before replying. "Quick fact check, what year is it?"

"It's 1821, and the British are at the door to avail us of our ancestral lands," he said, playing along, then scrubbed his face as if to invigorate his mind to the present. "Before there were Vikings attempting to claim this land, Celts were here, and before them, the pagan Picts who swore the first MacLaoch was born straight out of the sea. This bank man is only one man, and I'll pay his dues; he just needs to give me *time*."

I could hear the argument in his tone; it was an argument he had had with the odious bank man often, it sounded like.

"I hear you. Time is a fickle master. Maybe trade him a valuable item for a new due date? If you can't make it, then he can sell the item and default the loan?"

"You haven't dealt with our bank folk."

I set my mug down to pour his; he was too focused on his internal musings and our conversation to attend his own caffeinated needs. "No, but in the States, the sheriff slaps an eviction notice on your door; then you either leave willingly or in cuffs. I've not personally met our sheriff this way, but I've known folks who fell on hard times during the recession."

He thanked me for the mug and blew across its surface. "Aye, 'tis the same, only we have solicitors to fight this nightmare."

"Oh yes, same. Usually, though, if you're looking at bankruptcy, you can't afford a lawyer."

"We have just enough to pay solicitors—Casswell and Associates— but I'm trying to avoid that."

"I can understand. I thought here your name would have some sway, especially with such a long-time client like MacLaoch estate?"

"We're ten years in arrears. I think our name has had an impact."

"I'd say." I sipped my coffee. "What can I do to help?"

"How is it," he said, nuzzling up next to me, "that ye know just what to say to set me at ease?"

I looked up at him, surprised, then reached up and gently cradled his clean-shaven face in the palm my free hand. "When I'm not trying to kill you, it comes naturally."

That bit of darkness that had slithered into his eyes was gone now.

"Just having ye by my side is help enough. To know that I don't go through this alone and that ye don't judge me, very hard, for it makes it feel as though I might survive this nightmare. And knowing you want to help me gives me hope that maybe it wasnae out there," he said, nodding out the window, meaning down to Glasgow, "but right here with you and my clanspeople that I might find the solution."

He took my hand from his cheek and wove his fingers with mine and kissed the backs of our fingers, then looked down at me a promise in his eyes. "Our future babes, and their babes, will swim in that loch, so help me God."

I felt the hum in my veins answering his vow and whispered, "Mac-Laoch, be careful; your ancestor Lady MacLaoch had the power to incite a curse. I have no doubt that you hold that same power, and vows like that are dangerous."

"This is MacLaoch land, and no one will take that from us."

I set my mug down again and pulled him into a hug. "I believe you."

"Thank ye."

I leaned my head back to look up at him, and he down at me. "For what?"

"For believing in me. For giving me chance after chance to prove myself to you each time I bungle it up."

"Just remember that when I fall flat on my face—don't hold it against me."

"Never, not when ye are my air to breathe and the strength in my arms."

I shivered at his words. Our playful and serious lovemaking the night before swept into my mind, and the thought of having another round with him before heading into the field that morning had me groan-sigh in longing. His mouth found mine, and he promptly set me up onto the counter, bumping the mugs out of the way.

"Ye know I can't think when you groan like tha'," he murmured against my lips and made way for himself between my knees. "It reminds me of having ye naked while I'm deep within you. I want to make that sound come out of ye time and time again until I've lost my mind to yer body, lass."

I cupped his jaw and held him still while I devoured him. He matched me, heat for heat. Our heads tilting this way and that to get a better angle, to nestle our noses next to each other and breathe the same warm air of our home. My knees spread farther apart, and my heels jammed into his rear; I was going to need even more from him this morning.

He reached down and opened the fly to my jeans, and in the next moment, his hand was down the front of them. His palm cupped me as his middle finger slid up inside, making my pelvis voluntarily lift as I arched my back. "Oh..." whooshed out of my lungs as that electrical shock at his sensual touch zinged out over my skin and pulled everything taut as blood rushed to greet his hand.

He rubbed up and down while gripping the counter, keeping me balanced and arching off the countertop.

"Cum for me," he whispered against my breasts, which were begging to be free of the constraints of my bra and my cotton field shirt.

My mind skittered and swooned at his words, felt his finger deliciously thrusting against the entrance of me and his hand melting it all down into butter in his palm. I held on to the cupboard handle just as a shrill ring broke in.

Rowan cursed.

"Don't stop," I begged, knowing vaguely it was the ring of the landline.

"I—" he said as the shrill sounded again; then suddenly his hand was off me, but before I could protest, his own fly was open, and I was standing with my back against the refrigerator. I was still in a daze. I put my arm over his shoulders as he bent over and yanked my pants to my knees. Then, he lifted and put me against the refrigerator. My knees spread, jeans between us, my rear and tender parts were wide open and ready for his business.

The phone rang again, and Rowan cursed. "This will be fast," and kissing me hard, pushed into my wet and waiting confines.

I laughed at the delicious rush of him thick and stretching within me and felt gratitude that he did not stop but decided to pursue pleasure, even if it meant quickly. But I was ready, and he grinned back at me as the first few pumps of his hips made the refrigerator shake as my rear smacked against it. Then his erection lengthened, adding to the tenderness from his manual ministrations and a whole night prior; I quickly felt the orgasmic tightening of my pelvic bowl. The fingers of a warm, erotic pleasure pulled at my insides. "Oh yes, Rowan," I groaned.

With one hand gripping the top of the refrigerator's door and his other on my ass, he kept us up and against this sex support stuffed with perishables.

He moaned a sound deep in his chest that had my skin sizzling in response. His mouth on my neck, exhaling with each thrust, he rode us fast and hard until my nails dug into his shoulders, and I cried out in pleasure. Just behind mine was his soft exhale as he went up on his toes, pushing himself deeply within me before emptying with a groan.

His body relaxed save for his grip on the top of the fridge that seemed to now be the sole source keeping him upright.

The phone rang again.

He leaned back and looked at me, and I smiled, feeling the absurd laugh of just having had my mind wiped blank by this dark-haired Scotsman while the phone hollered at us both to answer it.

He grinned back. "I better get tha'," he said as he gently pulled us apart, and with red dick fat and happy and flopping free, he reached around the corner to pick up the handset.

"MacLaoch," he answered, sounding as if nothing was happening in his world; as I pulled my pants up, his eyes watched me, then suddenly looked away. "Oh aye?" Then: "Och, bloody hell. Aye, she's right here. I'll tell 'er." There was a touch more conversation that slid into mixed English and Gaelic. This gave my stomach a churn; he spoke to Reggie, the estate's head gardener, that way.

Rowan hung up after another affirmative; he tucked himself in, saying, "Seems that ye are needed up in the field—one of the trees was uprooted in last night's storms and fell into your field. One of the big ones, I'm afraid."

My heart sank. "Oh no..." I squeezed past him and was pulling on my wellies before Rowan grabbed me.

At my sharp look, he said, "*Ghràdh*, the back of your pants is wet."

He laughed as I cursed like him and wrenched my shoes off and changed. When I was cleaned up and back at the front door, Rowan grabbed a distracted kiss from me before I flew out the door.

Up the lower hill past the castle toward the research tent I raced. The field spread out, and my eyes scanned the far corner of the research site acres away. My heart sank—in the distance, the tree line was altered. Below the gap in the clear-blue morning skyline was a mass of yew branches in the research field.

I had a moment of déjà vu. I recognized the location and the sprawl of branches. Rowan and I had made love under that tree just yesterday. He'd asked me to marry him under that tree. A growing sense of dread filled my belly. I'd also floated off the ground under that tree in a supernatural haze that took me back in time and inserted me into my ancestor's body. I prayed that it was just the rest of the curse bleeding out of Rowan and me because of the power of the moment we shared. And not something more sinister, like Lady MacLaoch back for round two, wedding edition.

Following the path, I arrived at the base of the root mass. Holly was calling my name as she came up behind me.

"There ye are, mate! Can you believe—" she said but cut off as she took a good look at me, and her face cracked into a smile. "Looks like ye found a full-grown rowan tree."

I cursed and closed my eyes as she touched my unruly hair. "I might have," I said as I opened my eyes and pulled my orgasmic riot of curls back into a pony tail that barely allowed a second twist of the hair band.

"And I can see you're upset by the tree but also a little sad to have been pulled away from something else; you look like you just came...I was going to say from your bed, but I think I'll just leave that sentence as it is."

I worked my hands over my face, trying to scrub Rowan from my skin. "It's entirely accurate."

Holly burst out laughing. "God bless ye. Ye Americans are bold as brass. Poor laird, is he laying on his back somewhere feeling abused?"

I looked up and smiled; someone had excellent timing. Rowan leaned past Holly and handed me a to-go mug filled with piping-hot coffee.

Startled, Holly jumped to the side looking back at him, eyes wide.

Rowan said, "He's not; he's just fine, and thank ye very much for having concern for me. My legs are a bit wobbly, but I'll manage."

Holly burst out laughing. "Right you are, my liege," she said, giving him a half bow and a rolling hand.

Rowan gave her a long side glance and a shake of his head and gestured his own to-go mug ahead. "Shall we?"

Still laughing, Holly worked through the brush and branches ahead of us.

Rowan at my back said, "Reggie should be here. Ye alright? This looks to be..."

"Yes," I breathed and looked back over my shoulder and into his equally concerned gaze.

He then shared a similar moment to the one I'd just had, with me. "Fuck," he said at the confirmation that this was indeed the tree that we'd made love, decided marriage, and fought under. "I feel like I should say something like 'Grandmother, please don't return, we're just fine 'ere.'"

"Amen," I added as I ducked under a branch just as we came out at the crater the root ball made as a result of it being torn out of the earth.

Across the crater stood a few of my crew, Castle Laoch's head gardener, Reggie, and Marion and Flora. Reggie saw me and shook his head, calling over, "This is a sad day. That after all the years, after all the storms and war, one little squall with a big bluster comes knocking her over. Why, tha' sad little tree tha' was poked full of holes by worm beetle is half rotted and is still standing this morning," he said, pointing an old dirt-creased finger into the forest.

One by one the rest of the research crew started showing up, each of us standing at a distance both admiring and mourning the giant tree.

Rowan and I walked the length of the tree with Reggie as the researchers climbed atop it and took pictures.

"Oh aye, chief, what would ye like tae do with the wood? We can leave it for a bit and let ye and the wee ones," he said, gesturing to the researchers, "have a go at it."

Rowan looked to me then over his shoulder down the length of the tree as I answered.

"I'd like to do analysis," I said, thinking of the crown species we'd discover in both flora and fauna. "That would work great. As for the wood, Rowan, er, the chief—"

Reggie snickered. "Oh aye, I think it's all right, m'lady. We already know you're keen on him," he said and nodded at my ring finger.

Rowan turned back. "Reggie, how many board feet do ye think this is?"

Reggie took a deep breath and was about to tell Rowan what he and I had already deduced without even talking with each other. "I'm sorry, sir, it's so old, split and half infected, and with the diseased parts putting out extra branches like an octopus like its done, the wood isn't useable save for fire or letting it rot back intae the soil."

Rowan looked to me, and I nodded.

Reggie added a pointed pertinent detail that Rowan had known: "This is one of the legacy trees."

Rowan nodded. "How old, exactly?"

"Dunno, exactly. Early is all I know."

"How early is early?"

"Likely planted in the twelfth century."

Rowan looked at me, and we shared an "oh, shit" look.

"Maybe it's just the last of it," I whispered, talking of the curse.

Rowan nodded, a wishful-thinking nod of agreement.

Back to Reggie, he said in that voice I was getting accustomed to as "Chief Rowan MacLaoch Dictating," "Leave it for now, let the researchers comb over it, and we'll decide in the fall what more should be done."

"Aye, sir."

A holler came from the root structure back in the forest, and following the towering trunk, we climbed back over fallen saplings and smashed logs. The soil had mounded up at the base and the roots that had pulled up and out of the earth as high as a two-story house. Clambering over the debris to the shouting, I paused midway at the crest of the root divot.

"Wait, Cole! Right there! Right by your head!" Holly shouted.

Dr. Gillian was trying to climb up the soil-caked root system. "Right there," he said, pointing, then slipped as soil came lose under his foot. He grabbed an arm-thick root and righted himself.

Next to me was just a mass of tangled roots, some as large as my thigh; others no thicker than a blade of grass. "What am I looking for?"

I called over to them as I handed my mug to Rowan. His gaze was on Dr. Gillian and looking like he was about to shuck his shirt, swipe mud on his face, and go berserk.

I gave him a *Chill out* look and returned my gaze to Dr. Gillian.

"Oh aye, right there, Ms. Baker," Reggie said from below me where he'd worked himself down into the root crater. He pointed to something at my eye level.

"I don't see... Oh." Directly across from me in the knotted roots was a long mass coated in rich, black soil and caked in debris. It was just within arm's reach. I stepped up on the crest of soil at the pit's edge and, pushing other roots out of my way, reached for it. Out over the crater my fingers brushed against it, and heat shot up my arm, and I yanked my fingers back.

Dr. Gillian was close enough now to be able to reach the other end. "What is it?" he asked me. "Are you all right, love?"

Behind me I heard a low MacLaoch growl.

"Yeah," I said, leery. "I'm fine. I think it might still be warm from a lightning strike or something, just caught me off guard."

Dr. Gillian gave me an odd look.

I changed my footing and came up higher and grabbed the end of the oblong object. It was indeed hot, and as I grabbed it, the roots, it seemed, released it. The full length of it fell, and it weighing more than a sack of flour, I lost my grip. It tumbled down into the root pit below where the researchers descended on it.

I watched from my perch, the feel of it was still warm on my palm, and the unmistakable feel of ownership swarmed into my veins. *Mine,* it said.

I shook my hand out and made it down into the pit where Dr. Gillian had pushed everyone aside and with a few of his field tools broken off most of the dirt on one end. I heard him whistle.

"What is it?" I asked.

"You're not going to believe this."

I moved in closer to get a look over his shoulder.

"What?" I asked again.

"It's been preserved, and I have to uncover it at the artifacts station, but if I'm right, someone has bound whatever this is in muslin and sealed with wax. Judging by the length of it, there's a very good chance it's a Highland sword."

Goosebumps erupted over my skin as if someone had breathed down the back of my neck just before gripping my scruff tight.

*Mine.*

# Twenty-Four

I was standing at the upper edge of the field, the moody cloud cover added to the solemn feeling of having lost such a historic heritage tree. The green fluff of the fallen treetop surrounded us, its individual needles poking into arms and necks, while its new growth was lime green and soft to the touch. I held a small sprig between my fingers and rolled it back and forth as Holly and I talked.

"What I'd like for us to start with are two teams, root team and crown team, and we'll move together jotting observations and logging species," I said to Holly, who was making notes and nodding.

"Any preference on individuals making up the teams?"

"Just align them with their expertise."

"Aye, got it," she said and set off.

A few minutes later, I heard Holly's boisterous shout from within the forest at one of the interns, "Aye, anything else ye need, ye ijit? Like, me to wipe yer arse tae?" she said, her Scots thick as she came out of the brush smiling and saw my wide eyes at her quip. "Oh aye," she said and then intoned a nasally, whining child, "'Holly, I forgot my water bottle, can ye retrieve it for me?'"

I shook my head. "Need me to go get it?"

"Och no, he's stuck in the root hole and has been whining all morning, making the rest of us bitchy. I'll get his bottle...so I can pitch it like a football at his head."

"Holly!"

She waved her hand at me, giving a laugh over her shoulder. "Kidding!"

I was idly wondering if mediation between Holly and the intern might be needed—we were all a little stressed by the destruction the fallen tree had caused—when I was sidelined by the sound of Charmaine's heels in the gravel path through the Circle Garden. She arrived like an ill wind at the research tent below, blowing in and thundering something at Dr. Gillian.

My hand fisted around my coring tool like a dagger. I might have been mid-sample, but I had enough time to unscrew it and use it like a weapon. Standing in a cloud of deciduous needles, I watched as she took Dr. Gillian aside and said something to him, then pointed at the field and said some more.

Holly, I realized, was totally ignored at the tent but was anything but oblivious to the conversation. Or confrontation. I knew the moment Holly looked sharply up at me that the conversation was anything but amicable. I made to move down the hill to intercede when Holly discretely held up a hand for me to wait. Their conversation was something she wanted to finish hearing. It didn't last much longer. Dr. Gillian marched away; his stride was angry, and Charmaine watched him go before throwing her gaze at Holly, who swiftly looked down at the research table and shuffled things around. With an irritated huff, Charmaine pulled out her cell phone and marched back through the Circle Garden.

When she was out of sight, I made my way down to the tent.

"Mate." Holly grabbed my arm, her eyes wide, and looked around the area for eavesdroppers. There were none.

I looked at Holly; her caramel-colored eyes were bright with alarm. "What the hell was that?" I asked quietly.

"Oh aye, she went at him. Bold as brass confronting him about the Fund. I swear she didn't even see me; that woman is cold," she said, bristling at Charmaine's countenance. "She's out for blood, telling him he's tae to her bidding. To report back to the Fund that he's found nothing here. He tried to tell her that things have changed, to explain what we've possibly found this morning—the sword—but she cut him off and said it doesn't matter. I couldn't quite hear what she said next, but it sounded like she was calling him 'not a real doctor.' Then threatened to tell the Fund that their efforts are wasted here 'or else'—"

"What?" I felt my temper rise and reached for my rubber band and remembered its absence.

"Aye, and," she said, pausing for effect, "it gets worse. He asked why all this now, and she came right out and said it's all a con, that you're pocketing grant monies. She's angling for him to convince the Fund to revoke the grants."

I could feel my face go blotchy with rage. "That conniving—"

"Worse, mate—"

"Holly, I don't think I can take worse."

"He said no."

I wasn't sure, but that sounded like *good* news. I said as much.

"No," she said, the word so thick with Scots that it sounded like a dying *nae*, "it's bad. Charmaine is the kind of woman who'll take down Rome and all their allies just to prove she's right. Do ye get my drift?"

"Oh, she'll make life hell for Dr. Gillian?"

"Yes," she groaned out then grabbed my shoulders. She looked at me while she took a long, drawn-in breath, pondering if she should tell me something.

When she just stared at me, I asked, "What is it?"

She shook her head and whispered, "I dunno if I should say anything."

I could feel my brow inch up. Holly was forthcoming in everything. "Holly, if this is about what she's said regarding the site, I think you really should tell me."

"No, it's about Dr. Gillian."

"Ah," I said, "in that case, you should also feel free to tell me." When she didn't, I gave her a lighthearted prod. "Is it about you and he are sleeping together?"

Holly's eyes were at first confused then delighted. "Och, not yet, but I will, don't ye worry—"

"OK, if it's not that, what is it?"

"I think Charmaine is right about him. You know I've fallen for his pretty face, but I think tha' part of her rant was true."

Just then the slow gait of a lost-in-thought Dr. Gillian ambled up the lower trail, coming from the rear of the castle.

"Wait, what?"

I looked back and forth between them, wondering if I had enough time, when she swore softly under her breath, "She's taken the light right out of him, damn tha' woman."

"Holly..." I whispered.

"Shh," she said and smiled back at him.

I was torn. I needed just five more minutes with her.

Dr. Gillian smiled then waved.

"There you are, Nicole," he said and gave Holly a look that was something I couldn't place but maybe fear? Or caution?

His features brightened when he looked back at me "If you have a moment o' time for me, Nicole?" he asked and waved his hand behind him, gesturing toward the basement.

Looking at Holly, I weighed wanting to know what she meant about him and needing to deal with the urgent situation that was Charmaine the shark going after him. I gave Holly a nod and headed back down the trail with Dr. Gillian.

As we walked together to the basement, Dr. Gillian's face was in a relaxed, pleasant state, but his eyes were blazing.

"It looked like you and Charmaine were arguing about something just now," I broached.

He met my gaze for just a second; then he smiled to put me at ease. His mind, though, seemed was on a rat wheel of concern, before it was shuttered, and he turned to face ahead again. "Oh, it's nothing, really."

"Holly told me what was said," I ventured.

"Ah," he said then frowned. "How does that make you feel?"

*Damn*, I thought, that wasn't illuminating at all. I tried to be equally as vague. "I'm not happy Ms. Chevalier is going after you."

"That makes two of us. Anything else Holly relayed that was upsetting?"

"Something about you and the Fund. Is everything all right?"

I'm no mind reader, but I'm no slouch at picking up on vibes from others. Right then, Dr. Gillian was impossibly hard to read. He was the embodiment of a poker face.

"Please do not fret, Nicole. Ms. Chevalier is not a bother. Estate solicitors are old hat for me. They especially are peeved when they're not consulted on everything first. As you can understand, she's just been taken by surprise. Not to worry. I have the Fund in hand, and no one will be removing their grant monies, and they have insisted that I stay on as long as I deem it necessary. And with the possible sword discovery, I think a few weeks more is necessary." He gave me a wink.

I nodded, but the wink was a tell that something was amiss. I'd be calling the Fund again before the day was out just to make sure. In the meantime: "I'll let the chief know that she's interfering with our work." I reached out in my mind's eye to Rowan and felt Rowan's answering call. He was upstairs in the castle.

Dr. Gillian responded, "Nicole, love, that's not necessary—what is is our discussion of the cairns."

"What, now?" I asked and tried not to skid in the gravel.

He smiled. "What better time than when I have your full attention?"

I inwardly groaned as we came around to the rear patio and up the steps to the bowling green where I'd passed out a few days ago from a witchy tap to the forehead. It reminded me that I needed to see Ethel again.

"Let me be so bold"—Dr. Gillian was talking again—"as to ask you to dinner. One professional to another. I'm afraid we *must* finish our talks about the mounds in the field. We keep trying, yet we keep being interrupted. And I am sincerely worried of interfering in your work to proceed by myself."

"All right, the cairns. While we're at it, we can also discuss the possible Highland sword?"

He paused for just a second. "Yes, of course, the sword too."

"Tomorrow works. I can schedule some time with you."

"Perfect, there's an excavated cairn site a short drive from here that I'd like to take you to. I'll pick up some sandwiches and a good Bordeaux for us, and we can have lunch there while we discuss what to do with our site."

I paused. "Sounds like a date," I said dryly as we descended the stairs to the basement. *Date* echoed off the stones like a note from a boom box back in my face.

Dr. Gillian looked satisfied with my observation and mildly embarrassed. "I don't usually involve myself with colleagues, but *you*, I'd enjoy purposefully spending more time with."

We were down the steps and to the wide-open artifacts room door. I was blunt and kept us focused. "I don't think so. Now, let's see what we have."

We were immersed into chaos as Dr. Gillian and I entered into the room. We both saw that the interns, with tools in hand, were arguing about whether they should continue with the gentle work of uncovering the artifact in our absence.

Dr. Gillian rushed into the room and commandeered the tools and had them all take one step back. As I watched the scene unfold, I thought again about his date idea and realized he must not know Rowan, the chief of Clan MacLaoch and laird of the MacLaoch estate, was my fiancé. In a world where no one seemed to not know—and where our relationship in fact seemed to keep some people up at night— it was never my first thought that someone wouldn't know about us.

The basement artifacts station was a haphazard arrangement of abused wood desks in one of the larger stone rooms off the basement staircase. The desks that crammed the room were once used in every part of the castle when correspondence was done by paper and quill. Now, in all shapes and sizes, they took up the room, from elegant, curved legs to sturdy tops and tree trunks for legs.

On each one's worn top were puzzle pieces: pottery, bone, carved, broken, and decaying wooden things. Three of my researchers were cataloging and tagging items, and the rest were listening to Dr. Gillian's instructions.

I was just inside the door as Dr. Gillian went to work, his voice amiable and soothing. He pointed out obscure details about the tonality of the soil he was dusting off and what that meant for the potential of any preserved organic matter still within the decaying muslin. He rattled off muslin decay rates, and I slowly edged around the room, unable now to actually leave. Getting closer made me want to pick up the artifact and raise it over my head. To avoid any She-Ra moments, I moved to the nearest desk and sat on my hands, watching Dr. Gillian work. His field case expanded to another kit that he'd had: brushes, dental-tool-looking things, and tiny clearer that he used to gently blow bits of soil away.

"Why don't you just cut off the muslin?" one of the hovering researchers asked, keen to get on with the discovery.

Dr. Gillian glowered at him. Then he looked back down.

After that, the interns were silent as he continued sucking, blowing, dusting, and picking until eventually the muslin gave. It yawned open, revealing a very rusted, very long sword.

The room suddenly was molasses. Memories pressed against my mind, telling me I knew that sword, had held that sword, and had seen war with that sword. I knew it better than any lover, and if I could hold it once more, I'd prove it. I just needed to touch it.

I reached for my rubber band to snap in some clarity of thought and got a naked wrist. I cursed under my breath as Dr. Gillian and the students droned on.

As theories about how it came to be buried, who carried it, what wars had it been in, how old it was, et cetera, trickled out, Rowan came in. He made his way to my side; the excited chatter of the interns was a hum in the room. Dr. Gillian was now like a surgeon asking for tools and being automatically handed them.

Rowan slid in next to me, resting his rear on the edge of the desk and crossing his arms. Under his breath, he said, "Ye were calling me?"

I looked over my shoulder at him and smiled; no matter how my day was going, the fact that he could hear me call to him was delicious. His dark brows were low, shadowing his blue eyes, making them like haunted sapphires; they told me he'd had a rough morning, and his tightly crossed arms—as if holding himself back—said he was going to need another dip in the loch that afternoon.

"I was calling you," I confirmed and offered up my lips for a hello kiss, my thoughts about the sword sidelined. His arms relaxed, and his lips brushed mine. Some of his darkness faded as a smile touched his face, an automatic gesture when he looked at me, I was realizing.

"This morning was rough, then?" I asked.

"Mm," he confirmed, and the darkness was back as he looked at Dr. Gillian, "but ye first."

"Right, well, Charmaine attacked Dr. Gillian like a hornet earlier. She threatened to call the Fund and pull my funding if he didn't say the site was worthless to his superiors. Something about me pulling a con."

Rowan made a scoffing growl. "I heard something of that in our meeting with her this morning. She's in a right state. Her plans didn't go well, and everything is not going as she scheduled. She'll calm down in a day or two. I told her in no uncertain terms tha' you are tae be treated poorly."

He was captain understatement. "Babe, she called me a con artist and is trying to destroy the project we're working on here."

"Och, I know."

I turned fully to face him. "Rowan James Douglas MacLaoch, use more words."

He looked at me, and I could see then the flint in his eyes. He was suppressing his temper about Charmaine. "I've spoken to her."

"And?"

"And there's not much more I can do until she hits the trip wire, aye?"

"What does that even mean?"

"It means that the next misstep for her is going to be her last, and I'll not shepherd her to make sure she does as she's been asked. It means I've set the rules, when she breaks them again, I'll act. If I act now, she hasn't had a chance to prove herself worthy. I need her to focus on her job and not ye. She just needs a few days to calm down, and she can see then that she was wrong about ye and move on with her duties. She'll be stronger for it if she can."

"And put this all behind us? Just *poof*, forget about it?"

"Och," he said from the back of his throat like a cough. Apparently, I was misinterpreting what he was saying, and he gave me a glare that said to be careful of my temper.

I looked down at my empty wrist and then to the tools and equipment behind me on the table and rummaged deep into one open box and found a rubber band. It was a bit dry, but I put it on my wrist anyway and snapped it.

"Aye, good. Don't ever take it off."

Only it broke in two and fell onto the desk between us.

I gave him a glare, and he returned it with a kiss and a whispered. "*Tha gaol agam ort.* Try to keep yer calm, aye?"

Equally quietly, I said, "I love you too, but Charmaine is trying to destroy me, and while I appreciate that you trust me to handle myself with her, she's now affecting those who need those grant monies for their summer jobs and schooling in the fall," I said, pointing to the team.

"What did Dr. Gillian Pretty Face say when ye spoke to him?"

"He said it was no bother, the Fund wasn't going to pull funds."

"See. All's well, then; Charmaine is just bluster—"

"Don't sweeten your words with me."

"Aye, OK." He seemed to relent. "She's a fucking pain in my ass and just this morning tried to get me to sign papers to wed her and keep ye as a side fuck off MacLaoch property. She showed me the Baker lineage and called ye a con artist to my face too. She and I locked horns, and now I have tae decide whether I move forward with the bank man without Casswell or work around her somehow with Casswell. I know the auld man there, but he can no longer review documents much less decipher his ass from a hole in the ground." Rowan sighed. "I'm trying to wait her out, to see if she comes to her senses..."

"But she's a woman scorned."

"Scorched, more like. After she and I minced words, she had tae go up against Clive this morning..."

"Oh?" This news was my joy, Charmaine now having to play catch-up and defend herself? Karmic justice was coming around fast.

"She's made an enemy out of him."

I thought of Clive and Deloris and how now they got on well together. "I'm not going to try to fix that relationship."

"Aye, best let that one lie."

"What did she do?"

"Called the legend a fairy tale."

I winced. "For being so well educated, she's not that bright."

"People," he said, thinking on it and nodded, "aye, just tha' people aren't her strong suit. She's had her way most of her life, including in her career. This might be the first time she doesn't get what she's wanted."

## Twenty-Five

"Oh, hey, the gang's all here," I said as Holly now stepped into the basement, soil caking her boots and dusting her pants all the way up to her knees.

"Oye, there ye all are." She caught sight of Rowan. "Chief, my liege," she said and bowed.

Rowan huffed out a laugh. "Miss Holly. How's yer da?"

"Good, still working. Tired, though. The distillery is what it is," she said as though there was history within that statement.

"Aye?"

Holly shrugged and then seemed to think of something. "Da' mentioned that you should come see him sometime, something about yer uncle gave him something and something-something," she said and shrugged. "He moans on and on these days about the way things were, aye? It's hard to listen to, usually a lot about how they don't get to taste-test like they used to, but that one he brings up a lot. It might just be a dirty joke that the old chief told him, so, take it as you will."

Rowan nodded and smiled back at her. "I'll get out to see him soon, don't fret; you've delivered yer message."

Holly gave an exaggerated sigh and lifted her shoulders up and down. "Finally, got that weight lifted off of me." Then she laughed and went to the group. "Oye! Enough show-and-tell time. Ye can see it when he's done with it—back up to the field!"

With protests and scoffs at her bluster, they filed out. She laid a soft hand on Dr. Gillian's shoulder, and when his gaze lifted to hers, it was absent of emotion. I watched as her lips asked, "Are you all right?"

That raw look from before appeared again, and an unspoken conversation happened between them before he responded, "Fine," and gave her his Dr. Gillian smile.

I looked back at Rowan. "Did you see that?"

He was looking at me. "See what?"

"Never mind," I said and smiled and waved at Holly as she followed her herd out the door.

Now that the students were gone and Rowan was with me, I chanced a closer look at the sword. Rowan followed, pushing himself between Dr. Gillian and me. Hands on his hips, Rowan took in the sword.

"Decent work so far, Mr. Gillian," Rowan said, not using his title. "Looks as if it could be a two-handed Highland *claidheamh dà làimh*. Early, verra early like."

Dr. Gillian grunted—an acknowledgment that Rowan had spoken but not an affirmative—and looked at Rowan then the long, metal blade.

I asked Rowan, "Did you just use a fancy term for claymore?"

"*Claymore* is the Anglo version of *claidheamh mòr. Claidheamh dà làimh,* 'clay da lav,'" he said, pronouncing it slowly for me, "is a two-handed sword, common here in the Highlands. Claymore, or *claidheamh mòr*, has a basket hilt and was more common in the lowlands."

"No" came Dr. Gillian's reply as he donned gloves before running his fingers down the flat surface of the blade, revealing the blade had been engraved, "no, this is not a claymore, nor is it a sword of the same century or millennia," he said, and what seemed like an alternative version of Dr. Gillian was bubbling below the surface—there was excitement in his eyes. "I've seen these in Volga trade route artifacts. This is a Viking sword made, no doubt, of Iranian steel. This is an Ulfberht sword," he said, breathless, as if he'd just seen his long-lost lover walk into the room in only a chemise.

"Gesundheit," I said.

"Ulfberht. Made in the early thousands, wielded by Vikings, only a known handful in existence. And none, I mean *none*, in this good of condition."

"Hmm," Rowan said, reading my mind, and took the few steps back to be next to me while Dr. Gillian continued his loving ministrations to the sword. Under his breath, he said, "It just so happens we get a wee storm, and a single bloody tree falls over, and it just so happens to have a rare sword stuck in its roots..."

There was concern in his eyes and firmness of his mouth.

"Coincidence?" I murmured.

"Not bloody likely, is it?"

I shook my head.

"I think something is happening with the curse," he whispered. "Maybe we should talk with Bernie and Angus."

"Agreed. They visited when you were out the other day. They said something about 'finish it or be careful,' and they asked if you'd made my stay permanent."

"The wedding, then?"

"Yes, I didn't know then about finalizing the hand-tie."

Rowan picked up my hand and touched the band on my ring finger. "But we've taken steps, aye? So, it should be fine?" He looked up; the question was in his gaze.

I just shook my head. "I don't know."

"We'll need to see them."

"They're coming this weekend to see us both. We can ask about the curse then?"

"Aye, good idea—"

Dr. Gillian interrupted, nose still in his work. "Curse? What are you two on about, love?"

Rowan had already had a hard morning, and I groaned internally at the term of endearment. It was the second time today that he'd called me that in front of Rowan. It might be his last.

Rowan visibly bristled and looked over at him with disdain souring his face. "She's no' your love, *mate*."

Dr. Gillian looked at him out of the corner of his eye, and I swore I saw mischief dance in them. "Oh, I'm sorry, is she *your* love, then? I've been here for days, and she's not said a word about you. I thought you were the absentee chief, who let's others do his bidding whilst he sleeps his way across the land."

I felt my jaw go slack.

Before Rowan could move, I put my hand on his arm.

"Get the fuck out," Rowan said.

"Rowan..." I implored.

"I've never met so many women in one town that breathlessly tell me all about you, most of them having intimate knowledge of you."

This was a whole new side to Dr. Gillian. My brain said to push Rowan out the door, but a shock in my veins was making me instead want to pick up the sword.

"That's an interesting playbook yer working from, Mickey. Where have I heard tha' crap before?"

Dr. Gillian straightened. "I'm stating the obvious: that a woman like Nicole shouldn't be with a philandering neanderthal like you. But it's the power you have over people, isn't it? Money, influence, a rousing good time, everyone loves you. Frankly, go back to your other women. Nicole and I were having a fine time until you showed up. Perhaps it's you who should leave?"

"Now, hold on a minute," I said.

"I understand, Nicole—he's got a temper. When he leaves again, we'll continue where we left off. We'll have our date to study the cairns and the kiss you have wanted to give me since day one," he said and looked up with a grin and a wink.

Rowan looked back at me just as I remembered. In the field his first day here, the moment that Dr. Gillian had stepped in close, and just like closing a car door, I responded, nearly locking lips with him. *That fuck,* I thought.

Dr. Gillian was watching me too. "There, you remember. Had it not been for those old men who showed up, you would have kissed me without a care in the world." To Rowan: "It was a mighty beautiful day, and the stakes for the site were high, and still are. We don't know what resides under those cairn mounds, do we? But it's that educational excitement that you'll never be able to give her, *Chief.*"

My face was hot and blotchy with embarrassment and something else moving in swiftly behind it that felt like a volcano. Rowan's eyes were like steel on me, studying my reaction before they slid to Dr. Gillian.

"What the fuck are ye on about?"

Dr. Gillian was surprised by his question. "I thought I was being obvious, but since you are a neanderthal, let me be even plainer: She wants me. She belongs with her people of science, and that's me."

I wasn't sure Rowan was breathing any more. Then something like mirth broke his angry features. His laugh boomed off the stone and echoed out into the hallway. He sucked in a short breath and laughed even harder. "You?"

I couldn't help smiling myself, mostly in relief, as Rowan was now wheezing and doubled over, bracing his hands on his knees.

"Och, Lord, I've never heard such a load of crap said aloud with such a straight face!" Rowan regained control over himself and, with both of us staring at him, straightened his button-down and wiped the tears from his face with his arm. "Ah, fuck, tha' was good." Then suddenly straight-faced, he said to Dr. Gillian, his eyes having gone back to ice, "Touch her or otherwise imply that she's yours again, and once she's done with ye, I'll bury your body at sea—after I set fire to it and carve my name into your breastplate whilst ye still live."

I wasn't sure what Dr. Gillian's reaction was because Rowan's words stirred something inside of me, and I looked at the sword as if it had called my name. There was a war coming, and I'd need it. With it tucked safely at my side, I'd be able to defend Rowan and me.

The Ulfberht was beautifully made. It was grubby at the moment, but I could tell that the engraved blade would shine; the letters down her side would be dark where it was hard to polish. It was a sword that was worthy of being passed down from parent to child and so on for eternity. It was a sword that was the elite on the battlefield, a weapon worthy of striking fear into the hearts of his enemy.

"Cole!" Rowan grabbed my wrist. I looked up to find both Rowan and Dr. Gillian staring at me as if they'd called my name several times and I'd not heard them. My hand was open over the handle like I was going to grab it. Then point it at the heavens.

I looked at Rowan's hand on my wrist and looked at him and pleaded with everything in my body to take me out of the room, *or else.*

Rowan pulled me gently. "Ye have an appointment upstairs ye need to get to... Come now."

When I didn't move, he kept pulling until I took a step. Then another, until I was following Rowan from the room. Dr. Gillian watched with open curiosity but didn't say anything more.

I trailed Rowan out of the room and down the hall, and when he turned to talk, I said, "Farther."

Up the stairs and out at the dark rear hallway, I said, "Farther."

Up the grand stairs where the afternoon sun was just starting to creep, then into the upstairs conference hall that was shaded by the tips of the conifers outside. He opened a window and, standing next to me, poured himself a dram.

"Ye all right? Or do you need farther? I might have tae put you in a skiff and ride off with ye."

I leaned out the window and sucked in a lungful of cool salty air as he downed his whisky and hissed as it burned his throat.

"You might have to still." He offered me a sip of whisky. "No, I'm fine at the moment."

After a long quiet minute, I turned and sat my rear on the bookshelf beneath the window. He was quiet as he thought deeply while rolling up his sleeves, then stuffed his hands into his pockets.

"It calls to you," he said of the Ulfberht.

"Yes."

"It doesn't call to me. Could it have belonged to the seafarer, then?"

"I don't know, but with everything that's happening, it must have, right?"

He nodded. "Have ye had dreams like last time? Have ye seen Lady MacLaoch, then, and she's spoken to you?"

"No, but I keep feeling like it's mine," I said then whispered, scared about where this was headed, "But I've never owned a sword."

"Ulfberht is what Michael called it."

"Mickey," I corrected.

"Aye, Micah."

I rolled my eyes.

"If Marcus says it's Iranian steel, we know that old trade routes were used by Vikings that connected them to the silk road. If this is Viking, this is a Minory blade."

Hearing my ancestral name out of his mouth was like a church bell chiming the time; my skin lit up. "Yeah, it is. I want to put it in my hand and point the tip toward the sky, really bad."

"Don't."

I glanced at his worried face and agreed.

Rowan looked at me as we both tried to digest what we were experiencing. "We have no idea what's causing it?"

As soon as he said it, his eyes fell to the ring on my finger.

I read his mind. "Yes, ever since—"

"The forest."

"Maybe this is just some leftover energy or something from the curse? You know, like the symbolic use of the rings and all that?"

Rowan cursed. "Maybe and maybe Bernie and Angus come sooner than this weekend?"

I watched as he went white at a new thought. "What? What is it?"

"No, it's nothing."

"It's not nothing. What is it?"

"Energy, aye? Dr. Peabody said last year that it goes both ways: it stays the path as long as the laws, the rules of physics, stay in place to keep it going in that direction, aye?"

"Aye, I mean, right?"

"Well, we hand-tied. In the legend, she and the Minory *marry*."

"Right, a ceremony with witnesses, the physical symbols of our love, the rings, and all that. We're doing that..."

"But tradition has it hand-tie is a year to the day, after that one must marry."

"Perform the ceremony finishing the hand-tie binding, forever. Right, we know this."

"Aye..." he said as if that was the point.

I didn't follow.

"A year to the day. Tha's *today*."

I swallowed, doing swift mental math to confirm. "It is... So we need to...in order to finalize the destruction of the curse... *Today?*" I squeaked.

"The two were fully wed already when he was killed. If they were married, it makes sense that'd be expected of us too."

"But, but what if we don't? That's a lot to expect out of today... Will the curse be reversed? Can it even do that?"

"I dinnae want to find out."

I felt the need to take some action—now. If I were back home, this would be doable. I mumbled, "Something tells me a last-minute trip to Vegas is not what Lady MacLaoch had in mind."

Rowan's brow furrowed. "Vegas?"

"Our one-stop shop for licensing, marrying, pawning, and getting bailed out of jail."

"Not sure we need all four."

I looked at him. "The day isn't over yet."

## Twenty-Six

I put my forehead against Rowan's chest. He seemed to sense my tension.

"Before we sort this wedding, I have tae meet with my clanspeople and let them know of the castle situation. I'll try to track down the MacDonaghs too. Dinnae worry, we'll sort this together."

I tilted my chin, and he gave me a kiss. Warm beds, calming embraces, and soul-settling peace washed over me as his lips touched mine. My eyes fluttered shut, and I hugged his firm body back.

Thoughts, any thoughts, all thoughts, scattered to the four winds. His warm palm cradled my cheek as he said against my lips, "This is what I've missed the most in the last year. Where have you been, lass?"

"Right here."

"Aye, right here. Whenever I've needed you, you've been right here. I love ye, *tha gaol agam ort*." He deepened the kiss. "I'll be here now, with you, forever."

It had been a long time since it had been midafternoon and he was standing with me leisurely kissing my cheeks, lips, and tip of my nose. I felt as if I were at the ocean taking in a deep, relaxing breath of clean, salty air. And just behind that ocean air was the settling of my bones and a stir in my insides—I could do anything with his arms around me.

Rowan felt it too, and his hands pulled me in tighter, squeezing a groan out of me. I was going to need more; I was beginning to feel like an addict for his skin. I parted my lips, and Rowan fell into our connection right along with me.

Our tongues touched just as a stack of books were dropped onto the table from ten stories up.

The cracking sound shocked us apart. Charmaine stood at the table taking her calf-skin leather satchel off her shoulder and placing it on a chair. "Thank you," she said when she looked back at us, "I was afraid I'd have to get a bucket of cold water."

"Ms. Chevalier," Rowan said, his tone icing over as he acknowledged her presence over his shoulder. Back to me, he adjusted his shirt then his pants.

I gave him a wicked grin. His lips were red and wet, and his eyes were quickly recovering from their shiny dilation.

Charmaine nodded as she got her things out. "Mr. MacLaoch. Ms. Baker."

Now, well adjusted, he gave me a dark smile that promised we'd continue this later, wherever he happened to find me. Then, though neither Rowan nor I made a sound, I heard us both groan over this vetting business. The tree, the sword, my interns, Dr. Gillian's nonsense, the castle's finances, not enough time to do what I wanted with Rowan's body... There was too much for us both to deal with without having me do this dance with Charmaine again.

"I hope I don't need to remind you, Ms. Chevalier, that Ms. Baker is to be treated with respect as the future wife of the MacLaoch clan chief?"

I sighed. I was about to tell Rowan not to worry, that I had this, but then she looked at him with disdain before skating a scathing look over me, and I thought better of it. It was now between them, and he wasn't so much defending me because I couldn't but reaffirming their earlier argument. Their power tug-of-war surrounded me, but ultimately, it was between the two of them.

She gave him a cold smile before returning to her things.

I whispered to him. "It's fine, go. Send my regards to the MacDonaghs. And keep me posted?"

"I will," he said before giving my lips a quick kiss, then like the flip of a switch, was cold and distant as he spoke to Charmaine. "Do I have your word, Ms. Chevalier?"

She feigned a bored look as she glanced up at him. "Yes, fine, of course, I'll treat her with respect. She is the Minory heir, after all," she said. Rowan didn't see the look she gave me, but even if she had looked at him with the same expression, he might not have recognized it. It was the one that some of us girls had perfected by kindergarten, the one that said, "You're a little liar." Only now, as it was wearing adult clothes, it was more akin to what my mother called barnyard talk—she was calling me a lying sack of shit.

We were going to get along great.

Rowan whispered in Gaelic in my ear, making my ancient gold ring heat up. I heard that tumble of syllables, *ha g-eul ah-kum orsht*, Gaelic's *tha gaol agam ort. I love you.* Then he turned and left me to it.

I looked back at Charmaine and wasn't sure what to say that didn't start with an *F* and end in *U*.

I watched as she produced two pencils, two pens, and a legal pad tucked into a leather portfolio. Pens and pencils aligned parallel to the portfolio, she pulled out a third pen and clicked it. She looked as if she were ready to go to war gathering data. I felt intimidated and wished I'd brought some important things too: a rubber band; the sword; my fucking Blockbuster video card. Something to line up in a neat row against her pencils and pens.

Charmaine cleared her throat and said, "Let's now get the preliminaries out of the way."

"OK—"

"What we discuss is confidential. I will not share it with the world, and you will be expected to do the same. My final report, however, will be public and shared with the chief, the clan, and Casswell superiors. Upon receiving my report, Casswell will make a decision and let the chief know as a courtesy, then the clan through its registered members."

"Wait, did you just say the final report will be public? So, let me get this straight. I'm not supposed to talk about this, but in a report later, where you'll likely smear me, that will be available for all to read? What is this? A lunatic's version of a trial?"

"Ms. Baker, if we can't get past the preliminaries..."

I sighed and rubbed my temples. "Just start asking your questions, Ms. Chevalier."

She gave me a long, assessing glare then said, "As you wish."

The questions were severely innocuous at first, and they came faster and faster, as though Charmaine were as bored as I was. Where did I grow up, where did I go to school, who were my family's acquaintances what did my father farm what was my mother's career? Who were my governances? None. What estates was I entailed to? None, the farm would go to my cousin who was my father's lead farm hand. Credit obligations? It went on and on.

Then it got interesting.

"That completes the administrative and familial background assessment portion. If we have any further questions, I'll ask them the next time we meet. The next portion is for personal insight, and if my initial assessment of you is accurate, this section will find you most belligerent."

I tried not to hiss back at her. Instead, I asked, "Has anyone ever told you what amazing interpersonal skills you possess?"

"No, Ms. Baker."

"I didn't think so."

She looked askance at the ceiling then continued, "What exact date did you meet Mr. Rowan James Douglas MacLaoch, thirty-fourth clan chief of Clan MacLaoch?"

"Last year, around this time."

"I said exact, Ms. Baker, as in, day, month, year."

If today was our hand-tie, we'd met five days prior.

"I see. And what date did you begin seeing him?"

"Seeing him?"

"Yes, when did you have your first date? It's not a difficult question, Ms. Baker."

"For Rowan and me, it is," I said, thinking that our first date was the gala, then again later at the hunting cottage where we tied our hands together and he showed me what it was like to make love to a real man. It had been beautiful and meaningful and world shattering. It was also not what people called a date, really. More like a life-altering event. The hand-tying included.

"It is important to establish the timeline. When did Chief MacLaoch start courting you?"

I wanted to ask why the heck any timeline was needed. I felt like I'd committed a crime, and they were getting to the bottom of it. "When I attended the gala with him, I suppose?"

Charmaine froze then scoffed. "Lies are unbecoming, Ms. Baker. The MacLaoch chief has never, and swore he would never, taken a date to that event. Nor to any other MacLaoch event. So, let's try again. When did you—"

"The gala," I said dryly.

She was quietly seething when she turned her gaze on me. "While you might consider meeting him there and you two having a jolly good time at it, that's not the same as he specifically asking you—"

"I was handed a formal invite, on MacLaoch stationery; his hand-written note was on the bottom. It's in my keepsake box back at the cottage—need me to go grab it? Oh, and he paid for my dress and let me wear diamonds that belonged to his family. I found out later that they'd belonged to his—"

"—mother," she finished for me. She made notations on her paper that made the tip of her pencil snap. She picked up another, and it too broke. Forcefully sweeping the snapped tips off the paper, she finished with a third pencil and continued while looking like an ulcer about to burst. "This date is only a day before you were hand-tied." She sounded disgusted.

"Is that a problem?"

"Of course not, Ms. Baker," she said, sounding the direct opposite. "Convincing a man who has over one thousand subjects to shirk his clan chief duties and impulsively enter into a union with you, an American, whose only previous experience with responsibility was a farm in Georgia, is not a problem. It's a disaster."

I could taste my response on my tongue it was so bitter and reached for my rubber band, but just got skin. Instead, I chose to say, "I feel like you just called me a dimwit."

"If the shoe fits, Ms. Baker, if the shoe fits," she said, making another note. "Let's continue, shall we?"

It was a rhetorical question, and I glared my response.

"For the purpose of heirs—speaking of responsibilities—would you or are you interested in conceiving a child for the chief?"

"Excuse me?"

"Are you open to having a family, Ms. Baker?"

"Yeah, but—"

"And have you and Chief MacLaoch been intimate?"

"Hold on now—"

"This is for the purpose of compatibility. We have found over the years that an over-abundance of intimacy prior to the nuptials translated into frigid behavior in the bedroom afterward. Thus, making the likelihood of bastards increase."

"Sounds like a question and explanation from two hundred years ago."

She looked up from her paper. "These vetting questions are tried and true, Ms. Baker. Clients who follow our recommendations lead happy, successful lives."

"Right...but in what century were these questions crafted, Charmaine? Obviously in one that was filled with heir-apparents and bastards tucked neatly away under porch steps."

"Ms. Baker, are you refusing to answer the question?"

"No, I— It's just not anyone's business but mine. And Rowan's." All I could think of was what my mother would do when I told her of this question. She'd drop down in a dead faint.

"Yes or no, Ms. Baker? It's quite simple; we're not asking for your favorite positions."

My mouth opened then closed. No, I was wrong, this was when my mother would fall over in a dead faint.

She went on, gaining steam; my floundering was giving her small fragments of joy in her ice-cold heart. "I tell you what, Ms. Baker. I'll share with you my favorite positions the chief and I indulged in, and you can tell me yours. That way this questionnaire won't be so one-sided."

I needed to snap my rubber band a million times. Instead, I imagined this wasn't real life. I imagined I was in a movie, one where I was punching her lights out.

"Desks were always fun. We worked oh so hard..."

I was actually going to punch her lights out.

I did my best to close my mouth; she had to be baiting me. Still, a dark, poisonous feeling flooded my veins.

"If he was in London, we'd take dinner in my flat and end the evening on my king-size bed. Do you have a nice, wide bed? He's so athletic you must have one."

My skin started to heat with the voluminous anger that was detonating behind my breastplate. My ring finger was aflame.

"You'll have to tell me," she said, taking my silence as the nod to continue as she made swirls in the margin of her notepad, "if it's the same with you, but he loves to take me from behind."

"Loved," I said. In all the tangle of responses, how that one slipped out without toppling the others I didn't know. "Loved, as in, past tense. As in, you are past tense. You are in the past for him. You could not pass this test, Ms. Chevalier, as much as you hope I fail. Too much sex before marriage."

"I don't know, Ms. Baker," she said, smiling to herself, but something unfurled within me; the room seemed to grow darker, as if the clouds outside the window clustered heavily over the castle.

"He and I slid so easily together the other day, even after a year apart. I was reminded of old times—"

She glanced at me, and her face froze. "M-Ms. Baker?" she stammered.

"Charmaine," I said, and my voice boomed more than I'd intended. The chandelier above us tinkled, the crystal drops tapping each other as if the building had shaken. "Be quiet."

She nodded, looking to my hair then back to my eyes; she flinched. My scalp felt on fire.

"You taunt me with the unknown, press your tongue like a blade against my throat, and then beg me to not to speak as if that might threaten your knife edge deeper. I've had enough." I stood. The room flashed with lightning from the darkened clouds, and I thought I couldn't have timed that better.

"W-we can be done."

Towering over her, I said, "You're goddamn right we are."

Thunder rattled through the castle as I hit the stone stairs. Flora and Marion had been looking outside the tall, double-glazed windows over the heavy oak doors of the castle. They turned as they heard my boots on the stairs.

"Oh, my lady, it looks like rain..." Marion's thought drifted off at the sight of me, and Flora next to her genuflected.

I gave them a raised eyebrow and kept walking. As I ripped the door open, the heavens dramatically clashed, and rain began to dump in earnest. I wasn't quite sure where I was going but, in the deluge, found myself wanting to go back into the basement. I knew better. Instead, I found myself on the back terrace and face-to-face with the legend placard. Its letters jutted at me in a meaningful way as if there was something in those words I was meant to understand. Once again, I found myself touching the letters, but it wasn't the letters that caught me this time but my hand. It was too small. It was my hand, but I was suddenly perceiving it from the perspective of someone who was much larger. I had the start of a headache and, closing my eyes, took a deep breath and followed the sounds of the waters behind me, crashing on the cliff, lapping up on the shale, and moving into the loch at high tide. I smiled to myself. I'd never really noticed the time of day the tides came in or out. Only, right then, I felt an intimate association with them as if I knew them as I did my own breath. Something was awakening within me.

I shook and snapped my eyes open.

I looked at the wet stones beneath my feet and the dripping needles of the conifers just off the stone patio. "What's happening?" I whispered.

Looking down at my hands, I turned them this way than that. They had returned to being "my hands," and in a moment of desperation, I thought I needed to head down to the docks and see if I could find the MacDonagh brothers along with Rowan. I might not be dreaming about Lady MacLaoch, but there was definitely something in the air.

"Miss Minory, how fortuitous" came Clive's voice from next to me as he stepped down into the bowling green; his office was on the other side of the castle wall. I smiled and thanked the spirits that were watching me that he didn't flinch in response to the sight of me. Instead, he adjusted his spectacles and looked put out in his brown argyle sweater as he looked at his note in hand. "I've just been instructed that you're needed at the Misty Cliffs."

## Twenty-Seven

I was soaked to the bone by the time I reached Ethel's cliffside church. The wind was howling up over the ridge, blowing my rain-soaked hair back off my neck. I felt like a tern behind a jet engine.

I went to grab the handle, but my hand refused to open the door. Already in a lather over Charmaine, I found my temper began to grow again.

"Goddamn son of a bi—"

The door threw open, to a harried looking Ethel.

"Good, you're here at last. I've just returned from MacLaoch lands," she said and spat back over her shoulder. She continued, "Should I never return, it'll be too soon. But that's not the way of things is it, now that you and the chief—" She cut herself off.

Ethel's eyes scanned me from head to toe. "Oh, my eyes see now why you've been called to me," she whispered as I huffed out an impatient breath.

"I don't want to be here. I need to be elsewhere," I said, still physically unable to come into the church.

"What has happened?" She looked like she knew the answer but wanted my interpretation.

I shifted my weight, feeling like an insolent adolescent. "Nothing. Everything," I said, thinking of Charmaine again. "That whippet of a woman," I growled, feeling a direction in which to point my anger. My face burned again at the thought of her and Rowan together in the distant past. She was a pest, and the memory of them was the turd she'd left on my lawn.

I bristled.

Ethel spoke, and despite her being in the church and me standing in the wind and rain, it sounded like she was whispering directly into my ear: *Come now, child, be calm, breathe deeply, and let your mind be free of it. Come in. It's safe in here. No harm will come to you. Let the past go.*

I froze and looked at her. Some part of my mind registered that my ears had heard the river-stone tumble of a language foreign to me, but another part easily translated her words and eased.

"What did you just say? I mean, I understood it."

Her eyebrows rose over her dark horn-rims. "Ah, of course you did."

"Why is everyone looking at me like that?"

Her eyes stayed on mine. It was damned annoying.

"You have two faces."

That would do it.

"Two... What?" I squeaked.

She watched me panic, looking for a mirror.

"Come in, let me take care of him," she said. "It, I mean."

I stumbled into the church.

"Breathe deeply and with purpose," she said, guiding me through the darkened church to the antechamber where the stove heated the room and the light was warm and welcoming. She sat me down and took the seat across from me.

I dropped my pack and lifted jars off the table, trying now for any reflective surface.

Unperturbed by my reaction, she continued, "One large lung-filled breath in and hold the life force. Good," she said when I obeyed. "Now, let it slowly out then take another."

I looked at her then back to the table, still wanting to see my own reflection to confirm what I thought I already knew. But after a reluctant pause, I did as I was told: breath in, hold, breath out.

She studied me like a hawk "What is it that you feel, child?"

"I'm fine, I'm, I'm," I said, returning to my reflection task, "I'm just stressed up to my eyeballs, and it's showing..."

She was quiet a long while.

"What?" I snapped.

"What has happened, child?"

"Nothing..." I said absently as I picked up a spoon. It just showed an inverted me, heinously blurred and pale faced with a wild red-and-gold mass of curls around it. "What do you mean, I have two faces?"

"His face was reflected in your eyes just now—"

"Rowan's?" I thought hopefully and put the spoon down, continuing my search for something better. I reasoned it would be Rowan, as he was the only one I'd connected with on this level. I *wanted* to reason that.

"No, child. You probably don't even notice him since he's such a part of you."

"Who?" I squeaked again, not wanting to hear the answer but knowing I had to.

She gave me a pitying glance and patted the table. "He's gone now. We'll drink tea and talk about it."

The tea was served, and instead of milk, she poured whisky into my cup of piping-hot black tea. I shivered as the rain started to sink through my clothes.

She wrapped her forest shawl around her, silver rings on every finger seeming to have a glow of their own. "What happened?"

I blew across the top of my tea. Her continuing to ask some version of that question was like a calming chant. "That damn Chevalier woman."

"She is the woman who says whether the Minory and the MacLaoch unite, yes?"

"No... And yes. It's complicated."

"I met her today. She will be an admirable foe. With the love you share with the chief, there will always be complications. And always, a MacLaoch actor set to destroy the union. She is doing what she believes is only right for the clan."

Ethel's matter-of-fact tone, like she'd lived for a thousand years in one lifetime, was frustrating. Charmaine set to destroy me was accurate, but I really needed someone to say that Charmaine would never succeed because the love between Rowan and me was too strong.

I supposed that was my line. "She won't succeed."

Ethel smiled as if she'd read my inner thoughts. "If you believe it, and Rowan believes it, nothing can break that bond," she said and took a tentative sip of her tea and placed it down with an "almost anything."

I chose to not dive down the dark tunnel of what she meant by "almost anything"; instead I asked, "She's here to vet me for the Casswell agency. I'm not sure, even if I tried, that I could get her to accept me."

"And yet you must."

"How can I when it's jealousy that drives her. That...that..." I tried to think of a righteous nickname for her that really pulled together all the feels I had about her and instead just intoned with enough vexation to skin a cat, "*woman* told me what positions she and Rowan enjoyed in bed!" I might still need to punch her lights out. I picked up the tea and downed it. Heat scoured my throat, and I winced against it as the whisky bloomed in my belly. I set the teacup down hard and felt my scalp prickle.

Yup. I was going to have to punch her lights out.

Ethel, it seemed, had been waiting for this moment. She snatched my cup and peered into its depths. I was just about to ask what was wrong, as her stricken expression told me something was, when she stood abruptly, staggering back as if she had witnessed a death. Her chair upended as my cup slipped from her grip. The chair clattered just before my porcelain cup shattered with a crash on the stone floor.

"Ethel?"

She didn't respond, save to grip her chest and mumble a stream of words at the broken pieces on the floor.

Worry slithered in. "It's OK, Ethel; they're just leaves." I came around the table to pick up the broken pieces, feeling a little spooked myself.

"No!" she shouted as I reached for them.

"Oh," I said and paused. "Ethel—"

"No." Electrified into action, she whipped open cupboard doors above and below her, searching. I saw small and large bottles corked with wax containing tinctures, tonics, and dried herbs, small animals, insects, and roots.

"Oh, wow," I mumbled under my breath at the cacophony of colors in the specimen jars. It was an ancient apothecary's end-of-the-rainbow dream.

Ethel reached for a yellowish liquid and in one swift movement, cracked the seal, unstoppered it, and tossed the entire contents onto the floor over the mug and tea. Some of it splashed onto my shoes.

"What is— Oh, shit." I stuffed my nose immediately into my elbow. Rotten eggs. I was sure.

Only Ethel wasn't done. She had another bottle, this an herb; she frantically poured a light-blue liquid into it, shook, and tossed.

The stoppered vial hit the floor with a pop, and glass shattered everywhere.

I flinched. "Ethel, what in god's name are you—"

Palms up and arms out, Ethel closed her eyes and tilted her head back, pushing her heart forward. I took a step back as her voice, crying, wailing, cracked through the kitchen like static electricity. She keened as if pushing out an intruder who had come in with me. She was speaking drawn-out words, a language that felt older than the Gaelic she casually used. The washed-out *W*s and staccato-harsh consonants shot into my ears and struck my spine, awakening an internal alarm like the sound of a wailing wolf on a distant cliff.

As the hairs on my arms rose, the combination of what had landed at my feet began to react and give off a faint blue haze as wind whistled in under the door.

"What in the hell," I whispered.

As suddenly as she started, she stopped, eyes and hands closing as if turning off a light. She turned and strode to the rear kitchen door and whipped it open. The wind burst in, tossing back her hair and shawl ends. My own hair was flung back as papers scattered into the air. A door slammed shut somewhere on the other side of the church.

She let out a sigh. Through the open door, I saw the rain-soaked green pastures beyond and looked wide-eyed to her.

"Now, then," she said with a faltering smile to me, "that's all done. Fetch me the broom in the hall closet."

"What was that?" I asked as I came back with a broom and a mop. Ethel was shouldering the door closed.

"Mm?" she said, thinking deeply still as she gently kicked the cup pieces into a pile so I could sweep them up.

"What was that, that just happened?" I asked, still feeling shaken by the exploding gases, her wail, and the thought that somehow, I should have understood it all. And that maybe I had.

She again looked at me long and penetrating as if searching for someone and then said, "Listen carefully to me, child. Find the MacLaoch you are bound to, and I'll meet you at the castle at sundown. I was hoping for more time, but there isn't any."

I swallowed; I knew then with certainty that neither Rowan nor I would be finding answers with the MacDonagh twins.

"It's the curse, isn't it? We need to be married today, don't we? It's one year and a day," I asked as I dumped debris into the metal rubbish bin under her sink.

She looked old then, much older than the spry seventy-year-old I was accustomed to. Her shoulders stooped, as if the weight of what lay before her was heavy as stone and the magic—there was no other word for her chemistry skills—she'd just performed had drained her.

"Sit," she said softly. "I named my firstborn son Minory." It sounding like *minnow-rie*. "It was an old kind of sea kelp that held fast to the sea floor. I named him this because he was a steadfast boy whose pioneering ways with metal—in a time of sticks and stones—made him a wealthy man." She looked at me, making sure that I understood she was telling me the roots of my Minory bloodline from her firsthand experience. "His sons worked the trade, save one. My Minory's firstborn had bigger, bolder plans. The outer isles were between two worlds then, the old Norse country and the burgeoning power of Scotland. It was in those between times that he surpassed his father's fortune and became a king in his own right.

"It is this man I saw in your face, my grandson, who fell in love with a MacLaoch woman, and not knowing of her power, or despite it, he attempted to marry her upon his ship this very day a thousand years ago."

I felt a shiver of recognition tickle down my spine as I sat down next to her. It was the feeling friends of mine have expressed when they've been to Ellis Island or some other far-away place their ancestors had been. Only mine was for connecting with a blood relative from a millennium ago. This was the moment Ethel told me of when we first met, the moment when I'd come to understand who she was. And I did. I hadn't gone to the University of Lady MacLaoch and gotten a degree in the supernatural for nothing—my mind could now bend around some pretty reality-challenging ideals.

Ethel was my grandmother, to the twelfth degree, or some such.

"Understand, and I suppose you do—these things are not new for you—that it is not this body," she said, gesturing to herself, "that has lived so long but this ancestral memory that has. My grandson was fearsome. He was what you might call a pirate. He was a Viking chief, a warrior, and the definition of unforgiving. He dominated the outer isles, and his knee touched the soil for no man. His head bent in reverence for only one, and it was a raven-haired woman of the MacLaoch clan. He did not wear the title of king, but those who went into battle with him, raided with him, supped at his table and kept his bed warm, bowed to him and called him their god, did. He grew hungry for more and would not heed my warning when the man they called Laoch, the chief of the new but powerful Clann MacLaoch, denied his request to marry his only daughter, Lady Orabilia.

"Love is foolish like that. He did not die peacefully, and I see now with the protection of his one love running out, he will come for you, to likely keep you from repeating his fate. How? I do not know. But Valhalla—if he was allowed entrance—would have been his sacred home. I have no doubt he will take you there, as is the way with him."

My thoughts, which had been put on mute, sputtered to life.

I homed in on the thing that was most alarming. "Valhalla is Viking heaven, right? It's...it's not for those who are alive and breathing... You die to get there. Or is it some nice city in Iceland I don't know about?" I asked hopefully.

"Valhalla is for Viking warriors who pay the ultimate sacrifice in glorious battle. Yes, you must die to get there, and warrior or not, you'll be taken with him. I have seen it in the leaves and now with my own eyes: he is erupting from within you. It should be seen as a warning."

My mouth opened and shut, and I looked down at the ring on my finger for what felt like the hundredth time that hour. "Fuuu..." I cursed softly and gripped the ring and pulled. "I really need more time. I should be able to get this"—I grunted as I pulled even harder—"off. Ever since I put this thing on, I've had experiences with that guy."

Ethel, with incredible speed, snatched my hand, pulling me forward in my chair. Tilting her head back, as if she had bifocals, she adjusted my hand forward and back until she could see it properly. "Mother of all that is Green and Good...this is..." She breathed. "It carries the heat of him still. It is the original the ring for Lady Orabilia. It cannot be..." she said not in disbelief of the ring's origins but of something else. She finished, "Therefore, it must be."

I realized she'd said it before, and now it registered. "It is...the original. Did you say Orabilia?"

"Yes, it was her name. The lady of the MacLaochs, my grandson's only love."

I tried out her name again. "Orabilia..." It sounded lovely and lyrical to say, like the gentle rustle of wind chimes. Then as if answering, Rowan's call skimmed over my arms and down my back, hugging me from behind.

"Oh..." I said, shocked at the power of intoning her name, then looked back down at the ring. I took my hand back and tried pulling harder at the ring. It didn't budge. It was like trying to pull off a freckle.

"Child, that is a direct link to him. It was cast from the dragon clasp around his neck. This is no ordinary metal; it is the ring he gave her upon the deck of his dragon ship while he wed her. He was wed to her for only a few hours before he was killed for it. This gold is spirit bound to them both through his spilt blood."

My chest constricted. The delicate thistle in bloom on it made me ache—she'd worn this and watched him. Where was his ring? Something like a growl answered me in the thunder that rattled the cottage.

"Child," Ethel pleaded, "you understand what I'm asking of you?

You must do this; you must satisfy the last of the curse's requests, or you must learn to control him."

"Yes, but how? How do I control him until Rowan and I are married? We need papers. And if it's not legal in the eyes of Casswell, then Charmaine will play her part in all this and break the union on grounds of legality in the eyes of the law."

Ethel was calm in answering. "Among my responsibilities here at the church, I'm also ordained by the coven and by the laws upon this land to marry any legal-age couple who wishes to do so. I can appease both worlds."

My skin from my head to toe pinched tight, and goose flesh broke out again. By now I was half goose. I put together the meaning of having this woman, who was the grandmother in spirit to the Minory who sired my lineage and bound me to the MacLaoch clan, do this for us. It had a finality to it.

Ethel looked as if she'd known all along that this would happen and was waiting for me to put it all together myself. "Actions have power, and they only hold if it's your own," she said, as though hearing my thoughts.

I sat chewing on the side of my ring finger's nail, as if maybe I could chew off my finger, starting with the end. "Good. Yes, of course, that's what we'll do." I was suppressing the weight of the moment, that before the day was done, I'd likely be married. If, and only if, I didn't erupt with a ghost before then.

My breath came short and fast.

I absently talked. "You know, Peabody said the MacLaoch estate is high with ancestral energy from the curse. It's in the soil, air, and rocks. He metered Rowan when he was here last, said his metaphysical energy was off the charts. That's why he was able to break the curse—he and his great to the whatever grandmama shared the same pain. Heartbreaking, really. But now it kind of feels like a year later, it's my turn, and I'm suddenly really unsure of what to do. How did Rowan figure everything out? How are we—"

"Peabody, to which clan does he belong?" Ethel said, interrupting my spiraling thoughts.

"Who? Oh yes. He's with Clan America. He's a professor...and also studies metaphysics as if it were his day job."

"Metaphysics..."

She was squinting, thinking of what it meant, when I helped her out. "Study of the unknown or unexplainable."

Ethel looked at me and smiled, a look that was defiant. "Science continually comes up with names for things that already exist, don't they? Witchcraft and worshiping the mysteries of the natural world were curated by Mother Earth herself."

I shrugged. "Metaphysics sounds like a more scholarly pursuit in uptight social circles than magic, Ethel. Think of it as societal camouflage."

Ethel scoffed. "To you maybe, but to the trained ear, it's the other way around."

"That might very well be true," I said as she got up and dug once more through her cupboards.

"Your mention of energies, that has given me an idea." She dragged a stool over, and digging even farther, she reached for a wooden box. Bringing it down off the top shelf, she blew the dust off it and stepped onto the floor, put the box on the table.

"While you work on your intent, in keeping him at bay and setting the course correct on your marriage to the MacLaoch, I have this."

Ethel opened it, and despite it being filled with cedar shavings, it gave off a distinct odor reminiscent of vomit and cow manure.

"Intent?"

"Yes, it may take you your whole life to learn, but if it's my grandson within you, then you'll grasp it all the sooner."

"Care to explain further?"

"It is quite simple—and it is this simplicity that is lost on new witches: it is the same machinations as opening a door when you intend to go through it. You don't think of each step; you just do. Same as this. My grandson is you, you are him—intend to keep him contained."

I opened my mouth to respond, and when no sound came out, she continued.

"This will loan us time to prepare. More than what the ones I just performed can give us." She looked pointedly over her shoulder at the floor where she'd tossed her herbs and tonics a bit ago.

"Oh, please, no," I said, looking into the box, knowing that I'd have to drink its contents, eat it, or wear it, and any action would be gag inducing.

She wound a delicate leather cord around the item. I'd be wearing it, it seemed. "The alternative," she said as she finished making the necklace, "will be infinitely worse."

# Twenty-Eight

Shaking the rain off my sweater, I headed through the castle from the rear entrance. The gray stone was darker and more foreboding than I remembered it. The floor was slick with water where the students had carried things back and forth all afternoon. A thunderstorm was not a good time to be working under a tent in a field.

"Oye, mate!" I turned to see Holly jogging up, her hair in dual French braids keeping a tight seal against the rain. Something I thought I should do more of.

"Hey—"

"I've been looking for ye. We've got everything packed up and secured into the basement. Dr. Gillian is down there and in a right mood, just a heads up."

I nodded. "I think I know why." I added, "You headed home for the night?"

"I might. Pops needs me over at the distillery. I made the mistake of telling him that I spoke directly to our liege, and now he thinks I'm some kind of conduit. But I might come by later tonight to check on Lord Grump," she said, talking about Dr. Gillian. "See if he needs any female comfort." She gave me a full-blown grin and a wink.

I shook my head. "Holly...rules. You can't hump him while he works for us."

Her face pinched. "So, I should have kept that from ye?"

I shrugged. "Yeah, probably," then laughed.

"Yeah, well, it's all for the best since there's some weird shit going on in town. Rumor is that a MacDonald is coming to reclaim the castle for his clan?"

My brows rammed together. "What?"

"Everyone is a private eye now, looking for any sign of an invading army. I swear my sweet small down gets more bonkers every year."

"I'd say so... Oh." I knew who the MacDonald was. "Rowan is spreading the news that the castle is going through bankruptcy, and I think the agent from the bank is a MacDonald."

Her eyes brightened then clouded. "Aw, fuck. I feared tha' we wouldn't make it. Da has been fretting for the chief since his uncle was in charge. But it explains the MacDonald business and the fortifications the auld-timers are taking on."

"Fortifications..." I repeated, not liking the sound and implications of it.

"Sheep and washed-out bridges. I swear, I hope we don't have an actual emergency; the medics might not be able to get to us without answering riddles three from the blue hairs."

"Aw, I love it. They're so protective."

"Primitive, ye mean? It's quaint when ye didn't grow up with it, hon."

"Fair enough," I said, looking at the rain out on the bowling green. "Stay dry, and see you in the morning, Holl."

She saluted before bounding off the back steps. "Aye, aye, Captain," I heard through the closing door.

I smiled as I headed down the wide rear staircase into the stone dungeons. Basement, I corrected myself. What I really wished was Dr. Gillian to be in his upstairs chambers soliciting advice, naked, from Holly. No matter how against the rules it was. Unfortunately, since I had just seen her, I knew that wasn't true. Worse, he was not just cranky but with the sword.

I really wanted to be alone with it.

Fiddling with the dried woven root around my neck, I tried not to breathe in its stench as I walked into the cool, damp study room. The desks were as they had been earlier in the day, only tags had been added to items, and it was looking like an official inventory of a research site.

A chair scrapped back.

"There you are." Dr. Gillian's tone was bathed in accusation.

I stopped at the door and took him in. He rested a hip on a desk and folded his arms across his chest, his sweater going tight across his lean shoulders. His hair was damp with rain, making the ends curl beneath his ears where they had been tucked. His eyes were only mildly accusatory, as if they held less conviction than his voice.

"Here I am," I responded while my eyes darted around the room.

"There seems to be a priceless artifact missing," he said, being more cryptic than I'd observed him be before.

I knew the moment I'd entered. "The sword."

"And a few hours prior you attempted to pick it up barehanded. So, my assumption is you know where it is."

I nodded, hearing him, but something else was reaching out for it, feeling for her heat and asking it to return my call. The smell of the root ripened to the point where I wanted to rip it from my neck. I stopped calling for it and turned on him.

"I wish. What happened?"

"You know, it's this kind o' thing that Charmaine is looking for from you so she can boot you out o' here. Tell me where it is, and I'll tell her it's been found, and if you want to keep your career, you'll tell me now, and we'll forget about all this."

I paused. A big, long pause. He sounded like he was doing me a favor. So, it took a nanosecond to realize what was actually happening. I kept calm. "I don't have it—"

"Bollocks. None o' the students would have taken it, and you, Ms. Let Me Hold That Sword Barehanded, coveted it like a prized jewel just a few hours ago. Where is it?"

"Right," I said then repeated, "I don't have it, so who else might? Charmaine?"

He shook his head as if he couldn't believe how daft I was and then looked down the hall. "I had a three thirty with her to catch her up on the artifacts we've found. That one was of special interest, and she would not have taken it. Just tell me where it is, and I'll make sure Charmaine doesn't hear of it."

"You know, that's all well and good, but if I don't have it, that puts me into a bit of a pickle, doesn't it?" I said and put my things down and looked back to the empty hall where there was no Charmaine, and if I really thought about it, there likely never had been Charmaine. "I don't think Charmaine is coming, Dr. Gillian. Why don't we walk through the last—"

"I'll not be taking the blame for this."

I raised my hands in a surrender gesture. "I'm sure it'll turn up."

I went to the first table that had pieces of artifacts tagged on it and bent to the chest below it.

"I can't believe you," he said from behind me. "You're just going to pretend that you didn't take it? Willy-nilly look through all the cases, pretending to look for it?"

I looked back over my shoulder at him and had a difficult time reading him. Something was amiss that I couldn't put my finger on. "Why would I take it?" I asked, stalling for time. Time that gave me space to think on what I'd walked in on. Charmaine was supposedly coming soon to, to what, exactly? It felt like Mickey was purposefully pinning the lost sword to my chest. All under the guise of showing Charmaine the shiny new artifact. It was an unpleasant thought. I'd been having those a lot lately.

I turned back to the chest and closed my eyes at the realization that I was a hare caught in a snare. I stood and took a deep breath, trying to calm the feeling that shot into my veins, obscuring my thoughts and making me feel large and hell-bent on vindication.

"You'd take it to see me ruined," he answered my question. "After this afternoon, nothing is quite the way it should be. Maybe your precious chief took it."

I turned sharply. "Careful," I warned and had the odd urge to smell the air between us. Could I actually smell a hint of Charmaine's perfume on him, Chanel No. 666?

He pushed. "I suppose he's as likely a suspect as you are; since he's so whipped, he'd do anything for you."

Recognizing the trap for what it was, I asked the plain question my blood was desperate to know: "Where'd you take the Ulfberht, Mickey?" I purposefully dropped his doctor title.

His brows rammed together, and the pulse in his neck ticked up; he was about to object when I cut him off.

I took a step toward him, curious. "What has Charmaine asked of you? Did she ask you to hide it?"

"This is not a game, Ms. Baker— What are you doing?" His eyes showed a fraction of surprise in their corners as they looked down at me crossing the room to him. I had been a conversation's distance away, but now I needed to be even closer, needed to smell him, to see if his fear was tangible.

"What is it that you believe I am doing?" I asked and felt the ambivalence of my question for what it was, a stall for more time.

He stared at my face as I sniffed the air in front of his body like a wolf. He leaned farther back over the desk until he hit tool cases. Stainless-steel tools clanged to the ground. "You're... I dunno."

There was a hint of real fear now. The kind that manifests across the skin and spikes the hairs down the back.

"I'm...too close?" I said and smiled at his confusion: fight or flight? He was trying to quickly make assumptions, none of them accurate. "Isn't this what you asked for earlier? A little Bordeaux and alone time with me? But now you keep the Ulfberht from me. Mickey, how desperate are you to have looked past the obvious?"

"The obvious?" His voice was hoarse.

"I'll get my sword back and bury you." I turned my head this way and that, loosening my neck muscles. Something was arriving, and it felt right.

He stumbled over nuance. "*Your* sword? So, you did take—"

"Stop messing around, Mickey," I hissed into his face, my scalp prickling. The smell of the root around my neck intensified.

I looked down at the foul thing; it was getting in the way of thinking clearly. I ripped it off and threw it.

·  ·  ·

Nicole's skin shivered and shifted; her eyes dilated and returned to normal. When the Viking within had her look up, he saw the man she called Mickey Gillian express a kind of triumph. As if what had just happened, the tossing of the root, was a kind of win in a game of one-upmanship. Only the Viking was now at the helm and done playing any kind of game.

Her voice, now his, said with a sonic boom, "Fool!"

The expression was wiped from his face. "I-I, Nicole?" Fright choked him, making him a soprano. But he was a man practiced with adversity. He stood still before taking a steadying breath and asking, "If, if you don't come clean, Charmaine will block you from marrying the chief... Is that what you want?"

Ormr in his granddaughter's body snorted; then they gave the other man a murderous smile. "No... No, no, Gilliansson. What we want," he said, putting Cole's hand to the front of the other man's sweater and gripping, all while studying his gaze, "is to cut you open and run our hands in the river of blood the wound makes. Maybe then the truth will flow from you."

Mickey paled into sliver moonlight. "That's pretty vivid, Nicole. Are you all right?" he asked, pushing her hand off and moving around end of the desk. He put the next one between them, and then the next, as he headed toward the door.

His question hit the Viking as being downright humorous, since it was obvious the man really did not care if his granddaughter were well or not. They barked out a laugh, and it shook the stone walls of the basement room. The space got smaller as his focus on the man and his dirt-and-forest calico-colored eyes got sharper.

The eighteenth-century wood desk between them felt like a shield. With one hand, they slid it out of the way, the wood legs scraping loudly over the stone floor. Artifacts jiggled and bounced across the top as tools and pencils rolled off and hit the floor with a clatter. Ormr worked them toward the man again, desks slamming against the wall as they did.

Mickey back-pedaled and put the next then the next exam desk between them.

"You...you aren't all right," he answered his own question. "Let me get someone to come help you." He looked to the door.

"Mickey Gilliansson." The Viking's baritone cracked like thunder in the small underground room. Mickey froze. The Viking's pronunciation of his name made it sound as if he were including his father in the conversation by calling him "Gillian's son." "What is it that you are trying to take from us?"

"Nothing. I was warning you, that's all. Your MacLaoch—"

"—is a faithful woman who will always be at my side though this life and into the next. I will see to it."

His face screwed up into confusion.

"Do you profess to stand in our way, Gilliansson?"

"No."

The Viking felt the reassuring clasps of metal around his granddaughter's wrists. It gave him the feel of immutable power and as they came to a stop in front of Mickey. He had her sniff the air again. "I smell the foul stench of betrayal upon you. Sell your mother for a pile of furs, would you?"

The Viking smiled as he clasped Mickey on the shoulder with Nicole's agile but smaller female hand. He then laughed like a bear at the water's edge. "Fear not, Gilliansson—it's a look I know well from my own reflection. What is it that you're keeping from us?" he asked again.

Mickey's eyes swept over Nicole's body and stayed on the hand at his shoulder. "Are you sure you're OK?"

He feigned camaraderie. "We've never felt better. Unburden yourself with us."

"I'm not sure I should," he whispered and slowly, as if fearing to spook her with his hand movements, Mickey touched his forehead, mid-chest, left shoulder, then right.

The Viking felt an odd smile tug at the corner of his mouth. Mickey would tell them everything. "Tell me."

Gilliansson swallowed and said, "Charmaine cornered me. She's threatened my reputation if I don't do as she asked. She's already called the Fund to report you and me as frauds. They asked for evidence..." He let the words trail off and what was left unsaid speak for itself.

The Viking squinted at him as if to make his watery words make sense. He scoured his face for the lie. Waited for the crease in his eyes, the change of color, anything, but it was no lie.

"Why are you telling us this?"

"Because, for one, you're scary as hell right now, and I can't decide if your face is changing or if someone else is looking out through your eyes."

"Both!" he barked, making Mickey flinch. "What else?"

"Charmaine told the chief the other day to forget about you and just accept some proposal she'd given to him. He said, fuck no, never, and he'd rather die a thousand deaths than to be without you. She said that going through bankruptcy and clan wrath would be just about that. She grabbed his arm, and when he turned, she said she would make him heel to the duty of his clan. She'll do it too."

Nicole's lip curled back in disgust. "Chevalier," they spat.

Then Nicole fed Ormr Charmaine's unbidden words from that morning—when she flaunted the sexual positions Rowan and she had undertaken. Her words telling Nicole that Rowan had taken her from behind, painted the picture of Rowan intimately thrusting into Charmaine's ice-cold body.

Gilliansson whimpered.

The Viking slid their gaze down as he listened to Cole. Mickey was shrinking down the wall away from them.

"Thank you," the Viking said. "She dies today."

This shook Mickey's sketchy hold on his courage, and as they made to leave, Mickey grabbed Nicole's wrist. "No!"

The Viking raised his granddaughter's wrist, as Mickey held on, lifting him squarely off the stone floor. Mickey's eyes went wide as he rose from his crouch. Gilliansson's hand was smooth, the academic that he was.

"What is this?"

"You cannot kill her."

"You have qualms now, do you?"

"I am many things, Nicole—"

"I am no Nicole Baker. My granddaughter holds me within her. I am Chief Minorisson, or as you may know me, the sea serpent, Ormr."

Ormr's vision was clear then; he needed to get to Charmaine Chevalier. And kill her. There was an internal protest now too, and he hushed his granddaughter into complete silence.

## Twenty-Nine

The light from the first-floor stairs spilled down into the basement hallway. The stormy light made the long hall macabre in the deep shadows of every corner. The air held the damp chill of a dungeon. The stark contrast between this and the ones of five hundred years ago was that this one did not stink of human putrefaction. Though Ormr was certain that if one was pressed up against the stones, a hint of humanity's self-inflicted hell would still be detected.

Nearly to the stairs: "Wait!" came from behind him, and Ormr stopped them and turned back to the Gilliansson man. "You forgot this," he said and tossed something into the air.

In Gilliansson's other hand was his granddaughter's satchel; they didn't need it, but instinctively he held their hand out to first catch the lightweight object that was arching through the air to them.

He reached for it then yanked their hand back. It was the offending root. Gilliansson was swift, like a squirrel, but twice as smart. Ormr let the root land soundlessly at the base of the stair. The stench of it burned their nose. He covered their nose and mouth with his granddaughter's arm but not before he had a moment where his granddaughter's command broke in, and he thought to pick it up and take a long, deep, burning breath.

He hissed, *no,* and glared back at Mickey. "I require none of these things." Then he turned heading for the stairs once more.

Ormr had them on the first step when they heard Gillianson's footfalls sprinting toward them. Ormr flexed their fingers as he turned them to face the younger man.

Mickey tossed the satchel and leaped. Ormr smacked the bag aside and twisted out of the way from the younger man's tackle. Mickey, off-balance from the miss, plowed headfirst into the staircase wall. He collided with a grunt against the stone before falling to the floor.

At the top of the stairs came "Oye, Mickey! What the fuck, ye prick!" That voice carried a hum through Nicole's body. The MacLaoch chief was swift-footing it down the stairs, Eli Campbell right behind. Ormr looked up, making eye contact with the chief.

"What the—" Rowan's voice broke off, and he missed a step. Eli grabbed him as they both stared at Ormr inhabiting Cole's body, in a mix of wonder and shock.

Mickey rolled over with a groan.

"Never you mind, boys; we have it," said the being below them. They held up one hand to Rowan and Eli and then leaned down and grabbed Gilliansson by the front of the sweater.

Mickey's eyes popped open as Ormr as Nicole easily lifted his fourteen-stone body off the lower stairs. The wool seams of his sweater stretched and creaked.

Eli cursed as Rowan said, "Mary Mother of God..."

With two fists on Gilliansson's front, Ormr twisted and threw him back down the hall. Turning back, Ormr shook their head as the smell from the offending root rioted in their nose again. It was at their feet, and he resisted the urge to kick it down the hall, lest the smell stick to their boot toe.

"Cole, love..." Ormr heard a pensive-sounding chief on the stairs. The MacLaoch had found his footing again and slowly took the last few steps down to Ormr.

Ormr looked out of his granddaughter's eyes and did not enjoy the

MacLaoch towering over them. Those MacLaoch eyes were the color of deep water, endless fairy pools, the ocean on a clear bright day.

"You have the look of her. I see why my granddaughter has fallen along the same path as I. Come, we must clear the way for you both to wed; we must rid your lives of the Chevalier woman. She has reminded us this very day that you and she were intimate, and clear in her manner of how."

Down the hall, Mickey was attempting to get back to his feet; Eli stood dumbstruck upon the stairs above them.

Rowan's eyes searched Ormr's face. The chief's rough-hewn hand went to the side of his granddaughter's soft, feminine cheek, and it felt like a threat. They flinched. "Do not touch us so familiarly."

Rowan's eyes hooded as if hiding something dark and threatening in them. Ormr wanted to challenge that darkness, to put it against their own, but Eli looking down the hall distracted him. He followed the man's gaze, and what he saw made him growl in frustration. The Gilliansson lad was up and continuing to once again be a nuisance. Ormr would finish this with him.

Only, the MacLaoch touched their shoulder, drawing his attention back. "Cole, come back. Cole..."

Ormr's gut lurched as his granddaughter instinctively responded. It tugged at him like a shirt tail to step into the chief, to accept the subtle tone in his voice that asked for reassurance that all was well.

Suddenly, there was a person around their middle. Gilliansson had tackled Ormr into the wall, knocking their head hard against the stone and their back over the handrail.

Rowan shouted at Mickey before grabbing him. Ormr seethed at both men as they smacked and wrestled with Ormr and each other; they both deserved a lesson in respect. With a roar, Ormr shoved the larger of the two back. Chief MacLaoch stumbled down the rest of the stairs, his eyes snapping to Ormr's. He'd underestimated Ormr's strength. The small body of the Viking's granddaughter would make these men feel an otherworldly wrath. There was a mad scramble, and then Eli leaped down the stairs, grabbing at Mickey. As Mickey wrestled him off and kept an arm around Ormr, he tried to reach for the root below them on the first stair.

Its stench burned Ormr's nostrils, and they recoiled.

"Remove that wretched thing!" he boomed, pounding Nicole's fist into the side of the Gilliansson man's head. Mickey hollered, his hands going to the side of his face. Now free, Ormr held the railing and kicked Gilliansson across the hall. He slammed into the opposite stone wall before slumping to the ground. Ormr turned his granddaughter's gaze then to Eli; he was a big man, the kind of man Ormr would take into battle.

Ormr had his granddaughter smile at Eli. "Come, son, you are a vision of me in my youth. Bring your might against mine, and let us create thunder in these halls." He clapped their hands, making the entire castle shake with it outside.

Eli went white and, with his hands up, staggered down the rest of the steps and back down the hall to where the chief stood. The chief stepped around him, motioning for the Gilliansson man to get up and get behind him.

The MacLaoch chief swallowed and pressed Eli back. When he looked back, his gaze said he was ready to fight. He reached for the hem of his sweater and pulled it up and off. As he wadded it up, he held his gaze to Ormr's before tossing his sweater down. He then tugged down his wrinkled undershirt that was taut across his shoulders and displayed musculature that had just been worked hard and red marks on his upper arms where hands had grabbed and shoved him.

"Come on, love," the MacLaoch chief said, "come, let's square off again."

"Do not call me love, young man—"

"What you don't understand, Minory, is that she's in there, and she's pulled me to her. Or did you forget that she and I are bound together? It's time ye stopped silencing her and asked her to come join us here."

Ormr laughed. The concussive sound pounded off the stone, echoing back and forth until it finally it went quiet. "You speak as if we are not one! She is here. She is commanding me."

"I doubt it. Cole doesn't flinch from me. She may fight me, but I'll be a cocky sod and tell ye that it's only these hands that can calm that body yer in."

Ormr roiled at his arrogance, at his conceit. "You? The only one? And how did you show it, MacLaoch's son? You call her love; you say her body only responds to your touch, and with what have you done to keep it so? Have you acted as your grandmother told you to? Did you? And now, look where you are at. No. No, you are not 'the only one.'

"And now I see as plain as day. I have been wrong. You are not like my love, Lady Orabilia—you are your grandfather, Laoch. He took his daughter away from me, slaughtered me in front of her, simply because he also claimed her as his. You had your chance to prove yourself; now you and the Charmaine witch will die. Then with the blood of the curse, I'll take my granddaughter to Valhalla where I'll keep her safe for eternity. No MacLaoch sword will ever touch Minorisson and Minorisdóttir skin again."

Something within Rowan broke. He grew murderous, as if an oily balloon filled with demons had been punctured and it bled out into his body. His eyes shifted in that dark basement hall into hard obsidian stones shining back at Ormr.

The visual change in Rowan affected Nicole within Ormr; the roiling in their body caught Ormr up, and for just a second, he wanted to stop this. The need to pick up the root and huff it gave him pause, made him look to it.

While he wavered, the chief did not.

MacLaoch charged. His arms were around their hips before Ormr could catch their balance. He made to push them off the ground but was lifted clean off before being tossed bodily down the hall. Like a cat, Ormr twisted midair before landing hard on all fours several paces away. Their palms skidded along the stone; Ormr also recognized a shaken sense of awareness.

Ormr shook their head and made to get up as he silenced his granddaughter's pleas. The MacLaoch's knee came down onto their lower back, forcing Ormr back onto the ground. His hands were at once on Ormr's wrists wrenching them back behind like a prisoner.

Ormr cursed the lot of them and wriggled like a landed fish, stringing obscenities together like beads on a string.

"Now, goddamn it!" Rowan shouted and reached for something. The volumes of Nicole's curly hair obscured Ormr's gaze, but he knew one hand on his wrists would not hold them. He yanked as the chief's sweater was shoved over their nose and mouth. Burning engulfed their sinuses, but Ormr yanked it off. Rowan grabbed for the root, trying to shove it back over Ormr's face. Ormr twisted their face this way then that, dodging a direct hit off the root. As Rowan and he wrestled for control over it, they grabbed clothing and hair.

The root effected Ormr's strength, and Rowan captured their wrists again. Ormr glowered into Rowan's eyes just before he bent to the side and rammed their elbow into the chief's face. Reeling, Rowan shouted obscenities. Ormr, like a wild eel, turned onto their back as Eli stood over him.

A devilish smile spread over Ormr's face. "Ha! You have us at an advantage, son!"

Eli reached down to grab their shirt front but was met with Ormr's feet. Ormr put all their might into the move, slamming both feet into the standing man's chest. Eli was a big man, after all.

Only Eli did not budge.

Instead, Ormr shot down the hall on their back. Halfway down the stone floor, their flannel shirt caught and their feet went up over their head, sending them tumbling into the empty dungeon room at the end of the hall. They came to a stop panting and on all fours. Cautiously, they made their way to standing. Shaking their shirt down, Ormr looked at the three men down the hall. They felt the clunkiness of the wellies on their feet. They were too heavy for real battle. Ormr yearned to bounce on the balls of their bare feet. To start a real skirmish, they'd need to. The three weak young men in one hallway had the righteous feel of finally achieving a fair fight. He rolled his granddaughter's shoulders to keep them loose so their strikes would be like snake bites.

He watched the MacLaoch chief move to the front again. Behind him, Eli stood and passed him the sweater.

Ormr confronted them. "Come now, boys. Let us not play with magic. Let us be on our way. We have a witch to hunt."

The Gilliansson man found his voice; he was slumped against the wall holding his arm. "O'aye, is that so you can hang her from the nearest tree, psycho princess?"

Ormr's eyes narrowed at him as the MacLaoch looked over his

shoulder, saying to him, "It's best when ye have a bear cornered, fuckwit, not to jab it with a dull stick, aye?"

Eli said something to the other men under his breath, and the chief nodded then brought his haunted eyes back to Ormr.

All four stood there for some time in that dank hallway looking at each other, Ormr to the stairs just beyond where Mickey was slumped. His eyes, however, were sharp and not missing a move. A twitch or change in expression—he saw it all. Ormr was surprised to see this and that he'd not run for his pretty little life. And Eli scrunching and releasing his fists looked wary at Ormr as if unsure if he should use his full strength. Then there was the MacLaoch chief, who was not questioning his strength against them. It was refreshing to have felt his full power, pure and uninhibited.

"Keep looking at me like that, Cole..."

"She is not here, Laoch's grandson. You have failed her, and now it is I you must contend with."

He ignored Ormr and said, "Remember the forest the other day? Remember our tussle? Let's do that again, Cole, *mo ghràdh*. Once wasn't enough..."

Nicole pushed forward an intimate memory of the chief and her. He could smell the musk of the forest floor; all of it came sweeping in like a tidal wave. Ormr still yearned to fight, but now it was laced with something more.

He pushed the memory back at Nicole as a movement down the call caught his eye. Eli had moved. No, it was the Gilliansson lad.

"Now!"

"So sorry, love," Rowan said.

Eli held Cole's satchel and overhanded it like a softball player at Ormr. It came in like a speeding arrow. Confused by their childishness, he swatted the bag to the side but right behind it was the MacLaoch chief.

Before he could defend, the chief was within striking distance. Looking at their hands, Ormr missed the other man's head and was struck on the forehead with the chief's.

Ormr's head snapped back as their vision crisscrossed, and the need to vomit swept up. Their whole body went stiff, and just before their vision went black, they felt the chief catch their hands.

# Thirty

Something awful was in my nose and in my mouth. It was the smell of funk: hundred-year-old gym socks, wet dirt, and Limburger cheese pureed together and left to putrefy. I recognized it as the root from Ethel's cottage, and overriding my instinct to gag, I took a deep breath. And another, and when I thought I might pass out from huffing it, I realized the smell had dissipated. But my head rang like it had been used as a gong.

"Cole..." Rowan said, and I recognized his gentle touch on the side of my face. Oh, those hands, those rough and capable hands... I turned into his palm and breathed him in deeply. I clasped it to my cheek then buried my face into it. Ocean, sweat, and aged oak whisky casks all went down into my lungs and filled me with his buoyancy. My eyes tentatively opened, and I realized I was flat on my back in the basement hall, the stone floor was cold and uneven. Rowan was on his knees next to me. The root had been fastened around my neck, and Eli and Mickey Gillian stood by the stairs as if they'd been instructed to do so.

"Ye all right?"

I groaned. "You really bashed me in the head..."

He gathered me up into his lap. "Oh, fucking hell, I'm so sorry, but ye had gone and lost yourself to a man who I think is the Minory from the legend."

"Ugh, he's really something..."

Rowan brushed my hair out of my face and then looked over at the other two men, "Mickey, go find Charmaine and make sure she leaves town. Tell her nothing of what you saw. If she pushes, and you know she will, tell her I'm going to put her down the fairy hole with the bank man for what she said to Cole this morning."

Mickey slipped up the stairs as Rowan said to Eli, "Help me get her to the library."

"Aye."

I held up my hand to stop him, and he flinched. "Oh, Eli—sorry, no, I'm not going to hit you. I just, I think I can walk."

Eli looked to Rowan, and he nodded out of the hall. "Get us ice and meet in the library?"

With a last frightened look at me, he left, thundering up the stairs in his haste.

I looked back at Rowan, taking in his sapphire-blue eyes and the beginning of stubble on his cheeks and felt downright bewildered. "What the holy heck just happened?"

"I think I know. I had a visit from your witchy friend, Ethel. Let's get you upstairs, and I'll tell you all about it."


I WAS ON MY BACK ON THE GREEN VELVET SETTEE IN THE library that Rowan used as his office for castle meetings, looking at a fretting Rowan. He had wedged his bottom next to me and was pushing a lock of hair off my cheek then another off my ice pack. It wasn't lost on me that I'd held a cold cloth to my head in the same spot after passing out a year before. It was like déjà vu.

"Aye, déjà vu?" Rowan read my mind.

"Yes," I mumbled, not loving that memory just yet.

"Only this time I didn't find ye attempting to dive down a fairy hole."

It was an old back-and-forth, one where Rowan knew that I'd had what I called a class four claustrophobia attack triggered by new metaphysical energy we'd discovered, but like the gentleman he was, he instead insisted that he was saving me from jumping down the fairy hole.

I threw my arm over my face.

"Och, come now," he soothed and pushed my arm down, keeping the sack of ice on my head. "Look at me." His eyes were clear, if a little strained at the corners, but they searched mine. "Truly love, are ye all right?" The backs of his fingers brushed along my cheek. "I had to tell myself I wasnae fighting with you but rather a very old Viking. When you shoved me off ye when I first got there, I would have taken you for Eli in strength."

I shook my head. "If you didn't stop me where would I be right now?"

We both knew the answer to that and looked down at the root around my neck.

"Best keep this on for now, aye?"

"I think so..."

"Otherwise, I fear Charmaine will be swinging from the nearest tree."

"Rowan..." I groaned and pinched my eyes shut. "That's so dark. I don't think I would have. Would I have?"

He lifted my hand and looked into my eyes. "It's done now... Forgive me?" he whispered.

I'd already forgiven him, but the way he kept wanting to see my eyes and asking me to forgive him, I knew he'd not heard it enough.

"Of course I forgive you. But like I said, there's nothing to forgive," I said and then put my hand to the side of his face and gently pulled him in for a kiss.

He received it graciously, and I savored the feel of him warm on my lips. Rowan noisily sighed into it. "I thought, and not for the first time this week, that I'd lost ye again. When ye recoiled from me, I felt something break inside." He'd come to rest his temple against mine and was speaking so softly it was as if he were talking to himself. "It wasn't like the forest where I could tell ye were mad—"

"Incensed," I amended; mad was for children and petty foibles.

"Aye, but even then, I could tell ye had wanted me, and it was that which was causing you strife. This, this was ye calm, telling me to bugger off, permanently." He swallowed and then said humbly, "I did not like that."

Remembering the way his eyes had gone cold as if he'd taken in hand an old darkness of his, I'd say "did not like that" was the understatement of the year. "It was strange to see your eyes," I said, thinking of how they'd dilated into obsidian disks. "Even in the forest, with everything we said and pitched at each other, you didn't look like that. But just now... I didn't mean what I did. I mean, I think you know that, but," I said, putting his hand over my heart, "I always want your hands on me."

He smiled and leaned back before smoothing more locks of my hair.

I continued, "I could tell that what I was saying was hurting you, but I didn't care, except for just a second where it flooded into me that things weren't right. I think maybe it was there that I was trying to come out? Sounds like I was a butterfly trying to emerge out of a cocoon, but it really felt like they were my own thoughts. Not like there was more than one person in there," I said, tapping the side of my skull.

He nodded; he was taking it all in stride. Really good strides. We'd lived through Lady MacLaoch and her shenanigans, so this was familiar.

"Oh," I said, remembering vital information, "Orabilia, and we wed at sundown."

Rowan shivered and blinked twice. "What?"

"Earlier today, when you heard me call to you?"

"Aye, I was talking with Bernie and Angus. They were telling me relatively jack-all about this next phase other than we must marry. Aye, the dinguses, of course we know tha'," he said and leaned against the back of the settee, pleasantly squishing me in the process. "I thought you called because I was getting peeved?"

"On the contrary, I learned a new name today," I said and watching him closely intoned with my whole body, "Lady Orabilia MacLaoch."

Rowan shivered from head to toe before launching to his feet as if electrified. "Ho-whoa," he said, shaking out his hands and legs. "What was tha'?"

I grinned at him. "That's your grandmother's name. All I did was repeat her first name at Ethel's place, and you chimed back."

I watched his expression as it morphed from incredulous, to surprise, to acceptance. "Orabilia," he tested.

Rain smattered as if in answer against the darkening windows.

We looked to them and then back at each other. "Best not use it, aye?"

"Agreed, her name is like a talisman of sorts."

"And we're to be married at sundown?" He squinted outside.

"Agreed."

"Married," he said.

The full weight of it hit me too. "Oh."

Rowan's eyes were wide and reverent, "Aye."

"Oh."

He nodded. "Aye."

"Oh."

"...Aye."

We were rapidly absorbing the reality of the situation and the subsequent effects this would have on our modern life as official husband and wife.

"We don't really have time for all the fluff, do we?"

He slowly shook his head. "No. I'm so sorry. I should have done all this earlier—"

"Sure, we can play the 'should have' game until the cows come home, but it still doesn't change the fact that we need to be married by sundown or...or..." I couldn't say it.

"Valhalla."

Rowan could.

Right then, an absurd thought burst through the pressure of the situation. "My mom's going to kill me," I whispered, gathering up his warm hand to weave my fingers through his.

"She'll understand," he soothed.

"It's entirely possible that I've spent the last year with you protecting you from the realities of being involved with a Baker. I've been so focused on the Minory bloodline that I've ignored the living people bearing the Baker name and everything that comes with it."

"If she's anything like the woman I've met on the video chats, she'll be understanding."

I sighed. He was blissfully clueless. My mother held the ability to damn a person straight to hell while simultaneously praising them to heaven. But it was all right. One crisis at a time.

We looked at each other then, eyes settling onto the other's, then down to our clasped hands. A touch here and there, and we sat there like that until the ice melted in the bag and condensation ran off it and into my hair and down my temples. Rowan swiped the droplets off my temple, and when he finally took the bag off, he gently touched my forehead.

"Aye, it's red but doesn't look like it'll bruise."

I put my hand over it; the skin was cold and damp. I sat up as Rowan moved to the green-and-red-plaid carpet and gathered my knees into his embrace; his cheek rested on my lap. I brushed his locks back and absently tucked the short ends behind his ear. We sat quietly, touching each other, not wanting to be separate lest reality wedge itself wide and imposing between us.

The questions, however, were piling up, and I peeked down at him. "Want to arm wrestle? You know, see if the strength is just when he's here or if I'm all brawn now?"

He grinned. "I was thinking of tha'. Ye were just as powerful as Eli, possibly stronger. When ye clapped your hands, I think the thunder struck outside."

Just then Rowan's cell vibrated in his pocket. "It's Eli." He answered it. "Mate." After a few terse *ayes*, and other miscellaneous guttural Scots sounds, he hung up.

I smiled. "Eli and you, back together again?"

"Aye, it feels good. I've had a cathartic day telling my people to prepare for a bankruptcy and a wedding. Eli was last on my list. I was there when ye screamed for me," he said, tapping the side of his head. "He mentioned on the phone just now that he will be back with Ethel in a bit. Apparently, she was waiting in his kitchen when he got home. Elsie and the kids are down visiting her sister; Ethel advised them to do so. Said she was just sitting there with a cuppa like a movie assassin."

"Oh, creepy. Yeah, Ethel can buck societal norms. She means well. I think."

"But why Eli?"

"I have a strong suspicion that Eli is also a direct Minory or Ormr descendant," I said. "Ethel is mine, and possibly our, ancestral grandmother."

Rowan looked at me a long while. I waited as he put the pieces together, drew his own conclusion, and the light dawned in his eyes as he nodded, "Aye, all right, fine," he said, wrestling with his own preconceived notions of the world and adjusting them. "It's too bad, not that her being your grandmother is bad—it's only Sean is not going to like it; he's been performing MacLaoch weddings for centuries."

"Centuries..." I mumbled. "Come again?" I knew Sean. He was part of the elder elite in the local clan and a proud kinsman who took only two things seriously: vows before the Lord and Scottish traditions. Use shortening instead of Highland butter in your Scottish shortbread recipe? You'll be hearing from Sean, Bible in hand.

"What is he, like, a warlock or something? How old is he?" At this point I was prepared for Rowan to say yes, as old as the castle.

Rowan had stood and gone to the brass liquor cart near the window. He stood with a hand in his pocket, looking out the window. I found myself across the room at his desk rearranging things from where they looked to have been hastily put back. As I waited for his answer, I realized why the items on his desk were haphazardly replaced. They'd been on the floor. Charmaine's hind end had shoved them off onto the floor, Rowan pushing her. His thighs had rammed against the front of the desk right where I stood. I adjusted the leather desk protector, aligning it perfectly with the desk edge, then the fountain pen, the desk plate, the lamp, and the pewter weight that had the clan crest embossed on its surface. I didn't have time to analyze how I felt about all that.

He looked back over at me. "No," he said, bringing me back to the present and my question about Sean.

"Ah, OK. Good. I'm not sure if I can take any more fantastical, metaphysical, magical or whatever shenanigans right now," I said. "It's important that Ethel perform our wedding ceremony—blood oaths are important to the Minory."

"Aye, I think you said—"

"I did not say—"

"He," Rowan corrected, "said something of using the blood of the curse to marry ye."

"'Complete the task, or I'll take my granddaughter to Valhalla.'"

"Aye," he said, and we both shivered.

"Then I think it's important that Ethel perform it. She is like," I said, dropping a glass paperweight into my opposite hand, then back again, "she's like Bernie and Angus."

"Secret Keeper, then?" he said and turned fully now.

"Yes. She's embodied her direct descendant like a witch, or Völva, as she calls herself. But yeah, a witch," I said and let my lips stay stretched after saying the word. I wasn't sure how it sounded out loud to Rowan, but to my own ears, it was new, and I expected someone to scoff at it. I also knew I was right.

"Witch," Rowan muttered as he turned back toward the window, and I heard the glass stopper clank from the whisky decanter and a healthy splash of liquid into a tumbler then another one.

He returned to my side and gave me a tumbler.

"That's a solid three-finger pour, hon," I said.

"Aye, I think it's warranted."

I sighed, like a release of pent-up steam. "Agreed."

We clinked glasses. "To the fucking impossible,"

"To the fucking impossible," he replied.

There came a knock, and Eli pushed into the room; in his wake was Ethel. Ethel's hair was pulled back and her glasses were pushed up on top of her head.

"Here you are," Eli said, wide-eyed at me, then gave Rowan a one-armed embrace as Ethel came to me and put her hands on either side of my face.

"Look at me, child." She searched my eyes. "No, not you. Let me see my grandson."

"It's just me," I said, "for now."

Ethel looked down at the root. "So, it works, then?"

"Yes, as long as I'm wearing it and breathing it in, I'm me."

"The instant she takes it off, he comes out. He's most unpleasant," Rowan said, watching her handle the root as if she were holding a grenade without its pin.

She studied me for a moment. "You're right, then, the energy of Ormr"—Rowan and I flinched at his name—"is coming directly out of you, specifically, the cells of you."

"My DNA?" I asked, getting even more specific.

"DNA," she whispered, "of course. This is very rudimentary magic, nature's magic that keeps him in, and it won't be long now before he surpasses the power it holds with his own. Then it will just be up to you, Nicole, to keep him at bay," Before I could ask her what that meant, her gaze went sharply to Rowan. "We meet again, all too soon. This afternoon was a tragedy."

Rowan nodded. "Tha' it was, but thank ye for coming."

"Lot of good it did. She's hell-bent and has taken up the MacLaoch aggressor in your legend," she said, looking from him to me and then back.

"She's been taken care of," he said.

Ethel nodded. "Yes, good. Where did you dispose of the body? Her energies could still pose a problem after death, but if—"

"Now, hold on!" Rowan said, putting out his hand. "Stop, no, she's still alive. I've sent a man to escort her out of town. She's been dealt with... In a normal, twenty-first-century way."

Ethel scoffed. "She has more power than you realize—she'll be back." She stepped up to him and put her hands up and then waved him to bend down; he complied. Ethel clasped his face and looked into his eyes.

She whispered in old Gaelic as if she were speaking directly to Lady MacLaoch: "Show yourself to me, Lady Orabilia, daughter of Laoch, the original MacLaoch chief. Woman who bore her first child and cursed her father and every man to follow him with her last breath. Wake." She gave his head a forceful jolt.

I held my breath watching Rowan, who was paralyzed, half-bent in her grasp. Eli was looking to her then to me then back as if one of us was about to erupt.

"Ethel," I said quietly, "she's not here."

She turned Rowan's head back then forward. "Not yet, but she must, mustn't she?"

Rowan answered her in his Gaelic. "Grandmother, she's not here; she's long gone."

Ethel dropped her hands. "This is not the way. There's something missing." She looked back at me. "He will take you to Valhalla if you cannot fight him. There is no magic I have to match his. He's been too long in the Spirit world gaining strength, and his knowledge of the earth magic he has learned at my knee."

I swallowed, feeling my throat go dry. "But—" My voice cracked, and I put my whisky glass to my lips and downed the glass in one gulp. Rowan rose a single brow as if asking me, *Oh, that's what we do with twenty-five-year-old whisky now?*

"But," I continued with a throat now lubricated and on fire, "I thought the wedding will appease him?"

"Yes. If you were married within the year and a day. That time is just minutes from now. Your wedding must go forward. Without his one true love, the reason for all of this, we are only guessing at what will get him to be at ease." Ethel looked at me pointedly. "You must not ever take that off."

I looked down at the root. "I won't."

"Good. Now, I have papers that need printing," she said then pulled her glasses down and looked at something written on the palm of her hand. "The papers are at w-w-w-dot—"

Rowan spoke up. "I have a laptop here we can use."

SOON THE ROOM WAS FILLED WITH MARION AND FLORA, Deloris and Clive, with Angus and Bernie on their way. Eli and Rowan helped Ethel at the laptop get to the site and print the papers. Rowan had called on the clan, and they had responded and were spreading the word: Castle. Sundown.

Flora was holding my hand on her forearm as Marion poured tea and passed around a tin of biscuits. Clive spoke animatedly with Deloris about what all this meant for the history of the clan, and it reminded me of being home at the holidays. This was family as much as my blood family in South Carolina. The Bakers would fit right in, like a puzzle piece that was waiting to slide into place.

I smiled.

Flora patted my hand. "Ye'll be all right love—we're here."

"Yes, you are."

She looked at me with a question in her gaze. "Aye."

"I've not known anything like this outside of my immediate family."

She nodded knowingly. "You're kin. You're clan, so you're kin. And you're our history, the one we've been told about since we were wee. We're the lucky generation that got to meet you, the one who returns to break the chief curse. So, of course we're your family. You may not have known about us, but we've known about ye, and in true MacLaoch fashion, ye'll be married by the light of the moon and by the skin of yer teeth. It's thought to be an ill omen at MacLaoch weddings if all goes smoothly—it means the bride or groom is destined to die. And not of auld age."

"Oh," I said, absorbing this new information, "then we're in good hands, then?"

"Aye, the best, and if there's a touch more tragedy before ye say yer vows, ye'll have a blessed and peaceful life together."

"Come now," Marion said to us both, "Flora and I have been thinking that with the garden flowers in bloom, ye should have a bouquet of them to hold tonight, aye?"

I hadn't even thought of that. "Yes, um, yes that sounds lovely."

Papers fresh off the printer and reviewed, Ethel said to Rowan, "It's time, grandchild of Lady Orabilia of Castle Laoch. Time to gather your clansfolk for a celebration, or a war. If I know you Scots, you're always prepared for both."

Clive raised his teacup. "Aye, tha' we are!"

Rowan nodded to them both, and then came to me. He put his tumbler down and took mine gently out of my hand and put it down too. He walked me to the door and whispered down to me, "Together, aye?"

"Together."

"Let us prepare for something beautiful tae happen. Let us dress for the occasion? Diamonds and silk."

I smiled. "I think I have that gala dress still upstairs in your old office."

"The diamonds are in the safe," he said then kissed my cheek. "Just the earrings." He looked down at the root.

"Yeah, I'm not taking this thing off for anything. Even if it's a mil worth of Harry Winston diamonds."

He gave me a dark smile and swiped this thumb across my cheek. "Despite everything, we'll do this our way, aye?"

"Yes." I gave him a quick kiss. "I'll change and be right back."

"Hurry."

# Thirty-One

Rowan's office up the steep tower steps still held a few things that he didn't want to crowd our small cottage with. His ceremonial kilts, RAF dress blues, old shoes he refused to donate, and weird polyester shirts handed down from his uncle. My silk gown from the gala the year before was hanging in its garment bag. I took it out and slipped it on. It slithered over my skin like oil just as it had the year before ,and with the diamond earrings from the safe it was like stepping back in time. Only this time it was for our wedding.

*Wedding,* I thought with some consequence. I should have felt apprehension or excitement, something, but I was on task.

I went to the bathroom to pull my hair back. Despite my having iced my face, there was a red-and-purple bruise beginning to bloom. I rummaged around in the medicine cabinet and found an old tube of concealer and tried to open it. The cap was stuck, and despite having the power to crack skulls earlier I was being defeated by a cap and clammy hands. My heart was suddenly pounding hard as I wrestled with the tube. I dried my hands on the hand towel next to the sink and tried again, only this time my hands were shaking.

I shouted in anger and threw down the tube before bracing my hands on either side of the sink and taking a deep breath. I held it and looked up at the ceiling, trying to count to ten. But my emotions cracked my veneer of calm. I didn't want to have a massive fist-shaped bruise on my face at my wedding. So many things were out of my control that this one thing, this tiny request to the universe, seemed like a gimme. I blew out my breath, trying to calm my racing heart. I reached for my rubber band and realized yet again I'd forgotten to replace it with one that wasn't a dried-out husk.

"It's OK. I've got this," I said and looked back down at the tube, and realized it had a flip cap on it. I laughed. "Geez, Baker, calm down. You got this." I flicked the cap open and squeezed. Just air whooshed across my fingers. I closed the cap and tapped it on my palm and tried again. Once more, just air.

I closed it again and tapped harder, opened it, and squeezed out air. I squeezed the tube between two fingers from the end to opening until a dried crumb tumbled out.

Rage gripped my guts, and I turned around in the small bathroom and whipped the bottle out across the office, making it ricochet off a window.

Seething, I tried to count to ten, but it was too much. The compounded nature of the things that had been concerning me caught up and sought my counsel right then: Charmaine. Rowan's secrets. Loss of a portion of the research field to a massive tree. None of my family at my own wedding. Loss of my life at midnight. Loss of all control.

I looked down at my shaking hands and flexed them open. Heart hammering, I went back to the sink, and with numb fingertips, I splashed water on my face. I grabbed the towel, buried my face in it before dragging it down and tossing it to the floor in a fit.

Like a flood gate opening in release of rising flood waters, the answer came from within me: *Let's solve this my way.*

My eyes went to my neck, bare in the mirror reflection, then to the towel on the floor, in whose folds I could see the ripped necklace. A panic that was only mine skittered across my skin. "Oh no," I said back to him.

But that righteousness that settled into my bones converted my earlier rage into direction. Pressure eased off my heart as strength returned with vindication, making me feel fully alive and in control. We didn't need magic—we had destiny on our side. I looked back to my flame-haired reflection, the water-droplet gemstones at my ears, and my haunted green eyes. The shadow of the woman I was there in the mirror nodding back to me. It was time.

FIVE MINUTES LATER, THE CLOCK TOWER IN GLENTREE struck the time, marking the witching hour of one year and a day as over. Ormr, feeling the power of his granddaughter's body, strode over the stone steps and down the main stairs and out into the research field. Around the downed tree and into the forest they followed the call of his old friend. Rain whipped and whistled, casting the MacLaoch lands into the fury of the gods. Even they knew what must be done that night.

Into the mud pit that was now the root hole, Ormr slid in and found it.

His hands, the slender and deft ones of his granddaughter, were filthy with the deep soil from the roots of the downed tree his grand-daughter called heritage. Only he knew more: it bore the blood of his Orabilia in the aftermath of her birth, and before that, it saw her fingers dig the soil and bury his war maiden, Ulfberht, beneath it. And with each dig their fingers made in the soil, she fastened it to her mortal energies like a map tying the Ulfberht to him and his spirit. Gilliansson, that squirrel of a man, tried to hide his war maiden from him. But her pulse he'd always feel.

Out of the pit and at the top of the field where Mickey had seen the hasty stone graves of Ormr's crew Ormr now stood.

Gilliansson. Ormr's sword in hand, the Viking could feel the man's betrayal to him upon her hilt. Gilliansson had lied to Ormr to keep him from her. Now it was time to add Gilliansson's name to his list of those who must die before Ormr left the mortal plane with his granddaughter.

First, Ormr needed to raise his men. His ship had plowed through the water like a hundred terns scouting for fish. On that fateful day, it was the wind at his back and his men at the oars. His men. His family.

Sword in hand, he remembered the last kill it made: his own. Ormr ran his granddaughter's palm firmly down her rusted edge, forcing her to draw his blood out once more. The edge had dulled over the centuries, and the cut was not clean—but it was effective. Blood oozed out of his agile feminine hand, and he squeezed it hard, pumping until a single droplet fell to the soil at his feet.

"Wake," he whispered with intention into it.

The Ulfberht blade, recognizing him within his granddaughter's blood, woke. It buzzed within his grip until the rust shook from its forged steel and shone back at him in all its great eastern steel glory. It would do his bidding tonight, cutting flesh open like hot metal through butterfat.

His eyes went back to the field; each of the cairns had taken on the same ethereal glow as his sword, and pleased, he raised his arms wide.

"Rise, warriors, Vikings—my men—and return from your spirit walk," he commanded to them as if he stood on the prow of his dragon ship once more. Using incantations he had learned at his grandmother's knee while she stitched shut sword wound after wound, he called them forth from their shameful graves.

"Rise and rise again. Come forth from the darkness. Walk and fight beside me once more. My blood to your bones, rise."

One by one, bones the color of gold-flaming white suns, sat up out of their rock beds and then stood. The field filled with the souls of his dead men, and he felt a thrill run through his granddaughter's veins.

Beyond their incandescent bodies, down at the base of the hill, he saw the MacLaoch chief. Behind him was a slow trickle of humans gathering; some carried laughably short swords, others axes, and some rakes. Seeing him gave his granddaughter's body a shudder; dressed in a dark-green hunter's tartan, the chief could easily hide on the grounds. The chief's gaze was felt on his skin as the chief stood tall, his sword running the length of him at his side. He was the image of his forefather, the man who took Ormr's head.

The MacLaoch chief had failed in his singular task. Now, Ormr would take his granddaughter with him once he quit the chief's lineage this night. No MacLaoch of his bloodlines would ever touch Minory skin again. His own love knew the fierce nature of her blood and thought that through the bond between them, their descendants could avoid more bloodshed. She had been wrong. He would step in now and end it. This was the only way.

Ormr suppressed his granddaughter's internal pleas until she was gone and it was only him now in her body, and he lifted an empty, beckoning, hand out. "Come, my brethren, and raise your weapons. Tonight we earn our place in Valhalla!"

As they lifted their ghostly swords and axes high, their war cry rose with it. The cry was inhuman, like the screech of a thousand owls wrenching open the night air with their sound.

Rowan stood at the edge of the Circle Garden and cursed under his breath as his stomach bottomed out. "Holy fuck," he said, looking up over the field toward Cole. He had been right earlier—after Cole left, he told Ethel that if his past was any consideration to his future, he'd need to prepare for the worst. In times past, they would blow the horn and the Glentree bell tower would ring, signaling his clanspeople to rally. Now, he'd texted them. He intended to have a wedding but had prepared for a battle. Then a cold chill had run down his spine, telling him Ormr had Cole locked away, and battle it was.

Now he stood at the edge of the research field looking up at her. She was powerful, towering on a stone mound at the top edge of the field, the forest at her back. She, barefoot like a bloody Celt and in the silk dress she'd worn to the gala the year before.

And like during the gala the year before, it hugged her curves, displaying not only the roundness of her breasts and hips but also the long muscles of her arms and shoulders that she'd gained over the last year neck deep in the research field.

Ulfberht in her hand, gold clasps on her wrists and around her neck, her hair snapped and crackled out, glowing in a golden light that made her look like an angel. An angel of death intent on lighting the very earth on fire. And despite his fear, or because of it, he knew he'd lose what was left of his mind if he extinguished even an ember of that fire.

His blood told him Cole was locked behind her grandfather Ormr, and this time he'd not underestimate her powers. It seemed like a doomsday proposition having her stand over them. The only reprieve was that they were on MacLaoch land. He knew every inch of it and knew he'd have to use that advantage in waging this very delicate war.

The green of his great-great-grandfather's war tartan was woven with black, brown, and brick-red lines. Tossed over his shoulder while crouching in the brush, he'd be unseen. He had called his clan to his back, and despite their bickering and in-fighting over the gala fallout, they were arriving. The thundering metaphysical energy of the estate helped set the reality that they were indeed at war.

War.

He'd gone to war for Queen and country more than once. But at a cruising altitude of thirty-five thousand feet. Now with the clan chief's *claidheamh dà làimh* grasped in his fist, the blade tip pressing into the soil, he felt the weight of history on his shoulders. He just wished to all heaven and earth the spirit he was about to go against wasn't forever inhabiting his one and only love.

There was a murmur around them as she arched her blade up in the air and ran it across her palm.

"Och, laird, isn't that your Minory lass?"

Rowan internally grimaced. "Aye, she's being possessed by her ancestral grandfather, the Minory of the legend, Viking Ormr Minorisson."

A handful of his clan genuflected.

There was no need to sugarcoat what was happening. His clan knew of the legend and believed it harder than he ever did. They were a sturdy, pragmatic group that believed what they saw. And what they couldn't see.

There was a rustle behind him, and bodies were being pushed out of the way. The gray hair of Ethel he first saw; then out of the darkness, Eli followed in her wake. He was a whole shoulder height over Rowan's clan and wore his Campbell tartan and a modern replica of a lowland claymore, only his sat comfortably in an impossibly large scabbard as his hip. The dark of his shirt blended in seamlessly with the forest green and deep blues; his tarten tossed over his pale skin and red hair, he too would be unseen in the shadows.

They clasped hands and patted each other's shoulders. "Is she...?"

"Completely Ormr," he said and looked up the hill.

Eli murmured a prayer. "We will get her back," he said, full of a confidence that Rowan did not feel.

Ethel stared wide-eyed up at Cole. "My stars..." she said then turned to Rowan, patting the basket she held. "I have my things. It won't be enough; you have given Nicole Orabilia's ring. Now it's time for me to hold yours; where is it, lad?"

Rowan was surprised by her request "We've never seen it. If it wasn't melted into a macabre souvenir, rumor says that it's encapsulated in the seawall."

"The seawall," she whispered, looking out toward the loch. "Until I return with it, you must keep Cole alive. Then, when I do, you must clasp hands with her so that I may perform the ceremonies."

Rowan looked wide-eyed to her and then back up the field where a possessed Cole's hands were raised. Back to Ethel: "Pardon my French, but how the fuck am I supposed to clasp myself to tha' Viking within her body? She's the strength of Eli."

"You have it, use it," she said, pointing to his sporran. "Keep that close. And while he's grown too powerful for it, don't underestimate your lass—she may need just a window to break through."

"I rarely remove it," Rowan said, and despite the pressure cooker situation, Eli snickered.

"Not your cock, lad, the root. I sense it in your pouch; you were right to bring it with you."

"Right."

"Just get your hands to hers," she said and then lifted her basket, "and I will do the rest. Now, I will need three agile people to take me to the seawall."

"Ye'll need more than three—"

Ethel shivered and looked back to the field—there, row upon row of skeletons were sitting up in the grass.

Rowan's jaw went slack as a general gasp and cry came from his clanspeople.

Ethel shouted, "Three people, MacLaoch!"

Rowan had to shake off the terror that gripped his innards and stabbed what felt like a fire-dipped iron through the bullet wound at his hip. There had been bodies buried in that field, and now their skeletal remains were alive. His head clouded with fear. It was his war returned. He was on his knees in the sandbox begging for mercy. It was Vick's head blown open. It was the battle cry and the headlong charge into his dark place.

He took a long, deep breath in and opened the black box that he held himself in when he was doing four hundred knots in the cockpit. He shoved it all inside and locked the lid shut. He would feel nothing. He couldn't.

He clenched his teeth as he trained his mind to drain out every extraneous thought and leave him focused on the task at hand. Turning to his clanspeople, he said, "Be calm. 'Tis nothing but some fanciful fairy lights. I need Shepherd Rupert, Mary from the forge, and Kyle from the swim team. Come forward." Wide-eyed, they did. Mary had been handing out daggers, mail, and short swords. "Thank you, Mary. Now, you three will go with Ethel, Witch of the Misty Cliffs to the lower seawall. Follow her instructions, and you'll stay safe," he said and gave Ethel a *Got that?* look.

"Yes, yes, I'll keep you safe, but things have changed. Ormr has risen his crew. Your blades and weapons will have no effect on them." She looked to Rowan in analysis, then to Eli, then out to the field, her lips murmuring in silent conversation with herself. Her gaze came back to Rowan. "It'll have to do." She put her basket down "Quickly now, your *sgian-dubh*," she said, holding her hand out to him but looking at the dagger attached to his leg.

He bent and slipped it from its sheath and held the hilt out to her.

Ethel captured his fist around the blade and pulled. Rowan hissed as it sliced his palm, but before he could tell her off, she had drawn the blade across Eli's palm as well.

"Clasp your bloody hands together," she said, tucking the blade into her worn leather belt. When they stood looking at her for an explanation, she said, "Now!"

They did, and Ethel massaged their forearms as if to squeeze every last bit of blood out; she worked until blood dripped to the ground. She closed her eyes and tilted her head back and spoke.

Rowan understood only a few words of what she was chanting, something about bones, blood, and rising.

A short gasp from the crowd behind him, and he saw first the butcher's blade illuminate in a turquoise fairy-pool glow. Then another in the crowd and another.

Rowan looked to his hand in his friend's giant one and then looked at him. Eli's expression was one of shock and surprise. Eli was still new to this kind of magic. Rowan nodded in reassurance.

"Aye, it's all right. We'll see this day through. Be strong and have my back."

Eli nodded, but Ethel interrupted them.

"Both Minory and MacLaoch blood has been spilt. I wasn't sure if the sight of you was just a trick of the eye or you really are the fruit from Minory loins making the brotherly bond you two share be enough," she said to Eli, "and thus match the strength of my grandson's magic. Yet you are, and it is." She allowed herself a brief smile as she noticed Eli's sword glowing golden, before letting their hands fall away.

Behind them, weapons from Mary's forge, along with rakes, garden shovels, pick axes and scythes, all glowed like incandescent moonlight. Rowan thought the humble never looked so mighty.

Ethel took the three clansfolk and headed toward the castle to skirt it to the lower seawall. Rowan watched her go. If the ring was down there, he prayed she'd find it and prayed it was powerful enough to bring Cole back and send her devil of a grandfather back to Valhalla—along with his dragon ship crew.

Rowan turned to his clan then. It was time.

## Thirty-Two

Down at the lower seawall, the water was beginning to crash up over the outer edge of the tidal flats toward its high-tide mark. The air was damp but still, as if holding its breath. Ethel held the steady hand of the brown-haired swimmer as the other two stood guard at the sea gate entrance. Over the rocks and up the small hillside Ethel made it to the seawall. Her fingers worked over the rough black rocks there. The strong briny smell of the low tide pools behind them reminded her that it was the ocean that bore the MacLaochs. It would be there, interned in that rock wall, that she'd find the ring.

"I have my cell phone if you need it?"

"What use have I of a phone call at the moment, child?"

"Oh, I..." he said and lifted it, and bright light illuminated the area.

"Ah, that's very good," she said and picked her way across the wall, all the while feeling for the power she hoped it still held. Centuries had passed; she felt the ring would be there, but would its power? Her hands scraped and pressed at every rock surface until there was a gentle tug at her heart.

"Yes, I'm coming. He needs you. Where are you?" she murmured.

"What's that?" the boy asked.

The object called back to her. The older woman whipped around, looking out at the tidal pools. "Of course," she said. Gingerly she and the boy picked their way back along the seawall to the gate and then down. They worked their way over the damp rocks, sand, and algae.

Halfway across the tidal flats, she stopped. "Of course. That's why you picked the boy," she said and then looked at the fit young man whom Rowan had called Kyle from the swim team.

"What's that?" the boy asked again, his light still in his hand.

"Give that here," she said and took the light and shone it down into the water. There below them was a deep pool. The light did not touch the bottom. They both looked at it and then looked out to the incoming ocean tide.

"You must go quickly, or the current will return and push you down under. Now, it is still, and it is the lowest it will be for the rest of the moon cycle. Hurry!"

The boy blinked. "But it's freezing."

"Ha! We did not have to break ice to get in there. Come now. I'll hold your clothes, and if you do it fast enough, we might have a chance to drink whisky and toast our success."

"And if I don't?" His voice squeaked at the end of the question.

"If you don't? We will all die. Now, are you a MacLaoch clansman? Show your worth!"

The man named Rupert caught up to them on the slime-covered rocks and said, "Och, ye best do it, lad. This here is a witch, and she'll rob ye of your speed in the water, and ye can kiss yer record-breaking legend goodbye."

This was the motivation the whip of an adolescent needed. He cursed and took off his clothes and made Ethel hold his things.

"Now, what am I looking for?"

"I dunno."

"What?!" he said, his teeth starting to chatter. "What do you mean you dunno?!"

"I mean, you'll have to get your scrawny arse into that pool and go to the bottom. Bring up everything that doesn't feel like it belongs."

With an incredulous look and a silent plea to Rupert to save him, he nevertheless moved to the edge of the arms-width pool in his underpants. He panted twice in preparation of going under and then was gone.

In the distance, Mary was shouting at them. Ethel said to Rupert, "Go see what she's on about."

Ethel waited and then waited more. The seconds seemed to roll like treacle out a narrow glass bottle.

Finally, the boy's head broke the surface with a shout. "It's colder than a witch's tit down 'ere!"

Ethel narrowed her eyes. "Well? Have you found anything?"

He gave her a big, toothy grin, "Aye," he said and tossed over the side five round objects.

She felt a pulse from one. It was covered over by life from the ocean's floor and several centuries worth of grime.

"Yes, you've done it. Out, child. Get your clothes on."

He obeyed as she picked up the nugget and looked around. She needed MacLaoch blood. She needed an incantation she didn't know. She cursed and dragging the boy back with her, got to the sea gate and stopped short. Two men were arguing with Rupert and Mary from the forge.

"Oh, for Earth Mother's sakes! What now?" Ethel stepped up to the old men. They looked to be her age, one with a broken nose, and the other clearly never saw a fight in his life. "And who might you be standing in the way of those trying to do a great amount of good?"

"Aye, well, I'm Angus, and this is my brother, Bernie."

"Ye have something of ours," Bernie said and nodded to the chunk of seabed in her hand.

It dawned upon her then. "I see—she's sent you as well."

"Aye, we've come at the behest of the chief... Understand she has departed this world, but her magic still lies upon the land and with it, her intentions."

Rupert and the lad looked confused, and Mary watched intently as if a brawl were about to break out.

"She needs to be brought back."

"No," the man named Angus said, "if she returns, we risk wiping the MacLaoch ancestral castle and lands off the face of the earth."

Bernie had been thoughtful. "Not if she willingly returns to take what is rightfully hers. We will not have to generate or take much energy to let her return upon a path she sailed a millennium ago of her own free will."

"Ah, you see it as I do. Starting with this," Ethel said and held up the rock.

As he held his palm up for it, she brought the *sgian-dubh* from her belt across his hand and rammed the rock into the wound. "Bring her back."

Bernie hissed.

Angus cut in, "Wait now—"

Ethel spoke. The least she could do with her magic was clean the surface of the thing so that they understood what it was they were holding. The power it had.

Her words caught the air and threaded it with golden silk; MacLaoch blood would make it shine once more. All the more powerful if Lady MacLaoch's direct descendant, Rowan, held it. But this Bernie fellow would do.

Only the air didn't hold a charge. Confused, she focused and repeated herself, and again, until it was obvious nothing was going to happen.

Angus took pity upon her and held his hand out to her. She gave him the small knife, and he slid it upon his own hand. "Bernie and I are identical twins. We must do everything together."

He grasped the top of the rock and the three of them invoked the energy it took to shake the grit from the object.

Once it was done, Angus removed his hand and there in Bernie's palm was a swill of black ocean scum. He poked into it until he grasped something and lifted. It was a ring. Gold and clean as the day it was created.

Mary, Rupert, and Kyle looked over his shoulder at it; there was a collective "Ahh."

"It's the ring Lady MacLaoch set upon her husband's finger," Bernie said.

"Who?" Kyle asked.

"Shh!" Rupert and Mary said to him.

Angus continued, "The same one her father took off his dead body and gave back to her. Telling her to save it for a man who was worthy."

"Aye, it 'tis," Ethel confirmed. "And now there's a MacLaoch who desperately needs it, and he can call her back."

"Call who back?" Kyle asked. "Lady MacLaoch or the chief's Nicole?"

"Aye" was all she said before gathering her shawl and leading them back up to the battlefield.

# Thirty-Three

As Cole descended, the Ulfberht flinted on the stones in the field, and flanking her were Ormr's small army of skeletons. The sight, Rowan knew, would be permanently burned into his memory and be the thing of his dreams, and his nightmares.

She was midway down the hill when lightning shot through the low cloud cover as thunder pounded the air like a defibrillator against his heart. Mother Nature was responding to the energy production their square of land was producing, yet again.

"Laoch!" her voice boomed. Her voice had taken on a baritone as Ormr consumed her. "The time is nigh for us to bring your might against mine! This time, Chief Laoch, son of the Devil, I see you coming. This time it is *I* who is coming for *you*!"

Rowan gave the signal for his rear clanspeople to begin trickling out the back and come around the upper bank of the field through the forest.

"I am not Laoch! I did not cut your fucking head off, Minory! Get with the times, aye? And thanks to your betrothed, I lived a life learning what hell means! Darkness is an old friend, and you're inhabiting the last good thing I have on earth, so I suggest you get the fuck out."

Cole's lithe body paused, and her head tossed back and laughed. It echoed off the stone walls of the castle behind Rowan. "That seems like a threat, Laoch! So, Chief, if I do not comply, will you remove my head again? It is the only way. You know this, don't you?" Her body was moving again. "Yes... Yes, I see it in your eyes. You know you must kill us both. You must honor us with a hard-won fight; you must secure our place in Valhalla. It seems that, yet again, fate has not smiled upon you." Ormr laughed. "You *will not* do it! You *cannot* do it! Kneel now to me, boy chief, and let this battle be done."

Rowan felt an icy finger run down his spine, making him shiver despite the heat of his tartan making him sweat. He really needed the beast of a man who was in her to step out.

"Are you sure of this?" Eli asked under his breath.

"Aye," Rowan said as Cole walked down the last of the hill toward them, her arms out and her eyes sparking, "and no. Take the skeletons. I'll keep her busy." It was a good idea, Rowan thought. It just might work. But it was his initial part in it that was disturbing the fuck out of him.

Disarm her.

*Right.*

He pulled his sword up into fight stance and let out a whooping cry. He and Eli had practiced it as kids, mimicking his uncle and clansmen before a hunt. It was the keening song of warriors who raced into battle for centuries in the name of MacLaoch, in the name of Scotland, and in the name of their way of life since the first foot was set down upon their land.

From the forest beyond, his people whooped a callback. A shiver of excitement and ferocity moved through them. Thunder shook the land again, and Cole's possessed smile went wide. Rowan gave one last holler, iridescent blade held high, and raced in toward her. Eli had his directive. He would have to be fast.

Crying out in unison, they ascended to the skeletons, who wielded short blades. Out from the forest came his clansfolk, running down into the field, smashing skeletons as they went. Metal struck metal and bone.

Ormr in Cole's body looked over her shoulder at the chaos behind and looked back with a satisfied smile.

"To Valhalla!" Ormr's voice roared out of Cole's body, and spinning the blade up into her hands, he held it aloft and leaped. The air shivered with an electrical charge, all the hair on Rowan's body rose, and he cursed just as lightning crashed down into the middle of the field.

The blast of it knocked him clean off his feet. He hit the ground going ass over tea kettle back down the hill.

He skidded through the brush as carefully laid lines snapped beneath him. Righted, and on one knee, he saw Viking Cole rushing him again. Eli was at his knees, disoriented but getting up.

Head still spinning, Rowan watched as she roared, her blade cutting in for a beheading blow. He hit the ground as the sound of the blade whistled above him. Scrambling to his feet, he moved back up the hill, drawing her to him. As she approached, he kept the length of his six-foot blade between them.

He saw the deep change she was under in her eyes. They were electric green. Possessed green.

The clash of metal upon metal rang across the field like ten thousand soldiers upon a battlefield.

Breathing heavily and feeling like he'd been blasted out of a cannon, Rowan said, "Give her back to me, Ormr. She is mine; we are to be married this night."

Ormr's baritone called back, "It is too late! You have shown your ineptitude, child chief. I will take her home with me after we wipe your bloodline from this earth."

"And ye are not your own kind of inept, Ormr? That you should plan to take a powerful clan chief's daughter and not expect that he wouldn't come for ye like a war hound to set an example of you to everyone within striking distance and beyond? How can ye not think as your head was cut from your shoulders that *you* were the one who was wrong and deserved the ultimate fucking ye got?" He drew him toward him as he stepped back out of his reach. Once more, then again. The forest was at his back.

His baiting worked.

"Deserved?!" Ormr cried and struck again. The Ulfberht in his two-handed grip would have smiled if it could, cheering her master on.

Ormr lunged, and Rowan blocked the strike. The sound crashed in his ears and reverberated up his arm. They clashed again and again;

Cole's power was frightening with Ormr's strength. She dealt him another blow, sending his blade to the side, and moved in. She'd effectively eliminated Rowan's sword's six-foot reach advantage as if she had spent her entire life in combat. Rowan arched to the side to miss her blade; his own came around but only the hilt. She ducked his strike and was up again, punching him in his diaphragm.

The fist was decidedly *not* Cole's.

Cole, he knew, struck hard and true. But she only had about one good punch in her a bout; having been raised rough with her brother and cousins, she naturally play-fought. This, however, was the might of Eli with the expertise that made her fist feel twice as hard as he'd ever been hit before.

Air blew out his lungs, and his diaphragm seized despite his clenching it. His face was in the grass before he knew fully what had happened.

Rowan's head was yanked back by his hair, and the Ulfberht slid in under his neck. "And now," Ormr's voice whispered against his ear as Cole's body molded against his back. His body responded to the warm feel of Cole pressing against him, a comforting balm in all other circumstances. His brain however screamed as the baritone of Ormr said against his cheek, "You..."

Then Cole coughed.

Rowan smelled the stench of sewage, and a faint iridescent yellow plume rose from his sporran. The root was reacting to Ormr being so close.

Acting fast, Rowan yanked on his and Cole's connection.

Cole gasped against his neck; grabbing her blade arm, he turned. Her eyes had dulled. "Run," she spat, "run, and save yourself, our people—"

"No, Cole, fight him," he pleaded and pulled her in against him; he kept the connection to her open—it was easy with the yearning for her in his belly.

"He's too strong—" she bit off and winced, pinching her eyes shut. "I don't know how I can put him back or push him out of me." She opened her eyes, begging Rowan for an answer.

"The root," he said, reaching into his sporran. As he did, he looked back down the hill for Ethel; she hadn't returned. The skeletons, however, had turned toward him. Something—someone—was calling them over.

Eli beheaded the first two while the clan attacked the others; only there were too many, and his clansfolk were on the far side of the field. As a sea of them ascended, Rowan slipped the root out and with fumbling hands put it up to her neck. Her body jerked back and rolled to the side, gagging.

"Cole, please..."

From where she was collapsed on the ground, her chin shot over her shoulder, her eyes beginning to glow. "Run!"

The skeletons were too close. He reached for her but brought his sword up instead as the disconcerting hammer of real steel hit his blade. In the cacophony of bones and blades, Rowan cursed and tossed the root to Cole. He defended another barrage only to look back at her and see her eyes were incandescent once more and the root gone.

He raised his sword to block another strike. "Cole, fight it!"

It was too late; Ormr was back. He, in Cole's body, kicked Rowan in the chest, sending him tumbling backward down the hill.

Rowan came to a stop, and the world cartwheeled as he staggered to his feet. Cole, eyes green flames, was flanked by her dead Vikings.

Ormr's baritone barked, "Ha! MacLaoch, you disappoint me! I felt that we would finally have our true mights against each other." Viking Cole paced in front of him now, her blade tip pointing at him in accusation. "You are a disappointment. When will you MacLaochs learn? It is on your knees in fealty that you do the most good."

Rowan still couldn't breathe; his blade had fallen out his hands, and he braced himself on his knees. He had to launch forward. Tackle her.

Cole's blade went high. "Goodnight, MacLaoch. When the last of your blood is spilt, have no fear—this blade will pierce my own heart, and I will take my men and fierce Vikingsdóttir back to Valhalla. I'm disappointed. I was hoping you would be a potent adversary—"

Eli tackled her from the side like a rugby player. They skidded across the hill through the dirt and into the gravel trail leading down to the lower part of the field; strings and flags flew into the air.

Eli stood and roared down at his possessed cousin, "Give 'er back, you damned man! I hate what yer making me do!"

Rowan saw the tears in Eli's eyes; he was well passed angry. He staggered forward as Cole looked up at Eli, and the smile was back. There was a sick twist in Rowan's belly; Ormr was just warming up.

Blood dripped out Cole's nose. She put her fingers to it and dabbed.

Eli shouted, "Ye made me do this to her! Get gone!"

Cole looked at the blood then slipped her bloody fingers into her mouth and sucked them clean. Rowan and Eli let her stand.

"Remember," Rowan whispered to him.

Eli nodded.


LOOKING AT BOTH MEN, ORMR FELT DISAPPOINTMENT COLOR his vision—he could easily break these two. He would not return to Valhalla with Elias Campbell. Not with a grown man who wept openly at besting an equal adversary.

Bitterness shook over him as he stood, and holding his blade out to Eli, he said, "Yield."

"I'm not going to."

Ormr smacked the Ulfberht against Eli's and brandished it again, "Yield!"

The clang of the metal reminded Ormr of the fires of a blacksmith and the sound of a forge hammer upon steel. The MacLaoch chief's eyes were sharp, looking for an entry point for his fists, his sword far flung down the hillside. The power of his granddaughter was impressive, especially when the eyes of the MacLaoch met hers. He called to her, and that steely gaze was the kind of call he remembered of his own true love.

*Now,* he thought and lunged, slicing his blade against Eli's. Eli stumbled back as Ormr twisted, punching MacLaoch in his chest, careful to avoid his gaze.

The chief, swift on his feet, moved back, making Ormr's blow only a caress. Twisted there, the MacLaoch took the advantage and grasped Ormr's feminine golden-clasped wrist and yanked.

Searing lightning shot over Ormr's granddaughter's skin. His call was commanding her. Ormr's skin went tight, and his eyes ached with the pressure of her trying to squeeze him out.

"Gah!" Ormr shouted and tried to yank it from his grip, but Cole pushed him toward the MacLaoch. "Rowan," his lips whispered, unbidden.

"I'm here," he said, trying to grasp her gaze. Ormr looked to the sky, but the pressure was too great with the chief's hands clasped to his wrist.

Ormr met that gaze and felt something he'd not felt in centuries, defeat.

"Cole..."

Ormr would not be drawn in. He yanked his wrist from the chief's grip, but the damage was done. The chief saw clearly within Ormr's eyes what he felt. MacLaoch had to die immediately; he had to kill this feeling of defeat.

Eli was back, his blade swinging at the oarsman who had come to Ormr's aid. Ormr lunged; his golden-clasped wrist came up, blocking it with a clang of magic. The MacLaoch defended himself against an onslaught, his blade gone but his fists proving to be just as lethal. He dealt with Ormr's men with a blow to the face and then an arm around the neck before twisting the skull free of its spine.

Ormr growled, focusing on the chief. He pulled his knee up and kicked the chief in the back. His granddaughter's white dress ripped up the sides. The MacLaoch stumbled back.

Ormr sliced his blade back at Eli. The big man arched away but not before the tip of the Ulfberht caught his shoulder. The wool of Eli's tartan gave at the slice and slipped off. Ormr's next would not miss the heart. He lunged. Rowan shouted and grabbed Ormr's thrusting arm, making his jab go askew. Eli, paralyzed with disbelief, watched as the tip of Ormr's blade touched the skin over his own heart.

Ormr growled then punched MacLaoch's cheek despite the screaming in his head. The MacLaoch's head snapped back, then with a two-handed beheading hold, Ormr swung his blade around. Rowan shifted his weight, and Ormr's arms collided with Rowan's side.

The chief recovered quickly and grabbed a fistful of the dress and yanked his opponent forward. Ormr tucked his chin, taking the head-butt properly. Ormr's head rattled as the chief stumbled back.

"Fool!" his voice boomed. "Do not brawl with me! I am set to kill you, not take your ale!"

Eli recovered and moved in on Ormr, forcing his focus off Rowan. With the Ulfberht's hilt in his fist, Ormr attacked, smashing it against Eli's face, then kicked him squarely in his clan jewels.

Eli coughed, and his knees snapped together before he hit the ground.

Arms wide, Ormr stood over the man. "This body may be that of a goddess, but she bears my blood. She has the strength of youth and the will to fight like a warrior. Do not hesitate, for now we mark today as the day you die."

Standing over the downed Eli, Ormr raised his sword.

MacLaoch's arm snaked about his neck and pulled tight. Rowan yanked him backward, keeping Ormr's balance unsteady, making his granddaughter's feet grasp for purchase. Ormr let out a garbled laugh, thrilled at being overpowered.


Rowan's heart hammered in his chest.

Against her ear, he whispered, "I'm sorry, I'm so sorry, love. Can you hear me? Come back; fight him, *mo ghràdh*."

His choke hold would have put Cole unconscious a minute ago. Ormr was made from a stock he was praying he never had to see again. As he held her tight, he hoped the fight he was feeling drain out was of Ormr leaving Cole's body, but he knew it would be the kiss of death if he let up and Ormr was not unconscious.

"Come back to me, *mo ghràdh*," he whispered again, his eyes filling with emotion.

Down on the trail Rowan saw Ethel coming with the three and an extra two. Hope soared through him at the sight of Angus and Bernie. They were running now. How many of his people there were left he couldn't be sure since something dripped into his eyes, mixing with the tears.

There was more shouting behind him, and Eli was hobbling back up to standing and wildly gestured at the group to hurry. Then he picked his sword out of the shrubbery and roared toward something behind Rowan.

Skeletons once more, some in pieces, some rearranged backward, and some missing heads entirely, all moved toward Rowan. They were coming to Ormr's rescue. It dawned on him this time that both Cole and Ormr were in trouble. Sickness struck through his belly, and he automatically dropped her.

She slumped down his front to the ground as Ethel ran through the chaos to him.

A single, sword-brandishing blue ethereal set of bones broke off and moved toward her. It moved in a horrifying parody of a real Viking warrior, sure-footed and menacing, down the hill toward the frail and elderly Ethel. In a few steps he'd strike her down.

"No!" Rowan shouted and held his hand out as if he could stop the Viking bones in its tracks.

Cole coughed under him and rolled to her knees. She was dazed, but he was sure it was still Ormr in full control and deadening their connection.

Ethel, running, hissed at the ancient warrior then spat in his eye like a peevish footballer after a bad call. The iridescent bones exploded into flames. He was ash upon the ground behind her, giving Rowan a renewed sense of awe and hope.

Eli charged through the descending skeletons and struck out. He bowled them over as skulls popped up into the air as he took two out at a time. Rib cages cracked under his blade as he became a sword-wielding tornado. The masses turned from Rowan and charged at Eli. Behind Rowan, the clash of his clanspeople still rattled the air.

Ethel ran toward Rowan. "Wear this!"

Rowan held his hand out to receive the tiny object when Ormr twisted with a roar, kicking her back.

"Ooof," Ethel grunted, flying back in a ripple of dark-green shawl.

As she fell, a small golden ring arced through the air off her fingertips. Blinking blood out of his eye, Rowan reached for it. A possessed Cole grabbed him around the middle and tackled him back into the field.

Rowan hit with a smack and a seizing sense of relief. Ethel had found it.

"I'm so sorry, love!" Rowan shouted before clipping Viking Cole's jaw with his fist. There was a special place in hell for him. She took the hit as if he'd simply patted her cheek, and climbing over his recumbent body, she reached for the ring in the grass above him.

He grabbed her thigh as she straddled his prone body, like he'd done a thousand times before, only this time instead of being sensually deep within her, he was as shriveled in fear as he could be.

"Cole," he called to her, running a hand up her thigh, unsure if it would bring her out or enrage the Viking.

Her head snapped down, and possessed green eyes looked back at him as Cole's upper lip recoiled into a wicked smile. "Yes, love?" Her hand slapped over his mouth, and she shoved. "Wish to die today? Let's make it come true."

Not being able to breathe, he nailed her in her solar plexus and pitched her sideways onto a pile of rocks. She was at least not the same mass as he imagined Ormr had been. She coughed and lunged again. He reached forward, grabbing into the grass as Cole kicked him in the back. The strike knocked him clean sideways. Ormr was gaining in strength. Rowan groaned as pain radiated up his back and through his body.

Cole was on all fours searching the grass as Rowan's head cleared. The hillside doubled then combined back into one vision as he sat.

"Where is it?" the deep voice of Ormr muttered.

Warm in Rowan's fist was a hard metal circle. He looked down at it. The golden ring winked back at him.

He looked up across the hill to Ethel and saw her flanked by the twins. Ethel was making motions with her hands at him. As his vision cleared, he saw her trying to tell him to fuck something...or to put the ring on his finger. He was already slipping it onto his left ring finger like a wedding band. As soon as the circle settled into place, Cole's head snapped around, and her eyes glowed like that of a goblin.

In a moment of inspiration, Rowan looked to the ring his ancestral grandmother had given to the Minory in love and murmured, "Lady Orabilia MacLaoch, protect us." His body shivered as words began to swim into his ears from the clearing, from the three elders down below.

Words could be felt pounding the air like hands hard upon war drums. Over the fracas, he saw the mouths of the three of them move. The boom of thunder hammered the earth as their voices whispered over his skin, making him shiver again as if with fever. Something more than releasing Cole was happening. It felt as if a power was being woken up and called forth to challenge Ormr and his men. Ethel and the brothers' hands went together, and energy rushed into Rowan's body. Someone else's breath shot into his lungs, expanding his chest. He tilted his head back as if to get above water, to gasp his breath back. His back arched as his mind felt as if it were attempting to expand out of his skull.

He shouted and put his fists to his temples, trying to ram his skull closed. Fog slithered around him; it was pulling his skin off, cell by cell, skin flake by skin flake. His dermis rippled as if fingers moved under it, ripping it from his muscle tissue. Rowan screamed. Just as his skin felt like it was about to tear clean off, it came out of him. A being had been created from his body, pieces of his DNA, and put itself back together. Then, using the energy of the field, it had shocked itself into existence.

Rowan fell back to the ground as Viking Cole roared through the air. She leaped from her high ground, sword hilt held high and its tip down ready to drive it through his chest.

"Stop!" came the thing's voice. It echoed over the field sending a shock wave through Cole and striking Ormr from her. He stumbled backward out of her like smoke out of a tube, leaving Cole as herself midair. Cole's eyes went wide, and then she screamed. Rowan twisted just as the sword tip hit. She crashed on top of him and the sword into the ground next to his head. Rowan grasped her, cursing at the blessed near miss, and clutched her to his chest.

# Thirty-Four

I was still screaming when Rowan hugged me in against him.

Face buried in his tartan, I said in a sob, "I'm so sorry."

"It's all right, *ghràdh*," Rowan said in a rush, pushing my hair aside and looking into my eyes, "Aye, my god, ye are back." Then he gripped me harder still.

We whimpered together as Rowan sat us up. He wiped more of my wild curls out of my face and kissed my lips. Blood was trickling down his temple and had dried in bits along his eyebrow and on his lid. A strawberry bruise was blooming like a potential unicorn horn on his forehead.

There was a noise. Behind us was a woman clad in gossamer trappings that resembled a dress from a world ago; her raven hair to her alabaster ghost skin shone from within like moonlight. Her eyes were bright blue, the color that electrifies and sparks. His ancient grandmama, Lady Orabilia MacLaoch.

Shirtless and standing midfield was my ancient grandpappy, Ormr. He was what I had imagined, golden clasps on his wrists, dragon around his neck, and shoulder-length strawberry-blond hair was pulled back into a tight, war-ready plait. He was the kind of brawn that commanded awe when looked upon. Possessing more than just power in his muscle and sinew, he was a tower of anger and cunning. It was in the flint in his eyes, it was in the red scar across his neck, and it was in the hard edges of his joints. The animal skins that made up his breeches and his naked shoulders where a tunic should have been made it clear he'd been a warrior. An unforgiving mercenary of death.

Lady Orabilia MacLaoch picked her way over the ground. Time and all its inhabitants stood still.

As she went to him, the fog slithered over the ground and around his legs as if caressing him. His eyes strayed no farther than her eyes as he pointed the tip of the Ulfberht at her. "Stop."

She shook her head as if he were daft and sidestepped it.

"Stop..." he said again, this time quieter, as if in pain, as she came up to him. She rested her hand on his outstretched forearm and pressed it down. Her other hand skated gently up his bicep, caressing his shoulder and then up to his cheek, where she cupped his face.

"You are dressed as I last saw you."

"I will not stop," he answered.

She looked at him in earnest. "You are no monster. Do not make my father's words true."

The fight drained out of him like water. His blade fell from his fingertips, and his hands took her up instead. He was a man torn by the thing he had intended to do and the bittersweet alternative that had appeared and called his heart to forget the world existed.

"He took you from me. He made you watch me die. You've cursed him. But it's not enough." His forehead rested gently upon hers.

The fog billowed up beneath her, pressing her up against his body. Her head tilted to the side, and her mouth fitted upon his. I felt a sigh move through me, and Rowan closed his eyes. Ormr's hand came up slowly as if he were drugged and settled against the side of her head. He held her there against his lips until she sighed and smiled at him.

"Love," she said, using the word as a nickname and a reason, "it's how the curse must end. We end this. Not death. Give us another chance." Her graceful finger unfurled, pointing to Rowan and me in the grass.

His eyes stayed on hers for three heartbeats before looking to where her finger commanded his gaze.

He took his eyes from us and studied the ground for a moment before looking to her, as if the thing he was about to say was heavy. "No."

"No?"

"He cannot live."

She studied his face before saying, "He is my son."

"He is the vision of your father returned."

"And yet, he is still a man innocent of the crimes you accuse him of. Can you not love him for for being the blood and bone of me?"

Ormr looked to Rowan there next to me as she continued.

"And she, she is you. They love each other as we once did. Can you see it?"

I looked at Rowan then. If Ormr disagreed... If they fought...

He looked at me and that same thought was plainly written on his face. "Fuck."

Rowan looked down at our hands, something dawning upon him. "We have the rings..."

Minory gold winked back at me off his ring finger.

Rowan grasped my wrists. I grabbed his, unsure what it meant, but Rowan seemed to know exactly what to do.

We came to our knees as Ethel crammed things into her pockets while she frantically looked at the two spirits and then to us. We couldn't hear when her chanting started, but we felt it. Our breath caught in our throats, and the skin on my palms where I grasped Rowan seared to him.

Rowan's eyes fluttered as he groaned. Whatever was happening, he was going first. Ethel worked her magic, it pulling on him as she worked her way over to us. Behind her was Eli, sword in hand.

Ormr's voice growled out; he'd seen her. "Stop this, Grandmother. It will not work, only in Valhalla will—"

"Valhalla," Orabilia's song of a voice interrupted. "Will your heart be still, in Valhalla? Or will it yearn, as it has been, for the thing it has lost? In Valhalla, you cannot wander this earth looking for it."

His jaw clenched as if he were loath to tell her the truth.

"I see," she said and touched his face; again her voice was like vanilla, warm and rich in the air around us. "Come, let us join them, be rid of your vengeance, let your soul be at peace."

He wrestled with it. I could see the dichotomy within him, wanting relief that she could give and the retribution against the pain that had torn him apart. He knew how to punish, and the men at his back urged him to do it, to fight, and the Viking in his blood knew of nothing else.

I looked at Rowan. "Come. We have to help him."

Only Rowan didn't respond; he was drugged under Ethel's spell, his lids were at half-mast and his pupils rolled into the back of his head. I got up and pulled him with me. He stood easily and followed. I was about to take a wild leap of faith with my idea. Only history would know whether it was my brightest or my last.

Ormr looked down at me. A cool breeze came off them as if they were subzero and sloughing the chill into the night air.

"What is it that you are doing, Granddaughter?" He spoke to me but kept a wary eye on Ethel.

Orabilia said, "Let her show you another path, my dear heart."

Under my breath to the semiconscious Rowan, I said, "Here we go."

Stepping into Ormr was like stepping into a coat. A coat five sizes too big. His energy was different now and bulky.

Something happened immediately. Ormr attempted control again just as our energies, his and Orabilia's, melded with Rowan's and mine. Like warm and cold air colliding, in a supernatural storm front, wind began to whip around us.

I held tight to my mind, and my hands stayed clasped to Rowan's, only now we had the ghostly representatives looming behind us. Their hands unwittingly mimicked ours, clasping wrists. With choice taken away from Ormr, the Vikings around us rioted.

Ethereal wind picked up, creating a gale that now engulfed us like a F1 tornado.

Lightning crackled across the sky. I looked to Rowan, whose hair whipped to the side, and the bright shadow behind him. Lady MacLaoch's shadow did the same, hers mimicking long ocean waves.

Just then Rowan's eyes popped open, and he looked over at me, startled to be standing.

"It's OK," I shouted, but I couldn't hear my own voice in the noise.

Ethel moved on to me as she made her way up the hill. Eli kept knocking skeletons into the air like human baseballs.

Ormr was watching. He fought me for possession, pressing into my mind like a vice around my temples.

Ethel's words, now for me ,were heard like a whisper in all the cacophony: "Repeat after me, child: 'I surrender to you, to this love, by giving you all of me from my bone, my blood, and into my spirit until my life is done.'"

I tried to repeat, but Ormr squeezed my temples, making me cry out instead. My pain was laced with his panic.

Pain begged me to end it, but tenacity said to find another way. Energy was a two-way street, while I was trying to block him, I was closing another avenue back into him. With a panting breath in preparation, I opened up. Ormr rushed in, bloating and blinding me as someone screamed from far away.

Then all was quiet.

*That was a valiant effort, Granddaughter, but now I will end this.*

Not sure about that, I responded, feeling a whole foot higher, like a spectator in the bleachers. *I'm fairly sure the conversation we're having right now is in your mind.*

I had him look over Rowan's head to Lady Orabilia and then touched on the connection between Rowan and me, pulling him to me. Rowan had been watching us, waiting for a moment when he could intercede, but now his eyes fluttered shut; his grip on my forearms tightened before there in my gut was his siren song. The shiver of fae wings over my skin. The undeniable energy echo we now used like a telephone.

"I know, you know what this feels like," I whispered in our heads. "Give in to this; trust this feeling and never let go, no matter what."

Chaos crashed all around the tunnel of wind we were in, but there, our hands clasped, was quiet. Our connection was warm flannel sheets on a cold winter's night, it was Rowan against my back kissing my neck, it was the sumptuous velvet of our bodies together, it was refuge.

Ormr fell under the spell of it and repeated what Ethel had said and I with him, "...Concede to me your heart."

Ormr's light was golden to Lady MacLaoch's silvery-blue moonlight, and for the first time, he glowed. The yellow gilded our flesh and then up and over Rowan's and Orabilia's fingertips until it blended into the blue. Their clasped hands were the incandescent mix of ocean and sun into the green of succulent forest moss. The feeling of being filled with water had my chin tilting up, gasping for air as Rowan had.

Ethel made her way through the whipping wind, her shawl yanking and snapping back behind her. Next to us, she held a quaich. Liquid sloshed out its hand-carved form as she made it to Rowan's side and put a stabilizing hand on his outstretched arm, lifted it to his lips.

"Drink," she commanded, and he sipped from it. The liquid touched his tongue, and he winced. With a nod, she then turned to me, and she put the quaich to my lips.

For a brief moment, her eyes drifted to Ormr's. "Grandson."

"Grandmother. This is not what you foretold."

"No, it is not. That is done. This is the fix to the damage created when in haste you ignored my warning and took what was not yours to take."

Ormr growled. "I took nothing."

"And yet, here we stand."

In her agitation, Ethel tilted the quaich heavily, and back in my own body, I drank down a healthy gulp. It burned like whisky on its way down, but more than warmth stretched out into my appendages. A tingling dip and tug here and there as if Rowan's and my souls were being stitched together.

The suffocating feeling released me, and our hands fell loose, we grasped each other's fingertips, unsure of what came next but very aware of the knife's edge we were standing upon.

Ethel worked quickly. Grasping my hand first, she slid Rowan's *sgian-dubh* from her belt and pricked my finger. She pulled a crumpled paper from her belt and smeared my blood at the bottom. Rowan was next.

Ethel tucked it into her belt just as the chaos surrounding us crashed in. Ethel was struck from behind; a sunlit Viking skeleton stood unperturbed in the vortex, a hammer of sorts held aloft.

Ormr looked down at his grandmother and repeated, "Your words condemned me to my fate. I took nothing."

Rowan and I reached for her. "Ethel!"

Clanspeople fought through the wind, tackling the skeleton ready to off Ethel.

Ormr roared with rage behind me. My connection to him severed.

Wincing, Ethel looked up, a hand to the back of her head. "Put your hands back!" she shouted into the winds.

Eli charged, shouting, "It's of no use! Our blades damage them, yet do not kill them!" To demonstrate, he turned on his heel and took a skeleton's head clean off in one swipe. The skeleton pieces began to recollect.

"Send them home, grandson; do not undo all we have done here!"

"You know not what you ask of me," he said and stepped back, reaching for the sword. Lady of MacLaoch made no move, save to look at him with disappointed curiosity.

Rowan's face was one of panic as he tried to move, but his body was still in the ceremonial restraints, tied to Lady MacLaoch, and she firmly kept her hands clasped in front of her.

Ormr in a feat of pure ethereal magic picked up the Ulfberht and brandished it at Eli. Without Ormr in my body, I had no idea how to fight against him much less how to move his body so that he didn't lay waste to my cousin.

Ethel was shouting.

I gave her a glance; she was shouting at me. "Intent!" Then pointed at Ormr. "Intent!"

Ormr lifted his arm to cut his blade across Eli. I looked at him and reflexively, simply opened my hand. His striking hand faltered. He looked at it with a questioning pinch of his face. Then brought it back again, and this time I found myself opening my hand, but the intent was to be Ormr releasing the sword.

He dropped the sword.

I smiled.

He swiped it up with his other hand.

My smile vanished as I followed suit and opened my left hand, making the sword fall. He hunched over, grasping for it. He glared over his shoulder at me.

"Stop this, granddaughter."

I didn't know how to fight with a sword, but I could play hot potato all day.

"No. I've asked you to forget all this anger business," I said, grunting as I opened my hand; he was actively setting his intent on his own hand controls. It was like a wrestling match over the game controls. "But you've flatly refused, wanting to instead play stabby-stabby with the people I love. So"—I wrestled again—"we're going to play this hot potato game until you concede to a life of happiness with the woman you love. Send your men home."

"No."

"My god, you are stubborn. Lucky for you, we're one and the same. So, deny yourself for eternity—I'll be here protecting my loved ones, just like you would."

"You don't understand what he's done—"

"Rowan has done nothing—"

He stopped wrestling for control to argue at me. "He has tied us down and beheaded us! He has shown that he has his grandfather's alliance. He'll no more care for you then he will slowly kill your spirit!"

"I may not know what it means to be tied down and beheaded, may I never know, and I feel awful about the whole damn thing! But do not tell me about Rowan. I know him down to his marrow, and he will not—"

Ormr barked out a laugh. "You mistake me," he said, pointing to his temple. "I am you, as you have said, which means that while you have not walked in my shoes, I've walked in yours since you were a babe. So, tell me, what of this Charmaine woman? Why was she not dealt with? Why was she allowed to fester like a wound for a year? Do not lie to us— I am you, and you are me."

Oh, Charmaine. I'd had it right up to over my head with people's opinions that she held sway over Rowan and me. She wanted to take Rowan from me, calling me inadequate and bullying me into running. And now Ormr wanted to blatantly kill Rowan simply because of who his ancestral grandfather was. I'd had enough.

I looked down; I hadn't realized I'd moved much less picked up the dropped Ulfberht. I held it there in my fists. I felt something of Ormr's anger detonate in my chest and flood up to my head, making the whole field go red. Magic within the liquid Ethel had given me still vibrated in my veins, and with my anger spike, it spilled out my pores, and I felt downright on fire.

"Don't," I said, hissing, "you dare tell me what to do, who to love, or what Rowan means to me."

I was uphill from Ormr, and we stared at each other, my eyes looked back at me.

"I do this to protect you! You must not succumb to the MacLaoch schemes as they will—"

"Is that what Orabilia did?" The field seemed to shimmer when I said her name. "Did she burn you? Or did she try to change her father's opinions and start something new with you?" When he gave me no answer, I bellowed, "She followed her heart!"

"She is of no—" he said and reached for the Ulfberht.

"I don't think so." I kept it out of his reach.

By this point, the skeletons were confused. Their allegiance had split in two. Ormr was their chief, but I was his blood and wielding the Ulfberht. And if I wasn't mistaken, my skin was on fire. Gold fire like a dragon's breath.

*Dodge,* whispered into my mind, sounding much like Rowan, just as Ormr lunged. I leaned back, but it was too late. He grabbed my neck with one hand and reached for the sword with his other. I tucked it behind me. I gaged and coughed as my esophagus touched my spine.

Rowan roared as Ormr shouted, "Stop this game! I will not be kind."

I hissed, gagging, clawing at his hand. "You forget that I am you a thousand years later. You lived a life that was hard and well won, but I've inherited more than just your looks."

Furious, he then lifted me up by my neck.

# Thirty-Five

It's an unusual feeling that, being held up by the neck. The elongation of the spine is nice, but the suffocation and blood pulsing against your eye sockets are wildly uncomfortable. But also, your feet are free.

Ormr yanked me into him to get the sword, and I used his power against him to ram him like a stick of wood over the nail of my knee. It is a universal truth that the nut sack of a human male contains micro tacks that explode when hit.

His breath exploded out, and I was back on my feet, but his hand at my throat didn't release but tightened.

Gagging, I used my fist with the Ulfberht in it to sock him in the jaw, hard and repeatedly, until I was convinced I'd dislocated all five of my fingers.

Ballistic determination mixed with my vexation, and air quickly depleting, I grabbed his pinkie finger at my throat and yanked. I was willing to rip the ghostly thing off if need be.

Ormr hollered and released me, but he was now a volcano of rage. We were a nice, matched set.

"Petulant, feeble—"

"Yield!"

"To what?!"

"To me! To your love for Orabilia. Yield!" Thunder smashed against lightning, shaking the earth.

"You know not what you—"

"Yes, I do! God forbid you will allow yourself to love, to be loved, to spend your days in the afterlife at peace instead of keeping hate as your best friend as it eats you from the inside out. Look at what you've done! Look! You're going to tear my life apart; the curse will not be done! It will be repeated! This is not the end; this is the beginning of a never-ending cycle!"

He was breathing through his teeth as he stood. "Petulant child! My men were slaughtered! Only in Valhalla will we be at peace, having won the war against the man who started this curse. Your Rowan will never have a descendant to continue this curse. That, I promise."

*Rowan will never have a descendant.* Those words felt like a threat I'd never felt before. It was then that something within me opened and spilled out. Something that was older than Ormr and woven into the genetic framework of humanity: *save your babies.* My brain didn't see them as something that didn't exist yet, but rather they were in me, and in Rowan, waiting.

A kind of sickened calm shook down over me. I viscerally related to the ancient MacLaoch chief who severed Ormr's head.

I stood. Ormr reached for me. With two fists on the hilt, I sliced the Ulfberht around. Ormr growled and blocked; the Ulfberht pinged off his golden cuff. But surprise crossed his features; he was unprepared to go up against himself.

I was Ormr, in a way, and in that way, I used Ormr's instincts. Instincts he'd honed in battle.

Using his surprise, I kicked the inside of his knee, and Ormr stumbled. I roared and brought the Ulfberht back; he leaned out of the way, and following the sword with my foot, I nailed his knee again. This time he turned the joint into my strike—leaving his legs open like a lunge.

Then things got dirty. I let out a whooping cry and put the Ulfberht over my head to strike down. He blocked. Only it was the wrong thing to block. I had one and only fight move, and it worked again.

Ormr staggered forward after my second connection with his nuts, and I helped him hit the dirt with a kick to the same knee.

There was a moment when I thought of taking off his head. He had thought that Rowan's lineage was the only kind that would take a man's head off. He was wrong. Mine, his, our lineage would do it too. To protect, to defend, to end the thing we could not control.

But I was not a man at war. I was a woman given a set of circumstances that were ripe for repeating, and it was up to me to end that cycle.

Ormr was down. I moved quickly, and without remorse, I pointed the tip of the Ulfberht at him. "Yield to my path forward, Grandpappy."

His narrowed eyes sliced to mine. "Do not negotiate the with the blade pointed at me. I will neither yield—"

There was a cacophony of bodies being struck as Ethel's voice called to me through Rowan. Over the howling wind, I heard: *He's too strong. He must be unconscious or dead with the Ulfberht wielded by you for you and the MacLaoch to finish your tie!*

I looked to Orabilia. "Please!"

She smiled in return and slowly shook her head. "He is you. There is no place for me between you."

Fed up, I whipped the Ulfberht across the field, and Ormr smiled as if I'd lost my mind.

I grabbed the lower jaw of his open mouth like it was a purse handle. He yanked back in surprise, but his lower mandible was firm in my grip, and like a crazed maniac, I punched him. His arm came up, but I yanked him forward, making his hand reach out for balance, then hit again. And again. There was a goodnight switch somewhere around his jaw. I knew this from human anatomy, and I'd fucking find it.

"No one"—punch—"I mean, *no one*"—punch—"Is. Taking. That. From. Me." Punch. Punch. Punch.

He grabbed and bit, and I pounded. It was me, my fist and the side of his face, over and over.

Wind slapped against us.

"Yield!" I shouted just before kneeing him in the gut and releasing his abused jaw.

Ormr was on the ground where he'd fallen back, face bloodied.

"Take me to Valhalla, granddaughter," he said, arms wide.

I looked to the sword in the grass. I felt the endless haunting of him like a talisman, and for one wild second, I thought of sliding it between his ribs.

"Do it!" he challenged.

The wind rustled what was left of my ripped dress and made the grass beneath him lie flat.

Just as I dove for the Ulfberht, Orabilia threw her arms wide, and the air vacuumed in off the ocean, flattening the grass in the other direction. Lying back in the grass, Ulfberht in hand, I felt the moment when we held our collective breath just before she brought her hands back in a clap. The clouds above us erupted as lightning struck the ground in a fiery rope. I covered my head as hot air blasted past me.

The air crackled with static electricity, and I groaned and rolled over. The ground was blackened, and the edges of my dress were smoldering. I cursed and came to my knees, smacking them out.

Ormr was on all fours. "What have you done?" he hollered at Orabilia.

All around us was blackened, and a low meadow fire slowly crept along the damp brush, unsure whether it should die out or turn into a bigger version of itself. Everything in the field was gone: strings, flags, plants.

"Fool." Her voice carried over the field.

He was panting now and stood. "What have you done?" he wailed, and it was then that I realized his skeleton crew was gone. Clansfolk staggered over the hillside, trying to get their bearings as their opponents were suddenly gone.

"Fool," Lady MacLaoch said again as she picked her way over to him, her hands out wide; energy was actively being siphoned out of the earth in blue flames into her hands. Rowan had been released by her. The ceremony stood broken now. Rowan looked as if he were done with all this shit, and he was going to marry me no matter what.

*I'm coming to you.*

Ethel whispered to him, and he nodded, quaich in his hand, and made for me on the other side of the field. And I made my way to him, a watchful eye on Orabilia and Ormr.

Lady MacLaoch continued, "Have you not heard a single thing your granddaughter has said to you?"

"Where are my men?"

"Is that all you care about?" she said, and that graceful finger unfurled again as she blew into the air. Out on the loch was a dragon ship; its sail caught her ethereal breath and left for the horizon. "They return to Valhalla, where you pulled them from. Were they all that you searched for, in this life that is no life, the between worlds that you called home for the last millennium? Or was it something more?"

"Wench, you will bring my men back to me!"

She tsked, and it sounded like a ticking bomb. "I will not."

But Ormr wasn't listening, he caught sight of Rowan coming to me and thundered, "No!"

I, Ulfberht in hand, hoped the intent bit that Ethel had explained to me still worked. I raised it and then plunged it in the soil, hoping for a protective shield around me that Rowan could enter. The possessed sword lit like sun fire, and as the tip pierced the ground, it drew a wide arch of blazing fire around me.

"Fuck," I whispered That was not what I wanted.

Fire surrounding me, I listened in disbelief as Rowan's voice warmed my skin: *Aye, good* mo ghràdh.

With a whip of his tartan end over his head, he sprinted through the fire and erupted through it with just smoke touching him.

I stumbled to him. "Oh my, Rowan—"

He was all business. "Drink this."

"My granddaughter is mine to take to Valhalla," Ormr boomed to Rowan.

Orabilia was now an active participant. "So, you will become my father? You will behead the man who loves her? You will make her watch, as I watched you?"

He looked back down at her, his protest on his lips, but he was listening to her.

I took the quaich into my hands before I realized Rowan was glowing blue with his grandmother's powers.

"Wait," he said and looked back at Ethel. Rowan, *sgian-dubh* in hand, stood next to me and whispered urgently under his breath, "Give me your hand."

He wove his fingers between mine and trapped the blade between our palms and drew it out. I felt the blade slice across my skin but felt no pain. I was sure it was going to hurt like the devil later and crack and bleed at every opportunity. But that was a worry for later.

I felt my hair lift as Rowan, taking orders from Ethel, put our blood mix into the quaich.

I had no idea what for, but I prayed we didn't drink it.

My prayers were not answered.

Rowan drank first, then put it to my lips. I shook my head but drank down the now bloody slurry. Then tried not to vomit it back up.

I gagged, and the quaich dropped. Rowan's hands were on my neck, pulling my body in against his.

"*Tha gaol agam ort,*" he mumbled against my ear.

"I love you too," I said, clutching him in return; chanting once again filled our bodies and minds.

Ethel with Eli at her elbow moved back down the hill and was now with Bernie and Angus once more.

Rowan pulled me in even tighter, "With your blood within me, I am now bound."

I repeated his words. "With your blood within me, I am now— "

"No!" screamed Ormr and pointed at Rowan.

Lady MacLaoch was at his elbow and touched him gently. "They are doing what we could not."

He looked back down to her. "I tried," he said at last.

"You did, and I did. I wanted you and no other man. I yearned to make something new, to watch your scowl turn into a smile when it was only you and I."

He scowled at her then. "It was not meant to be."

"No, it wasn't," she agreed. "However, that is done; it is the past, and here we stand face-to-face in a short window of time to remake our past, to do away with old angers and make a new memory, a different destiny, and bless the children who are us reimagined. With them, we may see our love realized and come to life through their children. Our children, a thousand years later."

Ormr, defeated, fell on all fours to the burnt ground, his head hanging. From down there he said, "How can I accept a life that will not be rewarded in heavenly splendor? Valhalla is where—"

"Where we are going," she said, confused as to how he could have thought otherwise. "Let us be free in the life that comes next. Let our souls be now at ease."

He gave into her power, and as he stood, I looked to Rowan. His eyes were on Ethel. Rowan spoke swiftly. "Bound to you forever, next to you, and within you. From this life into the next. I share with you my love, my bond, and this oath. For eternity," he finished saying down to me, his eyes searching mine for its match.

Orabilia held her hands out and pulled Ormr to his feet while speaking as Rowan had.

I knew my part now and responded, as did my ancient grandfather, "For eternity."

The earth shook beneath our feet as if tectonic plates were settling into place. It shook my insides, making the horizon tilt.

I gripped Rowan tight as I felt my feet come off the ground. Rowan wrapped his arms around me as lighting cracked the sky open.

Ormr Minorrisson stood unaffected by the wind and thunder, a gentle smile on his face as he gave in to the quiet power of his one true love.

Orabilia said, "Ours has never been an easy love, has it?"

"No," he agreed.

"But now it will be." She met his gaze, and I understood then what it took to love a man like him—more than strength, more than sheer will, it was patience and faith.

"And so it will be," he said, looking to us through the vortex.

She caressed his face as he bent and kissed her.

Rowan and I felt the sigh, the release of the fight. The ground shook again. "It's time." Lady MacLaoch said then to her great-grandson, "The future is now your own self-made destiny."

I held on to Rowan as he nodded. "Goodbye."

He bent his head over mine, his eyes the color of sapphires. I closed my eyes as our lips found each other in love and also in relief. We were there, together, now through eternity. Just as we sunk into the sighing gladness of the kiss, the air surrounding us detonated.

Rowan and I winced, his arms going vice-like around me.

Air pressure pushed down upon us, first taking us to our knees, then shoved us flat to the ground. The sky split open then, and in a flash of blinding white, the vortex we were in collapsed upon us.

Rowan cursed as it pounded down like a thundering waterfall of air. Air shot into our noses and mouths unwillingly, pressing in at all angles, making us feel as if we were drowning. My eyes watered, and just as I wrestled to put my hands over my face, panic gripped my guts. After all that, right there in that field of death, we would die too.

Then it winked out.

My hand flew out with the sudden loss of air pressure, and I blinked in surprise. Rowan and I expelled our breaths. The quiet night air crept in, like that with a door shut on a thunderous party. I continued to blink tears back into my dry eyes and catch my breath as I rolled over. Rowan sat back, hands on his thighs, breathing like a marathoner after the final sprint.

Clanspeople groaned and sat up. Others held on to others' helping hands as they slowly got to their knees.

The grass was trampled and blackened, and stacks of rocks now surrounded us on the hillside that had once been covered in thick layers of native meadow plants and detritus. I cried. I sobbed at the sheer destruction of the field, our near loss of lives, and also the intense relief that it all was over.

The people were bloody and staggering about on the hillside. In the quiet, Rowan and I took a shuddering breath and looked at each other. A sense of déjà vu—only this time he wasn't also shot.

The night sky had gone clear, and the moonlight shone bright upon the field. Rowan's alter ego, the man who'd seen war and the inside of a cockpit, looked at me. His gaze was dark and distant, "Ye all right?" he asked, pulling me into his lap, wiping away my tears.

Reality made me mumble as I looked around in an existential crisis, "All right? What does that mean, all right? I'm physically functioning, but is all of me right with the world? I don't know."

This made him smile. "Aye, you're just fine then, wife."

Then, like a grounding rod, I felt whole; the sound of Rowan calling me wife made me smile, "Yes, actually, I think I just might be, husband."

We looked at our rings, smiling like fools, then to each other, and I whispered the words he used so often I now knew them by heart, "*Mo ghràdh, tha gaol agam ort,*" then put my hand to his cheek before sealing it with a kiss.

"Aye, my love, I love ye too."

"Forever."

"Always."

# Thirty-Six

Rowan and I stood and dusted off ash, burnt soil, and fear for our lives. My dress was torn halfway up my hip, and droplets of blood were on its grass-stained front. Rowan shoved his dark tartan higher up his shoulder, and his knees were bloody and grass stained. The only thing clean and unbloodied about us were our golden rings winking in the moonlight. Rowan reached out and gently took my hand and looked at the ring on my finger. "Aye, it's over, then?" he asked quietly. The warrior who had come out, I could see he was desperately trying to put him back into the box where he lived.

"It is," I whispered and quickly made to touch his face, only Rowan flinched.

He looked away but wove my fingers through his and held tight.

"Aye, Ethel, Eli, ye all right?"

Eli was helping Ethel to stand.

She held up a paper. "Alive, and it's legal," she said with a rare Ethel grin.

There was a smattering of claps from those standing within earshot and a whoop from Eli. "We did it." He grinned at Rowan.

We made it to his side, and Rowan said, "Aye, mate, tha' was a good idea ye had."

They shared an inside grin about something I had no idea about.

Around us, people made their way to standing, and the look of shock and disbelief mirrored on every face on that field. His clanspeople began gathering toward him, looking to him to have something to say.

I felt my own gut quake at the expectant faces.

Rowan was an expert at the helm "Aye, Reggie," he said, nodding to the head gardener.

"Aye sir," the older man replied as he held the two halves of a broken rake.

"Take the wounded inside. Is auld Mac 'ere?" he called to the crowd. "We need a doctor." In seconds he rallied his clanspeople again into action. First, we'd aid the physically wounded; then we'd see to the rest.

I helped shuffle the injured up the castle steps into the library, then into the office where there was good lighting. Cots were being gathered from shuttered rooms where they had been stored and antiseptic and wraps were being brought up.

THE LIBRARY WAS FILLED NOW, AND AS I WRAPPED THE LAST sprained wrist and gave him a pat, I saw Rowan had in one hand three cups clasped between his fingers and was freely pouring whisky into them. He smiled at his men and women, told them they did a fine job. They'd made him proud, and as the whisky continued to flow, the stories began.

Kyle told his story of diving into a fairy pool and taking the legendary ring itself from the fingers of the silkies that lived beneath its surface. Enamored faces listened then clapped him on the shoulder for a job well done. Ethel gave him a wink just before throwing back her portion of the whisky. I wove my way through the beds and reclining bodies to where she sat. Eli was next to her at the end of the long wooden table. The volume in the room increased as the dispersal of whisky did.

Over the boisterous recounting of tales, I nudged Eli's side as he looked down at me.

"Hi," I said.

"Och," he said, "Hi, cuz, how are ye. Are ye all right? I cannae live with myself if I hurt ye."

"I think I'm the only one who doesn't have a scratch on me," I said. "Sorry for all the punching, kneeing, and sword-jabby business."

"Oh, aye, it's all right. Just the sword poke got me a kiddie-size bandage. I'll live."

I smiled at him, but his demeanor sobered, he had more on his mind.

He shook his head. "I'm not sure what I've just seen or what I've done, much less what tae do about it." He looked up, his gaze attaching to Rowan as he moved through the room, the mugs seemingly multiplying in his very grasp. "He's a magnificent human, eh?"

Rowan's hair was tousled like he'd stood under leaf blower that was trying to disintegrate him into the earth. His hands were cut on the knuckles and bruised, and his eye was still marred with dried blood.

"He is," I said of my husband. Something about him called to me; things weren't right. He was holding something inside; his gaze didn't find mine when my eyes rested upon him. It was our thing, to talk without talking.

"I hear you about not understanding what we went through today," I said taking a deep breath, "Not sure I ever will. But we went through it together, right?"

He grinned back at me. "Aye, we did."

"So, if you ever need to talk about it, we'll be here for you."

He took my hand into his and gave it a squeeze. "And I for ye."

"Thanks, cuz," I said and stood and hugged him while he sat. "Be right back."

I wove through our clanspeople smiling—it was the surefire trick I quickly learned that kept everyone confident I was not in Viking mode. I got to Rowan's side and touched his back before gently taking the mugs from him and handing them to Bernie, who was waiting next for whisky. "Would you be a gent and pass these out?" I asked, and at Rowan's raised brow, I took the bottle of whisky and handed it over too.

"Oh aye, and what do ye think you're doing?" He looked at me as if I were intruding.

"There's one last person who needs medical treatment," I said. "Come with me?"

A few whistles came from next to us. "Och, gow wit 'er. Finish what ye both started!"

He made a guttural Scots agreement, but he pointed at Bernie. "There better be some left when I get back."

Bernie raised the bottle up, Angus next to him with the cups. "We make no promises, my liege! Take yer bride and be gone with ye!"

Up in his fairy tower office, I had Rowan sit on the corner of his desk, his hands rested loosely on the corner between his legs. He was the vision of cool, save for the corners of his eyes where he held himself firmly in check.

I tilted his chin and dabbed antiseptic across his brow. Rowan sucked in air between his teeth but made no movement away from me.

"Sorry," I whispered and dabbed at the dried blood until it became like paste and finally came up on my ball of cotton.

"It's all right."

The night was still large outside, and gentle clouds had moved in, making dark dots above the moonlit loch.

With the last of his blood washed away, I put my things down and put both my hands on either side of his deeply lined face. Worry cut at the corners of his wide eyes, doing things he didn't want to do roughened his mouth, and the hardness of having to be war chief took a chunk of light out of his eyes.

I tilted his gaze up to mine; he looked me over, and then his gaze went down once more.

"What is it?" I whispered.

"It's to be over now, aye?" he said of the curse.

"Yes, I feel it, don't you?"

"Aye," he said but there in the low light of his office, away from the expectant faces of his people, he whispered out some of his darkness. "I think something dark came out of me tonight. I might not be able tae put it back. Likely, I'm full broken now."

My heart clenched. "Broken?" I cradled his cheek. "In what way, hon?"

He looked up at me, remorse fully in his gaze, "Watching ye be lifted by yer neck while I powerless to help ye... Before that, I choked the life out of ye and brought my fist against your face. I think of it, and it makes me sick. Yes, ye were the brawn of your ancestor, but my eyes show me over and over cracking ye across the jaw and my fist feeling it."

"No, don't do this to yourself. I didn't feel it like you did. You were a sparring partner to him; I feel nothing other than the exertion of a fair fight."

My words didn't help. His eyes were anguished. "I hit ye. Like a monster," he said, his eyes glittering, emotion welling up.

I could almost hear other words: *Like my father.*

I groaned in pain with him. I wanted to bathe him in nice words, say that he was nothing like his father. But hard things didn't like softness. Instead of trying to reassure him, I dove into the heart of it with him. "You did hit me."

His gaze held mine.

"If I were doing anything else but trying to kill you while being possessed by a man twice your size, it would not be right," I said, kissing his cheek. "But as it was, if you hadn't, you'd have been dead in seconds. There was no other path. But you know this."

It was there within my words that he found his anguish and looked away. "I know it."

I brought his face back with my fingertips on his chin. "So, what is it, really?"

His eyes sparkled with restrained emotion. "What if this isn't the end?"

"What if the curse keeps coming for more?"

"Last year, I sat like this in the hospital, sure it was done. This time, it feels like it nearly took it all this time. It's only luck that has us sitting here, nothing more," he whispered then hit the nail on the head of his pain: "I just keep thinking that if I'd done something more, if I'd gone with you up to the room to change, we could have avoided all of this." He took a deep breath that shook his body with something that was deeper than the moment "Had I just tried harder... I've felt this way before. With Vick, had I done something different, I could have avoided it all."

"Oh," I said and pulled him into my embrace.

He hugged me back.

I nodded; the side of my head was against his as I did. "Luck is just the manifestation of a good plan. Sure, there's chaos to deal with, but it's not an accident. You made choices tonight that kept everyone alive. You couldn't save Vick, but today, the decisions you made saved me."

I felt another of his shuddering breaths under my arms. "I wish I felt the way you see it," he said and leaned back.

"You will. Maybe not today but likely tomorrow, definitely next week." I gave him a quiet smile. "If it makes you feel better, you can kiss all the spots you hit and remark on how miraculously unscathed my skin is. Seriously, Rowan, it's almost creepy that I haven't bruise on me."

"Magic," he whispered, looking me over. Rowan stood and gently took my chin in his fingers, turning my head from one side to the other. "Now, which side did I clock ye?"

I grinned. "I think it was my right?"

"Aye," he said and bent to kiss my cheek, his lips gentle. "Just for good measure," and he kissed my other one.

I looked up as he lowered his lips to mine, and there he placed the softest of them all and whispered, "I'm sorry. I'll never raise my hand against you again."

He smiled down at me, and I ran my hand down his stomach and braced myself there for a full lip-locked kiss. Rowan winced.

"Are you OK?" I asked.

"Oh, I'm fine—"

I didn't wait for him to finish; I lifted his shirt to discover a Cole-fist-size bruise over his diaphragm. "Oh, my stars, Rowan..."

"It's nothing."

But it was purple and ugly. I swallowed. I had been a lot more powerful than I'd realized. I'd scared the life out of our clanspeople, cousin, and now Rowan. I understood then like I hadn't just a bit ago, while full Viking, it was my face that Ormr used that scared the dark place out of Rowan and my face that nearly robbed him of everything, including his life.

My fingertips were gentle upon the bruised skin, the place where the muscles formed the valley between his abdominals. The humps of those muscles were worked and firm. I dipped my head and whispered against the bruise, "I'm sorry." And with the lightness of a butterfly's wings, I brushed my dry lips across the hot, angry skin.

Rowan hissed in.

I looked up at him in concern. "Do you think there's something broken inside? Maybe old Mac should see this."

He just shook his head. "My stomach is just bruised. It's been a long time since I've been struck tha' hard." He seemed to look at something in the distance and corrected himself. "No, I've never been struck tha' hard."

I groaned inwardly. "I feel like today might be the antithesis of the very idea of a wedding. I ache for the alternative, that we're blissfully happy and consummating our happy union. Instead," I whispered, "we've a survived a battle with ancients and come out alive, but barely."

I let his shirt down when he didn't answer. I had to see his other scar, the one on his shoulder. The one from the last encounter with Lady MacLaoch. I undid the first button on his Henley before his hand came to mine, stopping me. His touch was warm, but his voice was far from it. "Stop. I'm not ready for tha' yet."

"Oh, I, I just want to see it, your scar? From last year." I wasn't sure how I felt about him saying no to sex, but I pushed it to the back of my mind.

His eyes studied me for another second then released me. I finished with the last button and pushed his shirt and tartan aside. It was a neat, straight, raised line above the rod of his collarbone, the work of a talented surgeon unlike the one at his hip. He had two bullet holes and now a bruised diaphragm.

Apparently, Rowan and the man I descended from were men who knew how to fight, knew how to better their opponents. Rowan would feel better in a few days, maybe, but the work had to start now, or he might never see his way out. In another way he and Ormr were alike, when it came to the intricacies of allowing themselves joy and pursuit of love, they grasped at straws. Rowan knew dark things, knew the roads within hell like a well-read map. Out in the light of day, surrounded by unicorns and puppies, he didn't know how to grab happiness and ride away from the darkness. Seeing the bruise, I gave him on his diaphragm, I understood some of what he felt. And knowing him as I did, I understood how he couldn't ride from the darkness. Luckily, there were two of us now. I could show him how it was done.

I whispered, "This is your dark place, isn't it?"

"I just need some time." His hand skated up my arm, gently wrapped his fingers around my wrist, and pulled my hand off him.

It was quietly done, gently, but it felt as if the Grand Canyon was just placed between us.

"I should go," he said.

Several years ago, my mother had called me. I was in grad school across the country. TJ was home on a break from what seemed like an endless war in the middle east. His unit had been stateside for a week, and it had become apparent in the first two days that TJ was in a bad place. He'd been working with my dad in the fields, been surrounded by family, but something was wrong. He'd smile to me on video chat, but he was my brother, I knew a smile that was to make *me* feel better versus a smile that came from *within* him. I was on a plane and in his space in under eight hours. It took another eight hours of being a young pup pushing under his hand before he cracked. He was made from the same blood and bone, he and I. No one had dared to press him, and they didn't think they should. "He'll be fine." "Just needs time." I didn't know what he needed consciously. I knew I needed to be with him, and then I would figure out what needed to be done. I knew when to press and when to give in. When to crack a joke, when to hold his shoulders in a hug, and when to start a fight to get him talking. In the middle of the peach orchard, field ten, the day before I was to leave back for school, he cracked. There'd been two men, a downed plane, blood was everywhere, one man lived and the other they scooped his brain out of the sand and put him in a body bag. He shouted as he relived it, sweat it out in the South Carolina heat and then collapsed in a heap, sobbing for the horrors of it. We cried together that day. I walked alongside him within his darkness, and we dealt with it together. Darkness was like that; it was easier with a friend.

"Thank you for my hand back," I said now to Rowan. "I was worried it was going to get too cold up there all by itself."

He repeated, "I should see to my peop—"

"They're three sheets to the wind by now and no doubt emptying the kitchens. I also saw Marion and Flora down there; in their capable hands, I doubt *our* clanspeople will need you for days."

"Cole..."

I shook my head. "Remember what you said in the forest?" I reminded him quietly, "We do everything together. This is one of those together times." I felt out of my depth but knew that distance now could very well lead to something more complicated later.

"This is different."

"Different how?"

"This is about ye. It's about my mind," he said, jabbing a finger into his temple. "Being fucked up and not knowing what tae do about how I feel about ye. Am I scared? In love? Fighting for my life against ye?"

His Scots got thick, his tell that he was working a peaked emotional state.

I nodded. I looked down in my hands. "I'm fine. We survived but I understand; I have never been so out of control in my entire life too. Kind of makes me want to barf thinking about it."

His eyes quieted. "Aye, licking yer own blood will do that."

My own eyes fluttered shut before I had to pinch the bridge of my nose to keep the nausea in my stomach from taking over. "Oh, that was..." I let out a tiny burp. "Ormr was all *This is great; we're really fighting now*, but in reality, that's the most disgusting thing I've ever put in my mouth."

This made his lips twitch; he was amused.

"Oh aye, Mrs. MacLaoch, come now, is tha' why ye don't touch the blood pudding?"

This made my head snap back to his. "Say that again," I whispered and touched his lips with my fingertips in wonder at the beauty of what they'd just said.

"Is tha' why—"

"No, the missus part."

This made his beautiful angst-ridden mouth shake off the tight darkness at either side of it and spread wide into a smile, showing me a glimpse of his miraculously straight bone-white teeth. "*Mrs. MacLaoch.* Aye, I know yer name, it's not officially changed yet, but I like the ring of it."

"It's so possessive. Yet I want it. It makes my heart pinch with longing for it." I went up on my toes, brushed my lips over his. "I love you, my official husband, my Mr. Rowan James Douglas MacLaoch, thirty-fourth clan chief of the MacLaochs."

"And I ye, Mrs. Rowan James Douglas MacLaoch."

I laughed, both at the absurdity of losing one's entire identity behind their husband's name and the beauty of losing your full self in the one you've deigned to be your true love.

"I like it," I said and kissed him as his hand wove into the base of my hair and softly fisted it there. "Though I'll probably just add you to my already long list of names: Nicole "Cole" Ransome Minory Baker MacLaoch."

"That works too." He groaned, realizing something. "I believe we should tell Mickey the coast is clear."

"Or let him finish whatever it is he's doing to or with Charmaine."

"Aye, now that's a plan."

"Casswell and Associates... Charmaine is going to shit a brick when she realizes that we're legally married. I think that half the clan participating in it will be enough to keep her from demanding your chief title, but...something tells me she's going to be the vision of Woman Scorned."

Rowan's gaze stayed on mine. "Casswell, I'll deal with. The clan was here as witnesses, and it was done more proper-like than any other marriage on the books, I gather. As for Charmaine, she will be a right burr in our side, but I don't care."

I nodded and looked beyond him, thinking about how we'd have to deal with her. Her and her desk-desecrating ways. How she was able to make me look at desks and see not a useful place to write but rather an illicit surface perfect for destroying relationships was beyond me.

His fingers were on my chin again. "And ye, ye have your own dark place, Cole."

I shrugged. "It's just a desk."

His brows pinched together; he did not follow my line of thinking.

"Not dark, per se, but just wishing I had a mental erase button. But after everything that's happened tonight, it doesn't matter. It's like a pebble in my shoe. No, a thorn in my side. Or, no, like being attacked by a crow. Not all crows attack, but I might cross the street when I see another one in a tree."

He nodded, mischief in his eyes. "I see, a crow?"

"They're tenacious creatures."

"Mm." His chin ducked, and his nose tapped against my cheek. "Maybe, but let's put something to rest, aye? Put your bottom on the desk's front edge."

# Thirty-Seven

"Ew, why?" I crinkled my nose and laughed. "You're not going to make me reenact what I saw you and Charmaine doing in the library are you?"

"That's exactly what we're going to do."

Some might laugh and say, "OK!" but there was a twist in my brain, a twist that said, *No, that's gross*, a twist of pride that said I was not Charmaine and re-creating anything she did with Rowan would be like self-flagellation.

"Pass."

He nodded. "Sound reasoning. I only mention it because ye and I have never done it on a desk. A loch, cliff's edge, forest, settee, Persian rug," he said, looking pointedly behind me at said rug, then back, "and every surface in our desk-less cottage, but not this here." He pointed to its warm wood surface.

"Oh, Rowan, but that's comparing—"

"Nay. Not comparing. Let's call it a fact-finding mission, aye?"

"Fact-finding?"

"Aye. You trust me, right?"

I smiled at the glint that was still in his eye, "All right. Let's find some facts on this desk. Clothes on or off to start?"

"We'll get there," he said then thought better of it, "maybe."

He turned me just a bit and said, "That's how they all start. Just someone standing with their back to the desk."

"Is that a fact? Or conjecture?" I asked, smiling.

Only he answered with his finger. He gently pressed against my hip, giving me the gentlest of nudges, "Just stand in front of it, and we'll continue with this conversation."

I folded my arms over my chest and played along. "Sure," I said and sat my ass on the broad front edge of the desk. Pencil holders, brass note pad holder, and paperweights were gently nudged out of the way. "I am quite literate on how one might go about having sex on a desk, Rowan."

"I'm sure ye are. Now, will you help me, though?" he said, and his fingers went to his shoulder, "The end has come loose, he said, holding the tartan at his shoulder.

"Oh," I said, derailed from our conversation, "yeah, don't you need your clasp?"

"Aye."

I half expected him to tell me to tuck it into his belt, just behind his sporran, directly over his crotch. It would be the perfect segue into penis play, but he didn't. And frankly, he'd gotten a lot less lusty—he was downright dry and matter-of-fact.

I remembered seeing his clasp on the desk. "I think I remember seeing it..." I turned, looking over the desk contents. It was there on the far corner. I scooted farther onto the desk, and with a leg up to balance me, I reached over and got it.

I sat up with it and found Rowan innocently between my legs. "Mind if ye can pin it here? I'll hold the fabric," he said as he looked down to where his fingers held the fabric out to me.

I smiled and as I pinned it on said, "Well played, hon."

He looked down at me through his lashes, his eyebrows raised in question. "What's that?"

My feet came around the back of his legs and brought him in even closer, "You just happened to suddenly be so close."

He leaned against the desk between my thighs. "I just need your help with this." His breath was warm over my knuckles as I shoved the pin through the fabric and secured the metal of the clan crest over his heart.

He picked up my hand and put his lips to the backs of my fingers. "Step one. Now, ye know how you get onto a desk."

"And step two?"

"There aren't any steps, *ghràdh*," he said, being purposefully hypocritical, and gave me my hand back. I braced myself back on the desk. His desk was full of paperwork and a large calendar took up the center of it. The desk calendar was slippery. It slid, and I shifted my hand to the side of it, but it took up the entire writing area. I looked at the offending thing behind me and slid it as much to the side as I could. Rowan made to grab the pencil holder that threatened to topple, but I grabbed it in time. Only my other hand now had my full weight on the slippery calendar. It flew back, and things blew everywhere.

"Whoa!" I shouted as I fell back. My leg went up in the air, and Rowan lunged forward to grab for me. His hands caught my wrists as the calendar crashed to the floor with paperweights, papers, and writing utensils.

He pulled me up laughing; his eyes were twinkling gemstones. There, half back on the desk, my wrists braced in his strong grip, I realized we were in step two.

"Ye all right?"

I laughed with him. "I am. This is messy business, being on a desk."

He let my wrists go and came down over me, bracing his hands next to me, and bent his head. "It is."

I still wore the dress from the battlefield. The rip was right up to my thigh, and as things are when you're possessed and taken for a battle ride, you don't really think about what you're wearing until your husband is bent over you and whispering words over your chest. It's then that you realize silk is just opaque air.

His warm breath reminded me that I was cold in that upper castle room and that his breath was a stark contrast to the chill I felt all the way down to my dirty bare feet.

I shivered.

He looked up at me through the dark crescents of his lashes—his lips had been just above my nipple, but he was soon speaking against the tight peak of my left one as he said, "Ye seem cold?"

"A little bit."

He rested some of his weight on me, and as I was back on my elbows, my neck muscles strained, and suddenly I was flat as a pancake. Rowan brought me up to sitting. There he kissed me soundly.

"*Tha gaol agam ort,*" he whispered against my lips.

My neck craned back. "I love you too. Now can we go to our comfortable bed? My neck needs rest."

He smiled against my lips. "Aye. Of course. Help me with this again, then." He hooked a thumb under the clasp.

I did. The clasp fell loose, and with it in his hand, he held me up against him as he reached forward, putting it back in its box.

I breathed him in and automatically wrapped my arms around him. Soil, grass stains, and the iron tinge of blood welcomed my senses, and beneath it all was the musk of his exertion. The dried coat of salty sweat against his skin and ancient wool was a pheromone-filled perfume. His hand gripped my back to steady himself; he was not about to step out of our full-body embrace to reach the clasp box properly. His movements were jerky as he set the box then stood in front of me.

His lips came down to mine as my legs wrapped tighter around his thighs. I was going to need more of him before the bedroom.

"My hands are busy. Unbuckle my belt, will ye?"

My fingers moved through the fabric like a pickpocket until I found the clasp of his belt and undid it. His ten tons of MacLaoch tartan unfolded and fell to the floor with his sporran. The only bit still on was that which was thrown over his shoulder. And he was a right proper crazy Scot: there wasn't a damn thing he wore under it.

"Can ye tell me, lass, what is it that a Scotsman wears beneath his kilt?"

I laughed and looked up at him, our lips ghosting over the other's, absorbing the laughter in our smiles.

"Oh, I dunno, shall I look?" I asked as his hips rocked in and ran the full length of his hard cock up my belly up between my breasts.

"If it would please ye."

I looked down to his muscular bare legs, the black dusting of hair covering the bend and strength of his musculature. I ran my nails up the backs of his taut thighs and over the firm round muscle of his buttocks until I was under his shirt and draped plaid.

"Oh, absolutely nothing," I said breathlessly, pretending to be scandalized.

"Much like you, lass," he said as his fingertips followed the massive tear of my dress up the side to where it rode up now to my abdomen. He swept it aside and slid his fingers down over my navel and into my amber-colored brushland, following the path he'd studied so well over the last year. "Ye are so soft," he whispered, distracted and drugged against my lips.

Then as my thighs sighed farther open, he slipped his blunt fingertips within me.

I groaned out a reply, and as if I could swallow him whole, my legs widened farther. His thumb gentled upon the nub of my womanhood between the petals of autumn-touched forest. Rowan was drowning with me. One part intoxicated man, one part pleasure hunter. "Cole..." he begged as I fell back to my elbows again. I prayed they'd hold me until my blissful end.

His thumb swiped moisture from below and made things into a slip-and-slide of orgasmic joy. Rippling erotic energy gripped my guts and made me loose-limbed, and just when I thought I needed him up to his hilt within me, he slipped a finger inside. Then another.

I definitely groaned then.

"Rowan," I said and was surprised to feel sweat on my upper lip and absently licked it off.

He pressed his fingers deep inside of me, rubbing his palm over my clit as he watched my tongue like he was a bird of prey and it a tiny mouse.

"Get in me," I choked out, looking at the massive erection that was standing proud beneath his shirt and plaid.

He looked starved and bent over me, putting his mouth to mine, but I suddenly had noodles for arms. I was flattened onto the desk and out of reach of Rowan's mouth.

In the next second, I was cold. Rowan stood and with a growl tossed his tartan down and ripped his shirt off.

He tossed his shirt down and stood before me, a beautiful, battered Scottish god of war between my legs.

"Now, please," I begged him and came up on my elbows again and scooted forward to the edge of the desk. For someone less full of potent sex hormones, the height difference would have been obvious. This was a fact: Rowan was going to have to spread his legs like a giraffe at the watering hole to get in me.

His voice was raw. "I can't do a proper job this way," he said and with one hand on my upper thigh yanked me to him. I wrapped my legs tight around him and, in a whirl, he was seated, and I was astride.

My knees spread, and his warm, velvety cock slipped into my over-ready confines as if they were algae covered rocks and he the sea. Whimpering in gut-gripping pleasure of his full erection, I pushed him deeper. My knees slipped wider, taking him in to the hilt and stretching myself over his swollen cock and igniting every erogenous zone along the way. My fingers ran up into his dark hair and gripped tight as things shattered and smashed to the floor. Pencils clattered across the wood and stone as Rowan's hands gripped my rear in response sending sensuous tendrils of muscle tightening lust through my body.

I rocked him deep into me as our mouths and our skin slithered together with the thin layer of silk like powder between our bodies.

"Rowan," I begged.

And he helped set the pace, pulling me up then down; his breath caught, and a keening cry started somewhere in his chest before it slithered out and over his lips and caressed my breasts.

The sleeve of my abused dress slipped off, and with it the fabric dropped and exposed the top of my left breast. I kept our rhythm, the insistent pace toward the finish line that was flagged on by the fires that had erupted within us, urging us faster.

The plump dough of my breast was rescued by Rowan and now was cradled in his palm, his thumb flicking the nipple to stand before greedily consuming it whole.

Electricity struck through my nipple and dove down to where we were connected, fanning the heat of it, catching us in much bigger flames.

I praised God, Rowan, his ancestors, and rode him hard there on that old oak desk. We solidly lost our minds; my hands cupped his shoulders for support and his face, alternating as our lips set fire to each other's. His mouth opened, begging for more, and obliging, I responded.

My breath caught as the full combustion of his thickness within me pressed one last time against my ignition switch, and I shook with the explosion of it.

I pressed the gas and rode him harder as my mouth broke off from his in a gasp. Rowan's eyes closed, his mouth pinching in the pleasure pain of an orgasm so full that it wrung his body out from toes to the tips of his hair.

As we crescendoed off our cliff, Rowan pressed three last thrusts within me until he cried out with me, and warmth filled my insides, and I collapsed against him.

Breathing heavy and lying astride him, I was warm again, hot even.

I touched the side of his satiated face. "I love you."

He grinned back at me. "I love ye too."

Then with a smile, remembering we'd gotten on the desk for some sort of purpose I didn't remember quite well, I said, breathing hard, "Did we find...? Did we find the facts we were looking for?"

"Aye," Rowan said and swallowed, catching his breath. "All of them."

## Thirty-Eight

Before retiring back to our cottage in the early morning hour, Rowan and I showered in his old apartment and then rummaged through his closet to find clothes that were clean and didn't look like they'd been in a car wreck. We made our way downstairs and stopped in at the library. Only a few were awake, and at the far end of the room, the fireplace flickered and crackled, punctuating murmurs of conversation. Marion and Flora met us in the hall, had taken care of things and were pink cheeked with drink. Cots had been dragged into hastily dusted guest rooms and wool blankets tossed over bodies where they'd slithered to the floor happy with drink. Marion told us that there was general excitement that the next day would see a feast like that we'd never seen. Plans for a hunt then days of drinking in our honor had buoyed spirits to song and dance until sleep had taken hold.

"This night and the year before," Marion whispered with a sleepy Flora at her side, "mark a time we never thought we'd see. We've lived it like MacLaochs, survived it like MacLaochs, and with God as our witness, we'll celebrate it like MacLaochs. Like Scottish kings."

"Aye," agreed Flora, "celebrate, right proper, your homecoming, Cole, and the lives ye've saved."

Rowan squeezed my shoulders, and after the day I'd had, emotion bubbled up, and my lip quivered. I hugged them both and thanked them and let Rowan guide us back though the dark to our stone cottage before I fell to the floor with sobs of relief.

Rowan was quiet, holding me. As I settled, he finally voiced a response of his own, with a groaning sigh. "I don't know how we'll afford it."

I understood he was talking of the feast, and I just shook my head, hugged him. "We will, you'll see. And remember, one thing at a time. First, sleep; then, tomorrow, we'll tackle the rest."

I WAS BLOWING STEAM OFF MY COFFEE AS I SETTLED NEXT TO Rowan on our living room couch, wool blankets folded up around us. Out the large bay window we could see over the cliff and past the green of the forest to the Atlantic at the horizon. In the days of old, the morning would have seen the huntsmen up before first light, but it was modern times, and as such our modern peoples weren't ready for the battle last night then heavy drinking then a predawn hunt. Rowan had already sent out a missive that the hunt and festivities would start on the weekend, in two days. I powered on my cell and tossed it onto the coffee table and looked over at Rowan's laptop screen. He had it open to the estate ledgers.

"Find anything new?" I asked, snuggling into him.

He winced and readjusted. "Och," he said from the back of his throat, "not yet."

I was about to ask about his wince when my phone started vibrating across the tabletop then onto the floor.

"What the..."

I picked it up off the rug and looked at the screen. "I have 152 messages?" I croaked.

Rowan snickered. "Aye, *mo ghràdh*, and they're all from me."

I gave him a sly grin, and standing, I went to the window to listen to all his love messages. Only, by the third one, it was apparent that they were not all from him. My heart started to pound "That son of a bitch."

Rowan perked up. "And which son would tha' be?"

I turned around, seething. "Mickey, that candy-faced fuck."

Rowan's brows rose, unsurprised but curious. "And which part of Mickey-the-candy-faced-fuck has caused problems?"

"This," I said, pointing into the phone, "is message after message from the Fund." I sighed, calming down, and shook my head—it was just as well. "They've heard of Mickey Gillian, but despite his academic credentials, they did not send him. In fact, they tell me, he has been in locales where items have gone missing, but they could never prove it was him. Now we can add Castle Laoch to that list—he tried to take the sword, I'm sure of it. I will have to look into what else he sticky-fingered, other than Holly's heart and magnifier. Thankfully, since I'm not getting an earful about anything else"—I held up a finger as though to shush myself while I tuned back in to the message from the Fund I was listening to and then continued once I was at the part where I could delete that message and prep the next one to be played—"the part he told me about Charmaine, that she'd called and told the Fund that I was a con artist, seems to have been false. Who knows why, exactly, he said that. Could have been part of some scheme. Probably just projecting on his part. But that she assumed he and I were in cahoots—" I cussed resoundingly and stopped my voice mails and simply got on the horn with the Fund.

Thirty minutes later and just as many paces around the house as I spoke to the Fund, I hung up.

Rowan had been watching me like a field mouse from his den. "Well?"

I let out a long and exasperated sigh. "Sorted."

"And?"

The Fund is attempting to contact Mickey Gillian and has reached out to their Glasgow partners to get it sorted. We're not sure why he chose to say the Fund sent him here. I mean, he did mention wanting to find gold or something in the cairns but..." I shrugged. "After last night, I doubt we'll see him again. And"—I looked to the back of my hand where I'd written notes then to the front where they continued—"the Fund would like to ask you for permission to use your loch to transport heavy equipment to Orkney. Apparently, the roads aren't wide enough for a lorry to get through. They were having a hard time getting port permissions in a timely manner."

Rowan nodded. "Glentree harbor is one of the few deep ports that is still privately owned. And since you're the laird's wife, now ye personally can give him permission," he said and gave me a grin that was both prideful and also opportunistic—he was happy to be sharing the laird duties.

I grinned back at him. "I like the sound of that." My phone buzzed in my hand again and I looked down, "Oh."

"Oh, what?"

"My mom."

"Aye?"

I looked up, feeling a stress-sweat coming on. "She wants to chat."

Rowan shrugged, not understanding the gravity of the situation. "Aye, fine, I'll get her on now."

And before I could stop him or come up with a game plan, she was there on the screen of his laptop on the coffee table. I slapped my hand over his ring finger and buried mine under my butt.

Before I could say howdy-do, she said, "I spoke with Clive this morning."

My stomach bottomed out, and Rowan scooted closer and waved to her on the screen. It was a simple enough statement, but there on the screen I could see the tightness in the corners of her mouth. And that way she said Clive's name, intoning I should know damn well what they'd spoken about and the hot water I was in was boiling.

"Oh, you did? Great. He's still needing family documents then?" I pretended everything was just dandy and took a sip of coffee.

"I thought he might. Haven't heard from you in a while, so I thought I'd call him and see how my daughter was doing."

Rowan looked down at his phone, confused. "I didn't get a call."

My mother gave him a winsome smile. "Oh, darling, you're so busy I just didn't want to bother you. Clive needs documents from us, so it was two birds with one stone, you see?"

Rowan nodded. "Oh? Aye."

I hit the mute button and whispered out lips that were still smiling my mom's direction, "You're in deep shit too. She sounds nice, but you don't understand that tone. She knows and is far from happy."

We should have rehearsed what to say, like for us to tell her we were engaged and make a wedding date, which was really going to be just a reception, but she didn't need to know that. Part of me wanted them to jump on a plane now, but my father was a farmer, he planned his absences with the seasons.

"Fine," he said, also through a frozen grin, "but you don't think this is odd? If she wasn't suspicious, she is now."

I smiled big as I whispered, "Deep. Shit." And took us off mute.

"Sorry, Mama, hit the wrong button. You were saying?"

Just then, in the background, my father walked into their kitchen, work boots on, tucking a set of well-worn work gloves into his back pocket. He rummaged through the fridge before we heard the crack hiss of a can opening. My mother had turned and was waiting for him.

"Hi," he said as he squatted and waved at us. "Hi, you two. You get our care package yet?"

"Care package?" I asked.

My mother tsked at him. "Don't call your son that."

My stomach dropped full out. My throat closed. "TJ?" I managed.

"Yup." My father said letting the *P* pop in the air. "Your mother is probably pussy-footing around with it, but we had a real interesting conversation with Clive."

"Downright silly," my mother amended.

"On a fluke, your brother called us next. He's stationed in Germany right now, as you know. There's not a deployment on the line just yet, so he's taking some R and R to Scotland."

Rowan's hand under mine turned and squeezed tight. He was finally getting the picture.

"That's great. You know, we were just getting dates set for our wedding, and he can help us figure it out. After harvest this year, we were thinking. Dad, you'd be able to—"

My mother cut in. "Nicole Ransome Baker, don't you sit there and lie to us. You've already been married, and people up there are calling you Mrs. MacLoch Macklock or whatever already. Frankly, I'm disappointed."

Rowan tried to intercede. "My apologies. It's not as if we're keeping anything from ye; it's just hard to describe how—"

"Son," my father cut in and sat on a chair next to my mother and pulled the laptop close so that the screen shook a bit before it settled. "The way we hear of it, it sounds like it was a rush job. We have a saying here; they're called shotgun weddings. And there's a reason there's a shotgun involved."

Rowan swallowed.

I whispered, "Deep. Shit."

"Anyway," Daddy continued as if Rowan's color draining from his face couldn't be seen though the screen three thousand miles away, "he should be there shortly. Glad you two tied the knot, but before we really go at it with the felicitations, there're a few things TJ has been instructed on sorting out. Give us a call when he gets there. See ya, love bug," he said to me and then nodded to Rowan before closing the screen.

Rowan put his face in his hands and groaned loud and long.

All I could do was whisper wide-eyed into the room about the impending doom, "My family is coming to Scotland."

# Glossary of Gaelic Terms

**claidheamh dà làimh:** A two-handed sword.

**claidheamh mòr:** Known in English as a claymore; a two-handed basket-hilted sword.

**sgian-dubh:** Small, single-edged knife.

**ghràdh:** Love.

**mo ghràdh:** My love.

**Tha gaol agam ort:** I love you.

**Tha gaol agamsa ort fhèin:** I love you too.

**mo chridhe:** My heart.

**Tha mi gad ionndrainn:** I miss you.

**Tha mo ghion ort:** I love you with all my heart.

# Acknowledgments

I'd like to first thank my editor, Kristin Thiel. We started the edits of this manuscript just before lockdown in March 2020. Thank you for your hard work and keeping upbeat over the course of this long edit. You kept focus and dedication to help this manuscript be the best that it can be even when the pandemic and our city protests raged right outside your door, giving you every justifiable reason not to. This has been our most deliberate and meaningful collaboration yet, and I'm proud of what we've accomplished. Thanks for making me look so polished...*midden*!

Thanks also goes to Annie, my super-beta reader. We owe the line "He knew he'd lose what was left of his mind if he extinguished even an ember of that fire" to you. Thanks for reading this thing in all phases of its awesomeness. Even when right at the beginning it wasn't so awesome. I tried really hard to use the word *magic* (versus *metaphysical*) more—I did. I promise!

Thanks to the College Crew for showing up to the Coffee Chats we started in lockdown, I've needed them to reclaim my sanity over the last years. And your support through this publishing process has meant the world to me.

I'd also like to thank the people of Scotland I came to know about during my research, especially the YouTubers Laurenrhiannon and the VisitScotland channel for all their excellent videos on the Gaelic language. Being from Hawai'i, I understand it's easy for us outsiders to get it wrong. My trip to Scotland many years ago opened my eyes to the beauty of the place and how hard it must have been for my ancestors to leave. Please forgive any gross oversights; my joy for your culture and land, I hope, shines through.

And finally, thanks goes to the man who has always had my back, even a decade ago when, at the very beginning, this natural resources major said she'd write a book someday, and you never lost faith in me even when, at times, I had. We're several books in now, and I want to thank you again for your encouragement and steadfast belief in my abilities. *Aloha pumehana, mo ghràdh.* ♥

# Author Bio

Becky Banks is a bestselling and award-winning indie author from an old Hawai'i family, who currently lives in Portland, Oregon, with her husband and two children. Becky likes to craft dark romances that stem from her past and require love to see her characters through. When she's not crafting love stories, she's packing lunches for her little ones and breaking up *Minecraft* fights.

Visit Becky Banks online at beckybanksbooks.com and follow her on social media for updates on new releases and more.

facebook.com/beckybanksbooks

instagram.com/authorbeckybanks

amazon.com/author/beckybanks

goodreads.com/beckybanks

bookbub.com/profile/becky-banks

# Legend of the Brotherhood

*Enjoy this excerpt from The Legend of the Brotherhood, coming soon!*

---

## PROLOGUE
### *Loch Laoch, Glentree, Skye, Scotland, 1989*

Up on the black rocky beach four boats, half-cabin wooden skiffs, were being filled with not the ocean's catch, but untaxed whisky. They were lit by the moon's bright light on that cloudless night. The wet, cold bit at the men's heels as news from earlier of the tax man set to raid MacLaoch castle set a frantic rhythm to the otherwise clandestine and quiet pace required for aging raw spirit into Clan MacLaoch's Glentree golden whisky. The oak barrels from the Castle's lower caves were actively being evacuated. Clansmen sporting tight stone-washed denim, mullets, cigarettes between tight lips, and swatches of tartan tied around their wrists to protect against the metal bands on the barrels rolled, then loaded the five-hundred-pound casks into boats.

Rowan, a young boy then, vaguely remembered the way tobacco smoke hung in the air like a kind of misty layer over their illicit activities.

Then word came. The authorities were close. The black rocky shore made loading the boats hard and harder still when their high tops slid on the wet stones. News squawked over two-way radios: police were racing through Glentree toward the castle.

Men not carrying casks of MacLaoch gold were running on the beach, throwing their arms at the beached skiffs to, "Go! Go! Go!"

The last one to receive her heavy load was *Chief Desire*, Rowan's uncle's skiff.

Off in the dark, watery distance, a motorized engine, something large by the low tone of the hum, was coming up from the south, its searchlight a dot on the horizon. The authorities were coming by both land and water.

The last barrels were loaded when the searchlight and the yacht-sized vessel with the words HR Coast Guard emblazoned on the side crested the horizon. Out there beyond the break, it seemed like a ghost.

Cigarettes were flicked to the ground, indicating that things with the last skiff had gotten serious. The incoming tide had taken the remaining boats but *Chief's Desire*, who was still too heavy for the water lapping under her flat wooden hull, stood still.

The white sneakers of the man nicknamed Double-A streaked over the side of her hull. "Oye! Giver!"

The men rushed the bow and shoved in time with a low incoming wave. Aided by their force and the buoyant lift of the water, the skiff moved out with the retreating wave. All five men soaked their jeans as they gave her a final shove before climbing in.

Rowan remembered the sound of the outboard motors on his uncle's boat coming on. The sound caught another memory: his uncle's whisky boys talking about those overpowered white and shiny outboard motors the day they'd been installed. The clansmen had talked of the two hundred horsepower they combined to make and how it was all so American. That somehow, Miami Vice had gotten the better of his uncle all the way out there on that northern port of Skye.

As he stood on that beach, the searchlight of the incoming power-boat washing over the wave tops like an accusatory finger, did Rowan feel his uncle's boat, even with all that extra power, couldn't possibly outrun their English overlords. Even the skiff, with its half-Miami Vice overhaul, was still a blunt-nosed, sleepy wooden vessel whose original designs were for quiet fishing in the late nineteenth century. His uncle needed a pointed nose, a fiberglass bottom, and an unlimited fuel supply.

That man, his uncle, clan chief, and mentor stood beside him. He was the only one not to toss his tobacco; his cigar was clenched between his teeth. His uncle christened Seac James Douglas MacLaoch but went by Jacky, uttered a Gaelic prayer under his breath just as the winds changed, interrupting him with the request from the coast guard, "Cease activity and return to shore."

"They'll make it?" Rowan remembered asking.

"Lady MacLaoch willing."

Those words hadn't soothed him; in their legends, Lady MacLaoch was a woman who cursed them and all in her lineage, including him.

Then his uncle added, "And pray those engines don't rip tha' boat apart."

"What?" he squeaked.

Just then, Rowan heard the skiff's motors go full tilt, jettisoning it forward through the chop. The nose lifted at the first low, sloppy wave that struck the bow, making the men shout. The engine went slack, and two men were ordered to the nose and grip the wood rail. Double-A put power back into the propellers, and with the nose weighed down, they broke through the waves.

What it lacked in wave plowing ability, it made up for with its flat bottom in the shallows and the experts at its helm. The boat wave-hopped toward the channel, a line of low, slopping waves where the skiff could bypass the cresting waves more easily. Out of the protected bay, they'd catch the coastal rip current that sped north to the Orkneys. They didn't plan to go that far but Her Royal Highness' Coast Guard didn't know that.

The Coast Guard boat, however, was a wave-smashing colossus with a diesel motor built for high sea chases. It pierced through the outer chop, closing the distance to the running skiff at the open mouth of the bay like a boot about to bash a roach into the rocks.

"Uncle..."

"Dinna fash yersel'. Even with her load, she's made for the shallows.

Her royal highness' ship cannae be foolish enough to attempt what they are imitating to do." His tone went low and dubious. "I hope."

Rowan watched as the skiff hit the calm waters of the channel as the coast guard closed in. They were near to the mouth of the loch.

Next to him, his uncle whispered in their mother tongue to keep the men safe, the water to guide them, and for the MacLoach marshes to be ready to receive them.

Young Rowan ran then. Across the rocky beach, up the cliff trail where the smell of spilled whisky was heavy in the air. At the top of the cliffs, he watched the water chase as he ran, following their progress.

The large coast guard ship indeed looked to be preparing to ram the skiff; Rowan's heart went into his throat. He shouted for Double-A to stop. Stop this madness; they'd surely die. But there no way Double-A would hear him and did not; he kept to his course, following the edge of the bay. Then suddenly, the coast guard banked hard away from the skiff, allowing it to fly out the mouth of the loch.

Rowan shouted and punched his fist in the air - their first gamble was a good one - as his feet ran again toward the MacLaoch bluff.

He needed to ensure the skiff made it all the way, so he watched them. His feet stumbled over loose rocks on the trail.

The coast guard had righted and returned to the chase. They were much better equipped to fly through the ocean waters, and soon, they were once more on Double-A and his men. This time, the skiff veered away from the safety of the shallow waters. Rowan thought it wasn't a move they should have made as the coast guard vessel was on them again.

Commands echoed off the basalt rocks of the cliff's shoulders; they reached him in broken waves, sounding harsh. They were being ordered once more to stop. It had the underlying feel of "or else" in the command's tone.

The skiff wasn't going to make it to its final destination. That Rowan could plainly see. The English looked mad and ready to ram his clansmen with their massive white boat. Rowan lost them again as he ran into the forest following the trail, making his way through and to the forest cliffs on the other side. He popped out again just in time to witness the skiff dodging left again, pushing even farther out.

Rowan bellowed, "Nooo!" It was farther into the bigger ship's territory and a sure way to drown when the larger vessel's hull exploded the skiff.

The coast guard vessel followed and, anticipating a cut-back by Double-A, turned. Rowan screamed. The water frothed as Double-A indeed had cut back.

The *Chief's Desire* was surely cut in half from where he stood. The churning water, poor lighting with the spotlight, and not enough from the moon made the boat and the bodies impossible to see. Covering his mouth and his scream as if the authorities could hear him, Rowan felt hot tears sting his eyes. His uncle's men, clansmen who were second fathers to him, were surely killed. And he'd bore witness to the authority's brutality to an already brutalized clan. His stomach went sick.

Then the searchlight went mad on the water below, and in the moonlight, Rowan saw *Chief's Desire* running like a mud skipper over the water. The English boot had tried to crush them but failed.

Rowan whooped, punching his fist in the air, and sped along the cliffside trail again. The skiff, lit by searchlights, was headed straight toward the cliffs as the coast guard followed.

Double-A kept the motors blazing. He tore into the shallows, and while Rowan was relieved, the water there was riddled with underwater boulders that could crack the hull. The men were in a literal rock and a hard place. It was too dangerous to sustain. The coast guard vessel would pace them until they crashed, then pluck them from the water—those who survived.

It was as if the Coast Guard heard Rowan's thoughts and put on an extra burst of speed to trap them there in that gray zone of destruction.

The skiff, however, began to pull away as if they discovered they had another outboard motor and just remembered then to turn it on. Farther and farther ahead, the skiff led from the coast guard vessel. Another burst of joy surged through Rowan when he realized what was happening. Double-A had found the rip current that traveled to the Orkneys. It hadn't been out far where Double-A had been; it was close to shore that night.

He watched as the larger vessel turned its diesel engines on high—the growl of it reached Rowan—to catch the skiff moving with two hundred horsepower in a stream of water at eight feet per second. It was the equivalent of having the wind at their back.

The vessel kept on them, its massive searchlight trailing them. But then, in a blink, the skiff was gone. Rowan knew that Double-A made a hard right out of the spotlight, and by the time it took them to readjust it, the skiff disappeared. The Coast Guard worked in the area for some time. It searched the water and the shore for parts of the boat, and eventually, they discovered what his clan had over a millennia ago: a break in the cliffs that led inland.

Smiling and feeling righteous, Rowan ran back to the castle in a stream of whoops and hollers. They'd done it! They'd saved the clan's whisky; they'd be able to serve their clan's needs and make a tidy profit to fix the castle roof and help their clans people when they needed money for school or medical bills.

Rowan's feet slowed when the Castle came into view, and his jovial mood plummeted. Blue and red lights of police cars bounced off the upper turrets of Castle Laoch, a reminder that they'd not wholly gotten away with it.

The rest of the night was a blur. He remembered finding his uncle's hand and slipping his smaller one into his larger one. It gave him the reassurance he needed as the authorities boots moved up and down the basement stairs and then out to the lower cave. The rest of the MacLaoch gold was forfeited.

There was one pungent moment, though, that Rowan hadn't recalled in a long time. One where his present day circumstance pulled it up and out of his deep subconscious. His uncle was a colorful man who wasn't one to shy away from responsibilities, a party, or a fight.

"What'd you say, MacDonald?" Rowan remembered his uncle saying out front in the roundabout, the police and their vehicles the backdrop to their loss. The tone was one of aggression, and it made Rowan's stomach churn; his uncle was angry. Then, "Is that right?" just before the officer had his head knocked back.

The mayhem that ensued was foggy to Rowan, but that name, *MacDonald*, stuck.

Now, sitting before him at his office desk, a MacDonald too grinned, "This is long overdue, isn't it?" The underworked and overindulged man in a suit much too large for his shoulders but large enough to button around his rotund middle slid loan forfeiture paperwork across the desk to Rowan. "Ye can't outrun your bad blood, MacLaoch. And yer uncle was the worst kind. I'll finish what my own uncle started and be taking the castle from ye and yours as ye justly deserve."

That's what he'd said to Rowan before Charmaine had shown up, and turned things further upside-down. Now, though, looking down at the winking gold on his ring finger Rowan sighed, that was water under the bridge. But the bankman wasn't. If they had that confiscated whisky now, it'd be worth a fortune, and he could be done with the MacDonald bankman once and for all.

---

## CHAPTER 1
### Present day

The afternoon in our cozy cottage at the cliff's edge brightened as the summer sun began to break up the cloud cover outside. Beyond the front windows, the salt spray hung in the air, giving everything a gossamer glow.

Inside, the glow evaporated. I sat on the couch in the living room of our one-bedroom cottage; I could feel the tension beginning to build the moment we'd hung up with my parents in South Carolina. Rowan was next to me, still gripping my hand. My parents informed us that TJ was about to step off a C-130 and make his way to our part of Scotland. I was gauging how much time we had to change our address. That moment wasn't great for a family visit.

"Can a C-130 land at Eli's airfield?" I asked.

"Only if it wants to end in the water, there's not a runway long enough there. They'll land down Glasgow and then make their way north. We have a few hours to set up the welcome mat and clean things."

I looked around, "TJ won't care that we haven't vacuumed, babe."

"No, not that."

"Right, the field." Then I remembered, "Oh, the castle still has clanspeople in the upper halls."

"Aye, we just fought a mystical being, got married, and turned the library into a makeshift hospital."

He seemed calm when he started the sentence, but by its end, he looked panicked.

"I'm meeting your kin. And the place is a bloody mess. Literally." He shoved his hands through his hair and stood before looking around as if the answer was tucked under the couch cushions. He cursed resoundingly.

Now, we were getting on the same page. "That's more the reaction that I was thinking. We have a lot to do still. And this is a lot to try and explain to TJ – much less them – about what just happened. All my mother will hear is confirmation that we're married. And for her, doing that without her is...tantamount to murder." I felt a nervous giggle bubble up. I was a grown woman, but my parents still held sway over a small but consequential part of my brain. The brain that was still reeling from the day before but still instinctively wanted to make Mom and Dad proud.

Luckily, it wasn't them coming. TJ was amiable, and the secrets I had on him were akin to those of a priest to his local parishioners.

Getting up from the couch, I started, "Row—"

He was in the kitchen on his phone, calling Marion and Flora to get the front halls swept, foods ordered and rooms cleared. He hung up, and I noticed his skin was taking on a sheen.

"Hon, none of that stuff is necessary for TJ's visit—"

His slate blue eyes were wide, "Ye have family."

I looked around the room as if they were standing there, "Yeah, of course I do—"

"No, you're not an orphan. Like me."

"Right, I have—"

"I've even spoken to them, but now it's real. *They're real.* The things I've done, the things *we've* done. How do I face your da? And most importantly, your brother? They've every right to take my head off—"

"Whoa," I said, going to him, slid my arms around his middle, and laid my ear to his chest. His heart was hammering. "You've faced down much worse than a couple of rednecks like us, you'll be fine."

I listened to him take breath after breath until his heart rate came down. "Rednecks? Like..."

"I mean, we're country, we're nothing fancy."

I heard him sigh, "So...never mind."

"So, what?"

"Nothing."

I looked at him, "You're wondering if TJ is my brother-cousin, aren't you?"

He gave a nervous laugh.

"He is. Best to keep things in the family, right?"

"I can't tell if you're joking or no'."

I lead him on a little longer, "You'll finally meet TJ, you decide. Some people think we're twins. Our genetic code is so similar."

At this, he scoffed, "Aye, yer joking. He looks nothing of you. Tan and straight brown hair."

"You must be really rattled if you forgot that. Yeah, he takes after my father. I mean, when I said we're redneck, love, I'm using it in an endearing term that we're *very* country, and we do things our way, the rest of the world be damned. So, we won't expect formalities when TJ or my parents arrive."

"Ah," he said and kissed my lips since they were so close, "All right then, but if you allow it, we Scots are also a bit 'country' up here, and we've got a mind to stick to tradition like a wart on a toad so I'll be rolling out the red carpet to any and all of your family when they come."

"Fine, but when we mess it up. Don't come crying to me."

He laughed and kissed me again, "Ye know I'm a sensitive boy; dinnae make fun of me."

I hugged him tighter, and Rowan hissed, "Not so tight."

"Oh, right." I gently touched his abdomen, "Are you sure we shouldn't see a doctor about your bruise? It looked rough this morning."

Against my temple, he murmured, "Nae, nothing but a few days off of abdominal work, and I'll be fine. Dinnae fash yersel'" and his palm went to the round of my bottom. "So, none of this," he squeezed, "not until I'm recovered and your brother is tucked into a nice bed of his own far away."

That sounded like an eternity away, "That could be...*forever.*"

He kissed the end of my nose, "Then we never have sex again."

I grinned at him, "I think we're worrying about the wrong things."

"Aye, but it's a fun distraction. Shall we get to it then?"

I took a deep breath and grabbed the button of my jeans, "If this is our final time, yes, let's get to it."

Rowan laughed at my antics and inability to hear anything from him that wasn't a turn-on, "No. Cleaning and prepping for his visit. Let's head up to the castle."

I feigned a sad frown, "OK, fine."

Rowan held the door open for me as we stepped out into the weak sunshine of the early cloudy afternoon.

"I'd like to look at the field for a few hours to see what's left and see if we have to wrap up our research work with, 'Everything is a charbroiled briquette—the end,' or if there's an after story here. At university, we studied the aftermath of crown fires - fires that travel from tree top to tree top, leaving nothing but ash in their wake - and discovered solid ecological work to be done, even in the ash. We can study the regrowth over time though with lightning from an ethereal being, I doubt we'll be dealing with an elemental situation like a wildfire. But who knows?"

Rowan nodded; his eyes were on the charred hill coming into view. When he took a stabilizing breath, I looked up. The blackened soil came down from the research field, and after only several yards of walking through green grass, it began to change to yellow, then to brown, and finally to black-scarred earth.

I wove my fingers through his and gripped his hand tight. That charred grass was a reminder of the near loss of everything we held dear.

"I'm sorry TJ is popping in at a time like this. I can take care of him and let you focus on the clan's recovery and the bankruptcy proceedings —or rather, their lack thereof since he never showed up."

"It's just a matter of time with the bankman. When he was here last, he reminded me of our history. For him, it's personal. But we'll see it through. I've no idea how, but we must."

It was a minor mystery we had since he failed to show. It was like he disappeared with Mickey Gillian.

With Mickey, I could only assume he'd taken one look at the glowing skeletons and taken off, protecting his lying, cheating hide.

"We could just sell it," I said, returning to the bankruptcy as the field turned proper black and plant shadows were blasted against rocks.

"Och," he said again. He became nonverbal when there were subjects he didn't want to discuss.

With everything that had just happened, bankruptcy was the one thing that seemed fixable. "I'm just saying the Ulfberht sword—"

"And I'm just saying, while tha' may make a fine collectible in a sassenach's collection for several million pounds, I'll not sell the sword that is your birthright. It might bring tha' damned man *back*." His *back* sounded like he was hocking it out the back of his throat like a rancid piece of haggis.

"Yeah, yeah, so you have said. I'm saying that if it will help save the castle from the bank man's noose, as you so eloquently say, then I think it's worth it."

"Och, no."

"Fine," I drawled, then thought I'd poke at him, changing the subject from bankruptcy which was making him dark again, "You know I'm a sassenach, right?" I said, referencing the word that was sometimes used as a curse but meant outsider.

"Aye, and no. Now that you've reduced yourself to marry me, ye are no longer a sassenach but a Scottish lass."

I smiled at him and bumped him amicably with my shoulder, "Awe shucks, you say the purdiest things."

He grinned back at me, "And we both know what a load of manure tha' is; you are just as much a part of these hills and dales as I. Just ask Ormr Fucking Minorisson."

"If it's OK with you, I won't."

"Aye it is—"

He broke off as we squinted into the distance into the circle garden, where we both caught sight of a brown-haired figure with a high and tight haircut cutting through at a swagger's pace.

Suddenly, I was back home in South Carolina laughing, trading bawdy jokes, and eating Mother's tooth-achingly sweet pecan pie, which she made whenever he and I made her 'stressed to the gills.'

"He's not... that's not... actual skipping," I said as if I had to explain why TJ walked the way he did, "He just walks like he owns the world and he's on a stage before millions."

We stopped, and I waved as Rowan released my hand as if scalded. It was as if holding my hand was a dirty little secret. He wiped his hands on his pants as TJ, in his civilian gear, held a green pixelated camo ruck-sack over his shoulder and came at us smiling.

I mumbled, "And it's never a good sign to see TJ smiling like that. He's up to something."

His eyes were bright and clear. He was on cloud nine, and when he saw me, his smile broke into a genuine grin of joy.

I grinned back at him and felt that familiar sensation of being home, and I'd missed the hell out of him and his hijinks.

"Well, my my, if it isn't Miss Nicole Ransome Baker!" he shouted.

I couldn't help but laugh. Seeing him made me remember every funny moment we'd ever shared. "TJ, you jackass!" I exclaimed with love, "How the hell are you?"

"Great!" he said as he got close, "Hold this," and tossed his rucksack to me.

I narrowly caught the fifty-pound sack.

"Oof!" I grunted just before TJ socked Rowan squarely in the stomach.

---

## CHAPTER 2

Rowan's breath shot out as he doubled over. TJ smoothed his hand over Rowan's back and patted, "That was from my folks. They didn't like you getting my sister pregnant and marrying her without Pop's consent. Mom, though, wants the baby to be named." He paused, looking at something written on his palm: "Fredrick if it's a boy and Francine if it's a girl."

He gave Rowan a double pat as if that settled it.

I loved my brother, I really did, but when he socked my husband only hours after we'd just survived a mythic battle? I returned the favor.

I dropped his rucksack and lunged. My fist caught his surprised cheek, "You waste of breath pissant excuse for a human being! He's injured—"

TJ blinked in surprise as my fist turned his cheek. He grabbed a handful of my sweater absently as I tackled him into the cosmos bed. Pink and white petals blew up into the air. I sat on him and tried to sock him in the face again. TJ dodged to the side again and again.

"Whoa!" he shouted.

"And," I said as I punched missing.

"I'm not," *punch.* "PREGNANT!"

He was surprised enough to stop and say, "What?" Just as I clipped his jaw.

"OW! Stop it!"

"YOU, stop it! You hurt him! I'm not pregnant, and he's my damn husband, and if you were born with ears that worked properly and an actual brain between them, you'd have asked! Damn you—"

He looked beyond me to Rowan, "You OK, man?"

I slapped TJ across the head for good measure and looked back at Rowan, who was on all fours on the gravel, one hand clutching his abdomen. He'd gone ashy and was struggling for a breath.

"Shit," I scrambled off TJ and gripped Rowan's shoulders in time to catch him from fainting face-first into the gravel. I murmured to him, "Rowan? Honey?" And as he went to dead weight, I caught his head on my thigh and pulled him into my lap. "TJ!" I hollered, "You damn shithead!"

Only TJ, whom I sometimes forget is an army medic who buzzes into active war zones to save people, was on his cell already.

"What do you mean he's injured?" TJ asked, putting his fingers to Rowan's neck pulse to make sure he'd just fainted and wasn't dead as a doornail.

"I mean, he got hit yesterday, hard, in the stomach, and it made a huge bruise. And why the hell are you here at all?! Mother and Daddy said you wouldn't be here for another day!"

He shouted back, "I caught a ride!" TJ cursed, "He's got cuts all over him too; what the hell was he doing?" he said, examining Rowan's prone body before gingerly rolling him over and lifting his shirt.

"He was...a tree fell," I improvised.

TJ gave me a dead-eye stare, "Yeah, right. You don't get knuckles like his if a tree falls on you. You suck at lying." He gave Rowan's abdomen a gentle *tap-tap* with his fingers over the purpley bruised area. Then cursed again as someone answered his call.

"Yeah, you still with your transport?" he said to the person on the other line, "Roger that. Standby." And pushed some buttons on his phone, "Can you get a geo locate on me?"

I piped up, "Just tell the paramedics we're at Castle Laoch, they'll know how to get here, at the circle garden." Panic slithered in, having not gotten far enough from the events of the day before; all I could think was how shitty it would be for Rowan to survive everything, and a single punch from my jackass brother would kill him.

TJ said, "Yeah, you heard that? Know where Castle Loch—"

"Laoch."

"Right. You know where that is?" he said into the phone, then, "Roger that, ten-four."

TJ hung up and tucked away his phone before gently tapping Rowan's face, then his collar bone calling his name. He checked his eyes, pulling his lids up.

I filled the silence, "How long did they say they'll be here? Sometimes, they have an ambulance sitting at Glentree. Was it there? Shit, TJ, this feels serious. He's unconscious, Tee."

TJ didn't look up but put his ear to Rowan's chest and tapped. Then stood abruptly and went to his pack and rummaged through it for a secondary bag that had been smashed into the rucksack; it was the primary guts of the bag. He unzipped his med bag, dropped it next to us, put his stethoscope to Rowan's chest, and tapped again.

I heard the distant purr of a machine and thanked the heavens that the ambulance was indeed at Glentree. Only the purr of the motor got louder and turned into a *chop chop chop* sound closing in quickly. I recognized the sound of a helicopter as, TJ's phone rang.

"Go," he said then, "Yeah, put it down in the flower bed. Yeah, the circle one. Yeah, I'm sure!"

Wide-eyed, I looked around us. "Here?!" I said, thinking of the royal coastguard chopper out where Eli worked; it wouldn't fit.

TJ just ignored me, and within moments, something more frightening peaked over the trees in the distance. The helicopter was something out of the wet dreams of every child who wanted to decimate their opponent on the G.I. Joe battlefield.

"Good Christ, TJ is that what I think it is?"

He didn't respond to me; it was obvious the black war bird he usually rode around in when he was saving asses was about to land in the circle garden or on the corner of the castle. My head felt like it was going to roll off with the force of the wind under the rotating blades as it paused high over the top of us.

TJ stood as I ducked over Rowan's face, protecting him from flying debris, and tried not to think about what it meant if TJ thought it pertinent to have his taxi driver come back and get us.

TJ gestured to the pilots like a robot on a runway as they gingerly took the chopper down. The flag atop the castle's parapet flicked and snapped in the wind until it gave up and ripped off. The thunder of the rotor wash pounded through my chest and roared around us. I watched under my arm as the experts behind the stick slowly set the wheels down like a snail through the garden (with a tornado attached to its tail). The power was reduced before the blades relaxed to a whine.

Everything from there on was a blur of TJ running, the co-pilot assisting, and Rowan being braced for flight. His eyelids fluttered when he was moved from the ground to the backboard, and he groaned. We were in the chopper and airborne within minutes. I advised them on the nearest hospital. It was over the ridge where our lone surgeon was in residence. The same hospital I flew with him to the year before when he'd needed his bullet wound stitched shut. There was radio chatter of Rowan's description mixed with acronyms, numbers, and the occasional words I understood like unconscious, breathing, and unresponsive.

The drone of the engine and helicopter blades became white noise, and I watched TJ go through his paramedic motions of listening to Rowan's breathing and pulse and setting him into an IV.

It was a short flight. If the pale gray Rowan's face didn't scare the piss out of me, I would have found the quick trip humorous. We were on the concrete helipad in a minute, and for the second time in my life, I never wanted to see that chipped white paint of the air ambulance cross on the tarmac or the weeds that were trying to crawl up through its cracks, ever again.

We were out. Rowan was put onto a waiting stretcher. TJ was running alongside the stretcher, yelling things over the rotor wash to the surgeon. Again, once inside, I was stopped at the surgery doors and asked to take a seat in the waiting room.

No matter how many times it happened, I would never get used to that feeling of despair when those doors shut on me.

This time, though, my brother was there. He was still out at the helipad speaking to the helicopter's personnel after peeling off the stretcher once the surgeons were briefed.

By the time I reached him, the chopper was airborne, and he was walking back to me, the sober, all-business brother in place.

I started the conversation, "You piece of shit—"

"He didn't fall out of a goddamn tree—"

"How could you? Two seconds, you're with us, and you put my husband in there," I whipped my pointer finger to the squat concrete building behind me in case he was as dumb as I thought he was.

"He should have been in the hospital yesterday. And don't fucking lie, Nicole. What the hell?"

I took a deep breath, and guilt crawled into my stomach. I knew it. I knew Rowan should have gone to the hospital last night.

Instead, I shook my head and crossed my arms. In the distance purply highland hills towered, and even though we were inland, we could smell the faint brine of seawater.

"Well?" he asked. "He's got level three contusions on his abdominal muscles, and when I hit him, it ruptured something internal that had ruptured before causing a hematoma, and by the bruising, I'd say it was less than twelve hours ago. Did he catch a missile with his flack jacket on? It sure as hell wasn't my damn love punch."

"Love punch? That's what you're calling it?"

"*He* has internal bleeding, but yes, let's focus on me."

I sighed, feeling defeated, and put my face into my hands; the tears were there before my hands touched my face, "I knew we should have taken him."

"We who? And why didn't you?"

I dropped my hands and said with some heat, "I don't know if you noticed the scorched earth behind us when we met?"

"Hard to forget. Forest fire?"

"Something like that. Look, it isn't very easy to explain. And knowing you, you'll have to see it to believe it, so I'll save the explanation for later. Right now, I need to contact Marion; she'll want to know why all the second-floor windows have been blown out. And maybe Clive," I mumbled, thinking he'd been Rowan's right-hand man these days. I returned to the hospital's emergency side entrance, wiping my tears, TJ behind me.

"Nicole... Pipsqueak," he said, using his nickname for me, "If he sneezed today, he would have ruptured whatever it was. I'd say he had some bleeding yesterday, and related or unrelated, he also got himself a nice internal hematoma, and I just so happened to be the sucker that burst it. So would have a cough, or eventually just sitting up. Don't be pissed at me."

I turned on him at the doors, "I'm not—no, wait, I am. Of course, I'm mad at you! YOU PUNCHED MY HUSBAND!"

"He deserved it! No one in our family really knows who he is! He's just some Harry Potter wank that's convinced you to stay up here in the boondocks in some ancient pile of rocks he's pretending is some historically important functioning castle."

I was taken aback, way back, as in back the train up to the station. *"Everyone* thinks that?" It was way worse than I'd assumed, then amended, "No one thinks that!"

"Yes, they do, but they're too damn nice to say anything. Mother and Daddy, no, check that; Mother is pissed. As in, if you weren't in another country, she'd be sending you *pie*."

"Oh," I said, feeling my mother's ire sideline me from my own. Mother baking was bad. Despite being raised as a good Southern woman, she wasn't a baking sort of gal or an eloquent home cook. She had her rebellion when she married my father, a farmer, who liked to cook and never requested her presence in the kitchen. So, when Mother did step into the kitchen, it was a loud pronouncement that she was doing something she hated, and therefore, everything that kitchen produced was ire in edible form.

"What kind of pie?" It mattered.

"*Pecan,*" he said it like it was a sharp metal dagger.

"Oh," I said, not liking the drama or pie guilt that I was being subjected to.

"Yeah," TJ said, gaining steam, "So, now you're lying to me about him being hit before. Did *you* hit him? You've got a nice slice on your head. Did he hit you first and you got pissed and nailed him back with something big? You're ready with the lies and not even a day into your marriage. Fuck ya I nailed him. When he's better, I'll do it again!"

TJ really knew where my big red button was and loved to sit on it, "FUCKER," I shouted as the receptionist inside, on the other side of the glass entry doors, looked up concerned.

"Tell me I'm wrong. Did you hit him?"

"Ugh! You don't understand!"

"Explain then!" he said, throwing up his hands.

"Ugh!" I responded, "TJ, I can't just explain everything like they're instructions on how to make a peanut butter and jelly sandwich!"

"Try!"

"Fine!" I marched through the double doors into the waiting room and to the reception desk. I recognized the two women there from my last visit. "Hi," I said with an aspartame smile.

They gave me a kind but wry smile in return looking at my brother and then at me. They immediately updated me, "He's still in surgery."

TJ rested his elbow on the bar height reception counter next to me, "Waiting."

I threw my thumb at him, "Would you be so kind as to tell this moronic paramedic here who I am?"

The receptionist closest to me answered, "Mrs. Rowan Douglas James MacLaoch."

"Ah, right," I said as TJ scoffed, "I mean before Rowan and I married."

She smiled and crinkled her nose, "He won't understand."

"I know, but let's tell him anyway."

"All right then. You're the Minory lass."

I looked at my brother behind me, "See?"

"Minory lass? Grandpappy's real last name? So what of it?"

I waved her to continue and she eagerly complied, "She saved the laird of Castle Laoch by marrying him and being his one true love destined to break the curse from birth."

I turned to him, smiling, "Still think you know what's happening here?"

He looked from the woman to me, "Bullshit."

———

*The Legend of the Brotherhood* is coming soon! Turn the page for Becky Banks' other contemporary suspense titles that are available now, and be sure to visit beckybanksbooks.com to sign up for her author newsletter and get book release news and giveaways sent right to your inbox.

## CLAN MACLAOCH CURSE SERIES

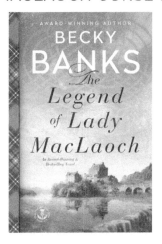

The Legend of Lady MacLaoch. *Book 1 of the Clan MacLaoch Curse Series.*

Centuries ago a vengeful curse buried itself deep into the history of the MacLaoch clan and became a legendary tale told by all those not cursed by its words.

In present-day Scotland, the laird and chief of the MacLaoch clan is an ex-Royal Air Force fighter pilot who has been past the gates of hell and returned a changed man. Rowan MacLaoch does battle with wartime memories and a family curse that threaten to consume him—unaware that his life and that of the history of the clan will be changed forever by the arrival of an American woman.

Cole Baker, a feisty recent graduate of a master's program, stumbles upon the ancient curse while researching her bloodlines. Moved by the history of the MacLaoch clan and the mystery of its chief, she digs into the legend that had been anything but quiet for centuries.

On their quest for answers, Cole and Rowan travel to places they have never before been and become witnesses to things they have never before fathomed.

The legend—one started with blood—will end with more shed as its creator finally exacts her justice.

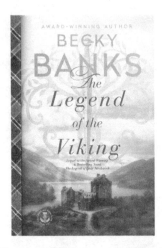

*Book 2 of the Clan MacLaoch curse series,* The Legend of the Viking.

In this second book of the Clan MacLaoch Curse series, we see our favorite characters, Rowan and Cole, return in their most passionate selves yet. Coming off the loss of the Gathering and the thought-to-be-extinguished MacLaoch curse, Rowan finally has a chance at his happily ever after. That is, until everything that he loves is put at risk, sparking events, that once set in motion, will not be stopped—except by love.

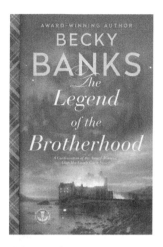

*Coming soon. Book 3 of the Clan MacLaoch curse series,* The Legend
of the Brotherhood.

In this third book of the clan MacLaoch curse series, Cole's two worlds collide
when her brother TJ stops by Castle Laoch for a surprise visit. His presence
upsets more than the status quo at Castle Laoch; Rowan struggles to find a
solution to the bankruptcy proceedings, which are starting to look like the end
for the MacLaoch clan. Cole and Rowan - fresh off the battle on the cairn knoll
- are bonded even more profoundly as they move to save the castle from
bankruptcy and a villainous bankman set on a generation's old revenge. While
Cole and Rowan's love is secure for eternity, the struggle for the ancestral
MacLaoch home hangs in the balance. Can Rowan's determination, the Baker
kids' ingenuity, and residual Viking power from Ormr Minorisson save the
castle and clan from ruin?

# ROMANTIC SUSPENSE TITLES

Flux. *Can one notorious hacker protect the women she's saved before her dark past finds her?*

Vega Flux, a notorious hacker whose single mission in life is to protect the weak from online trolls, crashes up against an impenetrable powerhouse of a man who wants nothing more than to slip the dark shroud off her persona and protect her from her torments.

In this smoldering high-stakes game of defense and one-upmanship, Vega takes a bet she knows she shouldn't and starts the largest hack she's ever attempted, against the only worthy opponent she's ever known, tech billionaire and ex-NFL tight end, Hoyt Kahoʻokalakupua. Master of his domain, Hoyt, welcomes the chance to flex his power in a true challenge. With the stakes dangerously high, and his heart on the line, he enters a game with a woman he wants it all from. There's only one fatal flaw: Hoyt and Vega are following different instructions to the same game. He's a law-abiding billionaire, and the world Vega lives in breaks every rule.

Dark passions ignite in this fast-paced thrill ride from award-winning indie author and Maui girl, Becky Healani Banks. As the torments of Vega's past breach her defenses, she reaches for the one man who is uniquely capable of providing the shelter she seeks. And in that process, she touches a power she's never known, real-life love.

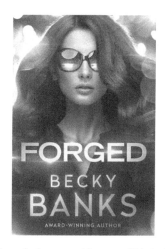

Forged. *First loves, dark pasts, and fast cars collide in this high-octane thrill ride.*

Managing editor of a Manhattan fashion rag, Eva Rodgers, couldn't believe she would ever step back into her old life, but the day her father called with his diagnosis, she had little choice. Returning home, and to the past she left behind, Eva signs up as editor-in-chief of the struggling Portland magazine, *Rose City Review.* There in the drizzling Portland metro Eva still holds firm to the New York city values that defined her time there: compromise on nothing. When her European auto, one luxury she missed in the walking and hired car world of Manhattan, needs fixing, she doesn't compromise. Even when the best European auto mechanic her assistant finds turns out to be an ex with a vendetta, Eva doesn't flinch.

Nathaniel Vellanova can't believe what the fuck just showed up at his garage. He'd gotten his life together, buried his dark past, and definitely put Eva Rogers in his rearview mirror. Right?

But fuck him if she wasn't standing right there in the pouring rain needing his help. He'd do it—help her out—just this once then forget all about her. Again.

In this dark and suspenseful story of broken first loves, readers will ride the smoldering heat of high-octane fast cars, glitzy club fashion, and tainted love and ask themselves, are first loves the only love?

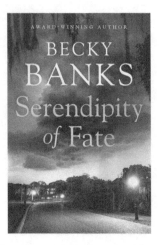

Serendipity of Fate. *Enemies to lovers romance. One war, one blood promise, and the love to save it all.*

It has been two years since Cason McPherson watched his best friend, Ryan Sparling, die in his arms. Now, with a blood promise tied to his heart, shrapnel in his hip, and a war behind him, he's focused on building a useful civilian life in his hometown of New Orleans. Living with Ryan's mother, a widow and retired nurse, he gives back the protection and care his best friend wanted. Only Ryan's sister, a woman whose well-worn picture got him through the darkest parts of the war, does not see it that way.

Savannah Sparling has spent the last five years building her career and life to the exacting expectations needed to achieve partner at Knight Interiors. And nothing could derail them except for the one person from her past who returned home a changed man. Cason McPherson and her brother Ryan had been her entire world once, but now she no longer recognizes him with his caustic attitude and effort to turn every conversation into a verbal sparring match. When a potential client, one large enough to secure her place as partner, requests her as lead designer, Savannah sets a plan for her final career move and Cason's eviction.

In a series of unstoppable events, Savannah's carefully laid plans backfire, and an unfathomable truth is revealed. In the aftermath, Cason and Savannah find that the only people strong enough to save them from themselves are each other. But will either one of them accept the help—and the love—that is offered?

# FUTURE SERIES

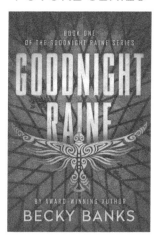

*Coming soon.*

Set one-hundred years into a dystopian future, this socio-political romantic thriller takes place in the sprawling catacombs of The Peoples Republic of Portland. In a world that has been punished by the misdeeds of mankind, one writer sets out to answer one simple question: What would happen if everyone had hope again? Absorbed onto a misfit team of ex-war machine operators, junior journalist Wendy Wilson, moves quickly to adapt or die while trying to save the city she loves and maybe, just maybe, change the hearts and minds of even the most blood-thirsty among them.

––––––––––

Be sure to visit beckybanksbooks.com and sign up for the author newsletter. Newsletter recipients are the first to get book release news and giveaway alerts.

14155739R00204